Derek Priestley
Peter Davies Ltd
15-16 Queens St,
Mayfair
London W1X , 8BE

KNIGHT
IN ANARCHY

By the same author
Imperial Governor

KNIGHT
IN ANARCHY

George
Shipway

PETER DAVIES : LONDON

Printed in Great Britain by
Cox & Wyman Ltd London Fakenham and Reading

To Juliet O'Hea
with gratitude

CONTENTS

		page
Prologue	December, 1135	1
1	January — April, 1136	5
2	April, 1136 — January, 1137	20
3	January — June, 1137	28
4	June — August, 1137	45
5	August, 1137	62
6	August — September, 1137	83
7	September, 1137 — June, 1138	97
8	June — July, 1138	113
9	July — August, 1138	127
10	22nd August, 1138	140
11	May, 1139 — May, 1140	157
12	January — February, 1141	671
13	June — September, 1141	191
14	September, 1141 — October, 1143	209
15	October, 1143 — September, 1144	228
Epilogue	October, 1144	45
Author's Note		47
Glossary		049

Prologue

December 1135

Nature had created the clearing in the Forest of Lions, and covered the rocky crust with a thin blanket of poor soil. Trees found no anchorage; bramble and briar mottled the surface. Later on, man hacked this covering away, and raised a few poor huts of timber and thatch. Wooden ploughs furrowed the earth; in the shallow scratches peasants scattered seeds of starveling crops. Lacking a church, they invoked a saint and called the place Saint Denis.

On this grey, moist December morning a great concourse filled the clearing. Striped and chequered pavilions overshadowed the rude village huts. Beyond, pressed against the forest bulwarks which surrounded the place like a gigantic palisade, the sombre tents of armed men ranged like a bastion against the serried trees.

The voice of the assembly was a low murmur, like surf on a tranquil beach. The mournful baying of hounds penned in a staked enclosure was an antiphon to a subdued chanting; the voices blended to sound a knell for the passing of men's souls.

A king lay dead.

In the centre of the crowd a procession formed: grey-mailed horsemen and black-gowned monks, proud-faced men in flamboyant cloaks, servants clad in leather and russet wool, and a pendant of pack-animals and carts. Twelve oxen dragged a huge four-wheeled wagon whose timbers, newly tarred, absorbed the dawn-flush and returned no light. On this, flaunted like a crown, was a coffin draped in cloth of crimson and gold.

The procession left the forest clearing called Saint Denis and straddled a rough track that led to Rouen, twenty-five miles distant. Armed men rode ahead, lances at rest, shields dangling from shoulders. Black Benedictines tramped beside the bier, muttering prayers, chanting antiphons, clutching the wagon-frame to sustain their weary passage. Behind them rode the rich and powerful, great men of Normandy and England, on caparisoned horses whose lineage was unsullied as their own. Retainers followed, men at-arms and servants; and a body of armoured knights guarding the wagon-train.

The rain misted down, beading cloaks and beards, and pecked tiny rust-spots, like flecks of blood, on mail-rings and helmets. The pace was laboriously slow. The funeral wagon lurched like a top-heavy merchant hoy. The coffin jolted athwart the platform; a corner of the pall slapped against a wheel, and gathered mud and clay. The column halted. Men clambered on the wagon, tugged and knotted ropes. The driver cracked his long whip; the oxen lowered their heads and strained under the yokes. The cortège lumbered on. Riders reined fretting horses against the slow crawl, and sweated in the unseasonable warmth of a Norman winter.

Four hours' travel brought them to a metalled road bequeathed by the Romans. Here, with relief, they halted again, and the nobility bade farewell to their king. They gathered round the bier and knelt in prayer on the muddy pavement, and bowed in homage to the insensible coffin. They remounted and clattered back the way they had come, happy with the relief which swift movement gave to aching muscles, back to Saint Denis to collect their several entourages and go their separate ways to castle and fief. A small gathering, some thirty armoured knights, monks and foot-soldiers, servants and carts, remained to convoy the towering black hearse.

They crawled onwards and, at the approach of dusk, made camp beside the road, still twelve miles short of Rouen. A low-voiced consultation between knights and monks, a tentative move to unbind the ropes, ended inconclusively. The bier retained its burden. The night was still, windless and warm. Candles burned, hardly flickering, beside the coffin. The monks whose duty it was to intone prayers throughout the watches clambered from the platform and continued saying their offices beside the wheels. Sometimes a stifled retching interrupted the litanies. Sentinel knights leaned on shields at a distance, and wound scarves round mouth and nostrils.

The king was four days dead.

At dawn they harnessed the oxen, but the driver, a forest peasant, violently refused to mount the wagon. A knight dealt with him roughly, using a lance-butt. As a concession they flung him a strip of linen soaked in wine, which the wretched man bound about his face. The column rolled forward; but the Benedictines no longer walked beside their charge, and the escort rode well ahead, and a wide space behind.

The Constable of Rouen, his dignitaries and prelates, received them at the gate with solemn pomp. New voices swelled the funeral dirge. The procession plodded to St Mary's church through narrow streets thronged with bystanders who yielded as though lashed with whips when the wagon passed. The knights, grim-faced, unloaded the coffin, bore it shoulder-high to the chancel and laid it on trestles before the High Altar. They conferred urgently with the Constable, and departed, and left their charge to the monks and a glory of candles whose flames, tipped with smoke, towered as though striving to reach beyond the miasma of corruption.

Next day six knights returned and bore the coffin to an outhouse, a wooden store-shed in the church precincts. Here were no monks, no candles – only rough peasants, burdened with tools, bulging sacks and ox-hides. A carpenter prised open the lid and released a choking stench. The servants ran in terror to the doors. The knights stood fast and gazed with clenched jaws at that which had been their king. They lifted the body and stretched it on an oaken table. They called a name, and drove the owner into the room at sword-point to do the work for which he had been paid. The man, a butcher and horse-doctor, wiped sweat from his face and wound a linen veil about his head, and advanced trembling to the table.

He laid an axe-edge against the neck, raised the weapon high, and severed the head with a single blow. A mess of stinking slime spurted forth and dripped dismally to the floor. With a small ladle he extracted the two putrescent globules which once had been eyes, and with hooks and strange implements of his trade scooped out the brain. He swept the glutinous mash into an iron bowl. With an air of growing confidence he stripped the sticky grave-clothes. He slit the belly from breast-bone to crotch and, plunging both hands in the cavity, pulled out bowels and entrails. Like a mariner coiling ropes he deposited the slippery tubes, turn upon turn, in the bowl. The liver, a liquid pulp, he poured carefully like precious wine.

The butcher took a knife and slashed the corpse from shoulders to ankles: long, deep, suppurating cuts. Then, seizing handfuls of salt from the open sacks beside him, he rubbed salt into the slits, filled the belly with salt, poured salt into the empty skull. That finished, he stood upright, clawed at the linen muffling his face and dropped to the floor without a sound.

3

A knight stooped, twitched the cloth aside and regarded the contorted face and staring eyes. He shrugged. "The last of the great host the king has killed," he murmured unemotionally. He rummaged through the butcher's clothing and found a leather purse, examined the coins and thrust the purse into his wallet. Seizing the dead man by the heels he dragged him from the room.

The tanner who waited outside with his pile of hides found nothing encouraging in the sight. The guardians forced him within and watched while he swathed the body, head lodged between thighs, in layer upon layer of ox-hide which he sewed firmly together.

Neither force nor an offered bribe – the purse given to the butcher for his services – could persuade any of the frightened servants to enter the store-room. The knights themselves lifted the iron bowl by its ringed handles and bore it within the church to a small grave hastily dug in the nave. They poured the stinking offal like gravy into the hole. Hastily they kicked in rubble and stamped it down and replaced the flagstones.

They tried to force the hide-wrapped bundle into the coffin, and failed. Abandoning the attempt, they carried their load into the church, placed it before the altar, and withdrew. The monks clustered around and lighted candles and resumed their monotonous liturgy.

During the night foul matter exuded from the body, soaked through the ox-hide wrappings and dripped to the floor. The monks, sickened, placed vessels beneath the bier. The bowls filled quickly and had to be emptied again and again.

At dawn the ghastly package was loaded once more on the wagon and departed, leaking stealthily but steadily, on the long road to Caen and the sea.

Henry of England was going home.

1

January – April, 1136

On a bleak January day I followed King Henry's funeral procession when they buried him below the High Altar in Reading Abbey.

Eight horses drew the hearse, lurching and bouncing between iron-hard furrows on a frozen road. The horses of the knights' escort skidded on ice-caked puddles. Cowled monks walked beside the wagon. Behind rolled a splendid column whose cloaks and trappings, scarlet and gold, emerald and blue, were a shout of colour in that leaden landscape.

The still air carried a numbing cold which struck like arrow-heads through layers of wool and leather. The company pulled gorgeous cloaks more closely around their shoulders and trudged slowly onwards, picking a careful way over the ruts. Here and there mailed horsemen, like grey rocks bordering a flowered river, rode alongside the procession. The horses's hooves stirred dry flakes of powdery snow; a moving mist, the frozen breathing of a thousand mourners, drifted like a gossamer curtain above their heads.

Henry's body had rested at Shinfield, four miles from Reading. Here the great men of England assembled like an army gathering for battle, and their pavilions and escorts and baggage surrounded the hamlet and made it the petty nucleus of a vast encampment. The counts were there: Ranulf of Chester and Robert of Leicester, each with his train of lords and liegemen. The bishops were there: Lincoln and Salisbury and London, with their clerics and household knights. And a host of lesser men, minor knights holding insignificant fiefs, had come to pay the ultimate homage to their lord, and to pray for his soul. In the midst of them all, in Shinfield's tiny church, King Henry's body lay throughout that frozen night.

When morning came they placed it once more on the wagon, draped with velvet cloth, purple and gold, and followed sadly on the last stage of the king's last journey.

Some in that great and powerful company mourned truly, for they had known Henry intimately, followed him on his endless journeyings in England and Normandy, fought at his side against Robert of Normandy and Louis of France. They may have loved him. Others shivered with more than cold, for death had bereft them of allegiances and scattered their loyalties; their paths were suddenly dark and full of danger. A few lugubrious faces undoubtedly concealed a keen anticipation: these were the seekers, the turbulent men whose energies, long repressed by the iron hand of an indomitable king, were now – so they thought – free to strike for power and wealth and dominion.

One among them could certainly not have mourned at all.

Golden-bearded, florid and blue-eyed, Stephen of Blois, Count of Mortain and King of England, strode at the head of his vassals. Thirty days ago he had been merely Henry of England's nephew, a man of might among others equally mighty, of royal blood but casting no shadow of royalty. Now he had England. Could he have truly mourned, as he followed with bowed head the robed and mitred bishops?

Far down the procession, as befitted our lowly standing in that glittering company, I walked with my father, Walchelin Visdelou of Bochesorne. Walchelin looked like an ageing falcon. From the ivory beak of his nose two furrows, grooved deep by weather and war, dragged like cords on the corners of his mouth. Greying hair brushed his shoulders like a coif. Once, in Red William's time, he had been a gay, young buck delighting in fashion's whims; from Rufus's effeminate court he had copied his mode of hair and beard and, disliking change, to this day mirrored their appearance.

My elder brother, William, rode far ahead, armed and armoured, leading the cortège among other knights of the funeral escort.

We passed the scattered huts and steadings of Reading village and entered the abbey gateway. Founded by the dead king some years before, the building was still unfinished; masons' scaffolding enfolded walls and towers. A troop of knights buffeted aside some gaping peasants who crowded the entrance arch. Sergeants eased the coffin from the wagon and transferred it carefully to the shoulders of four counts and four great barons. Preceded by chant-

6

ing monks, followed by the nobility of his realm, King Henry passed to his rest.

Walchelin said, "Humphrey, go now and find William – look, there he stands. Anschetil and the horses are somewhere behind on the road. I shall meet you here afterwards and we'll ride home together."

He passed within, and I went to stand at William's stirrup. My brother was grim-faced, blue with cold, and stared to his front with lance at rest across the pommel. His voice was biting.

"Don't stand there, clod. Go to that tavern behind us and buy some mulled wine – hot, and a lot of it. If you aren't quick the place will be drunk dry. I have to stay here until everyone's inside. Move, boy!"

I moved, and ordered wine. Presently William came to the tavern, a miserable little hut which catered for the needs of poorer travellers on that road, and dismounted stiffly. He gave the reins to a sergeant, and flogged arms across his chest and sucked his fingers.

"Praise the Saints that's over. God's blood, what a duty!" He drank deep, tilting his head until the flagon's rim clinked against his nasal. He put down the cup and made a face. "Filth! But it's hot, and I'm cold as an Angevin's heart. More!"

The taverner poured wine. The small, earth-floored room became crowded, as more knights awaiting their lords pushed in to find warmth and wine. A smoky brazier and the press of bodies soon heated the place and stirred smells of sweat and sour breath. The taverner scurried to tap fresh casks. William cleared a place for himself on the only furniture, a rude table, and sat, cradling his cup.

"The end of Henry," he said thoughtfully. "May the Saints receive his soul in kindness." He crossed himself. "There's little enough left of his body."

I was startled. "The king died a natural death, surely?"

William regarded me darkly. "As natural as a bellyful of bad fish allowed him," he answered. "No, it's not the manner of his dying, but what they did to him after he was dead. I saw it all. I had to, being attendant on his body night and day."

A stocky, broad-shouldered man forced his way through the crowd and clasped William's arm. "Visdelou!" he said, laughing. "Trust you to find the only warm place in this perishing village. A cup together before we go our separate ways." He bellowed for the taverner.

7

The wine arrived. William and the newcomer saluted one another and drank. William flipped a hand in my direction.

"This is my brother Humphrey. Odinel de Umfraville."

De Umfraville's dark eyes surveyed me briefly from head to foot while I bent a knee. Without interest he turned away and spoke to William. The want of ceremony in William's introduction and something in my appearance had told him immediately that, although of gentle blood, I wore no spurs; although sturdy and muscular I was inexperienced in war. For him I held no significance. Such treatment I had met before: the chasm between knights and the rest of mankind was profound. Yet, because something about Odinel de Umfraville attracted me, I found his negligence vexatious. Irritation betrayed me into a breach of behaviour, and I interrupted my companions' chatter.

William regarded me without favour. "Patience, whelp! Have you forgotten courtesy? Twenty next Martinmas," he grunted to de Umfraville, "and still mannerless as a Flemish arbalester."

Odinel was amused. "Were you telling him that tale?" he asked. "The boy must have a strong stomach. Remember Rouen?"

"Never shall I forget. We had to keep the old man at Caen until he had leaked himself dry. By the time we reached England he hardly smelt at all."

To me this was incomprehensible. I sulked over my wine.

A sergeant entered with a summons from my father. The burial was over. I was thankful to quit the hot, oppressive tavern, and gratefully gulped the icy air outside. I dropped to my knee in farewell to de Umfraville. The knight's eyes held a glint of amusement.

"God go with you, Humphrey Visdelou," he said. "Perhaps we shall meet again."

2

The first Humphrey Visdelou, my grandfather, had received Bochesorne from William the Bastard within a year of Hastings. Life had not been tranquil then, and Humphrey promptly built himself a castle on a hummocky spur which jutted like a fist from the downland escarpment above the river marshes. He dug a ditch around the spur, throwing up the spoil in a mound, and on the mound he built a wooden keep of oak-trunks riven from the forest, so that the castle stood on a flat-topped hill surrounded by marsh, moat and fosse. Along the plateau's rim he erected a timber palisade to guard the bailey.

The place, though not impregnable, was quite strong enough to defeat any dispossessed Englishmen, who were all that the castellan feared at the time. The attackers never materialized, and old Humphrey's villagers settled down peacefully under his rule. He endured the discomforts of his wooden fort until a few years before his death and then, prodded by ungentle hints from his suzerain – for the Bastard had never given him a warrant to build the castle – moved himself, his family and retainers to a more congenial abode across the river, and built the Hall.

The oak timbers of this rectangular house framed flint-rubble walls, dressed with stone and plastered inside and out. Humphrey, glad to be freed from the castle's restricted confines, measured a ground-plan thirty paces long and fifteen broad. The walls were eight paces high. Then his memories of life in turbulent Normandy counselled caution. He allowed only a single door, set high in the wall, and reached it by a wooden ladder. He pierced four narrow windows, two on each side, little more than arrow-slits – the interior of the Hall was always dark. At doorway level he built a floor supported on stone arches and made the space beneath a store-room for victuals, as though the Hall were indeed a castle, always provisioned for a siege. The steeply sloping roof was thatched; the hearth-fire's smoke escaped through a central hole. Humphrey lime-washed the walls, surrounded the whole area with a palisade, and was planning a fosse when he died.

Walchelin endured the troubles of Red William's time and saw King Henry's peace settle on the land. There seemed no longer any need for the semi-fortified inconveniences his father had imposed. A flight of stone steps replaced the wooden ladder. He added, at one end of the Hall's interior, a second floor, shielded from the main room by leather curtains, which made a bower for himself and the women of his family. Two of the four windows lighted this room; the rest of the Hall became more gloomy than before. Old Humphrey's palisade, robbed for firewood in the course of many winters, gradually disappeared.

Weathered by forty years of rain and sun, the house had settled into the landscape like a man in a comfortable and familiar bed. Like a vast white ship, foursquare and strong, the Hall floated serenely on green downland, while lesser craft – stables, byres, kitchens, mews and granaries – nudged her sides. Across the river the rotting timbers of Humphrey's castle reared like decayed teeth – a desolate place, disused, and avoided by the villagers. Water-weeds choked the moat; nettles and brambles smothered the eroded fosse. Only the gallows were kept in good repair: here, from time to time, Walchelin still hanged criminals whom he could lawfully punish.

When he abandoned the castle old Humphrey gave tenancies on his land to most of the men-at-arms who had formed its garrison. Some served in the Hall as guards, armourers and horse-masters. Others escorted the baron when he travelled, or followed him when he went to war. Their descendants, in his grandson's time, still held their tenures by fulfilment of the same duties. Doyen of these was Anschetil, son of a sergeant who had been at Hastings, himself a veteran of King Henry's wars who had fought at Walchelin's side at Tinchebrai and Bremule. This dour old man, still tough and wiry as a sapling oak, was now Walchelin's steward, and ruled his domain with brazen fists.

3

Altar candles gleamed like pale spears in the half dark of a January dawn. Light-sparks splintered on a silver chalice, gleamed from a belt buckle, and brought into wavering life the garish paintings on the walls of the little church. Along one wall Our Lord on His donkey rode towards the turreted ramparts of Jerusalem; on another the Dolorous Procession was fixed for ever in harsh blues and reds and greens, faded now in the gloom; the flickering candle-glow fluttered the pennons of Roman knights. Ranulf the priest, from whose brush these pictures flowed, murmured the final offices of Mass. A first glint of daybreak pierced the narrow windows.

Walchelin Visdelou rose stiffly from his knees and turned to survey the villagers. Heads bowed, muttering their last devotions, they crowded the tiny nave. For a moment he stood, peering into the darkness; then, with a sharp summons to his reeve, he limped to the doorway. I followed briskly, glad to be leaving the warm confinement and the smell of candle-fat and unwashed bodies. In the churchyard I stumbled over a burial mound and clenched my teeth on an oath.

Pale amber streaked the eastern sky. Stars gleamed faintly over-head. A horse snorted and blew: I walked over and spoke to the groom and stroked the bay stallion's neck. My father conferred with the reeve, as was his daily custom at this hour. He finished with an emphatic thump of his staff, and called my name. I went to receive my orders for the day: this also was usual at that time and place.

"Two men and a woman absent from Mass. Find out who, and why. Stay here and check the reeve's allocation of field work. I think he's miscalculating the boon days: it's high time they started building that weir below the mill."

The old man stumped away. I lingered impatiently while Ansgar, the reeve, detailed each man's task for the day, which he did every dawn in the churchyard after Mass. The villagers clustered round him, were named one by one for the day's work, gathered tools they had left by the church door and departed for the fields which they would not leave till dark.

I mounted Chanson, fought him rapidly to submission and trotted happily across the ford to the tilt-yard on Rood Hill. There I schooled him until the sun rose above the elm-trees.

I returned to the Hall, left Chanson at the stables and found my father and Anschetil eating at a table in the courtyard. Walchelin loved the sun: seldom could he be found indoors while a trace of warmth remained. He now sprawled on a stool, his woollen robe pulled open to expose his chest, a hunk of bacon in one hand and a parchment scroll suspended distastefully from the other. I rolled a log to the table with my foot, sat and drank deep from a flagon of watered wine. Schooling Chanson was always thirsty work.

"A writ," Walchelin growled. He dropped the parchment on the table and rubbed his fingers together as if cleansing them of garbage.

I nodded, unsheathed my dagger and sliced the bacon. "Have you sent for Ranulf?"

"I have. Meanwhile, Humphrey, you can exercise your learning and tell me something of Hamo de Neufmarché's latest move."

I flattened the roll, glanced at it and shook my head. "Latin," I answered briefly. "Beyond me."

My father grunted. Himself quite unable to read or write, be-lieving that such arts were a waste of time, utterly incompatible with knightly dignity and the profession of arms, he had neverthe-less insisted that I should receive some schooling from Ranulf the priest. For two years, under Ranulf's kindly tuition, I had struggled unwillingly with grammar and letters and quill and ink. The lessons occurred at infrequent intervals; they seldom lasted long. I could haltingly read simple passages in French, wrote hardly at all, and knew no word of Latin. I took pains to conceal my ignorance from Walchelin, who persuaded himself that his son was become something of a scholar. Moreover, to my shame, he was apt to boast of this misconception to his friends so that they, all hard-bitten knights and illiterate as himself, regarded me with wonder and more than a touch of scorn.

Ranulf entered the courtyard, prodded a liam-hound from the midden with his staff, stepped carefully across miry puddles and bowed low before his lord. The priest, who was to become my saviour, friend and companion in the dark years ahead, was my bastard half-brother.

Walchelin who now sunned himself benignly at his breakfast table, had spent most of his youth fighting at King Henry's side in the Norman wars. He found campaigning so attractive that he spent years together in Normandy and France, and accompanied the king wherever he went. His valour had become legendary. In the pursuit after Bremule he received a lance-thrust in the thigh, which healed badly and made riding painful. Walchelin recognized that his days of active soldiering were ended, and settled permanently in England. For nearly fifteen years he had lived at Bochesorne, acquitting his annual knight-service with sixty days' guard duty at Marlborough's royal castle where, with other warriors old and maimed like himself, he grumbled about his peaceful existence and told endless stories of the ancient days of onset in Normandy.

It was not altogether surprising that a man of his nature and outlook should treat his fief in England, on the brief occasions when he returned between campaigns, as a haven of relaxation rather than the corner-stone of his fortune and degree. The older villagers remembered his sojourns with awe. With two or three knights, staunch companions of many a siege and skirmish, he would hunt all day and roister all night. My mother, the Lady Hawise – whom I barely remembered, for she died in giving birth to my sister Isabel – and the ladies of the Hall retreated to the bower during these carousels. The household wenches and village sluts could not escape so easily. Walchelin demanded his rights and exercised them boldly. So, as the years passed, an increasing number of young men and girls in the village carried the Visdelou brand: a cast in the left eye. To the men it gave a sinister aspect; to women it added allure.

Ranulf the priest was the outcome of a twenty-year-old debauch, with the significant difference that his mother had been Lady Hawise's handmaid. Walchelin's wife, a woman of strong character, was extremely angry when her favourite tirewoman delivered a child wearing the tell-tale squint. When her husband next returned she insisted that he make provision for the boy and he, growling, arranged for Ranulf to be sent in due course to Abingdon Abbey for training as a clerk. Thence, some years later, Walchelin retrieved him and gave him the living of Bochesorne.

To this priest, now, as he bent his knee before his lord and father, Walchelin handed the scroll and bade him read.

4

With his first words my attention wandered. The parchment, a writ delivered by the Sheriff's sergeant, concerned an old dispute over a worthless strip of scrubland which joined Walchelin's Speyne estate to that of his powerful neighbour, Hamo de Neufmarché. It was an ancient, complicated and inherited quarrel. A Neufmarché fief, bordering Speyne, had been escheated by William the Bastard and added to the Visdelou Honour. Red William recovered the fief, held it for a time, and then returned it to Bernard, Hamo's father. These successive alienations had not made for friendship between the families and, during the changes, possession of the ill-defined scrubland border remained unresolved. Throughout the years sworn inquests, juries of recognition and Hundred Courts had in turn deliberated, argued and come to no conclusion. The land was a running sore, so expensive in litigation that Walchelin was content to let the matter slide. Hamo de Neufmarché, apparently, was not; the writ called for Walchelin's attendance in six months' time at the justiciar's court in Marlborough.

"God's bones!" he exploded. "Can Hamo never rest? he has fiefs all over England which return him thirty knights. Is he so land-hungry that he must seize another few hides of marsh and scrub? I have a mind to give him possession and rid myself of a nuisance."

Ranulf's squint set an incongruous leer on his round, mild features. He rolled the writ slowly in his hands.

13

"You forget Aelfric, my lord."

"Yes." Walchelin pulled his lip. "By the Bastard's mandate my father took the border strip from Aelfric's father; his family have become tenants where once they ruled. A free man, although English." He rose decisively. "Neufmarché shall not have my vassals. Look up the precedents, Ranulf: they are in my coffer. We will fight the case again before the king's justiciar."

He limped indoors. I stifled a yawn and grinned at Ranulf, happily unaware that Aelfric's miserable holding was to ruin Visdelou and change my life.

5

Springtime's warm rain dissolved the iron of winter. At Bochesorne ox-ploughs crumbled the brown earth which had for weeks been frozen and barren. A king had died; a usurper reigned in his place; life in England continued unchanged.

Walchelin, during that spring, travelled abroad much oftener than was his custom. I never accompanied him: I was told to stay and study the workings of farm and field, of byre and pen. "Some day," my father once growled, "you will be holding Speyne, and the bailiff there is a clever Poitevin who needs watching. You've got to know his job better than he does, or your peasants will starve and you'll be destitute." Then he climbed into the saddle and jogged down the track with Anschetil and his usual pair of armed attendants, pursuing some unknown mission to an undisclosed destination.

Visits from neighbours became remarkably frequent: Richard de Humez from Shaw and Gervase de Salnerville from Donnington often rode to the Hall. Sometimes they went hawking, although the kills were few. Walchelin's falcons were poorly trained and wild, which was largely my fault. The baron had delegated the mews to my care and I, unattracted by the sport, transferred my responsibilities to the falconer, an elderly man with little aptitude. But this was not the sole reason for their ill-success, and I was seldom reprimanded. Walchelin and his guests, usually engrossed in talk, were slow in casting the birds and accepted their failures complacently.

Sometimes Walchelin entertained his company with a hunt in the scrub forest above Bochesorne, or in Benham's wooded valley.

Boar and deer, the king's beasts, went unscathed. Walchelin's huntsman pursued foxes, hares, and wolves. The wolves were always with us. Visdelou held the Honour by the service of two knights and a fee in sergeanty which involved no more than the deliverance of three wolves' heads to the king every year: a relic from our ancestors who had been verderers in Ponthieu. Wolf hunting was my great passion; hounds, not hawks, were my comrades and disciples, the horse between my thighs an exhilarating vehicle to carry me from find to kill. From my forays the king could have had ten times his due.

Often Walchelin's guests neither hunted nor hawked, but rode the fields peaceably at his side, criticized progress of a crop, inspected herds, conferred with the reeve, whipped an idle villein. They talked a great deal, low-voiced, and ceased when anybody came within hearing. At the high table in the Hall, after meat, the baron and his guests mumbled over their wine far into the night.

I sensed, beneath the ordinary springtime routine of a prosperous estate, the stirrings of grave matters which had nothing to do with crops and cattle. My father was uncommunicative; he gave me no enlightenment. The only significance I plucked from these visits was that the visitors were all, like Visdelou, tenants-in-chief of the king.

Realization of this common link brought my curiosity to the boil. Knowing that one of the baron's closest friends was Philip de Peasemore, I asked with devious innocence why that knight had been so long absent from Walchelin's table and entertainment. My father's reaction explained a great deal that had been obscure.

"Philip," he mused. "Yes, we have seen little of him lately. A lucky man – he has no problems."

He fiddled with his rein – we were riding to the tilt-yard on Roon Hill – and glanced at me beneath eyebrows which bristled like frosted fur.

"Philip holds Peasemore of Hugh de Mortimer. He is Mortimer's man: where Mortimer goes Philip follows. His course – the thorny path of honour – is simple and straightforward."

His palfrey shied at a shrieking blackbird; he stroked its mane absently.

"When the Bastard took England he divided the land among his lords, and demanded from them in return that for sixty days every year they provide him with knights for his field army, or with knights to garrison his castles. A hundred knights, fifty, or thirty, according to the value of the fief. And so the lords parcelled out their estates and settled retainers on their lands in return for knight service. Fealty and homage are owed by such men to their overlords, and to them alone. Their ties of loyalty to the king are frail, and are broken, in necessity, at the middleman's command."

I bridled my impatience: what my father said was known to every man of gentle blood in Christendom. But Walchelin's eyes were empty, his mind far away; he murmured as though communing with himself.

"At Hastings' fight my father warded a sword-cut aimed at the Bastard, and was maimed for life. William gave him this fief. So we hold our estates directly from the king, with no intervening lordship, and of this we are proud. We are barons, in theory, the peers of mighty counts, of men like Robert of Leicester. There it ends. Robert has two hundred knights at his back; I have two. Pride, yes – but no power."

He reined, and gazed sightlessly at the thorn-forest which crowned Rood Hill.

"To a king of the old line, lawfully crowned and anointed, our duty is clear. His enemies are mine; his friends I support in peace and war; his command I obey without question. He, and only he, is my liege lord."

His horse stamped restlessly and plunged at the bit. Walchelin wrenched at the bridle with unwonted savagery.

"Stephen of Blois is king. Neither I, nor any of my neighbour tenants-in-chief, attended his crowning. We have sworn no oath to him. We were King Henry's men, and swore fealty to his daughter Matilda, whom the old king nominated as heir to England's throne. Where now is my duty?"

To my mind the answer was plain. "My lord," I answered impulsively, "our homage rests upon our vow. If you have sworn to the Countess of Anjou, she is our liege lady. We can have no truck with Count Stephen."

Walchelin turned his head. "Count Stephen, as you call him," he said softly, "is Stephen of England. I hold Bochesorne, Speyne and Benham of the king. He *is* king. If I keep my oath to Matilda I defy the king. The name for that is rebellion. With your brother William at my side, and you as my squire, do you suggest I make war on England?"

He talked on – an old, perplexed and tired man, torn by conflicting loyalties.

"This is the problem of small men like myself, and also of many powerful barons who hold great honours and command a multitude of knights. I do not yet see how it will end. England is still outwardly at peace, but turbulence ferments beneath the skin. The borders are stirring already. War in Wales, and five hundred English knights and sergeants killed in Gower. Invasion from Scotland. A fiasco, I agree, but a dangerous one: no one is happy about Stephen's truce with King David. These are all signs – signals for war. And to tell you the truth, Humphrey, I think I am too old to fight – for anybody, on either side."

I regarded my father with pity, but a fierce excitement stirred my heart.

"I am young, my lord, and eager for battle. All my life you have trained me for fighting. If we have to declare for our faith and our vow, I can carry your name and blazon."

"You cannot yet be knighted," Walchelin said tiredly. "You are under age. And would you go thundering to war for Matilda, and bring Fulk of Anjou to England's throne? Yes, you flinch. There are more complications in this business than you imagine. Men of wisdom but no power, men like myself and de Salnerville and de Humez, had better hold our peace and manage our estates and forget our vows. A greater lord may yet arise to lead us. Have you ever heard of Count Robert of Gloucester?"

"King Henry's bastard?" I said. "Yes, of course."

My father nodded. "One day he may sound the clarion. Until then, we wait."

He set heels to his palfrey and galloped to Rood Hill. Pondering the intricacies of politics, I followed slowly.

6

The last week in April was a blaze of heat and sunlight akin to high summer. Sweating after a hard contest against Anschetil's sword and shield, I thankfully discarded the quilted gambeson worn for practice bouts and strolled through the river-meadows. Lambourn, a shallow stream, flowed seldom more than navel deep; but at the mill-weir a foaming cascade tumbled, cool and inviting. I stripped and waded in.

The river was icy. I gasped like a landed fish, thrashed wildly and floundered to the bank. I rubbed myself from crown to feet with handfuls of gritty mud, daubing and splashing, and purged the winter's accumulated grime and sweat. Walchelin would not have approved : he believed that, in washing the body, water entered soft, unweathered skin and diluted the blood. He often quoted dire instances of knights who, immersed by mischance on campaign, subsequently expired of a debilitating fever. The baron himself bathed three times a year : at Whitsuntide, Midsummer and Michael-mas, in a half-cask of heated water. Great anniversaries they were, with all the servants at the Hall in a flurry. I had heard that certain wealthier lords built bath-houses in their yards or castle baileys, and bathed once a month. My father declared this practice to be both effeminate and dangerous.

I stood beneath the weir fall and let the tingling cataract cleanse my body. Then I stretched myself on the river bank, and warm sun sucked water-droplets from my skin.

Content and happy, I lay with eyes half-closed and dreamily watched willow branches dance and shiver against a velvet sky. The problems of a strained and discontented England faded from my mind. I was in my twentieth year; before next winter I would be given my spurs and tenancy of Speyne. Then, by all means, let the country blaze in war. I had no problems of loyalty; I was the baron's man and followed him whither he commanded. Fight the Countess Matilda and her Angevin dog of a husband? With pleasure. Contend against Stephen of Blois? I had seen him once, at Reading : he looked a personable man; he was, they said, a good knight – but he had no right to England's crown. I sighed happily. Let them but postpone their quarrels until I could take part, charging beside my father into battle. Or was Walchelin, as he had hinted, too old for fighting?

A bough shuddered and a dry twig cracked sharply. I sprang to my clothes, cursing, and whipped dagger from sheath. A wisp of movement flickered behind a tree-trunk, dangerously stealthy, like a thief or murderer on the run, or a discontented villein with a grievance. The English were always mad and unpredictable; no Norman was ever really safe. To be caught like this, unarmed, alone and naked, was wanton carelessness.

I lowered the blade and laughed. English, indeed, but not danger-ous. A wench I had tumbled, more than once, in a hay barn during the winter, the daughter of a peasant who worked at the mill upstream. She was young, golden and coarsely beautiful. But she smelt; I was clean and she was not. I stripped her clothes and bundled her, gasping and giggling, into the water and scrubbed her lovely body. Then, panting with exertion and desire, we rolled upon the grassy bank.

Three times I proved my manhood, for she was a demanding girl. At last, satiated, I lay with head in her lap, and her dexterous fingers sought and crushed the half-drowned vermin in my dripping hair. I drowsed, relaxed and sleepy, and utterly content for the last time in my life.

The sun dipped below the tips of the willow branches. My sweet friend's hands wandered from my hair. I spread her thighs and bestowed within her a fourth and final token of affection, slapped her rump and sped her homewards. Lazily I donned my stinking garments. Summer was here, and a change of raiment awaited me in the household presses.

2

April, 1136 – January, 1137

Sowing was all done; our horses grazed in the meadows, and the pigs had been driven to the forest. Shearing was long past. The fleeces, heavy that year, brought a good price in the markets at Reading and Hungerford. The silver pennies rattled steadily into Walchelin's treasure chest; he seemed content and relaxed. His doubts were resolved. His liege lady, the Countess Matilda, lingered far away in Anjou. In April the nobility of England, Walchelin among them, assembled at Oxford and swore fealty to Stephen. The fact that Count Robert of Gloucester had also taken the oath removed my father's last lingering hesitations. Stephen was king indeed, and England peaceful. Rumours of Welsh wars reached our quiet haven – but the Welsh were always fighting. They were the Marcher lords' problem, not ours.

William Visdelou rode over from Benham on a golden morning when I was idling time away in the bower, playing checkers with my sister Isabel. Walchelin dozed in sunshine that cascaded through open windows whose shutters were flung wide and linen curtains drawn.

William's face showed a vicious temper. He knelt to my father and came directly to the point.

"The sheriff's sergeant yesterday delivered a writ at Benham. We have been summoned for service."

Walchelin, who was nodding into slumber again, opened his eyes. "A mistake," he said comfortably. "A chancery error. I stood castle guard at Marlborough for sixty days last autumn, and you, in Normandy, gave King Henry three weeks more than your fee service. Have you been paid for that yet?"

William shook his head impatiently. "This isn't a matter of some clerk misreading the records. I talked with the sergeant. King Stephen is raising an army to march against Exeter."

My father came fully awake. "Exeter? What nonsense is this? There's no fighting nearer than Wales."

William said grimly, "Robert of Bampton has rebelled, and Baldwin de Redvers has fortified Exeter against the king. You and I are ordered to join John fitzGilbert's retinue at Marlborough. He marches within five days."

Walchelin, staring from the casement, idly counted the browsing cattle in the meadow below. Sunlight snatched false gold from his silvered hair.

"So it has come at last," he said dreamily. "Matilda's liegemen are taking the field. What now?"

"This is no political intrigue," William answered, "but a private war to right personal wrongs. Robert of Bampton's lands and castles were made forfeit because, in a drunken fit, he pillaged a neighbour's possessions. The king's judges tried him and fixed the penalty: a legal decision which he is refusing to accept. The man is a glutton and a fool. Baldwin de Redvers comes from a different mould. He is well born, eminent and commands many knights. They say he has revolted because the king would not give him the County of Devon in fee."

"Yes, I know Baldwin. A reckless knight. A good fighter. And Exeter, I believe, is a strong fortress. Probably a long siege." My father spoke absently; his gaze was remote; his thoughts wandered.

Rashly I interrupted. "War in England! A chance for brave men to win glory, to overcome, to gain ransom and booty! If only I —"

Walchelin glared at me. His squint was pronounced; his nose jutted like a kestrel's beak. "War in England," he repeated softly. "You half-grown cub! You know nothing. You have seen nothing. For thirty-four years King Henry's peace has held England. For thirty-four years no man has marched against his neighbour, no town has been sacked, no crops burnt. Knights ride the roads, but where are their hauberks? In pack-horse panniers, or carried in carts. How many men in armour have you seen outside the fields of tourney, or training under bannerets? What do you know of war's devastated wastelands?"

William said, "A few weeks in Normandy would open brother Humphrey's eyes. If he survived the first pillaging raid," he added sourly. "But we waste time. We have fulfilled our service debt for the year. This summons to arms is either mistaken or illegal."

"It is neither, William. You shall go. I am fit only for castle guard – I cannot take the field again. Summon Ranulf the priest."

We waited in gloomy silence. Walchelin unlocked the heavy iron-bound chest where he kept his treasure, extracted bags that clinked, counted money. Ranulf came, his hands earth-stained from work in the glebe fields.

"Inkhorn and quill, Ranulf. Write to the sheriff. Tell him that age and wounds prevent me marching with the king's army — which he knows very well. I owe two knights. William I deliver in person. By his hand, in my place, I send shield-money. Sixty days at sixpence a day. Thirty shillings. With these fitzGilbert can hire a knight to fight in my stead. Take the money, William, and the letter."

He locked the chest laboriously, fiddling blindly with key and hasp. I saw, astounded, the tears trickle down his cheeks. Slowly he descended the ladder into the hall and limped, leaning heavily on his staff, down the outer steps and across the courtyard.

William said, "Never before has a Visdelou failed to answer the king's summons in person, with hauberk and helmet, horse and sword." He hefted the bag of pennies in his hand. "Two and a quarter marks! Away go the profits of the wool crop. But I do not believe that was why the old man wept."

2

Walchelin aged more than his sixty years during the winter. He was, of course, a very old man. Few people lived so long and, in the years ahead, life became shorter yet. Except when nominated for jury service he went seldom abroad, and the supervision of our estates at Bochesorne and Speyne devolved more upon my shoulders. I spent less time schooling destriers and fencing with Anschetil; rarely did I range the woods with hounds at my heels, or cast a falcon. Instead, I rode the fields, inspected hay-barns and cattle-byres, numbered sheep and pigs, directed fence repairs and conferred with reeve and bailiff.

One such task took me, after the Christmas feast, to Speyne. I rode with Anschetil and a groom; a couple of liam-hounds which needed exercise trotted behind. All day we quartered the three vast fields which the bondsmen shared and tilled in strips: one already sown with winter wheat and rye, and a second under plough — Speyne possessed nine plough-teams — in preparation for a spring sowing of barley. The third, where sheep grazed on scanty stubble, lay fallow. The Poitevin bailiff, whom my father mistrusted, was nevertheless capable: no villein had fallen behind the rigid time-table of farming operations and the tillage of every piece was identical. Nowhere did I see that sure sign of lax control: un-ploughed or unsown strips in the midst of a cultivated field.

I slept the night at the manor house, an uncomfortable building which had never been a castle. Dawn brought an ice-barbed wind and powdered snow upon the fields. Shivering, we kicked the fire to life, made our devotions and breakfasted on barley cakes taken from the saddle-bags. The bailiff and reeve arrived and, seated at a rickety table, together we checked accounts. The audit was tedious but simple, and I found no mistakes. The estate had made a useful profit.

I counted pennies received from freemen's money-rents, returned the silver to a leather bag, slipped the account rolls inside and drew the thongs. My part was done. Later on Ranulf would trans-cribe the bailiff's entries in a flowing script which I had, in the past, so unsuccessfully tried to emulate. Then he would bind them in the ledgers, piled within my father's coffer, that recorded Visdelou's profits and losses since the Bastard's reign.

I rose from the bench, stretched stiffened limbs and kicked open the door. The scattering of snow had vanished; the wind had dropped. I glanced at the amber veil which hazed the sun.

"Past noon. Anschetil, saddle the horses. Figuring has numbed my brain and sitting petrified my legs. Let us take the hounds and find a hare or fox."

3

The liams raised a fox from a bramble copse and hunted lethargic-ally through thorn-scrub and woodland. Scent was poor: I regretted I had not brought my keen-nosed brachets. We cantered on slowly, watching the dogs puzzle a line which they could finally own no longer. We had come far from Speyne manor.

"Aelfric's tenancy," Anschetil replied to my query.

We found the man trimming a blackthorn hedge, a formidable barrier guarding his tillage against cattle, exceptional in that it grew, living, from the soil. The peasants built deadwood fences for the same purpose; a growing hedge indicated long tenancy under one family.

He was tall and square-shouldered, and grey eyes glinted like polished steel in a ruddy face. Gold still gleamed in his hair and beard. I greeted him respectfully. Aelfric was a freeman; his blood, though English, was pure as mine; no servile marriage, despite his family's descent from lordship to dependency, had sullied his lineage.

"The Saints guard you, Visdelou." He spoke heavily accented and halting French. "I saw your fox – he lies now in that coppice beyond the marsh. Shall I show you the trail?"

"No matter," I said. "The dogs are stupid today and the scent is cold. How was your harvest? Did you have a good year?"

He grimaced. "Fair. Enough to quit my rent. I saw little of the work. King Stephen claimed my services and I sat in siege-ditches before Exeter for two useless months. My sons carried the harvest."

I had forgotten. Aelfric, like all free English who held a certain hidage, was liable for annual service in the native levy – a relic of English custom from the days before Hastings.

"The first time I've been called," he continued, "thanks to King Henry's peace. My father marched against Robert de Belleme many years ago. Fortunately his helmet, spear and gambeson still hung on the armour-stand. The leather was cracked, the iron rusty, and nothing fitted too well. But I killed a Fleming in a skirmish and took his armour: ring mail and almost new." He grinned. "I may need it again soon. My Norman lords are restless nowadays."

I pointed my whip to men labouring in the distance. "If you are called again surely one of your sons can replace you?"

Aelfric looked upon the ground. "They are no longer free men," he said heavily. "My fields were once scrubland and marsh, like that which lies around us. The soil is poor; the produce sufficient to feed only a few. I pay danegeld, which bondsmen escape, and such other taxes as are decreed. My land no longer supports my family."

He raised his head and stared me proudly in the eyes. "We once were noble. To fill the bellies of wives and children my sons now work on Speyne manor and give boon-work at your bailiff's behest on your demesne lands. They have become servile. I am the last freeman of my line."

Aelfric turned away, retrieved his billhook and slashed the thorn-hedge. I could offer no comfort. The free English were a vanishing race; harsh necessity drove the few survivors into servitude. None

24

could help them, even if he so wished. I turned my horse and beckoned Anschetil.

"Let us, after all, try to recover our quarry."

The liams showed awakened interest in the copse which Aelfric indicated. The scent had improved, or the fox was lurking near-by. They led us, ranging widely among the trees, into deeper woods, and skirted a sodden meadow where dead-yellow reeds bristled like hostile spears. We plunged into a dense thicket whose brambles rasped our breeches and beaded scarlet droplets like strung rubies on the horses' flanks. From this place they bolted the fox and chopped him as he fled across a glade.

I dismounted, whipped the liams from their prey and rolled the torn body with my foot. "A fine beast. Aelfric's fowls will roost more easily now he is gone. Come, Anschetil. That ends our sport today."

I was wrong.

A crashing of undergrowth turned our heads. Two men rode into the dell, halted and silently surveyed us. The leader moved forward.

"By what right do you hunt upon this land?" he said roughly.

I regarded him: a dark-browed, thickset fellow, no longer a youth, who sat his palfrey with expert ease. His bearing and intonation told me he was gently bred, his age that he was probably a knight. I answered mildly.

"You are mistaken. I am Humphrey Visdelou, son of Walchelin of Bochesorne. We stand upon his manor of Speyne, on land held of him by Aelfric the Englishman."

The man glared arrogantly and drummed fist on pommel. "Land whose tenancy is in dispute, as you know well. My name is Richard Maluvel, a knight of Hamo de Neufmarché's household. By his order I ride the marches to rid his territory of rogues and poachers. Today, it seems, I have found both."

Tears suddenly clouded my sight. A scarlet mist shrouded Maluvel like a veil. I raised a hand.

Anschitel coughed. His warning rasp froze the movement. My eyes cleared.

"Maluvel." My voice was strange, with a hardness like the clash of swords. "Yes. I know the lineage. Descended from a strapper in Duke Richard's stables. Your manners betray you."

The knight gasped. Blood darkened his face and he spurred his horse towards me.

I stepped aside, placing my feet carefully on the slippery carpet of dead leaves, and grabbed instep and ankle. Either he did not know the counter-wrench or his reactions were slow. With a sudden twist I heaved him backwards from the saddle. The horse reared, brushed past and began to nuzzle a tuft of withered grass.

Maluvel's attendant dismounted quickly and ran to him. The knight rose slowly, his face mud-stained and doublet miry. Last year's leaves plastered him like scales. He crouched a moment upon hands and knees, head hanging, and breathed deeply. He clambered to his feet, faltered, and fumbled at his belt. The dagger came out.

"Devil's spawn!" he spat, and rushed.

I threw him quickly and easily, as Anschetil had taught, chopping downward at his knife-hand with braced forearm, kicking hard at a shinbone and letting momentum do the rest. Maluvel rolled twice, and came erect. I faced him, knife in hand, thumb along blade.

"No steel!" Anschitel roared.

I ignored him. A red transparency of anger bathed my enemy in a bloody light. Maluvel shuffled towards me, arm upraised, dagger-point high. A clumsy, unskilled fighter.

The knife descended – a wasteful, rustic strike which curved far from its target. I laughed, feinted once and lunged within his guard.

The point entered easily, jarred briefly on bone, probed deeper. Maluvel's leather doublet cushioned the hilt. I opened my hand and left it there.

His end was hard. He shrieked when he felt the knife, a noise like a hare's dying scream. He writhed on his back and squirmed like a wounded snake, and scrabbled at the hilt upon his chest.

We stood in silence, still as the trees, and watched him die.

Anschitel moved, walking stiffly, and wrenched the dagger free. Maluvel moaned – a forlorn sound, like the sough of falling wind. A small fountain of blood spurted from the wound. His body arched convulsively from head to heels, and he was dead.

Anschitel cleaned the blade on a handful of grass, returned the dagger to my sheath and tapped it gently home.

"It seems, master, that I have taught you too well," he said without expression. "Much trouble has been cooked in this stew, and the eating may scorch our lips." He beckoned the frightened servitor who stood trembling beside his horse. "Here, you. Give me a hand."

They lifted Maluvel's body, laid it face-down across his saddle and strapped stirrup leathers to hold it firm. Anschitel heaved the attendant on his horse – for the man shook so much he could hardly stand – and handed him the rein.

"Take this carrion to the Lord of Neufmarché. A present from Visdelou – the price of insult and trespass upon his domain. And, fellow," he continued, gripping the servitor's thigh with iron fingers, "see that you say truth at the inquest. You saw the quarrel; you heard the words that were spoken; you know whence the provocation came. If you lie I shall find you, and will surely slit your throat. Go!"

6

We called the hounds who, during the fight, had eaten all but the fox's fur and bones, and went swiftly to Speyne. There we collected the groom and rode for Bochesorne. Fits of shivering rattled my teeth and almost tumbled me from the saddle. Anschitel watched me sideways.

"Your first killing, master." His seamed, grizzled face split in a grin. "Never mind. Ranulf will exact a tolerable penance, and will give you absolution. You'll find they come more easily afterwards."

I shuddered again, and saw with relief the white walls of my home rise like a far-away sail upon the horizon.

The baron was in the bower. I climbed the ladder wearily and knelt before him and spoke formally, like a herald delivering an ultimatum.

"My lord, I have slain a knight."

3

January – June, 1137

Walchelin demanded details, and I cowered beneath his rage. Then he became calmer and brooded, chin in hand, for a long while. At last he spoke.

"Send a man to Benham. Tell William to ride here tomorrow morning without fail. We shall have to prepare our case, consider our plans. You, Humphrey, and your unbridled temper, have raised a whirlwind which may well topple our House and scatter the ruins. Go, now, to the church. Find Ranulf. Ask God and His saints to forgive your crime. Beg His intercession to avert the evils which I foresee."

Miserably I departed. Ranulf, when I told him, chewed his lip but offered no remark. I prayed long and passionately, until my knees were numbed and aching. Ranulf imposed a penance that would have shattered Anschetil's conception of the priest's tolerance.

A melancholy conference gathered in the Hall next day. William, frowning until his eyebrows were a sable bar across his face, forgot his acerbity and shot suggestions and expedients into the discussion like a bowman planting arrows. Ranulf, moon-faced and quiet, controlled the flow of our discourse and gently dammed meandering tributaries of argument. Walchelin drummed on the table, gazed at his dancing fingers and interrupted only to speak forcibly and with point. Anschetil leaned in the doorway, a barricade against intruders, supposedly beyond earshot. I listened silently in the shadows, and my opinions were neither sought nor offered.

The laws of England, inevitably, were the framework of their argument. Ranulf guided them through these complications, for my father's and brother's legal knowledge hardly extended beyond the scale of penalties exacted from peasants at fortnightly manor courts. Murder, he explained, could no longer be compounded by

28

fines graduated according to the victim's standing, as was the convenient English custom before Hastings. The Bastard had long ago decided to quell the turbulence of a newly conquered people by demanding a life for a life.

It seemed, finally, that three courses were open. I could seek sanctuary in a church, confess the murder and then leave England for ever. No further penalty was exacted. This, the coward's way, they unanimously dismissed. Or I could swear my innocence, supported by witnesses on oath. This process, known as compurgation, could result in my discharge – but we could hardly expect Anschitel to perjure himself, and Maluvel's servitor certainly would not. Both could bear witness to provocation: neither could deny the fact that I had killed.

That left trial by battle. My father had no doubt that I would have to face personal accusation and a duel, for Neufmarché's dignity demanded nothing less. That Hamo would press the king to declare our manors forfeit was unlikely. Such a punishment, leaving Visdelou landless and beggared, would drive me to servitude in England or to mercenary soldiering in Normandy – both beyond reach of his revenge.

William stated sombrely that, whatever might be the combat's outcome, the king would escheat Speyne and return the estate to Neufmarché, who had held it for a short time under Rufus.

"And, Humphrey, that will leave you, if you survive the duel, a landless knight – if you are ever knighted," he finished grimly.

The conference endured for longer yet. Knowing that the issue was already decided, I paid little attention. Anschetil's voice interrupted my unhappy contemplation of dust-motes dancing in a shaft of sunlight. The sheriff's sergeant entered and knelt to Walchelin.

He was an important official, the sheriff's representative in our district and responsible for issuing summonses and making arrests. He was also bailiff of the Hundred Court at Kintbury and, as such, well known to my father, who often adjudicated at the sessions. A considerable landholder, he held from his lord estates in sergeanty which rivalled the Visdelou manors in extent. I regarded him with respect and, under the circumstances, with some trepidation.

He opened a scroll and asked permission to read. The baron nodded.

"Whereas Humphrey Visdelou, son of Walchelin Visdelou of Bochesorne," he intoned, "is informally accused of the murder of Richard Maluvel, knight-attendant upon Hamo de Neufmarché, I,

John fitzGilbert, the king's sheriff, do demand that the said Walchelin Visdelou hold himself responsible for the custody of the said Humphrey Visdelou, who is in his mainpast, and shall bring him to the king's justices whensoever and wheresoever the king shall command. To which the said Walchelin Visdelou shall affix his seal in token of agreement. And if he cannot, or will not, take responsibility for deliverance of the said Humphrey Visdelou, then I command, in the king's name, that the said Humphrey Visdelou be delivered to me for custody in my donjon of Marlborough."

The sergeant finished, and wiped his brow. "Forgive me, my lord," he murmured. "I merely read what the clerks inscribe."

Walchelin took the parchment. "Wax and a taper, Ranulf," he said. "Humphrey, bring my seal from the coffer."

With his dagger he cut the parchment, threaded a linen strip through the slit, joined the ends and poured wax. He pressed Visdelou's wolf-head seal upon the blob and blew the warm medallion thoughtfully. The sergeant took the scroll and put it carefully within his wallet. Walchelin called for wine.

"A cup to moisten your throat, and to wash that legal jargon from your mouth," he said. "Now tell me, what was the outcome of that forgery case at the last Hundred Court?"

William interrupted to make his farewell, and I accompanied him to the stables, leaving Walchelin and the sergeant in amicable argument.

"What did he mean by 'informally accused'?" I asked.

William, foot in stirrup, paused. "Evidence given by a commoner, not of our rank." He swung his lean frame to the saddle. "The next accusation will be formal enough, and you will meet your enemy face to face. I hope you enjoy it."

He rode away, leaving me no happier.

2

Easter came and went. My penance ended – for thirty days, walking or riding, I had worn a hair-shirt and gone barefoot. A sheriff's writ commanded Walchelin to deliver me to the Hundred Court; and on a sun-drenched morning in April we rode to Kintbury.

The court deliberated in the open air, beneath the budding branches of an ancient elm. Four knights presided: men of substance, these, and important landholders in the Hundred. None was strictly of Walchelin's degree; none held his lands directly from the king, but was the vassal of some lesser lord. But this distinction made no difference in law. They adjudicated and sentenced according to a jury's verdicts. The jury – twelve freeholders of the Hundred – gathered in a group flanking the bench, and listened to evidence and conferred weightily among themselves.

Around them drifted a motley throng: plaintiffs and defendants, clerks and witnesses, idlers and peasants. With stave and boot three sturdy sergeants cleared a space before the bench. Voices babbled disharmoniously; hammers clanged from a near-by forge.

The leader of a group of horsemen standing on the fringes showed plainly the distaste he felt for the rabble's noise and stench. Sometimes he glanced, frowning, in our direction.

"The Lord of Neufmarché himself," Walchelin said. "Maluvel's killing must have angered him greatly to bring him here in person."

I examined Hamo's companions. A couple wearing helmet and hauberk – the only armoured men in that assembly – were household knights on escort duty. The third, a youth of about my own age, caught my look and glared venomously. Somehow I knew his face. I delved in my memory and found a portrait: eyes and nose and thin-lipped mouth belonged to Richard Maluvel.

The court considered a case of trespass. The witnesses were vociferous, the evidence contradictory, the jury perplexed and the justices bored. My father shifted impatiently in his saddle. Hamo's frown grew blacker and at last, exasperated, he spoke sharply to an attendant knight. The man shouldered through the throng and addressed the bench. The justices looked over their shoulders, saw Hamo, rose in consternation and hastily cleared the court. They conferred with the sheriff's sergeant, and gave orders. The sergeant stood before the bench, and commanded Humphrey Visdelou to surrender to the king's mercy, as personified in the Hundred Court of Kintbury.

I spurred forward and bowed to the justices. The babel ceased; the blacksmith's hammer rang more loudly in the sudden silence. The sergeant declaimed the charge, clearly and distinctly, in French and then in English.

"Who witnessed the crime?"

Richard Maluvel's attendant shuffled forward, and gave his testimony. He spoke truth, garbling only my insult to his master's lineage, for such niceties were beyond his understanding. The youth

31

with Maluvel's face beat a clenched fist upon his knee. The justices listened gravely, and talked again to the sheriff's sergeant. He, in truth, guided and directed the procedure of this court.

The sergeant paused consequentially, and addressed a rook circling lazily overhead.

"Who else witnessed the crime?"

A horseman reined beside me. I turned my head and saw Hamo's young companion.

"Enough of this farce," he said in a voice that grated. "You know very well that this murderer cannot be convicted on testimony alone. My name is Odo Maluvel, brother to Richard who is dead. I appeal Humphrey Visdelou."

The justices whispered urgently together. They no longer needed guidance – the law of appeal ruled nobleman and commoner alike.

"Odo Maluvel, will you prove the accusation with your body?"

"I offer battle. May Almighty God decide the truth between us."

A justice answered seriously, choosing his words with care. "We accept your plea, but trial by battle is beyond the jurisdiction of this court. We therefore remit the case to the royal justiciar, who will summon you to combat at such time and place as he may decide. Meanwhile, Humphrey Visdelou, you remain at the king's mercy. That is all."

I turned my horse, choosing the direction with intention, and shouldered Maluvel. He eyed me savagely.

"Control your mount, you oaf. Can't you ride? Is dagger-play your only skill? You'll need more than a villein's tricks when I start killing you."

"I'd have thought one of your blood would avoid mentioning villeins," I said gently. "Do not talk of killing. I shall leave you life enough to end it on the gallows."

Walchelin thrust between us. "Enough," he snapped. "Humphrey, come away."

I raised my hand in mock salute. Maluvel did not move. Hatred snarled his lips.

3

"What now?" I asked my father. "Does this affair drag through court after court?"

"No. The royal sheriff in these parts is John fitzGilbert. He is also a justiciar. His sergeant will take him a transcript of the Hundred Court's proceedings and fitzGilbert will summon you to the Shire Court. The verdict will not alter; that is foregone."

"How long will this take?"

Walchelin shrugged. "Who knows? A month. Two months. In the meantime," he continued, "I advise you to abandon your new-found zeal for farming and learn the manner of judicial duels. You may find it new – and alarming."

Anschetil was in the forge, watching the smith shoe Chanson. He knew nothing of Odo Maluvel but promised to make inquiries concerning his prowess at arms.

"Although," he added, "it may not tell us much, for this kind of combat requires unorthodox methods very different to knightly swordplay in battle. Steady with that rasp, man!" he bellowed. "You're paring the horn to the quick." He bent, examined the hoof closely, and straightened. "I think, master, I had better start teaching you as soon as may be."

My training began next day. The scene, as always attracted a scattering of spectators: a man-at-arms off duty, dawdling varlet, a brace of serving-wenches and a few children. But my fencing-bouts with Anschetil had years since lost their novelty. To our servants they were part of the Bochesorne routine, an interlude in hewing wood or grooming horses. Helmeted, attired in quilted gambeson, blunted sword in hand, I faced the sergeant. I was quite confident. Nowadays Anschetil seldom pierced my guard.

He shattered my complacency.

"No shield, master," he said cheerfully. "No helmet or gambeson either, but we'll leave you them for the time being."

Surprised and worried, I slipped wrists from enarmes and laid the shield aside. Anschitel faced me.

"Guard!" he cried.

His point flickered and swooped left. Automatically I warded with a non-existent shield, and the cut jarred upon my shoulder. Anschitel lowered his blade.

"You see?" he said. His cheerfulness was gone. "We have to start from the beginning. Shieldless, you are lost."

This was true. Horsed or afoot, a knight fought shielded. The long, convex, lime-wood frame embraced his body like a lover. The narrow expanse of hide was his main defence; the rough-surfaced hauberk was vulnerable to any pointed weapon. Shieldless, I felt naked as a newborn babe.

"First, your stance," Anschitel instructed. "Right foot forward, not left. Your only protection is your sword, and you want as much reach as possible. Guard!"

He feinted and lunged. I parried, wrist low, far too late.

"Look at your feet," the sergeant growled.

I looked. I had withdrawn my right foot unawares; my left shoulder, again advanced, bore the weight of an imaginary shield.

"We must stop this."

He cut pegs, malleted them into the ground beside my feet and corded my ankles to the pegs. Then he faced me again, sword in hand, and lunged. My effort to change stance was so violent that, with feet immobile, I fell upon my knees. A grin creased Anschitel's face.

"It will come, master, it will come. The sooner the better," he added.

The laughter faded from his eyes.

And so, for hours each day, my purgatory endured. On the fourth day Anschitel untied my ankles. For a while we fenced; like a colt released from hobbles I pranced around him happily. Anschitel warded my blade abstractedly, and watched my feet. Then he grunted and re-tied the bonds.

It took a week to unlearn the lessons of fifteen years. My shoulders and ribs, despite the gambeson's protection, ached from repeated blows. My helmet was dinted; my headache permanent. A blissful morning arrived when finally I pierced the sergeant's guard; the thrust, fierce and true, spun him to the ground. His boiled-leather features crinkled in a smile.

"At last, master! Now prove your hit."

Anschetil fought the bout with savage concentration. He used every wile of feint and invitation, thrust high and slashed low, his blade a lightning whirl. I warded with growing confidence, slipped a high-line point and cut right. His helmet clanged and he dropped like an empty sack.

"Good enough," he said, rising dizzily, hands to head. "Let's rest awhile. I'm seeing more stars than heaven holds."

We sat in the sun, panting. I removed my helmet and wiped the sweat from my brow. Anschetil cursed a cowman who, round-eyed, was watching our performance, and sent him about his business.

He said, "I have learnt something of your enemy, master. Odo Maluvel is a skilled and brutal fighter. Moreover, though too young to bear arms, his experience outweighs yours. He has taken part in private tourneys with Lord Hamo's knights, and fought, as his brother's squire, at Exeter siege."

The information was no great surprise. Richard Maluvel had been a household knight. He held no land; in return for food, shelter and a little money he guarded his lord's person, garrisoned his castle, escorted him on journeys and supplied one of the knights whom Hamo owed for seisin of his fief. Such men have no interests except arms and war. They give homage to their paymasters, but they fight for money. The territorial gentry, like Walchelin, regard them as little better than hired soldiers, descendants of those scallywag adventurers who infested the Bastard's army. Of this breed was Richard Maluvel. His brother, on the verge of knighthood could not be very different.

I had to face a practised professional fighter. That in itself did not frighten me, but Anschitel had worse in store.

"This sword-fighting is but preliminary to our real work," he said. Reflectively he fingered an ancient scar that seared his cheek. "Maluvel wields a guisarme."

I had never faced the long-staved hand-axe, and told him so.

"I have," the sergeant said. "They can be very nasty. It's a light one-handed axe: nothing like the heavy two-hand battle-axe the English use. I have had the smith make one for practice."

He went to the forge, and returned twirling the guisarme.

"The trouble is," he said gloomily, "that whereas I know the wards and counters to this weapon I have never used it myself. Spare me your blows, master, while I learn the art."

4

John fitzGilbert's writ desired my father to deliver me at his Shire Court in June. Three weeks were left.

Anschitel imposed a régime which left me little time for thought. Dawnlight tumbled me from my pallet and sent me running the tracks and meadows. All morning I fought the sergeant, sword against guisarme. In the afternoon, stripped to our breeches, we wrestled. His teaching went far beyond the ordinary holds and throws practised by rustics on the churchyard green. I learnt buffets and clinches which could maim and kill. While the shadows of the elms lengthened across the pastures I performed, under his instruction, curious exercises designed to strengthen belly and back, arms and thighs. At the day's end I fell on my straw exhausted, and slept without dreams.

Bread disappeared from my diet. I ate only meat and fish and strange green vegetables which Anschitel culled from the fields. Wine was forbidden. I had neither time nor opportunity for dalliance, because Anschitel had said something to my favourite wenches which sent them running like startled hares whenever they saw me.

He wanted the farrier to file my front teeth. I refused. "This is no time for vanity," the sergeant complained. "Your teeth can be a potent weapon. Remember the rules which govern your duel." I was adamant; and he contented himself with sharpening my toe- and finger-nails until they resembled a wildcat's claws.

During the last few days I faced Anschitel's guisarme without the protection of helmet or gambeson; my feet were bare, and I felt naked as an oak-tree stripped by December gales. Agility and swordplay were my only defence. The axe never found my body, and Anschitel swore he was not deflecting his strokes to save my skin. I tried to believe him.

5

In the darkness before dawn of a windy day in June I went to Mass and confessed my sins. Outside the church Walchelin waited with brother William, Anschitel and our armed retainers. Visdelou's entire war cavalcade – two knights, seven sergeants, five archers and a brace of pack-horses – rode for Marlborough.

During that journey across downland, through thorn thickets and tree-dark forest, while wind thrashed the branches and tattered clouds fled across the sky like charging pennons, I became convinced that I was riding to my death. Judgement of my crime belonged to God. Ranulf had told me, as we knelt in prayer, that none could hold me guilty until His verdict was known. I remembered the anxious distress in the priest's face, ghostly pale in fluttering candle-light. But I knew my guilt, and expected no mercy from God, and none from man. I prayed silently for forgiveness and a quick ending; and the creak of leather and rustle of mail-rings were a monotonous anthem to my invocations. In the end, when Marlborough's keep towered on a forested horizon, I knew a sort of peace, a resigned tranquillity. All fear had gone.

I was to learn, much later, that in this kind of acceptance, in this calm consciousness that there is nothing left to lose, a man will always fight his best.

We rested that night and all next day at a village tavern of the better sort. Walchelin made no claims on fitzGilbert's hospitality in the castle, as was his due. He seemed, in his withdrawn mood, to regard me as a pariah, an outcast whose contagion isolated us from our fellow men. Anschitel alone crossed the drawbridge to make our arrival known to the sheriff's officers.

On the second day the summons came, and we entered the castle. The Shire Court, held in the great hall of Marlborough, was a gathering very different to the rowdy concourse at Kintbury. Dignity ruled, and men spoke softly. There were no spectators; litigants and witnesses waited in the outer ward until the seneschal called their cases. Men-at-arms guarded doors; a jury – fur-mantled knights in long-sleeved tunics – lounged in chairs; the Marshal himself, enthroned in a high-backed settle, presided with a forcible precision that needed no guidance from sergeant or clerk. John fitzGilbert's rounded shoulders and stooping stance diminished his height; dark hair, lank as seaweed, framed a sallow countenance, whose eyes, gleamed like ebony beads, flickered restlessly from face to face. Suspicion was his nature; intrigue ruled his life. He was not a man to tamper with.

Odo Maluvel stood among a group of retainers. Hamo de Neufmarché was not with them. Having launched his vengeful missile, he was content to let God's justice carry it to the mark.

The proceedings were short. A clerk read aloud a transcription of evidence from the Hundred Court. Maluvel and I were left standing side by side before the Marshal. Maluvel made his appeal, low-voiced, with none of the blustering arrogance he had shown at Kintbury. fitzGilbert nodded, and spoke to the jury.

"Are you agreed, my lords, that this crime should rest upon God's judgement, that Odo Maluvel should prove his charge by his body in accordance with the king's laws, the customs of the realm, and the rules of judicial combat?"

The knights conferred briefly. Their spokesman rose.

"We are so agreed."

37

The Marshal regarded us, his face expressionless, his eyes cold and hostile.

"Odo Maluvel and Humphrey Visdelou, tomorrow you shall attend the Execution of the Verdicts, between the hours of terce and sext. There you shall fight, and fight to the death. In the outcome God will manifest that you, Humphrey Visdelou, are guilty or else guiltless of this foul murder. By the issue He will declare that you, Odo Maluvel, have made false accusation or have borne true witness.

"May Christ have mercy on your souls."

6

I slept heavily, like a drunkard drugged with wine. Anschitel roused me before sunrise. He played the light of his horn lantern on my face and grunted disapproval.

"Outside, master. Naked as you are. You need freshening."

We left the squalid room, where the baron and William still snored upon their pallets. It had rained in the night. Low clouds obscured the dawn-pale stars. Anschitel filled buckets from a trough and hurled torrents of icy water on my body. He bundled me indoors and scrubbed with a rough blanket until my skin glowed. He dressed me in breeches and woollen tunic, lacing the points with care, and put shoes on my feet.

"This rain has greased the ground underfoot. Remember it when the time comes." He put a wooden dish of lean beef on the table. "Now eat, slowly, and chew your meat thoroughly."

The village stirred. Voices clacked in argument and greeting. A donkey brayed; axles screeched like fighting cats; feet squelched in mud and splashed through puddles. Anschitel squatted on the floor and unsheathed my sword. Lovingly he whetted edge and point, caressing the steel with slow, careful strokes. He laid the stone aside and glanced through the doorway.

"We shall not lack company."

The miry road was crowded. Peasant and freeman, farrier and priest, soldier and smith – the people chattered and laughed with the carefree abandon of pilgrims. No saint had named this day, but fields would remain untilled and oxen unyoked. They all moved towards the castle.

My father and brother came from the bedchamber, yawning and pulling on clothes. Walchelin clawed his beard, cursing the tangles, and combed impatient fingers through his hair. William hawked and spat, blew his nose and wiped fingers on tunic. Their toilets ended, they crammed food into their mouths and ate standing.

"The horses are saddled, my lord," Anschetil said.

We mounted and mingled with the crowd. William flailed his whip and forced a passage. None spoke during the short ride; and we came to the Execution of the Verdicts.

The place was a sward which spread like a green carpet from the castle walls. The wooden keep soared above it, standing foursquare on a mound which plunged steeply into an encircling ditch. A bridge leaped the fosse in a high arch and descended to the inner ward, an abode of barracks and armouries, strongly protected by sarsen walls. From this again jutted the outer ward, a palisaded peninsula surmounting the meadow where we stood. The ground sloped gently from the castle and drained, at the furthermost margin, into an extensive pond whose weed-spotted surface glimmered like a sheet of mildewed leather.

On the glacis of the outer sward the people sprawled like spectators at a tourney. Bright tunics and gaudy hoods marked a holiday occasion. Hucksters with wooden trays suspended from their shoulders sold cheap wares – barley cakes, carved crucifixes, watered ale – and called their goods in strident voices.

A bell clanged from the bailey chapel. The hours of terce. A horn brayed harshly. John fitzGilbert the Marshal, castellan of Marlborough, rode across the drawbridge attended by household knights in flamboyant cloaks and garrison knights in mail and monks in sombre gowns. Behind them men-at-arms herded a melancholy procession. These were wrongdoers of the common people, men and women without guarantees or sureties, penned for many days in stinking dungeons beneath the keep. On this grey-clouded morning they were delivered to God, to learn at His tribunal the verdict on their crimes.

Armed men quartered the meadow and drove laggards from the green. Monks in procession, two by two, crossed the sward and knelt beside the pond. They consecrated the weed-scummed element and made it holy, hallowed by the Church, sacred as Christ's own vestments. The water was become pure: no longer could it accept a body stained by guilt.

Jailers led a man to the edge and stripped him naked and trussed him hand and foot. They bound a long cord about his waist and forced him to his knees. Sweat gleamed upon a face where starvation and suffering had chiselled deep caverns of pain. A fat-faced priest, with greasy pouches beneath protuberant eyes, knelt before him and muttered prayers. He clambered to his feet and gestured to the jailers.

They seized the prisoner by shoulders and ankles, swung, and hurled him far into the middle.

The water exploded. Glistening meteors sprayed and curved over the body. It surfaced briefly and disappeared. A priest tilted a sandglass and watched the trickling grains. Silence was absolute. The priest lifted a hand. Men hauled upon the cord, dragged the sodden bundle to shore and loosed his bonds. He lay there retching, half-drowned, all but dead, his innocence proved.

The crowd buzzed like wasps on honey – a voice that might have been relief, or could have been disappointment. We could not tell.

The victim of the fourth ordeal floated. Desperately he rolled and twisted and plunged his head beneath the surface and fought like a barbed salmon. The priest watched his sandglass. At length he bowed his head and crossed himself. The man came ashore struggling, and uttered inarticulate, half-choked cries. Jailers loosed his bonds and drove him stumbling towards a group who stood apart, ringed by guards. Here were brazier and blocks and curious iron implements and cauldrons that hissed and seethed. Here also was the Marshal's executioner, a gigantic Breton, hairy and naked save for a cloth about his loins. They flung the wretch at his feet, and he looked to fitzGilbert. The Marshal made a downward chopping motion with his hand.

The executioner's assistants took the man unhurriedly, spread-eagled him and held his leg across a block. An axe flashed. The foot fell away. Blood gouted. Swiftly they seized the stump and plunged it into a cauldron of bubbling pitch. The man screamed like an animal. They bound linen strips around the blackened mess, and let him lie.

The sheriff's sergeant stepped forward, parchment in hand.

"Siward son of Sawulf, in the eyes of God and man you are shown guilty of rape upon the body of Eadgyth of Pewsey. In the king's name I declare your house, goods and chattels forfeit, and order you to abjure the realm within twenty days."

Siward, senseless on the ground, heard not a word; nor, had he been conscious, could he have understood the formal phrases spoken in stilted Norman-French. A man-at-arms dragged him away. Another outlaw for the forests, I thought, if he recovered, or another beggar on some distant roadside. How could a maimed and ruined peasant earn a lawful living, or find his way across the seas?

7

The hours dragged on. Clouds, sullen and menacing, descended to brush the tree-tops. My thighs ached on the saddle, and I dismounted: stiffened muscles were a handicap I could not afford. Walchelin sat motionless, staring ahead. He seemed unaware of the movements on the meadow, which settled into a processional rhythm disturbed only by the screams of anguished men and the spectators' muted voices. Sometimes he bent his head, and his lips moved. Torn by pity and remorse, I watched his face. An agony of wretchedness scorched me like a fiery wind. I knelt before him.

"Forgive me, father," I muttered miserably.

He stretched a hand and stroked my head.

"You have long been forgiven, my son. Christ and His saints grant that you may prevail."

I laid my head against his knee, and wept.

Anschitel watched anxiously. Presently he laid an arm about my shoulders – a familiar gesture which I was past resenting – and drew me aside. Feverishly he poured water from a leather bottle and bathed my face.

"Body of God," he breathed. "This is no time for tears. Today, of all days, your eyes must be clear and keen."

William regarded us, and scowled. His gaze wandered across the arena and found Odo Maluvel, who reclined comfortably on a grassy bank and conversed unconcernedly with his friends. The comparison afforded him no comfort.

"Take a hold of yourself, brother," he growled. "Are you going into battle blubbering like a child? You had better —"

A tearing scream interrupted him. The verdicts of water were ended. Ordeal by hot iron, the test always imposed on women, had begun. Two only were present that day; the first had failed already. Unable even to grasp the red-hot ingot, utterly incapable of carrying it ten paces, she beat seared hands upon her thighs, upon the grass, and rolled over and over.

41

King Henry's laws allowed no mercy. Not for her the clemency of amputation and banishment. The executioners dragged her, legs trailing, to the gallows. There for a few moments she jerked like a mummer's puppet, and was still.

William nervously twisted a frayed thread on his sleeve. "Not long now," he muttered. "Are you ready, Humphrey?"

I walked a little distance apart and made water, aware of the a feeling within my bowels like coiling snakes. A bitter stench of burning flesh fouled my nostrils. The second woman, moaning, tottered her numbered paces. They prised the bar from her bubbling palms, bound the cauterized hands and led her away.

A knight rode slowly across the meadow. William raised his head. "Here is the summons."

I stripped my tunic and kicked off my shoes. Anschitel unsheathed the sword and put it in my hand.

8

Odo Maluvel and I knelt side by side. A priest joined his hands and muttered incomprehensible Latin prayers. Mounted knights, swords drawn, sat their horses in a loose ring some thirty paces across.

The priest ended his invocations, and departed. The Marshal's seneschal, a knight of high degree, advanced and thrust his sword into the ground between us like a naked cross. His voice stilled the tumult; the words dropped like stones into a pool of silence.

"Odo Maluvel and Humphrey Visdelou, you are delivered to God's judgement. On your bodies you shall prove His verdict. You shall fight with the weapons of your choice, save bow or arbalest, throwing-spear or seax, or any missile delivered from afar. You shall fight without hauberk or helmet, shield or chausse, with no covering for your body nor shoes upon your feet. If your weapons break you shall fight with hands and fists, feet and legs, nails and teeth. You shall fight to the death."

The seneschal plucked his sword and extended it between us.

"May God defend the right. Take guard."

He lowered the blade. I faced my adversary.

42

9

Maluvel advanced in delicate, cat-like steps, guisarme held across his body, blade resting on his shoulder. Warily I shuffled my feet and tested my foothold. The grass felt cold and slippery. I flexed my sword-arm, blade pointed at his throat. He moved right and came closer, so close that I had only to straighten my elbow to reach his ribs. His lips parted; yellow teeth showed in a mirthless grin.

"Why don't you finish it, Visdelou?" he whispered.

The axe-head flashed.

I parried hard and straight. The hilt twisted in my grip; pain jolted from wrist to shoulder. He changed hands, reversed the guisarme. The iron-point haft lunged at my face. I met the thrust on forte, leapt back and disengaged.

Sweat prickled my spine. The man was much faster than Anschitel, and much more agile.

The axe again rested on his shoulder. I slid to his left, feinted high, and cut savagely at his forearm. Maluvel warded strongly, the guisarme held two-fisted like a staff. Then he leapt within my guard. For six heart-beats we stood chest to chest, straining like wrestlers, weapons impotently wedged between us. With a convulsive heave I forced him away and jumped after him, blade flickering.

He gave no ground, and met my attack with a wall of steel. So for a space we stood toe to toe, and I beat at his defence with point and edge, and cut and thrust with all the skill I knew and all the energy I had. Iron clanged on iron like the hammering of a thousand armourers. Blood pounded in my ears; my lungs clawed for air.

I disengaged. The hilt was slimy in my grasp; my knees trembled. The enemy still stood, half-crouched, guisarme in the familiar slant across his chest, axe-head on shoulder. Sweat runnelled his ribs and beaded the hair on his body. Blood trickled from a cut; the rib bone gleamed whitely, like teeth in a red mouth.

"Tired, Visdelou?" He crept towards me – a stealthy movement, a leopard advancing to the kill. "Soon you will rest."

I knew myself finished. Maluvel was a better fighter; he wielded his terrible weapon with unimaginable skill; he was stronger, harder and more experienced. Nothing remained.

He read the desperation in my eyes, and grinned. His limbs dissolved in a blur of movement. The axe-head swung for my neck.

I warded, blade vertical, and felt the steel shudder at the shock.

I remembered, far too late, Anschitel's reiterated order to glissade guisarme cuts – the best sword ever forged could not withstand a straight, full-armed axe blow. Maluvel swung again, and yet again, and pushed me step by step towards the immobile barrier of mailed horsemen.

Exhaustion seared my body. The sword in my hand was heavy as a tree; the axe a lightning storm. I gathered the last of my strength and lunged for my enemy's throat, and knew it for a slow and futile gesture, useless as an infant's love-pat.

Maluvel parried with the haft, reversed his axe and chopped hard on forte. The sword-blade broke with a sound like tinkling crystal. He shouted and jumped forward.

The ground, trampled and muddy, yielded beneath my feet and I fell on my back, helpless as a day-old leveret. Maluvel stumbled over my thrashing legs and crashed athwart my belly. I twisted and grabbed his head. My thumbs felt for his eyes, found them, and gouged.

He shrieked like a woman. I thrust deeper, scooped the eyeballs, tore them from their sockets. Then I left him, and scrambled to my feet, and stood trembling.

Maluvel moaned and flailed his head from side to side and scrabbled at the turf. I saw his face, and the things that dangled on his cheeks. Vomit rose in my throat.

The seneschal approached and stooped over him. He straightened with disgust upon his face and kicked the guisarme towards me.

"Finish it," he growled. "He fought well. You don't want him dancing on the gallows."

I set my foot on Maluvel's head, to hold him still, and put the haft's iron point against his throat, below the ear. I breathed deeply, and thrust with all my might.

4

Some years since, when I was a boy learning knightly courtesy at Lord Patrick's castle of Salisbury, I fought in my first mock tourney. For days beforehand I dreaded the event, although I fought the engagement with blunt weapons against children no older than myself. It all proved far less terrible than imagination had foretold, and I acquitted myself well. The relief, and reaction from long suspense, ignited a boisterous mood, lasting for days, when I bullied my fellows, over-ate greedily and became the ringleader in wild escapades.

The same kind of revulsion afflicted me now.

For weeks before the duel my life had been more austere than a Templar's. My nerves now uncoiled like the driving-ropes of a tripped mangonel. I drowned thought and memory in a prolonged debauch, beginning with a drinking-bout in a Marlborough tavern. On the second day after our return to Bochesorne I was too drunk to serve the baron at table and he, in a rage, banished me from the Hall until I recovered my senses. I staggered to the stables, found a strapper and saddled horses. With a wineskin slung from a shoulder and the stable boy for companion I departed, singing, for the empty manor at Speyne.

I cannot remember how long I stayed there. Days and nights were a blur, like a painting whose colours have run and intermingled. The Poitevin bailiff provided wine in quantity and sufficient food. He also found the girls I demanded, greasy sluts for the most part, but willing enough. I took them singly, in pairs, in complicated positions devised by the erotic fantasies of a wine-crazed brain. The stable boy readily joined these games, and invented new and ingenious pastimes. I searched all the curious byways of love between man and woman. I learned the expedients of love between

45

women: sometimes the girls who watched us copulating were so stimulated that, unable to wait their turn, they rolled together squirming on the floor.

There came a hideous morning when, awakened by a hand on my shoulder, I opened sticky eyes and saw Anschitel's glowering face. For a moment I lay without comprehension, gazing at him, and a kind of pity flickered in his eyes.

He said, "Time this ended, master. I have come to take you home."

He bent and heaved aside the girl who lay naked across my belly. She snored, thighs spread, and exposed herself to Anschitel's steady gaze and the grey light filtering through high windows. The sergeant put a hand under my arm and pulled me to my feet. I swayed and almost fell.

He looked around the room, and disgust wrinkled his nose. "We'll leave this carrion where they lie," he growled. "Come, master. Stir your senses. Where are your clothes?"

He dressed me somehow and led me outside and lifted me on a palfrey. I clutched the pommel and rode shut-eyed, crouching like a hump-backed cripple. Twice I fell from the saddle, and twice I was sick. Anschitel said nothing, but handled me tenderly. We came to a brook and dismounted, and he stripped my garments, plunged my shrinking body in the water and scrubbed shingle on my skin. He dried and clothed me.

"You cannot meet the baron in this state," he said flatly. "If you permit, master, I shall keep you in my cottage a day or so."

I could neither argue nor think. My bones drowned in a tide of lassitude; my brain was a sodden pulp wherein hammers beat and ghostly voices spoke unbidden. Anschitel took me to his dwelling, a thatched and flint-walled hut, and laid me on a pallet in a dark corner.

I rested there for a time, hardly conscious, and battled with nightmares and bitter remorse. The sergeant tended me like a mother, held me down when dreams flung me shouting from the bed, and bathed the sweat from my limbs. His wife, a grey-haired, sour woman with no teeth and a crippled arm, fed me milk and eggs and dry barley bread. At last I slept without dreaming. A morning came when I awoke and my head was clear and the evils gone, though every muscle, seemingly, had been stretched upon a rack.

Anschitel had brought fresh garments from the Hall. I dressed, trimmed my straggling beard and ate a full meal for the first time for days. The sergeant had horses ready. Before we reached the Hall Anschitel said, "Master, I have spoken to the baron. He knows something of what has passed."

I compressed my lips. I was afraid of Walchelin's anger. My conduct in leaving him without word or explanation was beyond excuse. I was his son and, more than that, his squire; my profligacy had broken all the canons of knightly behaviour. I deserved his punishment, and feared his rage.

I left my horse at the stables and entered the courtyard. My father sat in the sun, and fiddled with a mail-coat spread on the table in front of him. He looked up briefly as I approached, and returned his attention to the hauberk. I bent a knee and stood in silence.

"The armourer has spaced these discs too widely," Walchelin growled. "They don't overlap at all. This is your job, Humphrey, and it's high time you attended to it."

He raised his eyes and gazed upon my face – a long, searching, considering look. Then he nodded slightly, as if he had discovered the answer to a question.

"You have become a man," Walchelin said quietly, "and for that I am not sorry. Your boyhood has been stretched beyond your years. The fault is partly mine: I have kept you too long by my side and shielded you from trouble."

He slapped the hauberk.

"This may protect your body, but a man needs more than mail if he is to survive in the modern world. He must have a hardness of mind and a callousness to armour his heart. He must discard all weakness, all compunction or remorse – the emotions that sent you to seek forgetfulness in wine and debauchery. They are sentiments you cannot afford, Humphrey. Remember that – always."

He bent again to his work.

"Now," he continued briskly, "you can cut away the faulty discs. There are six, just below the plastron. And you will deal harshly with that armourer."

Walchelin took his staff and limped into the house.

2

The long, hot days marched into high summer. Peasants worked from dawn till dusk in the hayfields, and reaping hooks sheared the brittle grass and whetstones sang shrilling songs. Haystacks climbed like miniature castles. Ansgar the reeve rubbed his hands in satisfaction: winter fodder, he declared, would be more plentiful than he ever remembered; far fewer cattle need be slaughtered in the autumn.

The baron began to make preparations for my knighting, and grumbled mightily at the expense. He called me one morning to the bower, where he sat swathed in a furred cloak, though sunshine blazed through the windows and a heat haze shimmered on the meadows. Often, lately, the old man complained of cold while the world sweated and sought shade beneath tree or hedgerow. Seldom, nowadays, did he sit absorbing sunlight in the courtyard.

"Hauberk, helmet, sword, shield, lance, destrier and saddlery," he groaned. "All these you must have. At least twenty marks. More than Bochesorne's revenues for an entire year."

This was more than I expected, and I rejoiced silently. When I was knighted I could acquit, with William, the service of the two knights due from our Honour. Therefore I had thought that Walchelin would transfer to me his own mail and war equipment. The baron's armour was serviceable but ancient. Old Humphrey wore it at Hastings and, although the leather gambeson had long been replaced, most of the mail discs saw the English axe-men who guarded Count Harold's standard. Anyway, the technique of mail construction had improved since then: flat, overlapping discs were becoming unfashionable.

My father continued, "There's a fellow at Hungerford has lately made a hauberk for Gervase de Salnerville – he showed it me last time I rode to Donnington. A sound piece of work. You'd better let him take your measurements. I've forgotten the man's name – Anschitel will know."

I ventured on tricky ground. "Does he make ring mail, my lord?"

Walchelin turned his head and glared. "What do you mean? Rings are no good. Cheaper than discs, certainly – less metal. Very poor protection. A sergeant's armour."

"Not flat rings," I explained patiently. "I mean overlapping rings arranged in bands."

Walchelin drummed on the table. "Yes, I know. Each band looks like a pile of coins toppled sideways. Proof against anything except a crossbow quarrell. I saw the stuff when I was on castle

48

guard, though there's not much of it about. Do you know its disadvantages?"

If I were to have my way this was not the moment to argue. I shook my head.

"Weight. Inflexibility. Expense." He stabbed his finger at me with each word. "Banded ring-mail is the heaviest armour yet devised. Also the least supple. And, because it contains five times the iron of any other armour, you have to mortgage a manor to buy it. Stop talking nonsense, Humphrey. I am not a count, with revenues from a hundred fiefs."

His face softened, and he smiled in his beard.

"Even if I were, I should not give you a hauberk which transforms you to an invulnerable dummy, like that banded foolishness. You would have chain armour."

I sighed. Chain armour was the ordinary knight's unattainable dream – a superlatively perfect and enormously expensive mail-coat, the perquisite of counts and princes.

"I shall ride to the Hungerford armourer tomorrow," I said. Walchelin's opinions on anything to do with war were always to be respected, although in this instance I thoroughly disagreed. But the old man had made up his mind, and I knew nothing would move him. "There is this for your comfort, my lord. When I am knighted you will no longer have to endure the windy embrasures of Marlborough castle for sixty days each year."

My father snorted. "Little you know, Humphrey. Visdelou owes two knights: by November three are enfeoffed. And the king will demand the services of three."

"But we hold our land by the service of two!" I protested.

Walchelin smiled bleakly. "A disadvantage of being a tenant-in-chief. If we held from a count or baron he could demand no more than our obligation. But we hold of the king, and he is above the law. In this there is no question of homage or fealty – only tax. The king – or rather his exchequer – can demand shield-money for every knight enfeoffed on an estate, irrespective of the actual obligation."

"He must be disappointed when all the knights serve in person," I said bitterly.

"Possibly. But you can see, Humphrey, that until I die your knighthood is a drain on our revenues rather than an economy. I think I am capable of garrison duty for a year or two yet, but if the king calls me to the field army again —"

49

"Merely an excuse to collect three marks' shield-money, although I should go in your place and fulfil our proper service. It seems, my lord, I had better forfeit Speyne and serve in another baron's retinue."

"You don't mean that seriously." Walchelin slowly shook his head. "A landless knight. A hired soldier. Little better than a mercenary Fleming. No, Humphrey. You wouldn't like that."

The old man shivered suddenly, and pulled his gown closer. "Cold," he muttered. "The sun has no warmth this summer."

I held his trembling body in my arms. It seemed improbable, I thought unhappily, that Visdelou would ever boast three knights.

3

Toa the armourer was a short, cheerful, bald-headed Englishman. A fiery red beard fringed a round, red face which glistened from the heat of his forges. I explained my requirements. With a true huckster's instinct he immediately tried to dissuade me from my choice.

"Scale armour, whether of discs, lozenges or rings, is no longer adequate, my lord. It's the old story of missile power against mail. Let me show you something."

He shouted to an assistant and led me through his workshop, past roaring furnaces and rows of workmen hammering and shaping, drawing and riveting. In a yard at the rear, littered with rusty ingots, broken tools and other rubbish, stood a straw dummy nailed to a post. The assistant draped a disc-mail hauberk over the dummy, and gave Toa a crossbow and quarrell.

"Stand with me, my lord. We have room only for forty paces, but the effect, I assure you, is the same at all ranges to a hundred."

I regarded with some qualms the fields and roadway behind the target, where cattle grazed and peasants tossed hay. The armourer saw my look and grinned.

"It is quite safe. I never miss."

He set his foot in the crossbow stirrup, drew the string with both hands and notched it. He put the quarrell in place, took aim and tripped the sear. The dummy quivered from the impact.

I inspected the hauberk. The missile had torn through the discs and buried itself to the feathers. Consternation stood in my face.

Toa saw and laughed silently. The cunning little eyes gleamed in amusement.

"This stuff" – he flicked the armour contemptuously – "is no more use than threadbare linen. What you want, my lord, if I may suggest, is banded ringmail or, better still, chain mail."

I rubbed my chin and studied the damaged hauberk. The man was stating the obvious. Of course I wanted the best armour available, and this demonstration increased my craving. But the whole business was arranged so smoothly that I suspected the foxy Englishman had often practised a similar display to persuade reluctant customers. Self-preservation will loosen the most miserly purse-strings.

"Arbalests are rare weapons," I said. "A man is as likely to be struck by lightning. What is your price for a ring-mail hauberk?"

"To you, my lord, son of my old client the baron Walchelin, I can make a coat for – let me see." He made elaborate calculations on his fingers, and his pig-like eyes, vivid as sparks, watched me shrewdly. "To you only eighteen marks."

I grimaced. "You are talking to the wrong man, Toa. I am not Count Ranulf, nor yet the king of England. Come, measure me for a scale-mail hauberk. Discs, if you please, of tempered iron, overlapping smoothly, sewn with thongs – not thread – on a gambeson of best quality ox-hide."

I strolled towards the workshops, and the little man trotted alongside, his beard jerking as he talked. He recognized defeat but his cheerfulness was unabated; he spoke learnedly of swords and helmets.

I interrupted his flow. "Would you repeat that experiment on a coat of banded ring-mail – the kind you are so anxious to sell me?"

Toa stopped and stroked his beard. The hair rasped like wire.

"I have but one suit in my shop," he said doubtfully, "which I made for Lord Patrick of Salisbury. I would not much care to damage it." He regarded the crossbow cradled in his arms, and added soberly, "This is a terrible weapon, my lord."

I silently agreed; but did not mention that I was more interested in the arbalest's potency than the proof of his wares. "So there would be damage?"

Toa pulled his lip. "I will be frank with you, my lord – especially as you resisted my blandishments and have made up your mind." He smiled briefly. "The quarrell will not penetrate banded ring-mail, unless it strikes exactly between the bands. Chain-mail it will not penetrate at all. But the impact, if true and square, can ram the rings into the wearer's flesh."

"And make a nasty wound."

"Yes. The fact is we armourers have not found an answer to the arbalest. The shield is nearly useless, although it may reduce the quarrell's velocity or deflect it. When the captains of battle realize what a paramount weapon this is there will be much carnage in war, and many good knights will die."

The thought of losing his customers seemed to depress him, and the smile vanished from his gap-toothed mouth. I clapped him on the shoulder.

"That time is not yet," I said. "Arbalesters are infrequent birds. Which is why I am ready to gamble on a scale-mail hauberk. Now, this matter of a helmet."

Toa recovered his gaiety, and wasted time and verbiage trying to persuade me to a very expensive helmet made of one piece of iron instead of the usual segments. I sighed and resisted. The second-best, again, would have to do.

4

In mid July, soon after my visit to Hungerford, a sheriff's writ called Walchelin to the Shire Court. The baron listened wearily to Ranulf's reading, and the lines were scored deeper on his sunken cheeks. For some days past he had not risen from his bed. The doctor who came to him from Kintbury, a Welshman named Gwyn, fed him incessant evil-smelling draughts; but seemed unable to locate his ailment.

"My lord is full of years, and his old wound still hurts him," was all he could offer." He must be kept quiet and warm, and should not exert himself with any business." He was a trim little man with quick brown eyes and a persuasive manner. I thought him a charlatan.

I took the Welshman aside and demanded a fuller description of my father's illness, and more definite remedies. Gwyn shrugged.

"I can do very little. If I had discovered the elixir of life I might do more. The baron is an old man. I cannot arrest the onset of age."

I let him go; and there and then assumed responsibility for

Bochesorne's affairs. I wanted to keep the writ from Walchelin, but Ranulf, on reading it, said the baron should hear its contents. Together we took the parchment to the old man in the bower.

From the pompous rigmarole of lawyers' language emerged a summons to show reason, on a day barely a fortnight ahead, why Hamo de Neufmarché should not have seisin of that strip of land which had so long been disputed between our families. The message was a confirmation and reminder of the summons sent many months before.

Walchelin said, "Very well. For Aelfric's sake I shall oppose Hamo's claim. Ranulf, look at the precedents and prepare the papers. Warn Aelfric. His testimony will be needed."

I said, "My lord, you cannot make the journey. Let William go in your place. There is nothing new to be said in this cause, and he can plead as cogently as you."

Walchelin closed his eyes. After a long silence he said, "Yes. That seems reasonable. He shall go. Write to the sheriff. Tell him William has my authority."

William, when he was informed, complained bitterly that his hands were full with preparations for harvest. This was William's way and nobody took any notice. Under Ranulf's guidance he studied the petitions and arguments – learning them by heart – which the years of litigation had bequeathed and, still grumbling, departed for Marlborough on a sultry August morning.

Four days later he returned. Dust powdered his mantle and caked the sweat on his horse's flanks. Only driving necessity could have compelled William, usually so careful of his horseflesh, to gallop his palfrey through the heat of a summer's day. I helped him dismount, and felt an unreasoning disquiet.

"I must see the baron," he said brusquely.

I told him the facts. Walchelin's state had worsened; he slept, or was unconscious, for long periods and, when awake, his mind often wandered. He seldom understood what was said to him.

William tugged his beard. "So. For the old man's peace it is probably as well. We have been dealt a heavy blow, brother. Speyne is lost to us."

I sat him down and placed wine and food before him, and he told me the story. When the case was called Hamo de Neufmarché's bailiff advanced all the old pleas and propositions which had been rehearsed in numerous courts for nearly half a century. William, in turn, outlined his arguments and Aelfric supported him. John fitzGilbert listened with a bored look on his sallow face. At the end he picked up a scroll from the table, surveyed it briefly and flicked it towards William.

"The cause is void," he said. "Read that."

William gave the parchment to Ranulf, and listened to his low-voiced translation of the Latin script. From a mountain of loquacity a meaning slowly emerged which stunned him. The king had escheated Speyne manor and taken it into his own hands. William, in disbelief, examined the seal. There could be no doubt. King Stephen, horsed and armoured, bestrode the wax.

My brother's senses staggered and he had no words. He looked at John the Marshal, whose black eyes flashed malice. William shivered. The fieldstone walls of Marlborough's hall were chilly with the accumulated iciness of many winters, but he knew that the cold lay within his heart. He started to withdraw. Hamo de Neufmarché, who lounged in a chair upon the dais, stopped him with a gesture and rose gracefully to his feet.

"With your permission, my lord Marshal, we had better hear the final disposal of this estate."

fitzGilbert nodded assent. Hamo waved a negligent hand at a clerk. The man unrolled a strip of parchment and read aloud.

His Latin was unintelligible to everyone except the clerics. When he had finished Hamo, without impatience, said to him, "Translate."

The charter bestowed Speyne upon de Neufmarché, with sake and soke, toll and team and infangenetheof, for the service of one knight.

Hamo said gently, "Perhaps, Visdelou, you would care to inspect the seal?"

William, bemused, took the wax in his palm, and saw again King Stephen's mailed effigy. He looked Hamo in the face and saw no triumph – only a hard, determined hatred which struck him like a blow. The baron left his chair and strolled towards him, moving with the sinister grace of a cat approaching a wounded and helpless bird. A pace away he halted, and spoke in a whisper passionate with loathing.

"You still hold Bochesorne and Benham, Visdelou. I give you my defiance. Within fourteen days I shall come with my liegemen and destroy you and all that you possess."

He passed on. His face was politely impassive. The words might have been no more than a courteous farewell.

William ended his tale and gulped his wine. "So there we are, brother Humphrey. Our estates and revenues have been cut by a third. No one," he added irascibly, "has mentioned any reduction in our obligations. We still owe the king two knights."

I sat and thought. In myself was the origin of this disaster. I had no doubt that Speyne's forfeiture was an additional punishment inflicted by malice and a lust for revenge. In this there was no justice. I had extenuated my crime; my accuser was dead; and God was my witness. Was the king greater than God?

I raised my head from my hands. "What prompted Stephen to this iniquity?" I asked dully. "He is still in Normandy, concerned with great affairs. He must have little time for the giving and taking of insignificant fiefs."

"*Who* prompted him, you mean. Hamo de Neufmarché, of course, acting through John fitzGilbert. The Marshal is a royal castellan, and sends reports to the king, wherever he may be, at regular intervals. He probably wrote persuasive reasons why Speyne should be escheated. I wonder," William added, "what favour Hamo has done him in return?"

He finished his meal and washed his hands. "Much as Hamo may want to slit your throat, Humphrey, he still has to consider his risk. The king has given him Speyne; he has not given him permission to harry Bochesorne and Benham as well. Hamo holds fiefs all over England – he has far too much to lose."

William dried his fingers and flung the cloth to a servitor. He rose and smacked dust from his garments. "It is done, Humphrey, and cannot be undone. We have at Speyne a few possessions which we must remove. I shall send wagons from Benham tomorrow."

William departed, and left me to my thoughts. I sat alone at the high table in gathering dusk. Servants came, arranged trestles and benches, set flagons and trenchers and prepared the evening meal. I saw them as ghosts, a dim background to the terrors haunting my mind.

Of one thing I was sure, despite William's comforting words: Hamo de Neufmarché intended to strip Visdelou to the bone. We could expect no help if Hamo came against us. Nor could we prevent him. I knew that his household retinue at Newburgh contained eight knights, and he had enfeoffed four others on the

Honour. Within hours he could lead a dozen knights and fifty sergeants across our marches. They were enough.

Against him Visdelou disposed less than twenty fighting-men.

It was not a matter of preserving our lands, or crops, cattle and possessions – it was a question of saving our lives. I needed a stronghold, a place where a few tough-hearted men could endure for a week or two. This was a peaceful part of England. War was a dim memory. A raging siege would astound the king's custodians. Even John fitzGilbert might be compelled, however reluctantly, to act in our defence.

Thus I paddled in the waters of delusion; and the last rays of sunset fled from the Hall and servants put sputtering torches in cressets. I rose stiffly from my chair and went to the courtyard. Saffron and emerald flamed in the western sky. Tattered clouds trailed the horizon like smoke from a burning town. Across the river the ruins of old Humphrey's castle lifted like the fingers of a mutilated hand.

I knew the castle as a childhood playground, a place of adventure and pleasaunce in daytime and a limbo after dark. By the reed-fringed, weed-scummed waters of the moat I had chased water-rats and found the secret nests of moorhens; in the fosse I played seek-thief with my companions among the purple heads of fireweed and rank nettles and pungent elder-flower; in bailey and keep we hunted rats from the dilapidated timbers of granary and stable. At the day's end we always retreated. The mound and broken keep seemed to shrink when darkness came, but the gallows beyond the fosse towered against the sky like a doorway to eternity.

For a long time I gazed and played with memories. Then, a decision made, I turned and went heavily to the sick-room in the bower.

Anschitel, next day, did not seem much surprised when I told him my plans. He had talked with Aelfric, and knew about Speyne. Together we waded the ford, climbed the castle mound and inspected the keep. The walls – oak trunks planted deep in the ground – had stood for seventy years and would endure another century. The top floor, which was also the roof and fighting platform behind the battlements, had collapsed under ravages of time and weather. The floor beneath, the living-room and armoury, had rotted and needed repair. The keep's only doorway, four paces above ground level, opened on this floor. Below was a store-room and granary.

"Three days' hard work for a dozen men," Anschitel said. He

stood, hands on hips, in the dark cellar and gazed upwards. "Nothing seriously wrong. Merely a matter of re-flooring."

We went to the bailey. The palisade had vanished, robbed for firewood long ago. A forlorn post or two leaned drunkenly like stumps of an old man's teeth. Anschitel paced the perimeter, muttering to himself.

"Two days' work for sixteen men," he said finally. "Eight cutting timber in the forest and eight to plant the stakes." He regarded the spinney that crowned Hoar Hill, a half-mile distant. "And four carters for haulage."

The sergeant gloomily examined the stagnant moat. "This will be a long and dirty job. Weed-cutting, dredging, digging mud." He stirred the murky water with his staff. Bubbles popped on the surface and released a putrid stench. "Hard to say, exactly. Probably four days' work for ten or twelve men."

I said, "What is the total labour force at Bochesorne?"

"Forty-three villeins and thirteen women, master. Also eight freemen and their servants, if we can persuade them. Let me see."

He squatted and scratched marks on the rain-pocked earth. At last he straightened with a grunt and stroked his beard. "I reckon we can repair the keep, build a palisade, dredge the moat and clear the fosse in seven days, working from dawn till night and employing every hand we have."

I nodded. The work would restore the bare defences of Bochesorne's broken castle. Much more was required to give the place strength.

Next day the fields were deserted, and men swarmed on the long-abandoned castle mound. I watched for a time, and saw the sullen faces of peasants driven from their husbandry at the most crucial time of year. Incomprehension was there, too; and this I regretted. Men work better when they know a reason for their labours. Impossible to explain. Sooner or later stories must trickle across the countryside, beyond our marches, that I was rebuilding Bochesorne castle. The news could precipitate Hamo's attack, despite the fortnight's grace of his defiance.

I sent a rider to Hungerford with money and a message for Toa the armourer. The man returned, carrying a crossbow and ten quarrells; he said Toa promised delivery of another thirty quarrells within three days. I had not countermanded my order for hauberk, sword and helmet: the armour would not in any case be ready for two months; and one could not foretell the future. But armour I must have immediately.

I climbed to the bower, drew the leather-curtain partition of the baron's bedchamber, and knelt beside the bed. It was a grey day; the narrow window shed a niggardly light. Walchelin's face was the colour of old parchment. The hand he raised feebly in greeting dropped limply on the coverlet.

"My lord," I said gently, "I have come to tell you of a crisis that concerns us all, and to ask a favour. Do not try to speak until you have heard my tale."

I chose my words carefully, so that he should have no trouble in understanding. I told of the forfeiture of Speyne, and of Hamo de Neufmarché's threat; and I described how I was re-fortifying the castle. He stared at the ceiling and listened and, at the end, closed his eyes.

I awaited an answer, but none came. Hesitantly I added, "If we are besieged I shall take command, and must expose myself. I shall fight as a knight. But I have only a squire's haubergeon." I drew a deep breath. "Father, may I have your armour?"

Walchelin opened his eyes. The watery film of sickness and old age had gone; his look was keen, hard and angry. "Do you think I cannot defend my fief? When Hamo comes I shall meet him on the battlements. Have my armour? What then do I wear? And you are not a knight."

The baron's voice sank to a murmur. He struggled to rise, clutched his throat and fell back gasping. I held a cup to his lips. He swallowed with difficulty and reclined, breathing heavily.

After a time he spoke again, in so faint a tone that I had to bend low to catch his words.

"I think you have done right, Humphrey. The king is overseas. We have no guardian. We must fight if we are attacked. Otherwise we are dishonoured."

Spittle ran from his mouth.

"I am a useless, dying hulk – when I am most sorely needed. Where is William? You have not told me. He must guard Benham. He cannot command here."

His breathing grew quick and shallow.

"You shall take my place, Humphrey. You must be knighted. I had intended, at Martinmas, to present you to the king. Now that cannot be. You must do without the ceremony, and the gifts, my son. I shall knight you myself."

"I am two months under age, my lord," I said unhappily.

A faint tremor, the mere whisper of a smile, stirred his lips. "Who will know, or care?" He rolled his head slowly on the pillow. "Fetch my sword – there, hanging on the wall."

I gave him the sword. Laboriously he reversed the blade, and put the hilt into my hand.

"Now you bear the arms of Visdelou, Sieur Humphrey. Guard our name, and do only what is right."

Tears fled down my cheeks. I kissed the baron's cheek, and held the frail hands in mine, and laid my brow on them and sobbed. Gently he stroked my hair.

"You are a knight, Humphrey. I do not know why you should weep. Take my armour. One promise I demand."

I nodded speechlessly.

"If I am still alive when Hamo comes you will carry me to the castle. You must not leave me here, nor send me away."

Unwillingly I gave my promise, for this I had not planned. The old man closed his eyes. Soon he fell asleep. I crept softly down the ladder.

7

Isabel and her tirewomen departed for sanctuary at Donnington, carrying a letter which Ranulf wrote at my dictation. I explained to Gervase something of our troubles, knowing that our friend would not refuse this small favour. None of our neighbours could help us against Hamo: their suzerains had not summoned them to war on our behalf.

I made time to practise with Toa's crossbow. Notching the string needed considerable strength. You placed a foot in the stirrup and pulled upwards with both hands. The string cut my fingers, and I pulled on gauntlets. Anschetil watched my efforts with amusement.

"You can always tell an arbalester by the callouses on his hands," he observed.

I used only three of the precious quarrells for practice, and padded the target with many layers of straw. Once I became used to the missile's velocity and flat trajectory my aim quickly improved. It was a far easier instrument to master than the bow. To Anschetil I expressed surprise that the weapon was not more commonly used.

He said contemptuously, "She's a slow beast. Your bowman can loose three arrows to the crossbow's one."

I shrugged. Arrows seldom harmed an armoured knight. The quarrell was irresistible.

After seven days the labourers finished work on keep, palisade, moat and fosse; and I set them to reinforcing the mound. The peasants grew more sullen; cornfields awaited the sickle; they saw their subsistence for the year starting to rot before their eyes. I spoke harshly, and drove them to the forests to hew wood.

I finished stocking the castle. The store-room beneath the keep could hold no more of grain and meat, water and wine. The armoury contained plenty of arrows. Behind the battlements I stacked long, forked poles to thrust off scaling ladders.

On the ninth day I summoned Bochesorne's retainers to the castle. From the Hall came Anschetil, four sergeants and three bowmen. Of the eight freemen on the manor five Normans answered the call, although they owed us no military service. The remainder, all English, did not arrive. They, likewise, had no armed obligation except to the native levy. I thought them fools. Hamo's men would not spare their cottages and crops; in the castle they might, with luck, save their lives.

I inspected the garrison's armour and weapons, and made up deficiencies from our store. I explained the alarm signal: a triple-rise call on a hunting-horn, repeated four times. I put them in battle-stations on the palisade, and practised quick retirement to the keep. Nearly all were mature men; few had experience of war. One or two had fought, years since, on the Welsh marches. Anschitel, whose tally of battles and leaguers outnumbered our entire garrison, viewed them with disfavour, and bullied them mercilessly.

To Ansgar the reeve I said, "The villeins will find no safety here. The castle was built to keep your people out; it has no room to shelter them. Tell them, when they hear the alarm, to abandon everything and fly to the forests, taking only what food they can carry. There they must stay hidden until the affair is decided. If we are overwhelmed they can return to the village and throw themselves on Lord Hamo's mercy. He is unlikely to harm them."

Ansgar pleaded with tears in his eyes. I left him impatiently. Anschetil said, "Get away, fool, and obey my lord's commands. If your lives are spared you can count yourselves fortunate. You of Henry's England have never seen a harrying. We shall all lose everything – houses and chattels, corn and beasts. Whether the castle stands or falls makes no difference. Nothing will be left to any of us – not to my lord, nor to me, nor to the poorest peasants. Win or lose, we are ruined. Now go!"

This hard decision had an unhappy sequel. Ranulf the priest declared that he must remain with his flock and share their dangers. I reminded him acidly that although he lived among the English he was still Norman, and the castle's purpose was to preserve Norman lives. His round face set in lines of unwonted determination, and defiance glittered in the eyes that were usually so mild.

He said, "My lord, I shall not desert the people who have worked for your family all their lives; whom you have now abandoned and left defenceless."

"You are both insolent and a fool, Ranulf," I stormed. "Do you think I enjoy sending our villeins to the woods? They are the muscles and sinews that provide our revenues; without them we cannot live. But you know very well that the castle can't contain them. End this folly. I command you, in the baron's name."

The priest smiled sadly. "You have not the power. This is not a secular matter. I have a duty to the Church and a responsibility derived from God towards the people in my care."

He stared me in the eyes. The Visdelou squint was very pronounced.

"Consider a little, my lord. You know my blood. Would you have me craven?"

I found no answer, and let him go.

On the eleventh day, an hour before sunrise, a watchman stumbled into the hall and roused me from my pallet. I read the expression on his face, and needed no words for his message.

A rider went galloping to William at Benham. I raised the horn to my lips and sounded the call, and turned to south and north, and east and west, and called again.

5

August, 1137

A household sergeant helped me arm. The baron's hauberk, although ancient, was in excellent repair, because I, his squire, had cherished it for years. I had polished and greased every disc, and knew every dint and scratch by heart. It fitted me well. Often, after cleaning the mail, I surreptitiously slipped it over my head and swaggered before my reflection in Isabel's polished steel mirror. Sometimes, when we were children, we acted the story of St Percy, and she was Andromède, and I rescued her from a dragon. A liam-hound played the dragon's part, and St Percy's terrifying grimaces turned him to stone. I pulled the most fearful faces, although the hound remained unaffected, and Isabel giggled. Once Walchelin caught us, and we froze in a rock-like trance so that the spell, for once, seemed to have really worked. He merely laughed and slapped the helmet over my eyes.

Now the helmet was a little tight, and the old-fashioned nasal, a narrow bar, rasped my nose. The sergeant bound protective hide-strips around my forearms. Only chain mail allows wrist-long sleeves: mail coats made of discs, scales or banded rings must end at the elbow, otherwise you cannot bend your arm to wield a weapon or guide your horse.

I slung over my right shoulder the baldric carrying Walchelin's sword. The shield, suspended by its *guige*, rode on my back. I strode to the castle. Men and women converged upon it, stumbling under the weight of such possessions as they could carry. I had promised sanctuary to all free tenants and retainers of Norman blood in Bochesorne, and to those who could reach us in time from Benham. I watched them doubtfully, and re-calculated numbers.

Servants carried the baron on a litter. Occasionally his eyelids fluttered and he muttered words we could not understand. Lady

Alice and her women walked alongside. Twice she stopped the bearers, and wiped the old man's face, and spoke to him soothingly. I do not think he knew what was happening – and I was thankful.

Hooves drummed on the wooden bridge. Horses were not needed in our predicament; fodder was limited; they were stabled in the vulnerable bailey. Nevertheless I could not bring myself to abandon our best – Chanson and two palfreys. We might need to send a messenger, or make a sortie. We might even have to eat them. Poor excuses, but Anschitel had not demurred.

Laggards hastened across the moat. We raised the bridge, closed and barred the palisade gate. Anschitel posted sentries on the battlements, and a sergeant herded non-combatants into the keep. Walchelin's litter rested in an alcove behind curtains. In the rest of the living-chamber more than thirty women and children crowded like cattle in a pen. Smoke from a central hearth drifted through a hole in the ceiling which gave access to the battlements. The privy, an iron cauldron set in a corner and decently curtained, they emptied through the doorway after dark.

Women moaned and chattered; infants bawled. Like chickens in a coop they quarrelled and elbowed and bickered over living-space. Anschitel finished posting his sentries and descended the ladder from the roof. He regarded the confusion and roared like a mating bull. He kicked women into place, threw children urgently to their mothers, and allotted living quarters as though billeting soldiers in a spacious town. When he had finished he faced them, hands on hips.

"You're very fortunate," he rasped. "You can all lie down at the same time. I've been in leaguers where they took it in turns to rest, and those who weren't sleeping had to stand. Luxurious, this is. Like the king's palace at Westminster. And now we'll have no more trouble nor noise."

I listened in admiration; then propped my shield against a wall and climbed to the roof. Aelfric, who had come to us from Speyne, leaned on the oak-trunk battlements, and watched the road from his homestead.

The sun peered above the horizon and promised a fine day. There was no wind; a white mist, light as thistledown, hovered over the river. A cow called her calf in the meadows; a cock, in lonely possession of the Hall's midden, crowed triumphantly. From Bochesorne village, half-hidden by trees, came a confused murmur like the babble of a shallow brook. Aelfric jutted his beard towards the sound.

"Like prodding an ants' nest," he said.

I saw figures streaming across the fields to the wooded hills above the village. Peasants driving cattle and pigs lagged at the tails of these various processions, striving to preserve a remnant of all they had in the world.

"Fools," Aelfric commented. "Beasts make a noise. Nothing like the call of livestock to attract a pillager."

His gaze lifted beyond the village and roved the valley lands which led to Speyne.

"The enemy are here, my lord," he added quietly, pointing his spear.

Black smoke pillared lazily above the distant tree-scape and climbed upon itself in ascending coils. I watched, and swallowed hard. My throat was dry.

"Robert of Ownham's cottage." I looked for him in the bailey below, and saw Robert leaning against the palisade, talking idly to a comrade. "I don't think he can see it from there."

Aelfric said, "What does it matter? He knows – like everyone else in the castle – that his house is doomed. Will you man the defences?"

"Not yet. We shall be long enough at battle stations. We'll await the outriders."

Time drifted past. The sun rose higher and warmed our faces. It was going to be a radiant day. A young blackbird, the last of summer's broods, alighted on a merlon and flew off again, shriek-ing alarm. More smoke soared to the sky, lighter coloured, grey and diffuse; the spirals rose and mingled in a cloud.

Aelfric said, "There goes Robert's harvest. They've fired his corn-fields."

I gazed westwards, to the track which crossed Rood Hill and straggled to Benham. From that direction I expected William and his sergeants. There was no one on the path.

Steel glittered in the coppice beyond the Hall. A horseman rode slowly down the road. Sunlight flicked sparks from his helmet. Two more followed at a cautious distance. I shaded my eyes and scrutin-ized their armour. Two knights and a mounted archer. Hamo's out-riders.

The leading horseman disappeared among the Hall's outbuildings. The others advanced on the trackway leading to the ford. Soon I could see them clearly, lances aslant their bodies, glancing around vigilantly. They threaded the tree-belt bordering the marshes, saw the castle and reined. For a time they stood talking and gesturing; then swung their horses and cantered back to the Hall.

Hamo had found us. I never discovered whether he had expected an easy killing in the open. If he had, his scouts must disillusion him; soon we should know his response. With a last look at the Benham trackway I left the battlements, retrieved my shield and descended to the bailey. Anschitel squatted beside the well. I told him to man the palisades.

When the garrison were in station I went from man to man, addressing each by name and saying a few words of encouragement. Some gave hearty replies and cheerful grins; others remained gloomy, silent and unsmiling. Whether they had any confidence in my leadership I could not tell. I was their commander and a knight – it was usually enough.

From the palisades we could see no more of the Hall than a thatched roof and high windows piercing lime-washed walls. Aelfric, on the keep, bawled his observations. Twenty or thirty men, mounted and afoot, were gathered round the building. More were in the village, breaking into the huts and riding past the church. Presently he announced the approach of a single horseman.

The rider followed a flint-packed causeway that crossed the marshes to the ford. His shield was slung and he carried no lance. I knew him for a herald and shouted a warning to the bowmen. Itching fingers were plucking at the strings.

The knight reined at the ford, raised an arm and shouted words which distance made inaudible. I stood above the palisade and waved him on. He splashed across the river and halted twenty paces from the moat. I could not see his face, obscured by helmet, coif and a splayed nasal of the modern type; the hauberk embraced a graceful, long-legged body.

"I carry a summons from my lord of Neufmarché," he called "Do I speak to Walchelin Visdelou, lord of Bochesorne?"

"The king, and he alone, summons Visdelou," I said. "I am Humphrey. By whose warranty does Hamo de Neufmarché and his followers trespass on our lands?"

"My lord has come to redress a grievous wrong. My message is for Walchelin Visdelou. I have no authority to treat with underlings."

65

I snarled at him. "Say to me what you have to say, or go. Your situation is too dangerous for insults."

The man shrugged. "As you will. Hamo de Neufmarché says this. He demands from Walchelin Visdelou the person of his son Humphrey. When Humphrey is delivered to my lord's keeping, Walchelin Visdelou and his liegemen shall be free to depart unharmed from Bochesorne, to go where they will, taking their arms and household goods."

"Your lord is indulgent," I sneered. "What if I refuse?"

"War," he said simply. "Your lands will be harried and Visdelou exterminated. Hamo de Neufmarché swears he will give quarter neither to you nor your men." Suddenly the knight swept his helmet from his head and let it dangle by the coif between his shoulder-blades. His was a young face, fresh-skinned and ruddy, his hair the colour of autumn oak. The blue eyes opened wide in frank appeal. "Humphrey Visdelou, we bring sixty warriors in mail against you. You cannot withstand us. Will you sacrifice the lives of all your garrison to save your own?"

This I instantly recognized as an overture to the men who, leaning upon the palisade, listened with rapt attention. "You go beyond your office, herald," I said. "Take this answer to your lord. Visdelou defies him and will fight him to the death. That for the formal challenge. You can add this as a private message. Already I have sent two of his men to hell. I shall relish the killing of many more."

The knight bowed, and his hair swung over his face like a tawny waterfall. Without a word he raised an arm in farewell, turned and rode away. I watched him splash through the ford; the water sprayed his armour.

Anschitel helped me from my perch on the palisade. He saw the trouble in my eyes, the doubt and melancholy, the shadow of guilt and fear. His smile was confident and reassuring.

"Well said, my lord." He tightened the buckle of my ventail. "Whoever armed you deserves a whipping. There, that's secure. Now let's have some fighting, and no more speeches."

2

Men gathered on the track beyond the marshlands. A mailed figure in front pointed and gestured with scythelike movements of his arm. Hamo de Neufmarché? I tried to recognize a distinctive blazon. He wore a blue-painted helmet, like others of his household; I could see nothing on his shield to distinguish him from his knights. A pity. If I could kill Hamo the war was won.

The knights dispersed. Hamo – if it were he – remained on the path with four companions. The sun rode high in the sky; I began to sweat beneath my hauberk. The day was langorous, tranquil, brilliant with heat. A haze shimmered above the meadows, where cattle still grazed quietly. Far in the distance smoke eddied and drifted above Robert of Ownham's ruined steading.

Figures emerged from the willow-tree screen which bordered the marsh, and mustered on the track. The long shields showed them to be knights – fifteen or more, marching purposefully in close order. On either flank, in ragged lines, men stumbled into the marsh. Sergeants and bowmen, these, wearing haubergeons and leather jerkins that ended at mid-thigh.

I watched in disbelief.

Although unpractised in war I had listened for many weary hours, at home and on castle guard, while my father and his friends remembered old campaigns. They discussed tactics and shook their grey heads sadly over the mistakes of long dead captains; and arranged beakers, daggers and trenchers to demonstrate the course of ancient battles. I had absorbed the principles which govern the conduct of siege and onset. My military education was doubtless rudimentary – but I knew enough to realize that one did not storm fortresses in this formation.

The truth I discovered long afterwards. Hamo's men had ambushed William and his three retainers. William they killed. One of his sergeants they took and questioned. They learnt that Walchelin was sick, the garrison few in number, the castellan a youth with neither experience nor skill. Hamo expected little resistance.

While his force advanced towards the river I could read his intentions plainly enough. The knights were an iron ram to smash into the bailey. Bowmen covered the attack from either flank. A short, sharp and brutal assault which pre-supposed a very slight defence. In some ways he read the situation aright, but the marsh undid him.

The sergeants struggling in mud could not keep up with the marching knights. The flanks lagged and trailed like the broken wings of a wounded bird. The knights strode firmly forwards, their eyes on the castle, totally disregarding their supporters' difficulties.

The interval between the two parts of the assault force widened. Twenty paces, forty, fifty.

Hastily I recast my dispositions. I called my bowmen together and placed them beside the palisade gate. I stood among them and loaded the crossbow. We waited, taut as our own bowstrings, while Hamo's knights marched steadily nearer.

I allowed them to cross half way, until the water lapped their hauberks' skirts. Bows thrummed like hornets. The arrows flew. I sighted on the leader, and flicked the sear.

The quarrell struck him on the brow and tore the helmet from his head. A tawny mane flared for an instant as he fell. I bent to re-load, and knew a momentary sorrow that the personable knight I had encountered a little while since was dead.

The second quarrell struck a shield, and I saw for myself the truth of Toa's words. The shield-hide proved useless as a drift of feathers. The missile's velocity hurled the bearer backwards as though hit by a charging lance. I caught a glimpse of the quarrell, buried deep, protruding from his chest. Hide and hauberk were so much paper.

The ford was a confusion of shouting men and torn water. The river, knee-deep, hindered them as I intended. They stood packed close, irresolute, shields high, nuzzling the rims. Arrows whirred and thumped the shields, clanged on helmets. The knights looked for their bowmen, and found them far behind, and bellowed angry orders. The men in the marsh stood and drew. The range was long, and none of us was hurt.

I loosed the arbalest on a target a blind man could not miss. The victim screamed – a high, terrifying shout. The group shuddered, swayed like trees in a wind-gust. Panic whipped them; they retreated and floundered to the track.

Two were brave, or foolish, or had lost direction. They came on, splashing through the water, knees lifting high like prancing horses. They found land and advanced at a shambling run, one behind the other.

I waited. The leader came within thirty paces. He stumbled on a boulder, and his shield went wide. I shot him in the belly. The quarrell pierced the scaled hauberk, soft intestines, and the hauberk again; and struck the knight who followed on the leg.

I do not think he was hurt, but he turned and ran. He was half across the ford before I could re-string. The quarrell took him between the shoulders, and he fell face down. The current drifted him slowly downstream; the body rolled over and over and an arm came up like a dying farewell.

The survivors trudged sullenly towards the willow-screen. Hamo's bowmen, thigh-deep in marsh, loosed desultory arrows. In the bailey men cheered and laughed and danced and slapped one another on the back. Aelfric roared approbation from the keep. I eased the strung arbalest, and returned quarrell to quiver. The string had savaged my fingers, which oozed blood.

An arrow, almost spent, tinkled on my helmet and recalled my duty.

"Keep under cover, God damn you!" I roared. "You're still under shot."

They returned swiftly to the palisade. Anschitel lifted the cross-bow like a priest handling a sacred relic. He looked to the ford. The river flung plumes of spray over bodies like steel-grey rocks. Beyond the shallows, where the current ran slow, red streaks drawled like rust stains on a polished mirror.

"Five quarrells, five dead, and the assault broken," Anschitel said. "Christ's wounds, it's a terrifying weapon! Why haven't we got more?"

"Why not, indeed, and the men who can handle them?" I said. My knees suddenly were jelly. I parted the slits of my hauberk and sat on the grass. "How many arrows went, Anschitel? Forty? Fifty? And not a kill. Arrows are wasted against shielded and armoured knights."

"Without the arbalest we were taken," Anschitel said soberly.

"Without the arbalest, and without the most reckless and ill-planned attack ever conceived, we would surely have been taken. Hamo de Neufmarché must be insane."

I got to my feet and gazed over the river. The enemy bowmen were retreating; soon they disappeared behind the trees, and the knights on the path went also. Nearer at hand, the knight whose stomach I had torn was dying a difficult death. There was nothing to be done about that. I could not risk opening the gate – although I coveted his hauberk. I told the garrison to stand down, leaving only sentries on the keep.

I said, "Those knights had not faced an arbalester before. They offered a close-set target, shield to shield. A shield-wall is proof against arrows – worse than useless against quarrells. Also they were unsupported. Hamo will not repeat his error."

A gentle breeze caressed the willows. I felt its coolness on my cheek, lifted my helmet and let it hang. The iron was hot. My whole body burned and ran with sweat; the hauberk dragged heavily on my shoulders.

I climbed the ladder to the keep, and saw with shame that my hands trembled on the rungs.

3

The heat in the chamber struck like a blacksmith's furnace. Sweat, filthy clothing, children's vomit and the overflowing privy compounded a stench that stopped my throat. Above it all floated the smell of fear. The women huddled like frightened ghosts. The attack had been a noisy business, for men do not fight silently. They had heard the shouts, the whistle and thud of arrows, and the uproar after the enemy had gone. But they had not seen anything at all, for the arrow-slits, unmanned, were shuttered and latched. Imagination had painted ghastly pictures.

Briefly I reassured them; and went to the corner where Walchelin lay. The baron lay propped against the wall, restless, rolling his head from side to side. His eyes were wild and sightless. There was a hectic flush on his cheeks; the bones seemed ready to crack the skin. The clamour had roused him, not indeed to consciousness, but to a waking nightmare where he re-fought long-forgotten leaguers and babbled the names of knights and sergeants many years dead.

I went to the battlements, and breathed untainted air like a swimmer surfacing after a long, deep dive. The sun slid towards the western tree-tops. Shadows flowed from the skirts of oak and elm.

Aelfric was still on watch. Elbows propped on an embrasure, chin in hands, he stared intently ahead. I touched his arm.

"What are they doing?"

"There's great activity around the Hall," he said. "Perhaps they're preparing another attack."

I followed his gaze. A commotion of men and horses eddied round the building. I saw burdened pack-horses led into the yard, and guessed that Hamo intended to make the Hall his quarters. I reflected, wryly, that he had no qualms about settling in a place absolutely without defences. He knew a sally was beyond our power.

Aelfric said, "They're moving. None is coming this way."

Horsemen rode to the pastures where our cattle grazed, and scoured the downland hillsides where sheep browsed like old dun rocks. Hallooing and shouting, trampling the standing corn and rising feathery dust-clouds, they herded the beasts across the fields to a fenced enclosure where we kept our breeding stock in winter. When they finished, Bochesorne's pastures were cleared of livestock, empty and lifeless like a land swept by murrain.

Aelfric sighed. "Lord Hamo learns from his mistakes. Thus war should begin : first to destroy the land and then one's enemy. He has left nothing, neither in forest or in meadow, of which in the evening you may have a dinner."

"Hamo has not finished yet," I told him. "Look."

Riders and footmen went to the grey-thatched hovels of Bochesorne village, to mill and church and fields where ripe corn rippled in the breeze. Torches flamed pallidly in the sunlight.

Wheat and barley burned in crackling fiery sheets that leapt to the skies. Trees, green and living, flared like torches. The mill tilted slowly to the river and collapsed in weltering steam. Bochesorne burned from end to end in a lake of flame that brimmed the vale. Cinders swirled and smudged the faces of the men who watched, appalled, from palisade and battlement. Heat like a corroding wing stung their eyeballs and parched their throats.

The smoke-fog drifted, settled over the meadows and blotted the Hall from sight.

We watched till the sun went down. As daylight waned the fire-light strengthened. The fields were carpets of glowing embers. Flames fluttered like tiny banners on skeletons of blackened trees. Smoke spread a murky ceiling that hid the stars.

Bochesorne was gone. Now we had nothing to lose except our lives.

4

I sent for Anschetil.

"Do you think they will attack at night?" I demanded.

The sergeant sucked his teeth. "It has been done. Not often. Only after a long leaguer, when the enemy has learnt the ground. Hamo hasn't had time – he has found other occupations." Anschetil rasped a finger down a smoke-grimed cheek. "Although he might —"

71

The sergeant crossed to the sentry who watched the northern face. "Have you seen anyone on the downs, Raoul?" he asked.

The man eased his iron cap, rubbed the back of his hand across a broken nose and spat from a dry throat. "Yes," he growled. "Five men – sergeants by their mail – trying to round up fifty-two sheep. Five halfwit children would have made a better job."

"You kept a good watch?"

"I saw the burning," Raoul said sadly, "but I have not moved from this place. I know my duty, Anschitel. No enemy has been prowling on my front."

Anschitel clapped him on the shoulder. "I believe you, Raoul." To me he said, "Just a chance that Hamo might have reconnoitred while we were distracted. He hasn't. He won't attack in the dark over completely strange country. We can sleep sound tonight."

I changed the sentries and arranged a roster of reliefs. The sun had gone, leaving a crimson afterglow flaming through the murk. Voices carried faintly from the Hall. I found time to wonder why an errant spark had not fired the thatch and burned the house about Hamo's head.

I crossed my arms on the parapet and stared into a night that matched my thoughts: a black void filled with the darkness of despair and lighted only by blood-red fires of hatred.

5

The riders came with daybreak. A sentry roused me from my resting place on the roof where I lay, fully armed, wrapped in a cloak. The dawn light was grey, deceptive, shrouded in heavy clouds. From the parapet we saw armoured horsemen, hazy and insubstantial as ghosts, cantering on the downs, probing the thorn scrub on Rood Hill, crossing the river marshes to the east. Horsemen were no menace to a fort. I did not wake the garrison, but moved round the battlements and watched.

Soon it became obvious that they merely reconnoitred. The riders quartered the ground, diverged, met and gestured and consulted. Sometimes they were near enough to hear voices. The light grew stronger. Women wakened in the chamber below; a child wailed; cooking-pots rattled and a blue wisp floated through the hole which was both ladder shaft and chimney. I smelt food cooking, and felt suddenly hungry. The horsemen ceased their wanderings, converged upon the downland crest north of the castle and stood in a group. Then they trotted off in a wide arc and disappeared in trees behind the Hall.

I went below to break my fast. Walchelin was awake and conscious. I told him of the previous day's onset, and how we had repelled it. He answered nothing; I could not tell how much he understood.

A lookout's hail brought me again to the battlements. A lone figure, leaning on a staff, trudged slowly down the track. Sometimes he paused, shoulders bowed, as though unable to go farther. He came nearer, and hesitated at the ford. I recognized Ranulf.

They opened the gate and brought him in. Ranulf sank tiredly upon a truss of hay. His garments were in tatters, his feet bare. We gave him water; he drank thirstily, and looked at me with haggard eyes. I asked a single question.

"Yes, they combed the woods and found the villeins," he answered. "They killed some and took the rest. Last night they used the women for their entertainment, in the encampment near the Hall. Even children, girls seven years old. I was made to watch —" His voice broke and he covered his face.

This was no time to grieve over ravished peasants. "Why are you here?" I asked brusquely.

"I come from Hamo de Neufmarché. If you do not surrender within the hour he will kill every man, woman and child in this place." He sighed, and dropped his head on his hands. "I do not bring this message willingly. I was compelled."

I saw blood staining his torn robe, and gently parted the rents. Red weals like raw meat scarred his back.

Ranulf said in a muffled voice, "They whipped me until I could bear no more, and bade me say to you what I have said. I am sorry, my lord. My flesh is weak."

I shook with anger. Ranulf was only a priest and a bastard, but he was part Visdelou and he was my half-brother. I helped him to his feet, and told Anschitel to take him to the keep and dress his wounds.

The daylight strengthened. A thunderous sky shut in the heat like a blanket. I dispatched the sentries, in turn, to get food, and told them to eat well. They would be lucky to taste another meal that day.

A sentry called me to the keep. Presently I saw men in formation leave the Hall and, half hidden by trees, move to right and left. They carried burdens, and followed the routes of the daybreak horsemen, keeping a long distance from the castle. None was mounted.

I sounded the alarm. The garrison came to battle stations on keep and palisade. I waited on the battlements and watched the enemy.

They moved slowly, in three groups, often concealed by trees and scrub, sometimes plodding across open ground. The baggage they bore hindered them; frequently they stopped and laid the burdens down. I strained my eyes until they watered, but could not recognize, at that distance, the nature of these peculiar loads.

The three columns crossed the river. Two stopped: one in the western meadows at the foot of Rood Hill, the second on the scrub-ridden slope to the east. The third continued, and eventually halted on the northern scarp.

"This sword has tree points," Anschitel muttered in my ear.

A horn sounded distantly from the downs. The prongs of the attack began gradually to close on the castle. As they drew nearer I saw that each group was divided into separate squads, and each squad bore a load: a flat package which they carried as men lift a raft to the water. They came on, rested at a signal, came on again. Soon they were near enough for us to distinguish, by their armour, knights from sergeants.

The enemy were close enough. I disliked these mysterious packages, and feared artillery; though it seemed unlikely that a small force, raised from the liegemen of a single Honour, could build siege-engines – work for professional engineers. I told a bowman on the western battlements to try the range.

The man notched his arrow, flexed and eased, pointed the barb at the lowering clouds and loosed. The arrow flashed in a high arc, descended and was lost. The enemy plodded slowly on.

"Try again."

The archer swore to himself, rubbed a seamed, sun-browned face and frowned at his target. He said, "It's a long way, my lord." The bowstring twanged.

One of the squads burst like a squeezed plum. A figure lay kicking on the ground.

The bowman grinned. "A lucky fluke. Much too far for accurate shooting."

A horn yelped sharply from the downs. The enemy dropped their loads, bent and heaved. Anschitel swore loudly.

74

"God's belly! Mantlets!"

The three groups resolved into quite different forms. Instead of men we saw dark rectangles with their bearers' heads peering over the upper rims. The shapes advanced slowly.

Anschitel uttered a long stream of complicated oaths. "Hay packed and wadded between sheep-hurdles. Impenetrable. Even for your crossbow. Christ tear Hamo's guts!"

I said calmly, "You have seen these before. How do we counter them?"

Anschitel sneered. "Mobile mantlets? Easy. A sally by mounted knights and a quick charge. They're heavy – can't be handled like a shield. Get round the sides and kill the bearers." He blew his nose vigorously and scrubbed fingers on the parapet. "A pity we haven't got the mounted knights."

"We have one," I said. I walked to the hole in the roof. Anschitel promptly barred my way.

"Are you mad?" he blared. "What can you do alone?"

"Kill some of them," I said, "before they kill me."

"And leave us without a leader? My lord, you shall not go!"

"Orders from a liegeman, Anschitel? You forget yourself. Stand by the gate; close it quick when I am gone, and take command of Bochesorne."

Another voice spoke. "You remain here, my lord, alive or dead. We do not fight without you."

I turned. The lucky bowman had his back to the battlements and reclined against the parapet like a labourer taking his ease. His bow was flexed, and the arrow pointed at my throat. He smiled a little, but his eyes were mirthless.

I do not know what my answer would have been. The whip and thud of arrows resolved the matter. The bowman flinched, eased the string and put a hand to his ear. He examined the bright blood on his palm.

"I am indeed in luck today," he observed to no one in particular. He turned and loosed viciously from an embrasure.

6

The mantlets ringed the castle to west and north and east on a radius of two hundred paces. Horn signals from the northern group directed the advance. Some of the mantlets were always halted, and covered those that moved with flight after flight of arrows. The garrison, peering over palisade and battlements, saw only helmeted heads and found little to shoot at.

I loaded the crossbow, wincing as the string bit raw fingers, and loosed at a head and shoulders target – a man standing to draw his bow. The quarrell hit the mantlet and penetrated to only half its length.

I missed again, and yet again. I had never practised downward shooting from a height: the trajectory was strange. I ran to the bailey, and two arrows quivered in my shield before I reached the palisade. The mantlets crept twenty paces nearer.

Bochesorne's archers answered vigorously, and made no impression. The dark blocks, like armoured monsters from the dawn of time, moved steadily forward, halted, sprayed arrows, and crawled on again. They were near enough to distinguish their casings – plaited hazel wands – and count the arrows studding them like spines. Too many arrows. I roared at the bowmen to shoot only when they had a worthwhile target. The flights from the castle dwindled.

I wasted three ineffective quarrells. The fourth was better, and I saw a helmet fly. An archer beside me cheered raucously; then screamed and clutched his face. A feathered shaft thrummed in his eye-socket. A sergeant sheathed his sword and dragged him to a stable. Soon he returned, met my eye and shook his head. He drew his sword and leaned against the palisade.

The mantlets neared the edge of moat and fosse. I loosed two quarrells at the nearest target. They sank to the feathers, but did not penetrate. The enemy was invulnerable.

The bailey had become a death-trap.

I shouted to Anschitel, who commanded on the western face, and to Aelfric on the eastern. Gradually I dribbled men from palisade to keep, and tried to cover them by swift shooting at the mantlets. No thought now of saving arrows. My men were most exposed when they climbed the mound and ladder; the enemy concentrated on these helpless targets. Four men reached the door safely, their shields prickling arrows like hedgehogs. Two were hit. One toppled from the ladder without a cry; the other wore three shafts in his body when they dragged him moaning through the doorway.

That left the two commanders and myself. I reloaded the arbalest, and no longer felt the pain in my bleeding hands. Anschitel took a bow and quiver, and shot steadily. I told Aelfric to go.

He wore a sergeant's haubergeon, without a coif. An arrow pierced the base of his skull before he climbed three rungs.

I called Anschitel. He dropped his bow, slung his shield and scurried up the mound to the ladder's foot. He saw Aelfric, face down and motionless, and frowned. With a run and a flying leap he arrived halfway up the ladder and bolted through the door like a squirrel into a drey.

I slung the crossbow like an ox-yoke round my neck, pulled my shield close, rim to nasal, and backed awkwardly up the mound. Arrows thumped the hide and rang my helmet. I climbed the ladder one-handed. A pain like a branding-iron seared my leg. Ready hands hauled me through the entrance, withdrew the ladder, slammed and barred the door.

Women in the gloomy chamber cowered in terrified silence. I stumbled across the room, replenished my quiver, and climbed to the battlements.

A horn blared, and the mantlets erupted men like a bursting dyke.

We could not stop them. They shouted war-cries as they waded the moat, waist-deep, and slid down the fosse and climbed the glacis and stormed the palisade. In an instant the bailey seethed.

We had three bows left. The arrows dwindled fast. The archers placed their shafts precisely, like women pointing embroidery. The noise was enormous. The enemy's war-shout – "Marché! Marché!" – rang like the clanging of bells.

I loaded the arbalest and started to clear the captured bailey. They had left no covering parties; the mantlets were deserted; the stinging arrow-hail had ceased. I leaned over an embrasure and tapped the sear. The target, close-ranged and close-packed, was impossible to miss.

I killed four, and my bowmen three, before the enemy realized their peril and the snare which held them. Then the shields came up, and they ran for shelter. Three knights stood defiantly by the well-head, looking up and shouting and brandishing swords. One I shot. The others ran before I could reload.

Anschitel was right, the arbalest was a slow beast.

The gate was open; some of Hamo's men scuttled to the mantlets' protection. The rest crowded the sheds which housed our animals and fodder.

I loosed at the thatched roofs in turn, and heard the sweet voice of pain. They stampeded, cramming the gateway and scrambling over the palisade. We skewered only a few during this rout: it happened too quickly.

The mantlets retreated, slowly and spasmodically, with none of the coordination they had shown during the advance.

I told my men to ease their bowstrings, and looked round the battlements. Twelve were left, and myself. We had lost the bailey and won a transient victory. Penned in the keep, we could not survive for long.

I dropped the arbalest and looked at my ruined hands.

Anschitel came to my side. "Bandages and salves," he said. "Why did you not wear gauntlets? Come below, my lord. We have time. Hamo will be in no hurry to renew his attack after that buffeting."

I stumbled to the ladder, holding my hands before me, palms upwards, like a beggar beseeching alms.

7

Ranulf tenderly washed and bound my bloody fingers, cut to the bone. The baron lay supine on his litter and stared unseeingly at the ceiling beams. Nobody asked how the battle went: everyone knew that any respite only delayed the ending for a little longer.

The gash on my leg was trifling; the blood had dried, and I refused Ranulf's ministrations. The man wounded on the ladder had died. The women trembled and muttered among themselves. The room was dark and fetid, a sad place, an antechamber to death.

I returned to the roof.

Two men kept watch; the others rested. I took the arbalest and tried to draw it; the agony bit like fire. Wryly I gave the weapon to Anschitel. He set foot in the stirrup and drew with all his strength; finally, with a grunt, he notched the string.

"God's bones!" he said, panting. "You need muscles like a mangonel's power-ropes. This is not for me."

Raoul of the broken nose was a famous wrestler. Smilingly he took the crossbow from Anschitel. The men sat at ease, backs propped against the battlements, and attentively watched his exertions. The sear clicked. Raoul regarded me with reluctant wonder.

"And you, my lord, draw the bastard as easily as a whore lifts her skirts."

"Partly knack." I examined my bandaged hands. "No longer. You will have to load for me. Find gloves."

I looked over the parapet. The blackened fields of Bochesorne, the cindered trees and charred rubble mourned beneath the funeral pall of a sullen sky. The mantlets moved again, no longer sundered, but joined like marching hedgerows. Smoke drifted behind them; we saw the flicker of flame. I looked at Anschitel.

"Torches for fire-arrows," he answered laconically.

I ordered bowmen to the parapet.

We had no defence against fire, no wet hides nor water-soaked palliasses to hang over the battlements. Even these were a meagre defence. The proper counter demanded a concentrated arrow-storm and a sally by mounted knights. We had three bowmen and one knight.

The mantlets came within eighty paces – a comfortable range. The arrow flights, like flying cinders trailing smoke, whirred towards us.

For the enemy it was easy shooting, their target the keep's square bulk. The shafts thudded home like separate heavy raindrops heralding a downpour. A shred of pitch-soaked, blazing wool wrapped every arrow below the barb, and charred a smouldering hole in the bone-dry timbers of the keep. We tried to pluck out those within reach. A whistling arrow-tempest beat us back. Two sergeants died, quickly and silently – for which I was grateful: our fighting platform was too small for clamorous and convulsive deaths.

The garrison crouched beneath the battlements while the fire-storm flew. Smoke raged skywards from the bailey, where arrows lodged in thatched roofs. The outbuildings burned like beltane bonfires. I heard animals screaming. Chanson was there, burning alive. I remembered him, and his savagery and his gentleness.

It was not cinders that stung my eyes to tears.

Smoke from the bailey enveloped the keep and hid the enemy. The keep began to burn; arrows lodged between oak-trunks set the timber alight; flames licked upwards. The women below were screaming.

In this moment of blind despair Ranulf's head and shoulders appeared through the gap in the roof.

"The chamber is on fire," he said calmly. "The women must come here or descend to the bailey."

I fled down the ladder. The room was in turmoil. Flames thrashed from a heap of straw. In stunned bewilderment I sought the cause; and saw two arrow-slits unshuttered. Some thrice-accursed bitch, wanting a little air, had opened the way to destruction.

The straw-fire caught a child's clothing, and leapt to devour a palliasse. The women, in panic beyond reason, fought like savages to gain the only opening they could see – the way to the battlements. I beat them from the ladder, mounted quickly and shouted.

"Out, all of you! To the bailey!"

The men descended to a terrifying cauldron of smoke and flame, the stench of cauterized flesh – the child burned like tinder – and shrieking, fear-crazed women. I ripped a smouldering curtain and took Walchelin in my arms.

Someone unbarred the door and set the ladder. Flames licked the shield upon my back. Carrying my father, I half-climbed, half-fell, and bore him to the foot of the mound and set him down. The bailey sprouted flames where men roved like demons in the furnaces of hell.

A scorching wind reft the smoke clouds. I saw armour glinting on the palisades, the loom of shields and swordblades red in the firelight. I shouted and charged.

"Loup! Loup! Visdelou! To me!"

Gleaming conical helmets surmounted five tall shields. Cut and parry, ward and thrust. Anschitel suddenly beside me, and Raoul on my left. Smoke billowing in gusts, flames whipping like banners. A clanging slash on my helmet. Counter-thrust through teeth and throat. Withdraw. Parry right. Shield across. Raoul down – a knight leaping his body. Shield left and cut aslant. Broken nasal and a blood-dark face. Shield centre – guard low. Anschitel gone. My right side open. Recover – quick!

The world exploded in fire.

8

I have no clear memory of what followed, or the proper order of events. Things happened without apposition, and remain imprinted on my memory like a series of pictures seen in a monk's missal when the pages turn. I remember the bailey, a smoky inferno, and a man bent over a corpse, stripping haubergon and weapons. On the well-head a sergeant ground his buttocks between a woman's thighs. He finished and withdrew, and tossed her down the well.

Later. I lay near the Visdelou gallows, and stared on myself stupidly, for I was naked. Nothing remained but the leather binding my forearms, and the bandages on my hands, Under the gallows a sergeant held my father upright, hands beneath armpits. Walchelin wore the grey linen mantle of his sickness; his legs and feet were bare. His grey head dangled on his chest, and around his throat a noose coiled like a snake. Ranulf knelt before him. The priest's lips moved.

The rope tightened like a bar. A prancing frenzy, a sudden injection of furious energy, seized the dropping body. The legs kicked in a final spasm.

Then I fell a long way into darkness, and an agony burned my temples, and unknown voices called from far away.

Merciless hands held legs and arms. I lay spreadeagled on my back. A man with a knife in his hand fumbled at my crotch. I stared vacantly. A livid scar creased his face from ear to chin; an iron cap sat askew on his greasy head.

A trumpet wailed. They lifted my body, and I floated to the clouds, and saw a burning, and a great concourse about the gallows, and a long column of armoured men.

Hamo de Neufmarché's face, spiteful, savage, the teeth opening and shutting in furious argument.

I fell into the void. A pain like sledgehammers beat inside my skull.

A voice pleaded. Ranulf. My eyes opened. The Devil in Christ's image gazed down. He reclined against his warhorse, arms flung wide along mane and quarters. His legs crossed negligently at the ankles.

Christ on the Cross. Satan in blasphemy.

Fine-meshed mail clung to his body like a snake's grey skin. Bare-headed. Glossy hair shining like black silk. Blue eyes, brilliant as sapphires, glittering in a lean brown face. The thin lips smiled.

Handsome as the Devil. A Prince of Darkness.

Ranulf, on his knees, arms rigid in supplication, prayed to him. The Devil spoke.

"One only," he said, and smiled.

The man with the scarred face seized me. The knife gleamed in his hand.

Understanding came in a blaze.

I prayed to the Devil, and besought his mercy. I was his man, I swore. He was my lord, and owned my fealty and homage. Let me follow him to Hell and beyond. Let me serve him for ever – only spare my manhood.

"Just one," Satan repeated, smiling.

The knife hovered, descended, and cut.

Agony unbelievable. An intensity of pain. A fiery orgasm that spurted blood upon my thighs.

Someone screamed. A dead sound, like a voice muffled by fog. He screamed for oblivion, for death, for release from anguish. Head between knees, he rolled over and over like a hoop.

I opened my eyes. I lay at the Devil's feet.

"Satan, you have betrayed me," I blubbered.

He hung upon his Cross, and smiled.

"I have saved you," he said. "You are still a man."

Ranulf's arms were round me. The shadows gathered.

"Why Satan?" the Devil wondered. "I am Geoffrey de Mandeville."

6

I remember very little of the journey that followed: Ranulf described it afterwards. The priest dragged my senseless body away from the armed men gathered at the gallows. None interfered; the tall knight leaned languidly against his horse and watched him go. Ranulf pulled me under a thorn-bush, realizing he would have to act quickly to save my life. A trail like crimson slime marked my passage. In that scanty shelter he tore his gown in strips, made a pad and bandages, and bound the wound tightly. The pad quickly became a sodden pulp; three times he renewed it, and little of his robe remained.

When Ranulf was satisfied that the flow had eased he lay beside me and considered what to do. Heavy clouds covered the sky; already it grew dark, although the castle, blazing gustily, flung a fitful light. A mailed column, led by the knight called Geoffrey de Mandeville, poured northwards into gathering dusk. Hamo de Neufmarché's men, seeking the last dregs of plunder, flitted like ghouls amid the fires. Presently they too departed, and Ranulf heard a faint echo of their voices from the Hall.

It was then quite dark, and the fires were dying.

I moaned and writhed in delirium. The priest tore his gown again, and lightly bound my wrists and ankles so that I could not wander. Then he crept cautiously to the gutted castle. He found corpses, some stripped to the skin, others still wearing vestiges of clothing. He collected garments and shoes for me and for himself, and found a linen mantle to make more bandages. Braving the heat, he crept into the bailey and lowered a leather bucket down the well. He returned to the thorn bush and loosed my bonds and, working by touch and the lingering firelight, bathed my wound and re-bound it, swathing the linen firmly round thighs and belly.

The bleeding had nearly stopped. He put a woollen tunic on my body, bound my hands and feet as before and went again to the castle.

In the litter of battle Ranulf found a short sword, some leather straps and bits of rope. He hacked branches from a tree and knotted them together to make a crude stretcher, fashioning it so that the shafts projected several spans at either end. Upon this he tied me. Taking the poles at one end over his whip-torn shoulders, so that at the other they trailed on the ground, he began to drag his burden from Bochesorne.

I think I remember the journey's beginning. The shafts bumped along the ground and woke me to consciousness and burning agony. I tried to pluck the pain between my thighs, but my hands were tied – I could only scream. Ranulf lowered the litter and dribbled water in my mouth from the dregs remaining in the bucket, and murmured soothing words I could not hear. He took the poles upon his back once more and, like an ox yoked to the plough, drew his load onwards into the dark.

I have no more memory of the night's happenings.

Ranulf's was indeed a desperate expedient. He had decided on his destination, but knew he had no hope of reaching it like this, for it was beyond his strength. Savernake forest lay twenty miles away. He knew, also, that before daybreak I must be hidden from Hamo's outriders. He found a sheep-drovers' trackway meandering westwards, and dragged me throughout the night, resting when his endurance broke, and taking up his load again, like Christ on His dolorous journey, and dragging, and dragging.

When dawn whispered in the sky behind him Ranulf had plodded, perhaps, seven miles, and had come to the end of his strength. He managed to turn from the trackway into a copse, a tangle of oak and bramble and bracken, lowered the poles and collapsed. For some time he lay in a waking coma, longing for sleep, tormented into wakefulness by his agonized shoulders – the stolen garment had shredded beneath the poles and his flesh was raw.

Ranulf woke to full daylight and drizzling rain. He pulled the stretcher farther into the ferns, and contemplated the occupant. I was still senseless, my face pale as wheaten dough – Ranulf doubted whether much life was left. He examined the bandage, caked in a mess of coagulated blood. He had no linen, no salves, and no more skill in doctoring than a village priest acquires in his vocation. He left the dressing as it was.

Ranulf found water in a puddle, bathed my face, trickled a little between my lips. He drank thirstily, bending on all fours and lapping like a dog. He squatted beside the stretcher, and raindrops pattered on the trees and shivered the bracken fronds; and he fell headlong into deep despair.

The priest had cause. His shoulders could not endure the shafts again, nor had he strength to draw his burden any farther. He had no food and no money and could not, while still so near Hamo's fief, risk revealing my presence by appealing for help. Meanwhile I, the reason for all his sacrifice and toil, seemed on the edge of death.

Ranulf dropped to his knees and prayed.

A jay screamed harshly. Branches swished and twigs cracked underfoot. The priest fumbled awkwardly for the sword tied at his waist. An elder branch, heavy with purple fruit, swayed violently.

Anschitel limped towards him.

2

His helmet was gone, and his haubergeon. Blood matted his hair and crusted face and beard; an arm, broken at the elbow, dangled crookedly. Mud and grime daubed him from head to foot.

He tottered forward and fell limply to the ground. Ranulf regarded him speechlessly.

"How did you come here? I thought you were dead," he whispered at last.

Anschitel opened his eyes. "So did I," he croaked. "Sword-cut through the helmet. Trampled in the fighting. Arm broken." His eyelids drooped.

"How did you find us?"

"Hid in the moat. Fainted. Crawled from the castle." He spoke with eyes closed, each word exhaled laboriously.

Ranulf repeated insistently, "How did you find us?" He recognized, with frightening clarity, that if this broken hulk could find him, Hamo's horsemen would have little difficulty.

Anschitel's tongue crept between his lips and sucked the drizzle that beaded his beard. The priest went to a puddle, soaked the hem of his tunic and squeezed water into his mouth. Anschitel drank, and lay silent awhile.

"Saw you go," he muttered. "Couldn't call. Couldn't move. Only half conscious. Then followed you. Two furrows on the path. Easy to track. Lucky you went slowly."

Ranulf knelt beside him and began gently to part his hair, seeking the wound. The sergeant lifted a hand.

"No," he said. "The pain is easing. Let me sleep."

Ranulf sat back on his haunches, and considered. For a moment his faith wavered. His fervent prayers had brought an answer – another wounded, almost helpless creature added to his load, while his resources remained exactly as before. Doubt hammered in his mind, and he closed his eyes and fought the heresy of disbelief. For a long time he spoke with God.

When his prayers ended a hog stood before him.

Ranulf and his sword moved like a blur of lightning. Five heart-beats later he cut its throat.

Anschitel sat in the bracken and watched. "Priest," he said, "you thrust like a soldier." His eyes roved to my face. "My lord has bled a great deal. Restore his strength. Give him blood."

He lay down again, and slept.

Ranulf obeyed. He mistrusted his own skill, and believed the sergeant, experienced in many campaigns, knew how to treat a dying man. He cut a collop of flesh, forced my teeth apart and dribbled blood down my throat. I was partly conscious, and some of this strange medicine went down. During the day he fed me repeatedly, and my understanding returned – I do not remember it – and I drank avidly. He himself ate the raw meat, and fed Anschitel. The sergeant revived, although he remained in great pain, and spoke intelligibly to Ranulf about their situation. The rain drifted all day and gently washed and cleaned their wounds. Their garments clung like fish-scales, but the air was warm with sultry August heat, and they felt no discomfort. Flies clustered on the pig's hacked carcass in the ferns.

We remained there for three days, despite Ranulf's fear that a strayed pig might bring a swineherd in pursuit. No one disturbed us. The priest went cautiously to the fringes of the wood and gathered certain worts, for he had learnt the healing properties of herbs. These he pounded and mixed with water to make an ointment. He bathed my crotch, spread ointment and replaced the bandage. The wound, a red and gaping horror, no longer bled. Ranulf set Anschitel's arm – an operation which caused even that hardened warrior to faint – and bound it between sticks with straps taken from my litter, and cleaned and anointed the cut on his head. His own scarred shoulders he ignored until the weals began to suppurate; then he had Anschitel wash them clean and smear ointment.

Our wood lay on the fingertips of Freemantle forest. We kept no watch, though Ranulf was astir at every sound. We ate raw pig with hearty appetite, reluctantly chewed bitter-tasting leaves which, the priest asserted, cleansed evil humours from the blood, basked in sunshine that followed the rain, and slept for many hours. During the third day I was sensible all the time, and the pain diminished. I remembered all that happened, and why I was hurt; but the memories were distant and without significance, so that the pictures they carried made no impact. Only the Devil's handsome face remained vivid in my mind. My companions never mentioned the siege and sack, and what followed: they discussed only our predicament and resolved plans for the future. The past was discarded as a snake sloughs its skin.

The journey to Savernake forest began after dusk of the third day.

We travelled by night along narrow paths which Ranulf knew. amid forest and scrub; skirted infrequent villages and barking dogs, forded shallow streams and, sometimes, waded painfully through marsh. Our progress was very slow. At first, despite my weakness, I found walking easy; gradually the pain between my legs dilated into a clutching agony, so fierce that my bemused imagination pictured an imprisoned stoat gnawing living flesh. Ranulf and Anschitel supported me, my arms about their shoulders. Often they begged me to rest, but I refused. I was determined to journey onward so long as the night lasted, and I could set foot to the ground, and could stay conscious.

At dawn we hid in a small copse: a dangerous place, for a village was not far away, and plough-teams toiled across stubbled fields. Ranulf feared herdsmen and wandering dogs. Although we could not safely stay there beyond nightfall, it seemed to the priest there was no alternative. I had collapsed, muttering, into delirium; and the strain of the march had re-opened Anschitel's wound.

All that day Ranulf feverishly tended his ailing comrades. He fed us the last of the pig's flesh, stinking and putrescent, which we had brought with us; found water and quenched our thirsts, washed our wounds, rinsed the bandages and re-bound them. He slept not at all.

My memories of that night are vague. The pain was paramount: a monstrous clawing which drove awareness of all else from my thoughts. There was the dim trackway underfoot, and the shadowy loom of great trees and crouching shapes where bushes lurked like animals. Ranulf muttered encouragement and prayers in my ear and held me upright. Fever began to rage and light-streaks like shooting stars split the darkness. Somewhere ahead, hovering in the nightmare, the Devil's sapphire eyes and smiling lips beckoned me onwards.

I obeyed and followed.

In the grey of morning we came to a great forest, to a hut in a clearing and a stranger whom Ranulf greeted. They carried me within, I think, and laid me down, and the pain reared like a wave and rolled me under and I drowned in roaring waters.

3

Satan, I trusted you. Why did you betray me?

Lucifer, Lord of the Day, Prince of Night, you own my homage and my fealty. Why did you betray me?

Archangel of Evil, your smile lures God's saints from Heaven, your azure eyes are stars lighting the highway to perdition. I gave you my faith. You are my suzerain. Why did you betray me?

Answer me, Satan. Your mouth curves at the corners, your skin is fairer than the morning's glory, your glistening hair blacker than the hell-pit whence you came. I worship you. You hang upon your Cross, and you do not speak. Why did you betray me?

Infernal Shadow of Darkness, you own my soul and my allegiance, my body and being is yours. I am on my knees, I prostrate myself, I beseech your favour and protection. Guard me, Satan, and lend me a little of your strength.

Why did you betray me?

4

The hut was eight paces long and four broad. Low windowless walls, half a man's height, made from dried clay daubed on hazel-wand wattle. In places the clay had cracked and fallen, and sunlight flashed in golden darts between the plaited stalks. A floor of beaten earth, without rushes, crumbling and filthy. Beech-branch rafters, crudely slotted into an oaken roof-tree. A sagging roof – birch and hawthorn twigs – black with age and greyed by mildew. The hut was very dark.

I called, and my voice was a whispering crack. The door opened. A figure bent beneath the lintel and entered, and knelt beside me. Ranulf. I spoke his name.

The priest grasped my fingers and bowed his head. He seemed to be weeping. He said, "You know me, my lord?"

"Why not, Ranulf? We travelled a long road together. Is this our destination?"

"You remember?" He was smiling, though the tears streamed down his cheeks and coursed the tendrils of a stripling beard. Ranulf bearded. "Thanks be to God. Could you eat? Are you hungry?"

"My belly feels empty as a Gascon's boast."

Ranulf grinned, ducked outside and returned with a bowl of barley gruel, fragrant and steaming hot. He made a pillow of sack-cloth and fed me from a wooden ladle. When the bowl was empty I lay back and looked him in the eyes.

"There is much I do not know, Ranulf. Whose dwelling is this?"

The priest hesitated and pulled the unaccustomed hairs upon his chin. A dun-coloured mastiff limped into the hut, collapsed comfortably beside my bed and rested head on forefeet. His amber eyes regarded me amiably. Three toes of the left paw were missing; the lawing, to prevent dogs hunting game, told me immediately that we were within the confines of a royal forest. Ranulf added confirmation.

"We have found refuge, for a time, with Brand the woodcutter, in the Broyle bailiwick of Savernake forest. This is a remote place, my lord. The verderers, of course, know Brand lives here; but he is seldom visited, and no stranger disturbs us."

"I remember our arrival. How long ago?"

Ranulf sighed. "For fourteen days you have been mortally ill, out of your mind, and recognized nobody. I thought you were lost."

A fly slid down a rod of light and buzzed about the dog. He gulped at it lazily. Ranulf continued talking. My thoughts drifted into the past. I recalled an agony beneath the gallows, and surreptitiously, under the coverlet, touched myself. Linen swathed my loins, and I could not find the evidence I feared. I was afraid to ask. The pain had gone, leaving a dull ache.

Ranulf saw the movement and stopped speaking. Lines of worry furrowed his face – a face less plump than I remembered. He hesitated again, plucking his lip, and then came to a decision.

"My lord, although you have suffered a ghastly mutilation your illness has been mainly in the mind. For many hours I have listened to your ravings in delirium. You surrendered the will to live. Worse – you wanted to die, and prayed the Devil to receive your soul. All this because you thought your hurt worse than it is: you feared you had lost everything that makes a man. You are wrong. God in His mercy intervened and sent the knight whom you believe to be Satan; and this knight saved your manhood and your life."

Ranulf paused and licked his lips. The fly settled, and the sun splashed jewelled rainbows on its wings.

"Hamo's executioner took only one testicle."

The priest leaned forward eagerly and watched my face, hoping to see a radiance of relief. I closed my eyes. I could feel no emotion at all; my mind was spent, weary, beyond the impact of words.

I said, "Tell me, Ranulf. I remember very little. They hanged my father. What happened after?"

He sought for words. At length: "The knights who struck you down in the bailey left you there, thinking you dead; and later the scavengers took your mail. Hamo de Neufmarché came and found the baron where you had put him, and him they bore away. He recognized you also, and carried you to the gallows. They poured water to revive you, for Hamo would not hang the baron until you could see him die."

The fly droned aloft and settled on the mastiff's nose. The dog snapped, missed, and scrubbed his muzzle irritably. A voice called distantly outside – a woman's voice – and a memory stirred and vanished.

"When you became conscious Hamo told you what your end would be. Do you remember?"

I shook my head. The nightmare closed around me like a swirling fog.

Ranulf told his tale, and the pictures unfolded in the darkened room like a living tapestry.

A trumpet sings wild and clear. Hoofbeats tremble the earth. Voices call harshly. The men around Bochesorne's gallows turn their heads, hands on sword-hilts.

Over the ford rides a column of armoured horsemen, pennoned lances and painted shields, and sergeants and mounted bowmen. A knight in a chain-mail hauberk in the van, bareheaded, his helmet dangling.

They ride unhurriedly to the gallows, gazing curiously at the wreck of siege and sack. The leader raises an arm and halts his troop. He looks at Hamo de Neufmarché's men, and the gallows' burden, and rests his glance thoughtfully on my prostrate body. Then he turns his head and gazes at the burning castle. Absently he strokes his horse's mane.

"A very pretty sack." A deep voice, resonant, clear as a bell. The tone changes, and carries an edge like a tempered sword. "Who leads this gang of thieves?"

Hamo steps forward. "I do not like your manner, my lord. This affair is private – the settlement of a debt. You had better go your way."

The knight gracefully dismounts. The tallest of men and the most handsome. (How well I remembered!) A thin-lipped, mobile mouth. Every movement a curve of beauty. From him emanates an aura of terrifying power.

A languid inquiry: "Your name?"

Hamo glances at his paltry retinue, and at the iron-clad column that follows his inquisitor. The knight watches him, reading his thoughts, and smiles pleasurably.

"Hamo de Neufmarché, I remind you that, although the king is overseas, private warfare in England is still illegal. That, however, does not concern me greatly – I am no guardian of the king's peace. But I am bound for Garston, one of my fiefs, which is only five miles distant. I do not welcome disturbances so close to my marches."

"I avenge a murder."

The knight's eyes rest, without interest, on my nakedness.

"Is this your murderer? What has he done?"

Hamo sullenly tells him. The knight listens indifferently, and leans against his destrier and spreads his arms.

"So. The boy killed one of your knights. In return you have hanged his father, harried his lands, burned his castle and slaughtered his liegemen. What more do you intend?"

"He shall be blinded, castrated and hanged."

Ranulf stands. All trace of the priest is gone, and a Visdelou speaks. He talks proudly, and flaunts my valiance, and boasts the assaults we repulsed and the enemies I killed. The knight listens; his smile approves. He looks at Hamo.

"I think you have done enough. Your murderer seems a true knight and a very brave man." His face is suddenly cruel. "I shall allow you a little revenge. You may take half his manhood."

Ranulf flings himself at the knight's feet, and prays for mercy in the name of Christ and all His saints. A mailed foot crashes into his face.

"Priest, you become importunate. I give your master his life and leave him the means to breed a race of paladins. Mercy? Never have I been more compassionate."

He addresses Hamo's executioner, who crouches above me, knife in hand.

"Be careful, swine, else I burn you alive. One only."

6

Ranulf was silent. I lay upon my bed, an arm across my eyes, living again the agony and shame.

I said in a shaking voice, "His name is Geoffrey de Mandeville."

Ranulf said soberly, "The Constable of London. A great baron, a man of power in the kingdom."

I said, "He is Satan Incarnate. I thought he had forsworn me. I am wrong. He saved me, as he said. I am his man, and I must find him again."

"I believe him to be truly wicked," Ranulf answered despairingly. "The Devil, in truth, lives in Geoffrey de Mandeville. Cast him out, my lord."

I said, "No. I worship him."

Within two days I left my bed in the hut and tottered outside. Dimly realized figures, half-seen in the vague shadow-world of my illness, I now saw clearly as the people who inhabited this forgotten retreat in Savernake.

Anschitel was there, of course, his arm still strapped in lath and leather, his wounds healing. The sergeant's greeting was strangely shy; he had listened to my delirious incoherencies and secretly doubted whether misfortune had left me entirely sane. The days which followed reassured him; but I think that, by some curious quirk of insight, he was more aware than Ranulf of the complete transfiguration of my beliefs. Ranulf, to the end, trusted that God would regain my soul; Anschitel had no illusions.

Our refuge, a sort of island which the arms of a stream embraced in a narrow oval two hundred paces long, lay in a marshy bowl whose slopes bore ancient oaks. Beneath them bramble, briar and elder wove a formidable barrier. The only access was alongside the stream, a boggy path discouraging to both man and horseman. Savernake, I discovered later, was mostly a series of straggling coppices linked by heath and downland. The woodcutter's steading lurked in the midst of a rare tract of true forest.

Brand was a surly Englishman about forty years old. Furry eyebrows met over a long and pointed nose; broken teeth peered between lips that were pink and wet and loose. He had a vulpine look; his eyes were restless and cunning. He greeted me without friendliness in a high and repulsively girlish voice, using his native tongue. And here, at once, a difficulty arrived in my relations with these humble English who had given us shelter. My command of their throat-stopping language extended to a few words connected with stable and field, and a handful of imperative verbs: go, come, fetch. Anschitel knew a little more; Ranulf, completely bilingual, was our medium of communication.

The ground between the streamlets was cultivated in a fashion that would have sickened Ansgar the reeve – did he still live? Moulting fowls scratched hopefully in sparse stubble. A strip of undernourished wheat awaited the sickle. On the fallow's coarse and scanty grass grazed two lean cows and four sheep. The hovel where I had lain, and two lesser huts of the same clay and wattle and tree-leaf thatch, clustered at one end of the island. A sagging haystack and a corral for the animals completed this sterile farm.

A bundle of rags and sticks propped against the haystack moved and spoke. A man so old, desiccated and frail that a puff of wind might crumble him to dust. Veins like tiny rivers patterned the bald skull; his nose, a ridge of gristle, curved like a talon over toothless gums. A milky skim filmed one eye; the other, ashen blue like a faded flower, watched me vividly. He saw me start, and the pallid lips emitted a faint cackle. An arm like a withered twig emerged from the rags, and a claw-like hand beckoned me closer.

"Norman, ain't you, young fellow?" the old voice whispered. "Killed a lot of you in my time. Nearly got your Duke at Hastings. That would have changed history, eh?"

My astonishment was twofold: first, that despite the English accent and senile lisp, this tattered hulk spoke French; and second, that he claimed to have fought in a battle seventy years before. He must be around ninety, and that was impossible.

The single eye saw my disbelief, and the dotard cackled again: a husky sound like the brushing of dead grasses.

"True enough, young man," he breathed. "The last of King Harold's housecarles, that's me. Tell you some stories, if you stay long enough."

His eyes dropped, and he sank into his private dreams – a shadow-world where Duke William and Red William still marched and fought and the White Ship foundered. Vastly interested, I sought Ranulf. There was much about this sanctuary and its inhabitants, and the reasons for our being here at all, which needed explanation.

"Impossible but true," Ranulf said. "The old man is Brand's father, and son of Aluric who held Savernake of King Edward. His name is Bovi. He indeed fought under Harold's standard, and was left for dead upon the field. For many years he lived disgraced, nithing, because he alone of Count Harold's bodyguard survived the fight."

I gaped at him. "Are you saying that Brand, this villainous wood-man in his wretched tenement, is grandson of a nobleman who held all Savernake?"

"Yes." Ranulf nodded sadly. "One of the many dispossessed after Hastings. Bovi was granted this small holding on condition that he cart so many cords of timber annually for the king's Warden of Savernake. He is, I suppose, a freeman: he does no boon work

94

on Henry Esturmy's fields." He looked about him, at the starveling fields and dilapidated huts. "Many a serf tills more land and scrapes a better living."

"True, Ranulf. Why, then, should this man shelter us? We bring him nothing but a rusty sword. We have no money. I am wasted, and Anschitel a cripple: we cannot yet work on his fields." Moodily I regarded Brand, who gathered the sickly wheat, chopping the stems viciously like a soldier dispatching wounded. "We have nothing to give, and we drain his miserable resources. What is his obligation?"

Ranulf's face closed. He chewed a grass-stalk and gazed at the sky. "I must not tell you, my lord. The seal of the confessional forbids an answer. But this I can say: years since, when travelling to Marlborough on a summons from the baron – God rest his soul! – I encountered Brand and saved him from a disgusting death. Under this obligation he has received us. But his gratitude is meagre as a hermit's dinner; he will not endure us for long. Indeed, he cannot."

The September sun, climbing above the encircling coronet of trees, shed a golden light on field and hovel. Brand's sickle flashed. A flight of swallows, summer's lingering heralds, skimmed the tree-tops. Anschitel sauntered up, asked permission, and dropped on the grass beside us.

Ranulf said, "My lord, we are safe here for a little time. What then? What do you intend?"

The lame mastiff snuffled my neck, and laid his head upon my knee. Absently I fondled his ears.

I said, "We cower here like outlaws. Why? Only my life is endangered, because Hamo de Neufmarché will kill me on sight. You he does not seek. Anschitel, you can always find service with another lord. Ranulf, a priest will never lack a living. I release you both from your fealty."

The sergeant scratched himself, and smiled. Ranulf chewed his grass-stem and stared at his hands.

"Forgive me, my lord, but a priest's sole fealty is to God, Who has charged me to recover your soul." He raised his head and looked me in the eyes. "We are your men till death. Let us not speak of this again." He spat out the stalk. "I ask only for your commands. What do you intend?"

I tickled the mastiff's ruff, and he grunted contentedly. "We are destitute, poorer than the woodcutter whose food we eat. We have

95

nothing, absolutely nothing but the rags we wear and a sword we stole. We can sink no lower; we can only climb. I am a knight. And so," I added definitely, "I must somehow acquire a sword and helmet, hauberk and shield, destrier and saddle, for without these things I cannot return to the world under the name I bear."

Anschitel found the louse he was seeking and cracked it triumphantly. "So. Those are your orders. About thirty marks' worth. We shall have to sack an abbey, or waylay a treasure convoy."

I said, "We must learn the byways of the forest, and discover who comes and goes."

Anschitel only nodded. Consternation stood in Ranulf's face.

"Yes. I am ready to kill and rob. Worse has befallen my House. Has it not?" I snapped.

The priest assented dumbly.

8

A herd of swine splashed from the stream and trotted into the clearing. Driving them was a woman whose face I remembered from the hazy vacancies of my fever, like a reflection glimpsed for an instant in wind-rippled water. She passed me without a look and penned the animals.

The girl was my own age, tall and slim, with the body of a boy. The face, clean-boned, was also oddly masculine, her mouth firm and unsmiling above a rounded chin. Her skin was tanned, and unblemished beneath the dirt, and her hair glowed like old gold.

I asked her name. She completed her task unhurriedly and stood before me, face expressionless, eyes downcast, and made no answer. I fumbled for my scanty English.

"Saiva," she said, and raised her eyes to mine.

They were wide and clear, and a brilliant green, the colour of springtime leaf-buds, of the emerald sky-flash at midsummer sunset.

In these still pools my reason drowned. I gazed bewildered, bereft of sense and speech.

I do not know how long we stood there, silent, looking one upon the other. She put her hands in mine, and raised her face. Gently I kissed her lips.

Then she was gone.

7

September, 1137 — June 1138

Saiva was a complication that nearly toppled from its eminence the object of my sojourn in Savernake. For days I wandered in a trance, seeking only her presence and dreaming of her hair and eyes and graceful body. The dreams were day-long: each morning she drove Brand's swine to the forest, for these were the pannage months of autumn, when the Warden permitted forest-dwellers' pigs to root for green acorns and beechmast — food which the deer would not eat until brown and ripe. At evening she returned to the island clearing. When the animals were penned and the day's meal cooked and eaten, we strolled the fields together or sat hand in hand beside the stream. At first we spoke very little, but as time passed she began to teach me English, and I, in turn, taught her something of the conquerors' tongue. Saiva was the apter pupil: soon we could converse, however haltingly, in passable French.

We were profoundly in love, but our love-making found no deep expression — only interlaced fingers and gentle kisses and embraces when our bodies never touched. I felt for her the pure, knightly love that the minstrels sing, the chaste devotion belonging to legendary heroes — a love I had believed mythical as the paladins themselves. The knights I knew in real life sometimes courted their ladies with all the circumstance of courtoisie; yet their aim was ever the same: to bed as soon as possible. From Saiva, at this time, I desired no more than the light in her eyes and the sound of her voice.

Beneath the level of my mind there existed a restraint that I never acknowledged. The wound which Hamo's executioner inflicted was healed; all pain had gone; I no longer wore a bandage. But tormenting doubts concerning the remnants of my manhood still remained. Was I truly a man, or merely a eunuch? The unconscious discipline imposed on my love-making during the day

97

broke uncontrollably at night, and Saiva appeared to me in lustful dreams whose ejaculations proved my fears unfounded. Nevertheless horror of total and degrading failure in the act of love fettered me like an iron chain.

We loved like children, and were happy.

I never left the settlement. Ranulf dictated this confinement. He told me the foresters knew that strangers lived with Brand – they knew everything that happened in the forest, because that was their business – but otherwise were not concerned with who we were or whence we came, provided we did not infringe the forest laws. Yet Ranulf thought, and I agreed, that the less I was seen the better. Possibly, after our experience of Hamo's vengeance, we exaggerated his tenacity; perhaps Visdelou's material ruin satisfied him. Ranulf believed otherwise: until the king escheated Bochesorne the devastated fief remained in Visdelou's hands; Hamo could not seize it legally. If he eliminated me possession might be easier.

So I loafed about the fields, and basked in the sun and fished the stream; and strength returned. The weather remained settled and warm – which was fortunate, since the lice-ridden clothes we wore were shredded to rags: I roamed the place half-naked and barefoot. Saiva, at dawn and dusk, wove garments from raw wool, the fleeces of summer's shearing. I sat beside her while she worked at wheel and loom, and watched her flying fingers. Brand watched also, and spoke roughly, clearly begrudging time and material spent on his unwanted guests. Saiva seldom answered; between father and daughter was a barrier of hatred which I did not understand.

I talked much with old Bovi, and listened to embroidered tales of Stamford battle, and the long march south, and the fight at Hastings. Of the years between he was unwilling to speak: they were years of humiliation, poverty and misery. He also told me something of the rigours that persecuted those who lived in royal forests. It happened, one noonday while we reclined against a hut and talked, that two roe-deer bounded across the stream and, after trotting aimlessly awhile over plough and stubble, came to the haystack and began feeding. I jumped to my feet and found a pebble, Bovi's alarmed shout checked me in the act of throwing.

"Do you want us evicted and fined, maybe blinded and maimed?" he croaked. "Put that stone down."

He told me that none was allowed to drive deer from a field once they had entered; moreover, forest dwellers were not permitted even to build fences to keep them out. Within the forest the deer was paramount; only the king, or the Warden by the king's command, might slay him. Savage penalties protected not only deer, but also other animals – boar, fox, hare, wildcat, badger, squirrel. Only wolves and birds could lawfully be taken – an empty concession, since none might carry bows or snares within the forest.

I regarded the roe-deer – fat, opulent beasts – tearing trusses from the stack, and my anger mounted. More than that: my mouth watered. Our daily fare was sparse indeed: barley gruel, coarse bread, small, bony fish taken from the stream. Never once had we tasted meat. Bovi read my thoughts in my face, chuckled, and uttered a sharp, gruff call from deep in his throat. The deer threw up their heads and trotted away to the trees.

"Makes you hungry to look at them, don't it?" the old man wheezed. "Norman, you'll be hungrier yet before the winter's out. You and your friends will bring us near starvation."

Hunger, here, was a permanent affliction. One cow had already been slaughtered; the meat, dried and salted, hung in blackened strips from the rafters. When the pannage months ended in November three pigs – half the herd – must be killed and the meat smoked. The remaining animals had to exist through the barren months on hay and the island's scanty grazing. Ranulf showed the grain stored in clay-lined pits. Three people, with luck and determination, might survive on these supplies during the winter: six certainly could not.

I pondered; and began fashioning a bow and arrows. I did this in secret, within a hut, but Brand knew and rebuked me angrily. I could not blame him: I infringed the forest laws and invited punishment. I waved him away and continued the work. Arrow-heads were difficult: there was little iron in the place. Eventually I filched a broken sickle, heated the metal and fashioned crude barbs. Anschitel killed an unwary mallard which settled on the stream; I used the feathers for flights.

Ranulf and Anschitel harnessed themselves to Brand's wooden plough, and the woodcutter finished his ploughing, harrowed a field and sowed winter wheat. The skies became greyer, the air colder; gales lashed the forest and stripped the trees. On a day in mid-November Saiva drove her hogs to the forest grazing grounds for the last time; all pannage thereafter was the deers' preserve. I helped her slaughter the pigs and dry the meat; and helped her gather firewood – all deadwood, this, for no living tree might be chopped – and helped her repair the hovels' gaping thatch. I was beside her all day, and a hungry desire swelled and gnawed like a living pain.

2

Saiva finished her stitching and examined the woollen tunic approvingly. I discarded the tattered rag I wore and she slipped the tunic over my head. Standing back, she studied the effect, her head on one side.

"A knight should have a Flemish robe," she said, smiling. "This is a sorry substitute."

I opened my arms and Saiva ran and clung. Suddenly she was crying. I smoothed her hair and tried to control my shaking limbs.

"I can bear this no longer," she whispered. "Come."

She took my hand and we went to the fields and crossed the stream. The water chilled our naked feet. She led me through trees to a clearing where frost-browned bracken blanketed the earth. The sunlight, pale and thin as watered wine, shed an illusion of warmth.

We lay together in the ferns and embraced and murmured endearments in a medley of languages. The urge mounted and rode my loins like a red fury. I put my hand between her thighs, and my power reared hard and strong. Then, like a cold grey snake, the ancient fear uncoiled and struck; emotions seethed in doubt and shame; desire collapsed and became a shrivelled finger. Muttering incoherencies, I thrust her away.

Saiva knelt beside me. Her face was set; her eyes an emerald blaze.

"I know what was done to you, Humphrey. I know why you are afraid. I know also that you fear without reason, and that you must not torment yourself, and me, for ever. Lie still."

She raised my tunic, unlaced torn and filthy breeches and drew them down. Tenderly she gathered me in her hands, and studied the scar of my humiliation. A tremulous smile curved her lips.

She said in a shaking voice, "Here is treasure enough for a woman."

Saiva lowered her head and kissed the wound.

Vigour returned and throbbed and towered. I reached for her. She laughed triumphantly and sprang to her feet.

"Wait."

100

She loosed her girdle and dropped her rope. The youthful body, small-breasted and slim-hipped, gleamed in the sunlight like an ivory statue. Her skin shone like silk, soft and unblemished save for the rash of vermin bites that we all wore.

Saiva sighed gently, and lowered herself upon me, and the lance impaled her.

3

The ferns embraced her body, gold on bronze, the altar of a three-fold sacrifice. I stood above her and raised my head and sang a paean, a thanksgiving, a babble of battle-cries and praise.

Lucifer smiled from the skies, and his eyes were a deeper blue.

4

Cold was the enemy, cold and hunger. We fought the foe like the garrison of a beleaguered citadel. We did no work beyond feeding the animals: the hay diminished rapidly. We lived together, by consent, in a single hut, and crouched around the fire all day, hardly speaking, striving to extract a mutual warmth from our bodies and the smoky flames. Our time-worn clothes were inadequate shields against the savage cold. By night we bedded together like a row of corpses, and brought within the hut as many animals as it would hold, and imagined ourselves warmer.

Christmas went unnoticed save by Ranulf, who made his solitary devotions. Afterwards the snow came, and for a space the cold relented. Then frost descended and gripped with claws of steel.

Food ran low. To save energy and appetite, we moved as little as possible. But it was a losing battle, and while the painful days went by we grew steadily weaker.

One night Bovi died. His fluttering spirit went without a sound; his body, when I lifted it, weighed no more than a bundle of feathers. We could not bury him in that rock-hard ground; nor could we leave him in the open, for we had heard hunting wolf-packs. I stripped his single garment and put it forcibly on Saiva, propped his brittle bones in a corner of the room and covered them with faggots. Thereafter we penned the pigs at night in one of the smaller huts. The consequence was disaster: maddened by hunger, they broke out and vanished into the forest.

The cow died. Her flesh was lean and stringy, and we devoured it raw, because we lacked the energy for cooking. Brand scoured the last husks from the grain-pits; and we ate the seed-corn. Ranulf tried to dig for roots, but the ground defeated him. After that nothing was left.

I looked at my companions, at the haggard, emaciated faces and the eyes big with despair. I took my bow and went to the forest.

The cold was a solid impact, an invisible onslaught that emptied my lungs. I plodded aimlessly with a vague intention behind my mind, a half-forgotten idea I strove to recover. Sometimes the ground receded, and I floated effortlessly above it; then the earth ascended, hard and dangerous, and jarred my rag-bound feet.

An alien sound behind me, a crackle like brittle straw. I turned slowly, plucking uselessly at an empty bow, and saw Anschitel following, sword in hand, head down, legs dragging. Wordlessly he waved me forward, and we walked on, moving with infinite effort across the frozen snow.

We came to a trackway, a depression that threaded the black trees which reared like skeletons, and found a man. He was not long dead; the snow had not covered him. He lay in an attitude of repose, as if asleep; but his face was the face of a skull and his body a rattle of bones. Anschitel squatted beside him, prodded the haunches, fingered his sword. Our thoughts were one, and saliva dribbled disgustingly down my cheek. I shook my head. Anschitel shrugged, and we went on.

By the edge of a copse we saw the deer, a roe-buck and two does, browsing on a holly-clump. The air was ice-fanged, windless, utterly still, so they did not scent us. We dropped on our bellies and began a slow, tortuous crawl, using every vestige of cover, and stopped, hardly breathing, whenever the animals raised their heads. At last we could come no closer; and the deer grew restless and suspicious, snuffing the wind and flicking their velvet ears. The nearest doe was forty paces distant. Awkwardly, moving with snail-like caution, I strung the bow and notched an arrow.

Flat on my face, I prayed wordlessly to the fallen archangel who was my god. A single movement carried me to my feet and loosed the bow. I heard Anschitel shout; then the snow was in my eyes, and sleep covered me like a soothing blanket.

The killing of the deer changed our fortunes. Anschitel dispatched the wounded beast and cut meat from a haunch. We ate voraciously and found new life glowing in half-frozen bodies. Moving the carcass was beyond our strength; the sergeant fetched Saiva and Ranulf. Brand, terrified by the felony, refused to come.

We left hooves and head in the hope of attracting wolves whose marks would confuse the signs of outrage. Slowly, with many respites, we dragged the carcass home, leaving a trail plain as a Roman highway for the foresters to read. No sooner had we crossed the stream than the last miracle happened: snow fell heavily and concealed our traces.

The bloody meat quickly revived us. (The mastiff, at his last gasp, frisked like a puppy before next sunrise.) Afterwards Anschitel and I hunted almost every day. Our rewards were various: an emaciated wolf, starving birds stunned by the cold, hares and foxes and two fallow deer. We learned to use every shred of cover which winter spared to hide the naked land; and the skill, born of desperation, that enabled us to outwit wild animals made avoidance of patrolling foresters a simple matter. Never again did we starve.

At Candlemas a wind blew from the west and the snow went and the land melted.

We buried Bovi, and buried also the evidence of our crimes: the hides and bones of the animals we had taken. With the snow gone, and the first awakening of leaf and bud, concealment became easier, and Anschitel and I ranged widely in our forays. The foresters' surveillance nevertheless seemed curiously lax. Soon we discovered they had greater problems than the depredations of individual poachers. Traffic in the forest byways increased daily while spring advanced, although few of the wayfarers were local inhabitants. One day, lying at the margins of a copse where the first green tendrils of bracken curled, I watched a party of mailed sergeants ride down and dispatch a deer. They made no attempt at concealment. Shouting and hallooing, they raised a mighty noise. Foresters arrived while they divided the carcass. After a wordy argument the sergeants surrounded the Warden's men, wielded vigorous sword-flats and pursued them into the woods. Flagrant, open violation of the forest laws became commonplace. Pressures were evidently generating somewhere that exploded barriers and released a flood of lawlessness. Events were happening in the outside world of which I was unaware.

I went to the highway, and watched from the trees, and saw armies on the march.

"Somewhere there is a war," Anschitel grunted in my ear. "Let's send Ranulf to inquire."

We clothed the priest in the best of our garments and sent him abroad. He was away for two days and returned with a bag of seed-corn, a new woollen robe, a little money and important news.

"While we were starving others have fought," he said. "David of Scotland invaded the north and devastated Northumbria. King Stephen went to meet him; the Scots refused battle and retreated. The king harried David's realm, but it was the season of Lent, and many knights refused to continue fighting. That, and lack of supplies, forced Stephen to retire. He is now in England."

I clucked impatiently. "War in Scotland does not affect us. What of the south?"

"Rebellion," Ranulf said. "King Stephen has broken many promises he made to the barons when he was crowned. Some he kept at other men's expense. The barons who supported him expected favours and concessions which have not been granted. He swore to restore all ecclesiastical estates seized by laymen; in restoring them he deprived the laymen." He smiled dryly. "You, my lord, are not the only dispossessed knight in England. Some of those who have lost their lands are holding castles against the king."

"Belly of God!" Anschitel growled. "They would not have dared in Henry's time."

"They think King Stephen soft," Ranulf answered. "That is not all. Powerful influences are stirring against the king. His very throne is threatened. The gossip is vague: I did not wish to appear too ignorant or probe too far. However, at this moment the king besieges Geoffrey Talbot in Hereford castle. William Lovel holds Castle Cary against him, and William de Mohun has sent defiance from Dunster."

I slapped my knees and rose to my feet. "Anarchy is salvation for such as we. Now, my friends – we have taken enough game to last a month. No longer will we hunt animals for their meat, but warriors for their mail. Then we shall leave Savernake and restore our fortunes in battle. We have prepared the traps – let us spring them."

"You speak for yourself," Brand muttered. "I stay here."

Saiva said, "I shall come with you."

I stared at her, began to speak – and realized I could not go any-where without her.

6

I had chosen three separate places for our ambuscades. All had cer-tain features in common : a sharp, narrow bend which would slow horsemen to a walk in single file, and tangled tree-branches over-hanging the track. We could not attack more than two opponents, so the pattern of our dispositions did not vary : I lay in the branches, sword in hand, ready to drop on the leader; Anschitel, hidden in undergrowth near-by, dealt wit hthe follower, Ranulf refused to kill or wound, so his task was to secure the horses. Saiva, concealed some distance away, gave warning when a suitable victim approached.

For days we were unlucky. Wayfarers were frequent, but mailed warriors rode in companies and solitary travellers went unarmoured. I changed location from day to day without result. When I nearly despaired, and contemplated some other means to attain our ends, we heard the vixen's mating-call which was Saiva's signal.

I watched the knight approach, and listened to his cheerful song:

> "Mais une merveille veoit
> Qui poist faire grant paor
> Au plus hardi combateor —"

I dropped on him and bore him to the ground. My sword point rattled his teeth and I braced for the thrust. His eyes, wide and unafraid, glared into mine.

Odinel de Umfraville.

A winter day when a king was buried. Reading Abbey. A tavern, and William's voice.

The curtains of degradation parted, and I saw myself for what I had become – a robber, an outlaw, a peasant. Odinel sprawled on his back, and dignity clothed him like a resplendent robe.

"Yield, my lord!" The sword trembled in my hand.

He stared along the blade into my face; contempt blazed in his eyes.

"I surrender to my peers. To you, pig's bastard, I give nothing."

Anschitel was suddenly beside me, whipping Odinel's sword from the scabbard, the dagger from his belt.

"Kill him quick, my lord," he rasped. "We cannot linger here."

I ignored him, lowered my weapon and stepped back.

"On your feet, Odinel de Umfraville."

He rose slowly, and leaned on his shield. I saw the perplexity in his face.

He said, "You speak French with a gentleman's voice. You know my name. You smell like a midden and look like an animal. Who are you?"

"Humphrey Visdelou."

"Humphrey Visdelou is six months' dead."

"Look at my eyes."

He murmured, "The squint. And the nose. Perhaps —"

Anschitel said urgently, "Saint Mary's womb! How much longer do we stand talking?"

Odinel turned and saw the prone figure of his attendant. "Have you killed Warin?"

Anschitel ground his teeth. "No. I am no bowman. My arrow missed. I clubbed him. I think he lives."

Ranulf and the horses had already disappeared. I pointed my sword at Odinel's throat and said formally, "My lord, either you yield and give your parole that you will not try to escape, or I must kill you. Have I your word?"

Odinel grinned. "Yes, Humphrey, you have. Now – what are you going to do with me?"

7

I led him to Brand's tenement. Odinel contemplated my dwelling-place and my companions with an astonishment that he did not try to hide.

"A poor exchange for Bochesorne," was his sole comment.

I set food before him. He regarded the crawling meat and flinched; and indicated the bulging panniers which his pack-horse carried. "You'll find cheese and wheaten bread," he said, "and a skin of wine. Please accept my hospitality."

I ate appreciatively, and savoured the wine with an appetite sharpened by half a year's abstinence. Then I studied Odinel.

He was a short, sturdy man, browned, brown-faced, with a clean-shaved visage that seemed to have been hacked untidily from a block of seasoned oak. Humour lurked in his eyes, and the lips smiled easily. They smiled now.

"This is an unexpected resurrection, Humphrey. I thought you dead. Will you tell me the story?" I narrated the whole series of misfortunes which had brought me down: the unpremeditated killing of Richard Maluvel, the trial by combat which followed, Hamo de Neufmarché's vengeance culminating in the sack of Bochesorne, and our rigorous sojourn in Savernake. I ended with a concise statement of our present intention.

"Wherein I am become an important figure," Odinel observed. "You want my armour, weapons and horses."

"And ransom."

"Yes," he said. "I see your point. How much do you demand?"

"Forty marks."*

"You do me too much honour, Humphrey. I had not considered myself so expensive. However, it seems I have very little choice. Perhaps I had better tell you my situation."

Odinel, second son of a baron who held Prudhoe castle in Northumbria, had served King Stephen in his campaign against the Scots. When this ended he still owed half his annual service, so he accompanied the king's forces southwards. Now, far from home, he sought employment for his sword in the western wars.

"Because there is nothing for me at Prudhoe," he concluded. "My fief is small and runs itself. I enjoy fighting. Besides," he added with a grin, "Stephen has lately increased the pay for voluntary knight-service – eightpence a day instead of sixpence – and has reduced the obligatory unpaid term from sixty days to forty. War becomes profitable."

"And your ransom?" I inquired politely.

Odinel said thoughtfully, "Prudhoe is a long way away. If you can spare one of my horses – it shall be returned – I'll send Warin to my father. This will take time – several weeks. I doubt the baron will approve the manner of my capture, even though you are, dear Humphrey, technically a knight." His glance rested speculatively on Saiva. "Meanwhile, what do you propose for my entertainment?"

During the days that followed I was forced to persuade Odinel that Saiva was not for him. In the end he accepted my ruling with

*Possibly £2,000 by present-day values.

107

humorous resignation, and ceased his advances – advances which Saiva did not discourage with the sternness I expected. I chided her gently. Since the winter we had lived together as man and wife, and used one of the smaller huts. Saiva sighed and pressed against me.

"Perhaps I am indeed a strumpet at heart. With my upbringing it could hardly be otherwise."

"Saiva," I answered, "I know remarkably little about you. So much of our time has been wasted fighting the elements and defeating starvation."

"And the rest we have spent making love," she said contentedly. "You do not bed with a peasant, Humphrey. My mother, whom I hardly remember, was daughter of a thane who died at Hastings. Brand, churlish though he seems, is descended from Cerdic – the first king of the English, Humphrey, of whom you have never heard. I am at least your peer in nobility."

"So. And do English knights always breed wantons?"

"No. If I am immodest, the fault is not entirely mine. Has Ranulf not told you?"

"No."

Saiva sat on the pallet and clasped her arms around her knees. Idly I traced with a finger the delicious curve of her spine.

"You had better know. Brand took me to his bed when I was eleven years old."

"Christ in Heaven!" I stared aghast.

"Yes. I saw no wrong. Who was to tell me? Bovi, even then, was senile – I doubt he noticed. For years I was Brand's daughter and his mistress. He fed me herbs to prevent conception. I use them still." She bowed her head and hid her face. "Humphrey, I enjoyed it. There was no one to warn me of my sin."

I muttered nonsense and groped for my clothes. "Body of God! This man must be punished. I shall —"

"No." Fiercely she grasped my arm. "He has been punished enough. Lie still, and hear me. We grew careless. One day he took me in the woods, and the verderers came on us and caught us.

"They seized Brand and bound him and took him to the Warden. On the way they met Ranulf, who went with them and interceded on Brand's behalf and begged for his life. You know the punishment for incest?"

"I know," I said grimly.

"Henry Esturmy listened to the priest, and spared my father's life, and remitted all the terrible mutilations save one. He castrated him."

I stared blindly into space. Sometimes I had secretly wondered at Saiva's astonishing aptitude in the arts of love. The mystery was resolved in a loathsome fashion:

I warmed myself at the fires which an unnatural beast had kindled; I harvested where the Devil had sown.

I shrugged. I belonged to the Prince of Evil – who was I to spurn his gifts?

Saiva cried bitterly. I took her in my arms.

8

I chafed against Warin's return with the ransom which would release me from my bondage.

Meanwhile we lacked neither food nor raiment. Odinel, I knew, could not have travelled so widely without money, although at first he happily denied possession of a single penny. I ransacked the rouncey's panniers without success, and at length went to him and said, "I am reluctant to search you, but necessity is apt to blunt my finer feelings. Where have you concealed your silver?"

Unthinkingly I drew his dagger from my belt; absently I stropped the edge on a piece of hide. He watched me a while, chewing his lips; then he laughed, rummaged beneath his tunic and flung a wallet at my feet.

"About six marks," he said. "Leave me a little."

I left him half. Ranulf took the rest and bought woollen tunics, cloaks and boots, breeches and jerkins of leather. He bought bread and corn, a cow and an ox, a boar and a sow. Brand grunted when he saw his stock replenished. He expressed no thanks.

Odinel's habit, whenever we came near, of keeping ostentatiously to windward and wrinkling his nostrils, finally goaded me to ordering a general washing of bodies. Ranulf looked distressed, Anschitel thunderstruck. I insisted; and took Saiva to a pool downstream, where we stripped and scrubbed each other. Then we plucked vermin from our heads and bodies, burned the tatters we wore and donned new clothes. I took the dagger to my hair and shaved neck and beard, leaving only a pad upon my skull. This was the fashion of our grandfathers, the conquerors of England. I appreciated the sense behind it.

Saiva's hair I also cut. When we left the forest a woman in our train might attract unwelcome notice. I decided she must be my varlet, and began instructing her in the care of horses and armour, using Odinel's equipment. After our cleansing in the stream I dressed her in tunic and breeches, girded a leather belt about her waist and set a cap on her cropped head. Her slight body perfected this disguise; but the result, to my eyes, was so extraordinarily lascivious that I had to hurry her into the undergrowth. I had promised Saiva to do Brand no harm, but his continual presence drove me from the steading – I could not bear contact with the brute. Sometimes I shot a deer: a transgression that was no longer rash – the forest lay open to depredation. Soldiers encamped near by, or riding through, broke the game laws with impunity, and the foresters were frightened to interfere with these ruthless pilagers.

At last, bored and restless, I took Odinel's armour and rode knight errant.

Some of these wandering warriors whom I have since encountered were true knights who faithfully believed that by offering their bodies to violence they fortified whatever troth they pledged: the Glory of God or their ladies' virtue or the Holy Grail. In victory they expected no prize save honour. Often they were poor and ascetic, nearly monks, living on the bounty of abbeys and monasteries; sometimes they abandoned their own identities and assumed the names of Arthur's knights, those fabled heroes from the minstrels' lays.

Such men were in the minority.

The typical knight errant was an unemployed mercenary, a soldier who profaned the tenets of knighthood in a kind of licensed brigandage. Inevitably a man of prowess at arms, he selected his victims with care and issued his challenges discriminately. A proper knight could not refuse a challenge to single combat and keep his honour – though it was occasionally done. When the robber – for he was little else – had tumbled his victim in the dust he demanded recompense, a prize for his petty victory. The unfortunate sufferer yielded his shield or his sword, his horse or his hauberk – sometimes all.

I became one of these gentry.

Odinel's hauberk, a well-made suit of banded mail, fitted so tightly that I had to discard the gambeson. His sword felt a little light in my hand. The destrier, fat and glistening from plentiful forage and

Saiva's grooming, lacked Chanson's speed and fire. Thus equipped, and with Anschetil at my back, I waged my squalid little war.

I am not proud of this episode, and shall spare the details. My favourite station was a deep ford in the forest where the trackway from Pewsey to Marlborough crossed a brook. The campaign in the west brought many armed men along this path: I did not lack victims. My choice was sometimes rash; frequently I was lucky to remain in the saddle when the contest ended. From the losers I exacted the tribute I desired: helmets, shields and swords, hauberks and haubergeons, four palfreys and a rouncey. I did not obtain a destrier – the only war-horse I coveted carried a knight of forbidding aspect: discreetly, lance aloft, I let him pass unchallenged.

Thus I armed, equipped and mounted my little retinue – and ever since have accounted it a stain upon my knighthood.

9

At the end of May Warin returned, escorted by two men-at-arms, and brought the ransom. Odinel watched silently while I counted the pennies. When it was done I returned to him the money I had already taken. Inscrutably he regarded the coins in his palm.

"And my horses and armour?" he inquired.

I answered gruffly, "Take them and go. You have served your turn."

Odinel's rough-hewn features crinkled in a smile. "Humphrey, your notions of honour are peculiar and unexpected. They afford me vast entertainment – a pleasure which I do not think I can forego. What will you do now?"

I bowed my head and groped for words. The utterance of my dream, my longing, was inexpressibly difficult.

"I go to London, to serve the Constable, Geoffrey de Mandeville. To serve him, and none other."

He contemplated me reflectively. "I also seek employment. Geoffrey, by all accounts, is a valiant knight. If you could bear my company, I think I shall go with you."

I said fiercely, "I hope you appreciate *your* company. I am a landless knight, soon to become a soldier, a pillager who lives by the sword. You babble of honour – with such as I you put your own at risk."

Odinel laughed outright. "Humphrey, I enjoy you more and more. You really must ride your humour on a looser rein. I think I can look after myself. Come, what do you say?"

"As you will."

I turned on my heel and left him, and tried to hide my gladness.

I went to Hungerford. This was the first time I had left the forest, and I found myself riding chin on shoulder, hand on dagger – the world seemed full of enemies. Toa's workshops were busier than I remembered, with more forges, new sheds, more workmen – this was a time when armourers throve. The red-faced, jovial Englishman pretended to recognize me, and swore that the hauberk and helmet, sword and shield which he produced for my inspection were the very ones I had commissioned on that carefree day so long ago. The accoutrements fitted well enough; the workmanship was excellent. I gave him money, and the armour to Saiva, who gravely loaded the rouncey. Nobody gave my varlet a second look – except for a willowy, long-haired knight who, in the intervals of fitting a hauberk, mistakenly sent her languishing glances and bestowed on me a roguishly envious wink.

Some days later our little cavalcade rode from the island steading that had been my home. No one bade farewell to Brand. An ox hauled his plough, and he gave his attention to the furrows. He kept his back towards us, and did not seem to see us go.

We left him the lame mastiff.

8

June – July, 1138

On the first day we travelled no farther than Hungerford. I took
the horses to a smithy and had them all re-shod, and visited a
saddler who repaired some of the indifferent saddlery which my
knight-errantry acquired. Lastly I went to Toa and bargained for a
crossbow and quarrells. The armourer reluctantly sold me his last
remaining arbalest – the weapon he used to demonstrate inferior
armour. "Like that disc-mail you're wearing," he said pointedly.
"The best suit I've ever forged, mind you, but not quarrell-proof.
I make no secret of that. Chain-mail, now —"

I cut short his huckster's chatter, paid more than the weapons
were worth and returned to the tavern where we lodged. Anschitel
received his gift with consternation.

"I am a swordsman," he complained, "and too old to learn new
tricks. Give this contraption to Warin."

Odinel's retainer grinned and shook his head. A cheerful, rosy-
faced man, with prominent blue eyes and a receding chin, he possessed much of his master's humour but was, I thought, simple
almost to the point of imbecility. "Not I," he said. "I am a bowman.
Bow and crossbow are different as fox and wolf. Besides, arbalesters
are unpopular: they're seldom given quarter."

Perhaps Warin had some sense in his head after all.

At Reading I bought a chestnut stallion and, with a sigh for the
memory of one better than he, named the animal Chanson. He was
a velvet-mouthed six-year-old, superbly balanced and clearly trained
by someone who understood mounted combat. During our ten-day
halt in Reading I spent hours schooling the destrier.

Saiva's masquerade, peremptorily inflicted on my companions,
roused none of the problems I expected. Odinel, whom nothing
surprised, leered lasciviously; Anschitel's weather-scoured features

showed no emotion; Warin's eyes momentarily bulged still farther from their sockets. She made no claims upon their tolerance; always she behaved and worked as her role demanded; soon they seemed to forget her sex. Her slim body concealed a boy's wiry strength; the longest day, the hardest task never defeated her. Anschitel, who once absently clouted her for clumsiness when off-saddling, and was immediately horrified by his lapse, listened in silent admiration to the scarifying language, French and English intermingled, that she promptly vented on him.

Ranulf treated her with a certain reserve. He had shed his priesthood, but he could not in a moment discard the tenets of a lifetime and the canons which forbade association with women. Ranulf was that rare creature: a parish priest who never took a concubine. Remembering that by birth he was half Visdelou, I always found his chastity astonishing. He did not, of course, dare to reproach me or Saiva for our transgression of God's laws; although a further development created by our odd relationship must have strained his reticence unbearably. Because lack of privacy forbade fornication when we encamped, I occasionally spent the night with Saiva in taverns on the way. Knights and soldiers frequented these inns; sometimes merely a slung blanket separated us from our neighbours – an inadequate muffle for Saiva's amorous gasps. Gossip returned to our ears by way of Odinel, who gleefully reported that my reputation for sodomy began to surpass Red William's. I laughed; but Ranulf, I think, was truly distressed.

The caution imposed by fugitive days in Savernake lingered with me still; I avoided strangers and seldom left the camp. Odinel, a gregarious being, went often to the village, and conversed in taverns with travellers of every degree. From him I learned that the war had taken a new turn, that petty rebellions in the west were becoming a full-scale civil war which could cleave the kingdom like a battle-axe.

"King Henry's daughter and her bastard half-brother have joined hands in Normandy," he said one evening while we loitered around the cooking-fire in midsummer twilight. "Count Robert of Gloucester recently renounced his allegiance to Stephen and defied him. He and Matilda gather armies in Normandy and prepare for war."

"What for? To topple Stephen and put Matilda and her Angevin husband on the throne?"

"You forget, Humphrey: Countess Matilda is the legitimate heir, to whom all the barons of England swore fealty."

"That was eleven years ago," I said. "Since then these same lords have given allegiance to Stephen. Including Count Robert. What does he hope to win by breaking his oath yet again?"

Odinel threw away the beef-bone he was gnawing, crossed to a pannier and poured wine. "Robert believes England belongs, not to his half-sister Matilda, but to her son. He supports Matilda to set a second Henry on the throne. Unfortunately the boy is only six years old."

I kicked a log into the fire, and sparks showered briefly in gathering dusk. "This is all high politics," I said irritably, "a business for counts and princes, far beyond our reach. Robert and Matilda and their armies are still in Normandy – their authority cannot sway us. How has Robert's defiance affected England?"

"Wareham, Shrewsbury and Ludlow have declared for Count Robert. Bristol has closed her gates against the king. King David of Scotland invades Northumbria again and besieges Wark and Bamborough."

"And where, in this chaos, do our loyalties lie?" I wondered.

Odinel drained his wine and laughed without amusement. "Mine to my father, the lord of Prudhoe, whose vassal I am. If his summons reaches me I go. Till then, Humphrey, I suppose I must follow you on your curious errand. And who do you think holds your own fealty?"

I said slowly, "King Stephen, by law and custom, who escheated Speyne. Bochesorne and Benham were ravaged, and he sent no aid. Am I still bound by homage to this man? I do not know. Not willingly will I fight against him; but my sword is for sale, and the chances of war are beyond my governing." I ground my fist against my forehead. "How, in this maze, is a knight to save his honour?"

"Humphrey, you take yourself too seriously." Odinel's tone was bantering, but his eyes were serious. "Have you not listened? All over England counts and barons and knights are breaking and re-affirming and again breaking their oaths. Why should you be different? When rebellion reigns only the faithless are true, for they swear fealty to themselves alone."

I said sombrely, "Without faith I cannot live. Mine reposes between the hands of the man who saved my life, a suzerain before whom I have not yet knelt in homage. I belong to him alone, and must serve him until death."

The fire was dying. I rose, stretched, and lifted my face to the stars.

"We have stayed here too long. Tomorrow we march."

2

Windsor castle loomed above the Thames like a gigantic fist splitting the earth's crust. The fortress had hardly changed since the Bastard built it. The keep, walled by mighty oak trunks three layers thick, reared on a mound that was high and steep. From the mound two baileys flared like wings. Duke William's wooden palisade still guarded the upper ward; around the lower bailey workmen replaced stakes with walls of mortared stone.

The castle's dominant might hit me like a blow between the eyes. Hill and mound and keep soared tier upon tier. Later in this history I saw London's fortress, and Colchester's, impressive and impregnable emblems of Duke William's might – but without Windsor's towering magnificence.

Tents and pavilions sprouted like garish toadstools on the meadow beneath the wards. Lances flaunted gaudy pennons; hauberks dangled from racks like desiccated corpses. Varlets groomed horses picketed in orderly rows; smiths and armourers beat on anvils; sergeants bayed commands; spearmen in squads marched and counter-marched. Bowmen practised at the butts, chaffering and wagering on their shots; knights in conroy wheeled in complicated manœuvres like steel-grey checkers on an emerald board. Among the tents and horse-lines and drilling constabulars flowed an iridescent concourse, lustrous as flower-petals floating on diverse streams – knights in blue and scarlet cloaks, women wearing robes of green and purple, saffron and amber, russet-clad sergeants and black-cowled monks. Above them the castle frowned like a menacing war-god.

Odinel contemplated the scene and said, "Here, if I am not mistaken, an army gathers. Here we may find work for our swords. What is your wish, Humphrey? If we join this throng we may find escape difficult. The king is our overlord, and these are the king's men – you would not find rebels disporting themselves beneath Windsor's royal walls."

"I seek the Constable of London," I said brusquely, "and none shall stop me. Ride on."

We threaded the encampment and pitched our tent on the outskirts. We met knights who saluted us and announced their styles and titles, and I heard the dignities of illustrious Houses: Roumare and de Senliz, Beauchamp and Mortain, whose blood has stained the battlefields of Christendom from Roncesvalles to Bremule. They greeted us well, and offered hospitality and made no comment on our humble equipage, for we were knights and all knights are a single fellowship.

Odinel and I put off our armour, washed the dust of travel from face and hair and donned tunics and cloaks. A friendly, voluble young knight, by name Drogo de Bevrere, stood by and chattered while we made ready. I asked the reason for so great an assemblance of knights and men-at-arms.

"Do you not know?" he said in surprise. "The barons of the north have sent to the king for aid. David of Scotland has crossed the Tyne."

"These names mean little to me," I grunted, struggling with the points of my breeches. "Have the Scots not invaded farther south before?"

"Never before. Look." Drogo pulled an arrow from Warin's quiver, squatted and drew lines in the dust. "Here is Tyne, and here, some thirty miles south, is Tees. Between the two rivers David has halted, and burns and devastates the countryside. I have heard," he added sadly, "that his followers pillage, rape and murder with a ferocity never before witnessed in a Christian country."

Odinel buckled dagger to belt and girded it round his waist. "What drives this man?" he said. "Is he not content with his own realm and barbaric subjects?"

Drogo glanced up from his map-drawing, a serious expression on his young, fresh face.

"David claims the county of Northumbria because his queen's grandfather held the land when Harold ruled the English."

"A ridiculous demand," I said. "As well might Brand the woodcutter claim Savernake. He has a better right."

Drogo was puzzled. "Brand? Savernake? I don't think —"

"No matter. Is the King of Scotland so keen to become an English count that year after year he harries the lands he wants to own?"

"No. There is more than that. David was the first to swear allegiance to Matilda of Anjou. He has never renounced his oath. Now he goes to war on her behalf."

"Which makes more sense," Odinel said. "If the Angevin ever succeeds, then the King of Scots will extend his fiefs to the Humber. Kings do not make war for petty rewards."

I said, "What of the northern barons? And the English levies? Are their retinues so small, or so lacking courage, that they cannot prevent invasion of their own domains?"

"They are frightened enough," Drago answered, "and with reason. The Scots crossed the Pennine mountains, there," – his arrow traced the dust – "and raided into Lancashire. Another foray penetrated Yorkshire, here. Meanwhile King David, in the moorlands north of Tees, is collecting a mighty army. They say that over twenty thousand warriors gather to his standard."

"Twenty thousand!" Odinel exclaimed. "An exaggerated rumour, certainly put about by the Scots themselves. There were not so many on both sides at Tinchebrai."

Drogo shrugged. "I do not know. I have seen no battles. However it may be, the northern barons sent Bernard de Balliol to King Stephen and asked for help. The king is fighting in the west and cannot go in person, but he sent his writs abroad and called his vassals to acquit their services, and named Windsor as the assembly place."

"When do you march?' Odinel said.

Drogo repeated, "I do not know. Certain barons are dilatory, and plead excuses: their retinues have not arrived. Bernard de Balliol chafes and bites his nails, and fears the Scots may forestall him." He grinned. "Bernard is an angry man. Do not cross him."

I stood, smoothed my tunic and slung my cloak. "Bernard is not my quarry," I said. "My destination lies elsewhere. I seek my lord, Geoffrey de Mandeville."

Drogo flipped Warin's arrow into the quiver. "Geoffrey de Mandeville?" he said casually. "You need travel no farther. He is here."

3

"Lord Geoffrey, I offer you my sword."

The pavilion was only a little smaller than the Hall at Bochesorne. Scarlet and yellow stripes banded the canvas; corded tassels, gold and scarlet, adorned the poles. Silken curtains blazoned the walls;

fresh rushes and aromatic herbs covered the floor like a field of flowers. In the centre stood a parchment-littered ebony table with ivory legs, fancifully carved. Three chain-mesh hauberks, dangling from armour stands among swords and baldrics, seemed alien in this panoplied magnificence as scarecrows in a bower. In a chair like a throne, lounging on embroidered cushions, velvet and silk, I found the man who was my destiny.

My mouth was dry and my knees trembled.

A sea-green robe of finest linen descended to his ankles; intricate designs in silver thread decorated the hem. The sleeves expanded at the wrists to arrow-length lappets tipped with little golden bells, so that a tiny music accompanied his every gesture. From his shoulders swung an azure mantle, ermine-lined, and pointed shoes of soft red leather covered his feet.

I raised my eyes to his face, and held my breath.

All was there as I remembered, in my dreams and in my waking reveries. The archangel's face, lean and beautiful, the smiling lips and shining night-dark hair, and the eyes like sapphire pools where the souls of sinners drowned.

Without thought or conscious volition, like a priest before the Rood, I crossed myself.

Geoffrey de Mandeville said softly, "Why do you sign yourself? I am not God."

"My lord," I said miserably, "I intend no offence."

He gestured to the squire who brought me into his presence. The bells tinkled a brittle tune.

"Leave us, Thibault."

The boy threw me a curious glance, bowed to his lord, parted the door curtains and went. Geoffrey de Mandeville spread his hands on the table before him.

"Now, Humphrey Visdelou, tell me of yourself, and why you want to enter my service. How many men-at-arms are in your train?"

"Do you not remember me, my lord?"

"Remember you? Why should I? Visdelou? A noble name – from Ponthieu, I believe. But I have not been honoured by the friendship of your family."

I gazed at him mutely, helpless, my world shuddering in ruins like a citadel struck by earthquake, my devotion running to waste like spring water in desert sands. For this I had not envisaged: that my saviour would not know of his salvation.

"Ten months since, my lord, at Bochesorne," I muttered. "The sack. The gallows. And —"

"No, I do not remember. Tell me, Humphrey Visdelou."

His eyes held no compassion, but his voice was gentle.

Stammering and incoherent, I told him my tale. When I arrived at my moment of shame I could not go on.

He raised a hand, and the bells chimed their melody. "You need say no more. Now I recall it all." He looked at me strangely. "And for this – shall we say – partial deliverance, do you consider yourself somehow in my debt?"

I said, "Yes, my lord. A debt that is beyond repayment."

He sat very still, and gazed at his hands.

"Humphrey Visdelou," he said at last, without raising his head, "you are an unusual man, and I am not certain that I comprehend your standards of obligation. Another in your position might have sought my life, not my service. However, you have your own ideals – and who am I to shatter them? I know you for a brave and stalwart knight, and I believe you to be faithful and true." The blue eyes lifted and looked into mine. "You shall become my man. If ever you are disloyal to me I will kill you."

He rose to his great height and sauntered round the table.

"Give me your homage, Humphrey."

I knelt and joined my hands in prayer, and put them between his, and swore the oath of fealty.

"*Gaufrid de Mandeville, jo sui vostre liges hum par fei e par humage.*"

I remained upon my knees, and prayed silently, and his touch was warm on my fingers and the tears ran down my face.

4

Next day I moved our camp to Geoffrey de Mandeville's tent-lines. My lord had a considerable following: in his train marched eleven knights and fifty men-at-arms, some drawn from the Tower household and others from fiefs he held in Essex. The king had directed his mustering writs to his vassals in eastern England, whose Honours lay mostly in the counties neighbouring London, so that great barons like Aubrey de Vere and Hugh Bigod of Norfolk sent contingents to Windsor.

Although Odinel knew I was determined to follow Lord Geoffrey, I had not tried to persuade him to the same course. Odinel's loyalties were more complicated than mine. I, a tenant-in-chief of the king, had elected to serve a baron who was also a tenant-in-chief: so long as my lord obeyed Stephen I committed no crime. But Odinel's father, the lord of Prudhoe, held his fief of a baron whose grandfather had done homage for his lands to Siward, the last English Count of Northumbria – the county now claimed by David of Scotland. That baron had no affinity with the Scots, but sympathized with Countess Matilda's claims, which had Scotland's support. Odinel's loyalties were therefore so involved that he could never know, until he answered Prudhoe's summons, on whose side he would fight.

Odinel solved the problem in his own cheerful way; and came to the horse-lines and told me about it.

"I am become a true soldier," he said happily, "a man who fights for money and owes no faith. I had an audience with that lord of yours – by the Lance, he's a frightening man! – and told him my circumstances. He understood perfectly, took me into his service – eightpence a day – and demanded no homage. He accepts that I remain a vassal of Prudhoe. And here I am."

"You're an enfeoffed knight," I grunted, "playing at soldiers. It doesn't matter. Hold this rope and get the horses in line. We're under military discipline now."

Our haphazard vagrant way of life was ended. My lord's captains were men of force and method. Ernulf de Mandeville, his son, commanded the conroy – the name given to a mixed unit, horse and foot, about fifty strong. A sullen unsmiling man, oddly staccato in his manner of speech, he resembled his father only in menace; he was stocky and dark and tough as an ancient oak-beam, and gave all his resolve and purpose to the ordering and conduct of war. Ernulf allotted us stations in the line, examined our horses, unrolled hauberks and haubergeons and tested the mail ring by disc, ran his thumb along the edges of swords, thumped shields and minutely inspected rivets, cast a disparaging eye on our tent and fingered the suppleness of saddle-leather. At length he finished his inspection and stood before us, hands on hips.

"I've seen worse," he grunted. "Somebody here knows his job. That palfrey's got a loose shoe, near-hind – attend to it. Who's your purveyor?"

I indicated Ranulf.

"Draw rations and fodder from our carts at dawn each day. Pay on the nail. We drill every morning. Parade before my lord's pavilion when the chapel bell rings prime. And you can throw that arbalest away."

I said, "I will not."

He glowered at me. "Foul weapons. I won't have them in my conroy. Slow and cumbersome besides. Do as I say."

"Ernulf," I said, "I shall use your advice in the ordering of my men and obey your commands in battle. I have seen that you are an experienced warrior with a keen eye to detail – indeed you have, in a short space, taught me a good deal. But the internal discipline and equipment of my retinue is a matter for my authority – not yours. They are my liegemen – not yours."

Ernulf glared, compressed his lips and strode away.

"Another dangerous fellow," Odinel observed, following him with his eyes. "Efficient, but mad in his efficiency. I'm glad you've put yourself between us and him. Heigh-ho," he yawned. "I've done no drill for months – doubt I can remember the commands. Humphrey, I think you've plunged us into a welter of work."

Work there was, during that golden June when the army lay in Windsor's meadows. Every morning two hundred knights and a thousand sergeants drilled and shot and cut and warded until the sun rode high in the heavens. My little retinue was all mounted. so we drilled as a constabular – a cavalry unit of ten or twenty horsemen – under Ernulf's long-drawled, singing commands. Later we joined forces with other contingents and thundered over the fields in squadron lines. I found the exercises exhilarating, and did not grudge the hours spent afterwards in grooming, greasing saddlery and polishing armour. Although no knight objects to working on horses, anything else is the business of squires and varlets. However, the humbler tasks proved too much for Ranulf and Saiva alone: Odinel and I took pity on them and scrubbed away willingly.

I found, among this assembly of fighting-men who were jealous of their privileges and touchy about style and title, that one had to be careful in using the word 'sergeant': a name reserved fairly strictly for those men-at-arms – swordsmen, spearmen or bowmen, mounted or afoot – who were landholders acquitting their tenure by military service. Landless freemen, whether household troops or paid hirelings, held a lower rank in the military hierarchy – not for them the dignity of sergeant. Occasionally, in my earlier days, some grizzled veteran growled, "No sergeant, he," when I affixed the title to an unmerited man. Nevertheless, even experienced knights employ the term very loosely to signify any man-at-arms; and so I shall continue to use it in my history.

5

Now that we lived among Lord Geoffrey's retainers Saiva's position became ever more difficult. I had bound my little band to secrecy about her sex – though I could not be certain of the foolish Warin, a babbler addicted to the ale-pot. Many women lived in the encampment. Some were high-born ladies: wives or lemans whom knights had called to Windsor to enliven the tedious waiting. These we seldom met; they strolled upon their lords' arms along the river-banks or rode hawking in the woods. The bulk was camp-followers of various kinds: laundresses, alewomen, wagoners' drabs and a heavy sprinkling of harlots. The stews, though set apart, were much frequented. These women moved about the tents and horse-lines at will, and sent Saiva many a penetrating glance and knowing smile. From women whose profession is sex, sex cannot be concealed. Moreover her lowly standing as a varlet exposed her to horseplay and buffet from men of base degree, sergeants and grooms; or else to amorous advances from perverts of every rank, knights included. Anschitel protected her as best he could, but it is difficult for a sergeant to rebuff knights. I could not take her into the company of my peers when I mingled with other knights to gamble, gossip or sup: she had to remain with the attendants at a distance. Once she was nearly raped – in her masculine role – by a hairy bowman behind a haystack. I sought the man's lord – none other than young Drogo de Bevrere – obtained permission and used my sword flat to beat him to a pulp. But the problem remained.

Eventually Saiva, irked beyond endurance, suggested a solution.

"Why can't I be your squire, Humphrey? I could then attend you at table and go with you anywhere."

"That I have considered," I said, "and it is impossible for two reasons. A squire must support his lord in battle, which you cannot do. A squire is noble, and aspires to knighthood, which you cannot have."

"I am noble," Saiva answered sulkily.

123

"You are English and a woman," I retorted. "Let's hear no more of it."

I resigned myself to the inevitable exposure of her secret; meanwhile I took care to be in her company whenever possible, and thereby enhanced my reputation for devoted sodomy.

Although I saw little of Geoffrey de Mandeville by day, he relished the company of his vassals when he dined. "For," as he once smilingly explained, "if I don't sup with them they will consume my victuals and grumble behind my back." If no great baron were present at the board he would often call me from my lowly place and bid me sit beside him, and I listened, entranced, to his conversation and melodious voice. He knew much of battle and the art of war, and quoted from great captains of the past, Xenophon and Caesar – for he was a clerkly man who could write and read in French and Latin. "They were warriors of organization and method, Humphrey," he told me, "whereas modern war lacks both. I have striven to impart some of their principles to Ernulf." He pointed his dagger at his son, who argued blackly with a companion. "Ernulf is thorough and systematic, but he is no innovator and lacks imagination. He would lose a battle by obeying the rules."

"My lord," I ventured, "I have ridden under Ernulf's orders these three weeks past, and I have much respect for his methods."

He smiled and sipped from a cup of hammered gold. "Ernulf bumps you around on horseback. Has he ever practised you on foot?"

"We are knights," I said in surprise. "Our business is to charge with lance and sword."

"There you are," my lord sighed. "My beloved Ernulf will not accept innovations – if such they can be called – which have been used for seventy years. Don't you realize that Hastings, where the English proved that mailed infantry behind a shield-wall can break a cavalry charge, has changed the face of war? Count Harold dealt our accepted battle tactics a fatal blow."

"My lord," I protested, "the stories told by veterans of the Norman wars are full of charge and counter-charge and the shock of lance on shield."

Geoffrey de Mandeville shook his head. "Predilection embroiders their memories. For consider: dismounted knights in close array won Tinchebrai, Bremule and Bourg Theroulde. In fact, a dismounted charge decided the issue at Bremule. And yet we still

image that heavy cavalry dominates the battlefield, a belief revived
forty years ago by the fights in Outremer. Unfortunately our enemies
in England are not light-armed, ragged infidels. Perhaps you'll find
the Scots are something of the kind; then you mailed and mounted
paladins can prove your worth. But I doubt it."

He laid a hand on my shoulder.

"Ernulf told me about your arbalest: you were right to cross
him. Here is something new, untried and invincible. I like intelli-
gent novelties and respect the mind that exploits them. You are
that rare individual: a soldier with ideas. When you return to me
from the north we shall discuss these matters further."

"Return to you? Do you not march with us, my lord?"

He smiled into my eyes. "Mind your manners, Humphrey. A
vassal should not introduce a new subject into conversation with
his lord. We talk of war, not politics." His dagger tapped the rim
of his empty wine-cup; the gold rang like a bell. "I am King Stephen's
man by faith and homage. If David of Scotland prevails against
him the way lies open for Angevin Matilda. Would it not be dis-
astrous if I in person were found in arms against her supporters?"

He saw my shocked amazement, and laughed, and the Devil
looked through his eyes.

"Politics, Humphrey. Do not betray me, my faithful knight."

The dagger-point rested delicately against my ribs.

6

Night air cooled my wine-fevered face; the grass, scented with
green bloom and rain, yielded a pliant couch. From the faraway
encampment a clamour of carousal reverberated like sounds of
distant conflict. Saiva lay upon my breast, her velvet lips like butter-
fly wings caressed my cheek; and I was content.

Presently she stirred and spoke.

"Tomorrow we march."

"Tomorrow we march," I agreed. "Not before time. News from
the north is not good: the Scots are raiding and ravaging. Nor is it
catastrophic, for King David still lingers beyond Tees. His vassals
seem dilatory as Stephen's in answering his call to arms. Not until
today did our last contingent arrive."

We rested awhile in comfortable silence. Moondawn paled the

stars and bathed the trees in silver. The noise of revelry abated, and we heard only the rustling reeds and the river's gentle pluck and ripple. High in the sky a solitary light glowed in Windsor's towering pile.

Saiva moved in my arms.

"Humphrey, you have found your God, or your Devil – your Geoffrey de Mandeville. What now do you propose?"

"To follow him until I die," I said simply.

"He holds you still? You have found no dross in your demon?"

I loosed her and sat gazing, chin in hand, over the moon-streaked waters.

"I have come to know him well. Although familiarity is an acid that flays the paint from a tawdry image, Geoffrey de Mandeville has lost no stature in my eyes. No longer, in truth, is he the satanic archangel of my fevered dreams in Savernake. He has become a man, but he reigns above all men; and I know that Lucifer burns in his heart."

Saiva was silent. A faint breeze rustled the grasses. I turned my head and saw tears gleaming in her eyes.

9

July — August, 1138

In mid-July the army departed from Windsor on the two-hundred-mile march to York.

Bernard de Balliol led the host — a testy little man with a face like an irritable sheep and an intelligence sharp as a Fleming's knife. All the great barons had gone their separate ways: Hugh Bigod to Norfolk, Aubrey de Vere on pressing business to Oxford, Geoffrey de Mandeville to his custody of the Tower. My lord made no advertisement of his departure. Taking two knightly attendants and a handful of men-at-arms he rode for London one rainy dawn and was gone before we were aware. He left the conroy under Ernulf's command.

The long and monotonous march set a pattern for many that I endured in the years afterwards. Our route lay through a countryside untouched by war. We feared no enemy attack, and our numbers effectively deterred robbers and outlaws. Progress, dictated by the wagon-train, was grindingly slow. A miscellaneous collection followed the column: carts of every description in varied stages of disrepair, drawn by all sorts of animals: horses, mules, donkeys, oxen — even by dogs. No one could impose a uniform standard of fitness on these vehicles, for every knight equipped his own retinue — as I did mine — and the outcome was variable as the owners' purses and inclinations. Camp-followers swelled the train: sutlers and wagoners and vendors and women; and numerous sheep and cattle — the army's travelling larder.

The first stage to St Albans — a little over twenty miles — took two days. The roads were wretched: rutted tracks meandered through forest and dissolved into muddy quagmires at every ford or downpour. Bridges there were none. Axles broke, traces parted, insecure loads fell off. On the second day Bernard, in a spitting rage, rode down the column, whip in hand, and lashed animals and drovers indiscriminately. This did no good at all; but in the evening he summoned constables and bannerets and used his tongue more searingly than he had his whip. Sawing and hammering kept the camp awake that night; wheelwrights and carpenters got little sleep. Afterwards we had fewer breakdowns and delays; but this, I think, was mainly due to the paved Roman highway which we followed northwards from St Albans.

In six days' marching the army covered seventy miles and approached Huntingdon. I surveyed the knights who rode in our company. Lances swayed like reed-clumps in a sluggish stream. Singly, in couples, in scattered groups, on the road or off, chattering and singing, they resembled a concourse bound for some fairground rather than an instrument of war. Our men-at-arms kept a vestigial formation; the knights none. The army, in its disjointed passage, used more than a mile of road, and the motley transport as much again. A fine target for a surprise attack, I reflected – but the enemy roved far to the north.

After Lincoln, a walled town where we halted for a day, the weather improved and the road worsened. We entered the freeholds of war, a countryside so scourged by Duke William's ancient harrying that the land had never properly recovered. Villages were rare, the harvest-ripe fields half tilled, the peasants pauper. We met few wayfarers – those diversified wanderers who travelled England's roads and enlivened the march: pilgrims and pedlars, minstrels and merchants. Sometimes we passed an abbot and his attendant monks, comfortably mounted on asses, escorted by vassal knights; or itinerant preachers – half-mad fanatics who, amid jeers and cat-calls, vehemently upbraided our passage.

Day after day the sun blazed from azure skies. By noon mailcoats became too hot to touch and sweat runnelled our ribs. Odinel donned a linen mantle beneath his armour, the skirts trailing to his ankles below the hauberk's hem: a fashion adopted by many knights and culled, so he said, from experience in torrid Outremer; and swore he was cooler.

"Mere foppery," I growled, "a hindrance flapping around your legs, a handle for unhorsing. Surely more effective, if you must, to wear mantel over hauberk, not under, so that the sun's rays don't reach the metal."

But no, said Odinel. smirking – that was not fashionable.

Not much remained of Rome's handiwork in the road we trod.

The causeway survived, a grass-grown embankment that flew straight as a quarrell over a bare countryside. The surface was eroded and broken; boulders and up-ended paving troubled horses and wheels. Gaps yawned where winter spates had torn the earth. Generations of travellers and marching armies and time's ravages rendered Ermine Street – for so the English called it – an obstacle rather than a road. None, in these parts, had troubled with repairs. So traffic flowed alongside, and wheel-ruts wandered in parallel paths extending a hundred paces both sides of the causeway.

On the twentieth day since leaving Windsor the walls of York thrust over the horizon like the snout of a fabled monster from the minstrels' songs. The army did not arrive unheralded; Bernard de Balliol had sent outriders from his last encampment. On this day the column rode in order, rank upon rank. Knights and ladies and burghers poured from the gates to welcome them. We pitched tents outside the walls, discarded hauberks and went within, seeking taverns and women and meat and luxuries which none had tasted since Windsor. The town suffered a riotous night. The brothels were crammed, taverns overflowed, and brawls reverberated in narrow streets. By morning half Bernard's army was a leaderless mob of queasy-bellied, sore-headed rapscallions.

Ernulf forbade his conroy the town, and held the half-mutinous men in camp by sheer personal menace. Later he sent quietly to the vintners for wine-casks, to taverners for ale, and procured some drabs of the better sort. The sergeants enjoyed their pleasures no less under a pretence of military discipline.

I had always respected Ernulf. I began now to like him.

We found no other army at York. Bernard de Balliol had assured us that the northern barons and the English levies were gathering for war; but we saw only the castle's garrison and a handful of knights and men-at-arms attendant on local barons whom Archbishop Thurstan had called to council. Day by day we watched these great men coming and going about the town on business that was clearly important. They disappeared for hours in the archbishop's palace and emerged wearing anxious faces. Nothing concrete, such as a force of armoured fighting-men, seemed to result from their deliberations. Our own leaders' comments daily became more cynical and caustic.

"They beg King Stephen's help," Ernulf observed, "and get it; then expect his thousand men to fight the Scots unaided."

Bernard de Balliol attended the meetings – which did nothing to cool his peppery temper. Finally he gathered bannerets and constables and addressed them in his pavilion. I waited on Ernulf, and heard Bernard's discourse.

"My lords," he said, "we find ourselves becalmed on a sea of irresolution. None seems able to decide what must be done. I do not accuse our Yorkshire peers of cowardice. I do not accuse noble knights, such as Walter Espec and Robert de Bruce, of hesitating to face King David. These men, and others with them, have often proved their valour. I do not say that suspicion and mistrust is rife among them. They are barons whose honour is unstained and fealty assured."

He paused and surveyed us, and smiled grimly.

"I make no accusations. This remains: the only man in York who wants to fight the Scots is an aged churchman, the archbishop himself. He and I together are striving, day and night, to persuade our friends to the same course."

Ernulf said, "What of the enemy?"

Bernard said gravely, "The Scottish army is mustered by Teesside. Our spies watch and report. They may advance at any moment."

"And if they do, we fight unsupported?"

"You should know better," Bernard answered testily. "My orders are to reinforce the army of the north. I do not intend that we alone should be that army. I have no love for hopeless causes."

He dismissed us. I was perplexed by the situation Bernard had revealed, unable to understand why the local magnates could not gird themselves to defend their territory. Ernulf glumly explained.

"Divided loyalties. Some of the barons are David's liegemen and hold lands from him. For example, Robert de Bruce and William de Percy. Bernard de Balliol, for that matter, is also Scotland's vassal – but he was forged on a different anvil. If David wins they lose. If David loses they are no better off. They dally and suck their thumbs and hope for compromise."

During this time of indecision the army, encamped outside the walls of York, grew restive. Vassals whose forty-day term had long expired, who saw no prospect of fighting, came to Bernard and demanded release. Irascibly he overrode objections, took them into paid service and persuaded most of them to stay.

A knight of King David's household, captured during a raid, gave Odinel news of his Northumbrian home. Prudhoe castle, he proudly informed me, still held for Stephen, despite a leaguer culminating in a determined storm. But the lands had been thoroughly harried. "My dwelling is rubble and my fields burnt straw, the villeins dead or enslaved. I have nothing to return to, and the baron my father seems perfectly capable of beating the Scots without my help. I do not think I shall leave you awhile, whichever way this business goes."

I took lodgings in the town above a saddler's shop; Saiva and I lived there happily enough. Odinel pursued a burgher's wife, a fat, fair-haired wench who should have known better, and disappeared on hopeful assignations at improbable hours of the night. Ernulf sternly eschewed all relaxation. He replenished the conroy's provisions, repaired carts, replaced decrepit draught-animals, inspected saddlery and farriery, bought fodder by the bale.

On a windy evening in early August riders galloped through the gate with news that shattered York's placidity like a boulder splashing into a stagnant pond. A thundering Scottish raid had crossed Tees and burnt villages and devastated fields in a wide arc for ten miles south. This was clearly a reconnaissance in force, preliminary to a general advance.

Archbishop Thurstan called the barons to council and, as Bernard informed us, spoke for the turning of a sand-glass without stopping. His exhortations prevailed.

We watched the outcome: messengers hastening on every road, a feverish gathering of supplies and fodder from the countryside, the barons galloping from the gates, homeward bound to collect their retinues. Odinel regarded the eruption sceptically.

"They'll have to be quick if we aren't to face David alone," he said. "I wonder how many will return."

His pessimism was unwarranted. Within two days the first contingents arrived. Tents and horse-lines and the panoply of war progressively covered the heathlands around York's walls. Robert de Ferrers returned, a mighty baron in Derbyshire, leading three hundred knights and sergeants, and William de Aumale, who brought from his Yorkshire fiefs not only Norman warriors but English levies – as, indede, did every knight who held estates anywhere near York. Not many of us had seen the English at war: curiously we regarded these long-bearded warriors and their round shields and feeble mail. Only the better-armed aspired to metal-studded leather jerkins and iron caps. They carried battle-axe, spear, or sword; and all went on foot. Because the English were a conquered people whom we had always worsted in battle, I tended to regard them as second-rate troops; but Odinel had seen them in Northumbrian wars, and thought differently.

"Poorly armed, admittedly," he said. "What would you expect? These English are freemen – perhaps noblemen – who have lost their lands. They have little wealth to lavish on hauberk and haubergeon. But they can fight, Humphrey – I assure you they can fight."

Eleven days after the Scottish raid the army was all assembled – a faster gathering, Bernard de Balliol sourly admitted, than he expected. On the twelfth day scouts brought news that roused the old warrior like a destrier pricked by spurs.

King David had crossed Tees.

2

A knightly throng filled St Peter's church and overflowed to the cobbled square beyond. This day ended the fast enjoined by Archbishop Thurstan: a precept the reverent among us faithfully obeyed. The archbishop celebrated Mass, and solemnly dismissed his congregation, giving them God's blessing and his own. Into Walter Espec's hands he consigned his cross, and a silver pix containing the Host, and St Peter's standard, and bade him carry them always before the army. Then he stood forth and addressed us.

Thurstan was an old man, so frail that two acolytes supported him on his feet. But the resonant voice soared to the oaken rafters like a banneret's call in the clash of conflict. His words were vehement, irresistible in their impact, uplifting the hearts and souls of men who were doubtful, and mistrusting, and a little afraid.

He preached a Holy War.

"The Scots who have in this land violated the temples of the Lord, polluted His altars, slain His priests and spared neither children nor women with child, shall on this same soil receive condign punishment for their crimes, since victory depends not on numbers but on the strength derived from Heaven."

I can remember, now, little of his oration; but this I know: the men who afterwards departed from St Peter's church had forgotten jealousies and bickerings, petty animosities and fears, and were united in a fervid determination to annihilate an enemy cursed by God.

At noon the army marched.

The order and method in our progression delighted Ernulf. This was a military movement very different from Bernard de Balliol's ragged embulation from Windsor. We did not fear ambush: Walter Espec's defiance had gone to King David days beforehand and, once battle has been formally offered, a treacherous attack is, in knightly eyes, almost unthinkable. But many of our leaders had warred against the Scots; they knew that David could seldom control his tribesmen's plundering forays. These bands might be encountered anywhere, without warning. They were no hazard to an ordered column, but stragglers offered an easy prey.

We did not straggle.

In the evening, after eight hours' marching, the army reached Thirsk, where Roger de Mowbray held a castle for King Stephen. His constable was glad to see us. Tides of war had scoured this place; cindered mounds and a gutted church marked the village. Fire-scars streaked the castle's wooden keep. Near-by, in field and moorland, mouldering bodies rotted and stank – Scottish corpses, these, to whom none would give Christian burial.

The army encamped around the castle. Bannerets ordered the lines carefully and stationed pickets; sentries were nervous and alert. At nightfall the barons went to the castle to debate the next day's operations. Some time during the second watch Bernard de Balliol came to Ernulf, sleeping cloak-wrapped by his horse. The low-voiced summons awakened me. I lay on my elbow and listened.

Bernard said, "I come to warn you for duty at dawn. We send an embassy to King David: Robert de Bruce and me. Your constabular and another from Robert's retinue escorts us."

"An embassy?" Ernulf said. "I thought we went to fight, not talk."

Bernard wearily seated himself on a destrier's battle-saddle. The lingering embers of a dying camp-fire painted dark shadows under his eyes.

"Thurstan's exhortations lose force with time and distance," he said. "My lords grow doubtful of the outcome; the protagonists of compromise have had their way. Robert de Bruce is chief amongst them: he is still David's man by fealty and homage. He

133

persuaded the others to parley. That decided, I had to reveal the bribe entrusted to my care."

"A bribe? Money?" Astonishment sharpened Ernulf's voice.

"No," Bernard said tiredly. "Not money. Stephen gave into my hands a charter, witnessed and sealed, assigning to David the county of Northumbria, which he will receive of the king's hands on condition that he withdraws his armies into Scotland."

"Christ's thorns!" Ernulf snarled. "We mobilize a host, we advance in full caparison of war against our enemy, and one march away we decide to give him all he wants. We shall be the laughing-stock of Christendom!"

A distant sentry challenged, men coughed and muttered in their dreams, horses stamped and snorted. The noises of the sleeping army merged in a murmur like the uneasy breathing of a slumbering giant.

"I could do nothing else," Bernard said. He pitched a pebble into the fire; a flame spurted and died. "Stephen's orders were precise. If the Yorkshire lords resolved on battle, well and good; if they wished to negotiate, Northumbria must be put in as an inducement. At the last moment they have decided on negotiation."

"Robert de Bruce is a traitor!" Ernulf exclaimed.

Bernard sighed. "I do not know his mind. It is true that he has much to lose. So have I. Tomorrow we ride together to the Scottish king, he to persuade, I to bribe."

He rose, gathered his cloak about him and strode away. Ernulf sat on the ground, spitting oaths. A cheerful voice spoke from the darkness.

"Don't worry, Ernulf. You'll have your battle. King David is after bigger game than a devastated county already beneath his heel."

And Odinel, having delivered his prophecy, rolled himself in his cloak and went back to sleep.

3

The road, a hoof-beaten track, slanted across the heath. A mist-haze, precursor to a blazing day, veiled the plan and drifted around the column like gossamer threads. The constabular rode fast, eyes wary and senses alert, swords loose in scabbards and lances balanced.

Two men in the lead carried green-leaf sprays, emblems of truce, tied to their lance-heads. No one spoke very much. Ears strained to pierce the familiar creak and jingle and thudding, and listened for alien sounds.

A peaceful embassy traversed hostile country where the enemy respected neither harbinger nor herald.

Sun-glow shredded the mist. The track unrolled to the horizon. Robert de Bruce swept dewdrops from his coppery beard and peered into the distance.

"Allerton lies ahead," he said. "We shall stop awhile at the castle."

There was no castle at Allerton.

Massacre's rust-red stains streaked bailey and ramparts. The keep was a blackened stump, the palisade timbers splayed like broken spears. Smoke-wisps coiled lazily above the ruins. Bodies sprawled everywhere, naked and mutilated, unrecognizable.

"These were women," Odinel muttered, pointing his lance.

They lay in a group, gathered together before they died for purposes we could only guess at. Then they were butchered. Severed breasts and ripped bellies, the foetus of an unborn child drooping like a blood-slimed doll.

The knights crouched over saddle-bows like figures carved in stone, and their eyes flinched from the grotesque abominations spread like sacrifices at their feet.

A fallen crucifix, forgotten loot of a ravaged church, impaled a head which still wore the lip-stretched grin of agonizing death. A sergeant dismounted, twisted the skull and laid it gently down. He thrust the crucifix into the ground among the contorted bodies, stood back and knelt in prayer.

The riders' hands moved to their shoulders, and they crossed themselves.

Bernard de Balliol said hoarsely, "Come away. There is nothing for us here." Savagely he scrubbed dry lips.

The constabular rode on, walking the horses, recoiling from the clatter they made in that silent and terrible place. They passed grass-grown mounds where huts and cottages, long since destroyed, once stood before King David's men had found them.

Ernulf said, "We parley with these animals. Have we no shame at all?"

On the plain three miles beyond Allerton a round-backed ridge swelled like a weal from the scourge of God. Bernard halted the constabular and turned aside, and rode the ridge from end to end. He paused on the summit and pondered, chin in hand, a lone figure graven against the sky. Then he rejoined us, still thoughtful, and made no remark. We went on, riding fast.

Soon we saw men in the distance, small groups wandering the moors. We passed them quickly, shields enarmed and lances ready. An arrow whipped harmlessly overhead.

"Scots!" Ernulf said through gritted teeth. His destrier swerved out of line.

Bernard looked over his shoulder and barked, "Keep your ranks!"

Mail-coats gleamed far ahead, and gaudy pennons fluttered like flower-petals. Robert de Bruce shaded his eyes.

"Knights, thank God," he said. "Now we are safe."

The outriders raised garlanded lances on high, and the constabular rode on at a walk. King David's knights gave courteous greeting, inquired our mission and led us to his camp. There they set food and drink before us and attended to the horses. They made friendly conversation, gravely discussed the chances of encounter, and begged news of friends in the Norman army. Odinel exchanged gay badinage with a Vexin knight he had once fought outside Prudhoe's walls. Presently a messenger entered, and asked permission to lead us to the king.

The constabular rode to the meeting-place, an open sward near King David's emblazoned pavilion. The barons of Scotland, mailed and mounted, stood in serried ranks behind their king, who sat his destrier in the centre. The line was an arc, the half of a circle; we arranged ourselves in like order opposite, so that the council became an armoured circumference. This is the custom when warriors debate; bishops and prelates and softer men prefer roof and walls and swansdown cushions.

Robert de Bruce and Bernard de Balliol dismounted and knelt, and put their hands in the king's hands, for they were his liegemen. Then they remounted, and Robert stood forth before his lord, and said what he had come to say.

Terse argument and stubborn stipulation have no place in these debates, always adorned with flourishes of polite usage and subtle divagations that barely hint at the ultimate purpose. While Robert intoned the formula of greeting, and conveyed in urbane language King Stephen's salutations, I had leisure to study the ruler who commanded our enemy.

King David was a short man, passing middle age, thick-necked and deep-chested. Watchful eyes contradicted an indolent expression. Broad, strong fingers tapped a march-tune on his saddlebow. A chain-mesh hauberk, so finely fashioned that it embraced his body like shimmering grey silk, ended above chausses smooth as beech-bark. Red leather straps secured golden spurs upon his heels. Jewels studded the golden coronet around his helmet, and his shield bore a rampant dragon, gules on vert. The destrier, a Flemish-bred skewbald stallion, pawed and lunged at his bit.

I wondered a little at such magnificence in a barbarian chieftain; then remembered that David had lived much in England and mingled with counts and barons of King Henry's court, where he rubbed off the tarnish of Scottish barbarism. During his fourteen years' rule he had nearly eliminated the rude clansmen from his entourage, replacing them by French and Norman knights – as the frowning ring of steel bore witness – and introduced civilized manners. Scotland, at the core, had become a Norman community; the flesh of this evil fruit was still a bestial horde whose atrocities the king directed and condoned.

The polite formalities came to an end; Robert de Bruce spoke in booming tones that rang like a gong.

"Sire, who are your enemies? Against whom are you leading your huge army? You propose to fight those very Norman lords who cleared your way to the throne and who have since helped to keep you there. We, the men you regard as enemies, are no different by blood and by brotherhood from those who now stand behind you."

"A good point," Odinel murmured, pretending to adjust his plastron.

"My lord, do you now feel so secure, so confident, that you can afford to lead Norman against Norman, vassal against suzerain, knight against knight? Do you really feel so safe and happy among your Scots?"

"Tactless," Odinel whispered disapprovingly. "There must be some Scottish lords in his retinue."

"Sire, our army is smaller than yours. We see the imminence of defeat and death. But if we are to fight we have chosen death, for you will not vanquish us alive. You do not know, my lord, how dangerous is despair."

"So? Fight to the last man?" said Odinel. "Nobody asked me."

Robert spoke in impassioned tones.

"My lord king, spare yourself, spare your kingdom, spare your noble vassals. You gamble everything you have, all that you are, on the hazard of your tribesmen's prowess in pitched battle. Have they met that test before? Have you so much faith in them?"

"A clever speech." Odinel spoke in my ear. "Tried to widen the gulf between Norman and Scot. Overdone it, I'm afraid."

King David listened. No emotion showed on his face; eyelids hooded the wary eyes; only his fingers, tapping a faster rhythm, betrayed any feeling. He seemed to ponder awhile; then raised his head.

"And Northumbria?"

Bernard de Balliol lifted a parchment scroll; waxen seals dangled in a cluster.

"Here is the deed, sealed by King Stephen, witnessed by his barons."

From the ranks behind King David a knight spurred forward, a young man with a twisted mouth and angry eyes. He reined beside the king and pointed at Robert, his arm out-thrust like a lance in rest.

"What value has a charter brought by such as you?" he shouted. "To my lord the king you owe fealty and homage. Why, then, do you ride in his enemies' ranks?"

The armoured circle stirred and swayed like tree-trunks shaken in a gale. Odinel soothed his horse, and whispered, "Henry, the king's son – a young hothead and a notable instigator of war."

Robert's face was white. His red beard flared like fire. The lance trembled in his hand.

"In using discourteous language, my lord, you do yourself dishonour." He paused, and contained himself by an effort. "I cannot answer you as I would, for the garlands of truce protect you."

He addressed the king.

"Sire, what is your will? What instructions do I carry to my lords?"

Henry blared, "Tell them that Scotland does not treat with perjured and faithless knights! If they are afraid, and must sue for peace, let them send honourable men."

Robert's temper snapped.

"Honourable!" he roared. "You prate of honour, and ride to war among savages who rape and murder and mutilate, who pillage churches, castrate priests and blaspheme God. Honour!" He spat. "Yours has drowned years since in the blood of slaughtered children."

A babble of voices tore the silence. Sloped lances suddenly levelled; hands went to sword-hilts; steel rasped on scabbard-rims; horses plunged beneath the prick of spurs.

King David spoke at the top of his voice. The clamour stilled.

"Robert de Bruce," he said quietly, "you have heard our answer. I regret only the manner of its giving."

Robert bowed his head. "As you will, my lord." He stared David in the eyes. "Sire, I hereby defy you, and renounce my fealty and homage, freely given and freely taken."

Bernard de Balliol ripped the charter across and across, and opened his hands. The fragments wavered to the ground like the sinking banners of a lost cause.

"Sire, I hereby defy you, and renounce my fealty and homage, freely given and freely taken."

He paused, and added in a voice like granite, "In the name of my suzerain, Stephen of England, I offer battle tomorrow on the moorlands north of Allerton."

5

None hindered our passage on the journey back. Bernard set a tempestuous pace. When we reached the whip-scar ridge he stopped and beckoned Ernulf.

"We shall fight here," he said. He looked at the sun. "A little past noon. Send two men, well-horsed, quickly to Walter Espec at Thirsk, and tell him to march immediately."

He regarded the ground thoughtfully.

"A good place. We shall stay to reconnoitre and plan our battle stations, and send scouts to watch the Scots."

Ernulf chose Odinel and me. We did not spare our destriers. Before dusk the army reached the long mound above Allerton.

There they rested for the night, and perhaps slept a little.

10

22nd August, 1138

Ernulf's voice roused me in the darkness before dawn.

Fog tickled my throat and made droplets on helmet and hauberk. Shadowy forms stirred round me, coughing and hawking; iron clinked on iron; numbed feet stamped the heather. A murmur of voices swelled in the night. Somewhere to the right torches sputtered and flared like smudged halos.

I leaned on my shield, cleared my throat and spat. My body ached; moisture seeped through cloak and mail, gambeson and tunic. A damp greasiness like cold sweat slimed my skin. The frail torchlight scattered specks like snowflakes from mail-discs and lances. Men groped for weapons and collided and cursed.

My friends were all around me, but I felt cold and alone, and more than a little fearful.

I slung my shield, fumbled with hauberk laces and ventail, withdrew the sword-blade a handsbreadth and tapped it home. Anschitel's fingers flitted over lace and buckle and he clicked his tongue disapprovingly.

He said, "My lord, the Scots are breaking camp."

Far away to the north, hazed by the foggy curtain, a luminous sheen glowed and faded, waxed and waned like starshine on a winter's night.

I said, "Fires. Do they begin harrying so early?"

Odinel, knuckling his eyes, emerged from the darkness. "What a God-accursed hour to start a war!" he complained. "No, Humphrey. The Scots have fired their bivouacs: a tribal custom before battle. Quite senseless – but a convenient warning."

Ernulf appeared, fully accoutred and very brisk. "No time for chatter," he rasped. "If you want to empty your bladders and bowels, do it now. Then eat – get something into your bellies."

We obeyed his anatomical instructions. Men wandered a little way into the night and squatted, or straddled and made water where they stood. A latrine stench nipped my nostrils, a stink that lingered pervasively and mingled later with the smells of blood and sweat and fear. This is the true scent of battle, whatever the troubadours may sing. I came to know it well.

I chewed a hunk of bread and peered into the night, The torches scattered enough light to show a little of the army, a shifting, indistinct, murmuring mass stretching away right and left on Bernard de Balliol's chosen ridge. A horse neighed shrilly; orders cracked like whips above the sough of voices.

Messengers strode down the line bawling for constables and bannerets. Ernulf disappeared. We waited, and talked in disjointed sentences, while a pearl-grey light, fragile as thistledown, filtered through the mist and paled the fires in the north. Faces became recognizable: Anschitel's oak-bark features and Odinel's sun-burnt mask.

"It's time they brought up the horses," I said.

We looked towards the wagon-lines. The entire mass of led horses and carts and followers, escorted by a dozen mounted knights, retreated farther to the rear. We watched incredulously, and saw them halt in a hollow four hundred paces behind the army.

"Christ's wounds!" Odinel exclaimed. "Are we to fight on foot?"

Ernulf, returning at that moment, answered promptly. "You are. And we're in the wrong place. De Mandeville guards the left flank. A particular honour." He smiled sardonically. "Three paces forward and follow me. March!"

Ernulf invariably addressed his knights like peasants.

The conroy trudged to the extreme left. The army heaved and shook like a monster awaking from sleep. Detachments straggled into new positions, formed line, elbowed for fighting-space, dressed ranks. Not all the horses had gone: barons on destriers rode from point to point and urged men into station. Odinel eyed them sourly.

"It's a remarkable fact," he observed to his shield, "that a horseman can run from a stricken field much faster than a man on foot."

Ernulf glared. The knights in the conroy chuckled.

I have barely mentioned, in my narrative, these seven companions of our fortunes: the men who carried Geoffrey de Mandeville's blazon to the field above Allerton. For this omission I can only plead preoccupation with my own affairs; and also, perhaps, that they combined in varying degree the characteristics and interests of Ernulf and Odinel, whom I have sufficiently described. Some drew pay, like Odinel and me; some were household knights like Ernulf; none held land. All, in essence, were soldiers whom I knew only in camp and on the line of march: blithe companions, fond of wine and wenches, touchy on points of honour, arrogant, often cruel, earnestly concerned with horses, hauberks and the appurtenances of war, seldom introspective though frequently highly emotional; and comfortably assured that the Holy Trinity ruled heaven and earth and controlled the destiny of man. They were simple beings, ordinary knights, with an uncomplicated outlook on their narrow world.

When the re-grouping ended – it did not involve everyone: the centre hardly stirred – I could see the heather-bloom beneath my feet. The mist began to lift, wreathing upwards in tenuous spirals like the steam from a boiling sea. Slowly the moorland's brown and purple billows unrolled into the distance. A glow like burnished copper tinged the eastern horizon.

Ernulf, thorough as always, set each in his place, man by man. In front were bowmen, a thin line widely spaced; behind them knights stood shield to shield; sergeants held the third rank. The knights' twelve-foot lances were gone with the horses – these weapons need a destrier's velocity and are useless for dismounted combat.

Ernulf inspected his dispositions, frowned, and said, "When the enemy come to close quarters, bowmen will retire behind the knights. This we will practise now."

It was awkward at first. Eight archers stood before ten knights, and dodged between shields, sometimes upsetting the owner's balance, sometimes entangling themselves in knightly legs. We cursed, and declared the tactic impossible; the conroy on our right – Aubrey de Vere's men – watched our antics and laughed immoderately. Ernulf scowled more blackly and persisted. Soon we learned to open a little when the bowmen retreated, and close shields rim to rim when they were through. The archers, ducking back and forth, entered into the spirit of the exercise and, when they were behind us, crouched and feigned to shoot between our shields, or stood on tiptoe and shot over our shoulders. Because of the damp-laden air they had not yet strung the bows; strings reposed safely in wallets.

Anschitel, encumbered with his arbalest, tripped and sprawled. He swore richly.

"Thirty-five years' service," he raved. "Four pitched battles, twenty leaguers and a hundred skirmishes – and here I am, dodging about like a hunted rat." Hatefully he addressed the crossbow in his hand. "And this I owe to you!"

I smiled at him. He grinned and shook his head ruefully.

Ernulf, satisfied at last that the bowmen were sufficiently nimble, finished his drilling. "The army's dispositions are these," he said. "The first line, bowmen backed by knights and men-at-arms, holds a front four hundred paces long from wing to wing. You," he said pointedly, "are in the first line. The second line has three divisions: dismounted knights and sergeants in the centre – there, on the summit of the ridge – and English levies on the flanks. The third and rearmost line is all English."

"And what is that?" asked Odinel, pointing.

We turned our heads. From the horse-lines men dragged a wagon to the centre of the host, and left it like a wooden crown upon the highest place. White-robed monks climbed on top and raised a pole, tall as a ship's mast, and guyed it to the frame. A painted standard hung limp in the windless air.

The first glint of sunrise pierced the lingering mist-shreds and touched the banner. Ernulf shaded his eyes.

"St Peter's standard," he said soberly. "Those are the sacred emblems Thurstan gave us."

He crossed himself, and dropped on his knees. Many followed his example, and knelt and bowed their heads and prayed.

I gazed at the standard, and fought for belief, and found none. A useful rallying-point, I thought – no more than that. With a sigh for my lost faith, and an uncomfortable feeling akin to self-disgust, I turned to survey the English behind us.

Little order was apparent among them, and they did not stand in ranks. I scrutinized them curiously. Priests flitted to and fro, and gave absolution to kneeling groups – parish priests, by custom, accompany their levy contingents to war. Huge men, crudely mailed, and fondling long-handled battle-axes, straddled in front and guarded the vulnerable open flank. They bore small round shields: I tried to visualize them, so encumbered, wielding the two-handed axes.

I learned later.

Horsemen galloped over the moor and swerved towards the

barons clustered around the standard. They gesticulated and pointed northwards.

"The scouts are in," Ernulf murmured. "Not long now."

Propped on shields or squatting in the heather, we made desultory conversation and idled away the strained prelude to battle. The sun had not yet risen, but the eastern sky was aflame. The mist swirled its skirts and disappeared. The moor stretched clear before us to a horizon shrouded in morning haze.

Sun-flashes prickled the haze like sparks.

Odinel, reclining full length on the ground, rose regretfully to his feet. "Here they come." He pulled helmet on head, rammed it down and drew the laces tight. "I hope," he said, "the next time I lie down I shall still be breathing."

2

Trumpets called to arms.

A shiver like wind-ripple on ripe barley went down the ranks. The archers strung bows, flexed and eased them, whisked arrows from quivers and fitted notch to string. Behind them, in the battle-line, three hundred knights enarmed shields and stamped down the heather to give firm footing. They measured fighting-space – sufficiently close for continuous shield-cover but with room enough for sword-arm play. Sergeants in the third rank covered intervals between knights, so presenting to the enemy an appearance of solid depth.

Blades rasped from scabbards and twirled to rest, point down, in three hundred sun-flashed arcs.

Ernulf paced our narrow front, six steps each way, and regarded us critically. He shifted a bowman a half-span forward, moved a knight a handsbreadth right. On our left lay empty moorland, the heather trodden flat by the army's passage from track to ridge; and the track meandering like a faded ribbon; and a few stray English who squatted, tunics over buttocks, answering belated rumbles.

The distant sparks assumed shape and form. Outriders of King David's army cantered along the track, slowed and halted. Some whirled about and disappeared; others left the trackway and traversed the length of a low hump parallel to our front. They gestured and beckoned. Voices carried faintly on the quiet air.

We looked beyond, and saw the tidal wave that followed.

Around an iron core of knights swarmed vast disorder, a motley horde without formation or cohesion. Sunlight splintered on innumerable spears. Their voice was a rolling growl like the mutter of faraway thunder.

We watched in awe. Odinel swallowed noisily, and cursed under his breath.

They enveloped the outriders and carried them forward like driftwood. The clamour mounted. For a few nerve-rending moments they seemed poised on the brink of a headlong charge. Knights galloped in front and shouted. The tribal multitude, swirling and eddying, ground to a reluctant halt.

Ernulf stuck his sword into the ground, and rubbed his nose beneath the nasal. "God help anyone who has to command those brutes," he said. He surveyed his bowmen, who had involuntarily retreated – even Anschitel – until their backs pressed against our shields. "You'll have to do better than that," he told them starkly. "Get back in station – three paces in front."

called shrilly – voices of protest and fear. The English swayed and called shrilly – voices of protest and fear .The English swayed and stared over our shoulders, round-eyed. The entire shield-line shuddered like a fern-frond rustled by wind.

The army's resolution ebbed.

Walter Espec, black-haired, full-bearded, rode slowly down the line. He paused to address the men in front of him, and moved on and spoke again. He arrived at our naked flank, reined and gazed keenly into our faces. His stature so dwarfed the destrier that he seemed to bestride a pony; his eyes glowed like points of fire.

He said, "We are outnumbered ten to one. What else did you expect? A gentle tourney, knight to knight, with ransoms given and feasting after? I cannot oblige you, my lords: the Scots have too few knights. Look at them!"

Walter swung in the saddle and pointed.

"Ten thousand bare-arsed savages! Not a mail-coat among them – even their shields are only calf-hide. And here you stand, helmeted, armoured, shielded from head to foot – where can they strike you? How can they hurt you?"

He smiled. White teeth gleamed in the sable beard.

"Numbers are useless without discipline. The Scots are a disorganized mob, as you have already seen. But I come, not to make speeches, but to tell you how the battle shall be conducted. The army will not advance. We stand our ground and let the enemy run upon our blades. Here, before your feet, is the killing-ground. Stand fast, and swing your swords."

Walter Espec dismounted and gave his rein to a varlet.

"Any who wish to leave this field," he said sternly, "will have to use their feet. We all fight dismounted."

He strode away. Odinel watched him go, and said, "Ha! I misjudged them. No fleet destriers to whisk our leaders away if things go wrong."

I said, "No advance, and no retreat. Walter is over-talkative. Kill or be killed is the order, my friends." I pinched my nostrils. "God's body! How those English stink!"

3

The Scots arranged themselves in a formation that seemed a near replica of our own. Bowmen stood in front of a tenuous line of dismounted knights, for they were few in numbers. The clansmen in the rear managed to pluck a rudimentary organization from disorder: they deployed in three companies, widely separated, so that the flanks extended far beyond the vanward line of knights. They did not do this without enormous confusion, all clearly visible from where we stood. Only four hundred paces separated the armies.

"Quite sensible," Ernulf approved. "Bowmen to soften us up; armour leading, to break our line; infantry following to exploit the gaps. Wonder if they're keeping any cavalry in hand?"

Apparently not. Only a few bannerets, busily engaged in marshalling an unruly army, were still mounted. King David's dragon standard floated behind the enemy's centre: his knightly bodyguard was also on foot. The king himself I could not distinguish, unless it were a horseman arguing heatedly with clansmen gathered round his horse.

Odinel's voice rasped like a whetstone on blunt iron. He pointed his sword.

"Christ's thorns! What are the Scots doing now?"

The enemy, before our eyes, began to alter his dispositions.

The knights in the van turned about and ran to retrieve their horses. At the same time the Scots in the centre – Galwegians, I learned later – rolled forward in a wedge, engulfed the archers and swept to the front. Their leaders strove to halt them. Furiously they tried to beat their men into a semblance of rank and order.

The movement brought the Scots within three hundred paces. Their army was in total disarray.

I leaped forward. "Now is the time!" I shouted. "Now! They are leaderless and lost – carrion for our swords!"

"Back into line!" Ernulf roared. "You heard the orders – we do not advance. Get back!"

I watched the opportunity spread like a golden harvest before our eyes. The Scottish knights were scattered, the army's centre in ferment. One charge, and the battle was won. And here we stood – obeying the rules.

I ground my teeth, thrust my sword savagely into the ground, parted the skirts of my hauberk and pissed. Then I turned and surveyed our ranks: the waiting bowmen, the wall of tall shields reaching away like a palisade, topped by conical helmets and broad nasals: a long row of identical masks.

I returned sullenly to my place.

Odinel patted my shoulder. "Too much zeal, Humphrey," he murmured. "You're right, of course."

Anschitel turned his head. "My lord is certainly right. We could have made an easy killing." He set foot in the stirrup of his arbalest, pulled and notched the string. "Not any more. Look at the knights."

The Scottish knights – for so I must describe them, although they were all Normans – plainly recognized the reckless hazard of altering dispositions in face of the enemy. Quickly they found their horses and formed a double rank before the tribal infantry on the right wing; and stood like an iron cliff directly opposite our flank. Odinel eyed them without affection.

"Don't think I like that very much," he said. He screwed his eyes at the banner which fluttered in the centre. "Prince Henry's blazon. They won't lack leadership."

I remembered the hot-eyed, crook-lipped man who had wrecked Robert de Bruce's peace parley, and found no comfort in the memory.

Like courteous hosts allowing their guests to dispose themselves in comfort, we watched the Scots perfect their new deployment. Prince Henry's cavalry, supported by tribal infantry, held the right wing; the men from Galloway, an amorphous, noisy mass, boiled in the centre; infantry held the left. Behind the Galwegians, King David's standard marked a reserve of dismounted knights.

A trumpet sang a lilting call which trilled high and clear above the din. Suddenly the battlefield fell silent.

Odinel said, "Here they come." He raised shield-rim to nasal; the tiny clink rang sharply in the stillness.

I lifted my sword, hilt behind helmet, blade resting on spine. My knees were shaking and a foul taste soured my tongue.

Dawn was an hour gone.

4

"Albany!"

Swords beat on shields – a rolling clash like tide-drawn shingle.

"Albany!"

The Scottish centre erupted and drowned the moorland.

They came in a wedge, a broad, blunt spearhead directed at the heart of our line where the standard flew.

Squat little men, shouting and bounding over the heather. Spearmen pointing ten-foot shafts. Round shields. Men balancing throwing-spears. Men brandishing swords. Saffron kilts and hairy thighs.

The bowmen drew until the staves curved like reeds, and sighted and waited.

Eighty paces. Naked chests and matted beards. A raging clamour like a storm of wind.

Three hundred bowstrings thrummed. The arrows flew.

They fell in swathes, and leapt the tumbling bodies and ran on, and more fell, and still they ran.

The archers plucked and loosed, plucked and loosed, and the bowstrings hummed like harpstrings and the arrow-storm beat like hail.

The men of Galloway died in droves; and the charge rolled on.

Twenty paces.

The bowmen ducked for cover; and the long swords whirled and struck.

Everything happened very quickly.

I remember a body banging my shield, hands scrabbling at my helmet, the sword-hilt twisting in my grasp after a cut to the breastbone, and the sturdy pressure of a friendly shield against my shoulder-blades. I heard Ernulf grunt when he slashed, and thought I heard Odinel singing – but that may have been a delusion born of stress.

I was getting very tired.

Then they went. The bowmen crawled out and sped the rout.

Ernulf shouted, "Not there, fools! Targets right!"

He grabbed men by the shoulders and twisted them towards the centre.

A roaring battle raged around the standard. I saw knights standing on the wagon, and swords swinging like flails. There, at the point of the wedge, was the enemy's greatest strength: there they had penetrated the shield-wall.

Our bowmen loosed into the broil. Ernulf ran on, called bannerets by name and pointed the target. Conroy after conroy joined the shooting; the goose-wings flew like sleet.

From Aubrey de Vere's conroy few arrows went. They had derided our drilling; and now five bowmen, slaughtered before they could escape behind the shields, were dying noisily in the heather.

Ernulf returned, panting. "How have we fared?"

One knight was down, helmet dented and coif slashed. Blood smeared his face. Sergeants dragged him to the rear.

"Close up," Ernulf said. "Straighten the line."

The onset in the centre failed. Hacked in front, stung by arrows from the flanks, the Scots began to go. In ones and twos they turned from the fight and ran. Soon the front was clear, and around the standard bannerets shouted and restored the line and dressed ranks.

Bodies littered the moorland like windrows in a hayfield. Maimed men crawled and moaned and tried to pluck arrows from flesh. Within sword's-length of the line lay those who had reached the shield-wall. Bowmen roved among them, daggers busy. Presently the wounded ceased to cry.

The survivors of the charge assembled between the armies, and tumultuously re-arranged themselves. Someone suggested we should follow and complete the rout. Ernulf indicated Prince Henry's horsemen, poised silent and unmoving, and shook his head.

"Just the chance they're waiting for," he said dryly.

The bowmen wandered farther afield and collected arrows which they tugged from shields and cut from bodies. Ernulf watched approvingly – quivers were half-empty – but kept an anxious eye on the Galwegians. Soon he recalled the archers. Once more they took station before the shields.

The enemy's courage burned low. They trotted slowly, shields high, flinching when the arrows struck. Gradually they came to a halt, and crouched behind shields, and flung ineffectual spears. Their van was forty paces away. Our bowmen notched and flexed and dealt them death.

A huge Scot, a man of mighty stature, burst from the ranks and bounded towards us. Hair and beard flowed like a gilded battle-banner in the wind. Madness flamed in his eyes. Hatred and terror and fighting-lust contorted his face, and the sword twirled in his hand like a glittering wheel of fire.

The bowmen laughed, and altered aim.

We heard the shafts thump home, in shield and chest and shoulder and thigh. He staggered, and ran on, and slashed with his sword at the empty air. The arrows clustered on him dense as a hedgehog's prickles. Weaving like a drunkard, his mouth open in a soundless scream, he fell on his knees at my feet.

I split his skull to the nostrils.

He was the last of Galloway to touch our shields.

5

The clansmen retreated unevenly, like leaves blown by wandering winds, a man here, a clump there. They halted beyond shot. Their chieftains bellowed and beckoned. The men listened sullenly. Then they turned and went farther away. Some were running.

Ernulf announced, "They're finished. We won't see that devil's-spawn again."

"Plenty left," Odinel said. He sucked a gash on his wrist and frowned at Prince Henry's knights. "I think there's worse to come."

We rested on our shields. The enemy's voice was a muted roar, like the thunder of fog-bound surf. Battle-wrack tangled the heath: bodies and shields and broken spears and clotted trails behind wounded men. Bowmen strolled out and scavenged for arrows. The English murmured behind us: a frustrated sound – their swords were clean.

My throat was parched. I sucked a heather-sprig and tasted blood. The hauberk pulled heavily on my shoulders; discs were stripped and the leather torn, though I had felt no blows. Someone in the next conroy retched violently; a knight bent over his sword and vomited. Drogo de Bevrere, by his armour: banded hauberk and

150

ring-mail chausses, helmet painted white and blue. Terror-haunted eyes in a grey face. He turned, pushed blindly through the ranks and vanished among the English.

It is sometimes salutary to remember that lineage does not always breed lion-hearts, and not all knights are brave.

A stir like the breathing of wind on a falcon's feathers rippled the Scottish knights. We saw, and clenched our teeth. Backs straightened; hands clutched shield-grips; feet scrabbled for footing in the heather.

Ernulf said, "Has anyone here faced a mounted charge on foot?"

Anschitel answered, "I was at Bourg Theroulde."

"What is best to be done?"

"Let the rear ranks close up tightly and press their shields against the backs of the men in front. Push hard when the clash comes. The line must not break."

Ernulf gave orders.

"Anything else?"

"Pray," said Anschitel tersely. He shouldered to the front, stood with the bowmen, notched his arbalest.

Lance-pennons snapped in the breeze. A trumpet called. The van moved slowly forward, knee to knee. When they had gone thirty paces the second rank advanced. Tribal infantry trotted close behind.

Two armoured waves; then a spate of footmen.

The trumpet howled. Lance-heads swooped and levelled; the pace swelled to a headlong gallop. A medley of battle-cries drowned thundering hooves.

We lifted swords, and rested the blades along our spines.

Bowstrings thrummed and arrows hissed – and glanced from shield and hauberk, harmless as falling leaves. The arbalest twanged. A saddle was suddenly empty, and another, and a third. The bowmen ran for cover.

The storm broke the shield-wall. I must tell you why.

A charging knight, mounted, mailed and shielded, is the most formidable missile man has invented. A deep ditch will stop him, or a stout palisade, or a poorly trained destrier or one that is too experienced. For this you must understand: war-horses are trained to ride down infantry by setting them at straw dummies and linen shields in line; soon the destrier learns that these are harmless and gallops over them without check or swerve. The first time he meets real men, and iron-framed shields, and the prick of swords he will, if staunchly ridden, bear down and crush them. But the shock and hurt he remembers afterwards, and becomes progressively less willing to face a fighting-line.

All constabulars have varying proportions of well-trained, first-time destriers, and wary animals who know what a shield-wall means, and knights a little less than staunch. A cavalry charge usually reaches the enemy in that order.

We were unlucky. Prince Henry's knights were brave and their horses did not flinch. I, perhaps, was unfortunate in my opponent, for he rode me down like a wisp of hay.

His lance-point scored my helmet; his destrier's chest hit my shield with enormous force, flung me backwards and drove the breath from my lungs. I turned on my face and drew the shield like a coverlet over my body.

Blows thumped on the shield-hide, hoof or blade – I knew not which. I lay there winded, gasping for air, and the fight raged over me.

A pause, a momentary cessation of tumult and pain. I clambered to my feet, groped for my sword.

Blearily I surveyed the ruined line. For fifty horse-lengths wide spaces yawned; men stood in little knots surrounded and embattled. Like rocks in a mill-race they fought off the second wave that seethed through gaps and beat upon the English.

The levies yielded and gave ground like a door swinging on its hinges. But the front rank, the axemen whose grandfathers won Stamford Bridge, stood shoulder to shoulder and did not break. Enarmed shields rode high on biceps; the murderous axes rose and fell. A war-shout like a clarion split the air.

"Out! Out!"

The armoured charge, like a spent landslide, glissaded off the rock-wall of the English axes. Our surviving knights turned about and beat on their backs and helped them go. I saw Odinel's sword cleave coif and neck; Anschitel, helmet dented and askew, tramped purposefully behind the horses and slashed hamstrings. There was no sign of Ernulf.

The enemy infantry, outdistanced by the knights, were two hundred paces away.

I ran among the mangled and intermingled conroys, grabbed bowmen and thrust them out of the fight. I bellowed instructions. Somehow we ranged a ragged line far out in the heather, and began shooting. I do not think that these few shaken men alone could have stopped the Scots; but bannerets in the centre, who were not engaged, saw our peril and sent bowmen running.

Arrows flew fast and thick; the enemy flinched and slowed.

I turned to the trampled wreckage where our shield-wall once had stood. The cavalry had gone. The English axemen dropped blood-streaked blades upon the ground, and leaned on the shafts and guffawed, and mocked the knights and sergeants who were trying to re-form ranks.

We had broken and they had not. We deserved their taunts.

I found Odinel and croaked a question. He swept his arm and pointed.

The Scottish knights streamed towards the wagon-park, far in the army's rear. The baggage guard rode to meet them.

Saiva was there, and Ranulf.

6

There was nothing we could do.

I watched for a little while, and saw the guard go down, and the compact mass of picketed horses split asunder. Riderless animals burst from the press, and knights rode whooping in pursuit.

Prince Henry's constabulars had turned to pillage. They were out of the fight.

Wearily I tramped the length of the conroys that had borne the brunt: de Mandeville, de Vere and de Lacy. Bannerets and constables lay dead or wounded. I took command and, with no ceremony and a whip-crack in my voice, shoved knights into line, re-built the shield-wall, arranged sergeants in rank.

Away on the army's right the Scots launched their last attack, and a new battle raged. We watched apathetically, glad the business was not ours; and saw the onset, scourged by arrows, roll to a stop far from the shields.

Our own immediate enemies, Prince Henry's footmen, retreated out of range. Bowmen hunted arrows and replenished quivers. We examined the fallen, left our dead where they lay and gave some meagre aid to the wounded. We found Ernulf, bleeding but conscious, with a broken leg, pinned beneath a dying destrier.

A strange lull brooded over the battlefield, and the armies watched each other like wrestlers seeking a hold.

Then the Scots began to go.

I gazed in a kind of tired disbelief. This was no organized retreat: the enemy hordes drifted apart like the petals of a blown rose. Individuals and groups and septs and clans straggled from the battlefield like an audience when the mummers' play-acting is over. The dragon banner advanced a little, hesitantly; knights crowded about it and I thought, for an instant, King David led a forlorn hope for a cause already lost. But horses appeared, and they mounted and rode away. The dragon dipped and vanished.

Trumpets shouted and barons came running, swords on high.

The army advanced.

7

I wiped my sword carefully on a Scottish kilt. The short skirt exposed the buttocks; I polished the blade on dead skin. Heedlessly our ranks swept past, and shouted and brandished weapons. English bodies collided with mine. I swore at them angrily.

Anschitel stood at my shoulder and swung his crossbow and guarded my back. Soon they were all gone. The noise receded. Now I heard that agonized lament, a threnody of pain, which the wounded sing. The convulsions of those who strove to die bubbled among broken bodies.

St Peter's standard lifted in the breeze and flapped heavily against the mast. The long pennons curled like serpents. Knights and a bevy of monks still stood on the wagon. They chanted a paean of praise, a thanksgiving for victory. The sunlight washed their robes and they shone like snow.

The sun. I blinked unbelievingly. My aching bones insisted on an eternity of conflict, yet the sun showed that dawn was but three hours gone. Between the bells of prime and terce this battle was fought and won.

Anschitel said wistfully, "The enemy's baggage will be well worth pillaging."

I sheathed my sword, and did not answer. After a little while I saw Odinel and Warin returning across the battlefield.

"I had forgotten, Humphrey," he said shortly. His face was drawn and tired. "Let us go."

We trudged towards the shattered wagon-park. Dead horses and dead knights – victims of the English axes – littered our path. One was not quite gone. He lay on his back, staring at the sky. Blood gouted from his mouth. A deep gash savaged his chest. Hauberk and plastron smashed into broken ribs which protruded like dead-white fingers. I knelt, loosened coif and put dagger beneath his ear. Odinel muttered a prayer for his passing, and crossed himself.

We went on.

Scottish knights galloped by – fugitives belatedly aware of defeat and route. They did not molest us. A victorious army lay between them and safety, but they were mounted and we were not; they would probably escape. Anschitel laid his sole remaining quarrell in the arbalest, and sighted. I cursed him, and thrust the weapon aside.

Destriers and palfreys strayed everywhere. We examined them keenly, seeking our own. Odinel shouted happily, and sent Warin scampering. The bowman returned, leading his war-horse. Odinel climbed to the saddle.

"I'll look for Chanson and the rounceys." He glanced at my face, and added with compassion, "That which you seek, Humphrey, you had better find for yourself."

We came to the wagons. Bodies were there, but not many; the knights had sought loot, not the useless slaughter of varlets and sutlers. Survivors cowered amid tumbled baggage; a great number had fled.

I found Saiva and Ranulf, torn and dirt-stained, crouched together beneath a cart. Ranulf gripped a spear, and gave no greeting. Until he saw my painted shield he could not know that we were friends, since all knights in mail, friend or enemy, are indistinguishable. I took my love in my arms, and her body trembled on mine. For a long time we embraced, and I caressed her shorn head and mumbled foolish endearments and strove to check my tears. She raised her face; lingeringly I kissed her lips.

Ranulf said miserably, "My lord, we have lost the horses."

He stood downcast and ashamed. I examined the spear that he had dropped. The blade was bloodied to the haft.

"You have killed, Ranulf?"

He nodded dumbly.

Saiva said quietly, "In my defence, Humphrey."

I took both his hands in mine, drew him to me and kissed his cheek.

155

"Brother Ranulf," I said, "until I thought you dead I did not know I loved you."

Odinel returned triumphantly, leading Chanson, gashed on the quarter and a stifle grazed. He trotted sound. I tightened girths and mounted, plucked a lance from the crooked rows planted among the wagons. Anschitel caught a stray palfrey and gave his crossbow to Warin, whom we left with Saiva and Ranulf.

Odinel bent from the saddle and laid a gentle hand on Ranulf's shoulder. "My friend, do not trouble yourself so greatly. Remember, too, that the brand of Cain – which you do not wear – was a sign of God's mercy and protection."

He felt his rein and glanced at the sky.

"Nine hours to sunset," he added briskly. "Plenty of time for hunting Scots. Humphrey, lead on."

We skirted the battlefield, where Englishmen and Normans strayed haphazardly and dispatched wounded, stripped the dead, looted the enemy's baggage; and rode north. A few knights who had found horses came with us, about twenty in all.

This was the only pursuit. Our leader had looked no farther than the battle.

I killed a great number of Scots during that long afternoon – I do not know how many. We found them everywhere: lying in the heather, running like sheep, hiding in streams, wandering bemused like drunkards. The majority had thrown away their weapons; very few showed fight. We caught four knights who escorted laden rounceys. They would not yield; we charged and killed them. The panniers contained gold chalices, candlesticks, jewelled crucifixes, and silver coins: part of King David's treasure, the loot from a hundred churches. Hastily we divided the spoil. I stripped from a dead knight his chain-mail hauberk and chausses, close-meshed and beautifully wrought. Towards evening we loaded our plunder on the captured rounceys and returned.

That night we slept where we had fought. Saiva and I made love among the corpses.

The barons long debated a name for their victory. None wanted to remember Allerton, so they called it the Battle of the Standard.

11

May, 1139 — May, 1140

Geoffrey de Mandeville said, "Nine months ago you fought the Battle of the Standard to save Northumbria from the Scots. Then the kings made peace, and Stephen gave Northumbria to David."

"Better so," I answered. "In generosity to a beaten enemy he has removed the cause of contention."

"The only cause, do you think?"

We stood on the Tower battlements and looked idly over London, basking in the brilliant sun of early summer. Houses and churches, streets and mansions spread below us like a map. Half a mile away the stone piers of London bridge strode across a greenly limpid Thames to Southwark's straggling purlieus.

"Prince Henry of Scotland is at Stephen's court — a valuable hostage," I said. "The north is safe. And last summer Stephen quelled the western rebels. Only Bristol still holds against him."

"Yes," Geoffrey murmured. "The king has been remarkably successful." He tapped his fingers on a stone merlon, and added thoughtfully, "I wonder whether he knows that Bristol's garrison are not the only active enemies he has in England."

I gazed from an embrasure. London Wall reached north five hundred paces from the Tower's foot to Aldgate. After curving west for a mile it angled abruptly south to the confluence of Fleet and Thames. Helmets of the watch and ward tinkled like jewels on a two-mile long diadem.

"Are there others, my lord?" I asked lazily. The hot sunlight was drowsily comforting, the stone warm to my touch, the bickerings of princes remote and unreal.

"Rouse yourself and listen, Humphrey," Geoffrey said sharply. "For nine months now you have lived in my household at my expense. I have given you rich clothing" – he tapped my embroidered mantel – "and silks and furs, destriers and coats of mail. You have wallowed in a luxury which you never before thought possible. Do you think I do this for the sake of your falcon's nose and squinting eyes? You should know me better."

I became fully alert. Geoffrey de Mandeville's irritation was a lesser man's blast of rage.

"My lord," I said, "I am grateful for the favour you have shown me; in return I have given you my homage and my fealty. I have always performed any service you command – and more besides.'

A merchant hoy sailed gracefully up-river and moored at Billingsgate wharf. The sail came down with a run. Geoffrey watched it abstractedly.

"You are a good soldier, Humphrey," he said. "Ernulf has told me – far too often: he is something of a bore about military affairs – how you saved the flank at Allerton. I appointed you banneret of the Tower knights: you command them well. The constabular of crossbowmen which you enlisted is a fearsome weapon."

St Paul's distant spire charged into the cloudless sky like a glittering lance. At the western limit of the city's mile-long riverfront a banner lifted on the ramparts of Baynard's Castle.

I said, "A weapon without an edge, my lord. Ranulf told me that the Pope, a month since, prohibited arbalests as unfit for Christian warfare."

"Papal decrees!" Geoffrey said contemptuously. "As well might he forbid the tides to ebb and flow. No man can stem war's inventions. Let it go. I was speaking of the king's enemies."

He glanced at the sentry, a man-at-arms pacing the far ramparts, staring eastwards over the meadow called Smoothfield. The sergeant was beyond earshot.

"Bishop Roger of Salisbury is chief justiciar; his son Roger is chancellor of the kingdom; his nephew Nigel is Bishop of Ely. Another nephew, Alexander, is Bishop of Lincoln. These four men have mutual interests and enormous wealth."

"I understand, my lord, that the Church supports the king."

"And so it does," Geoffrey said smoothly. "However, Roger and his kinsmen are also custodians, on the king's behalf, of eight great castles. Three guard the road to York; four others bar communications between rebellious Bristol and the Channel ports."

I closed my eyes and drew a mental map: two fortress arcs, widely separated, protecting Stephen's flanks on north and south during his drive to Bristol and the west.

Geoffrey continued, "Consider also another bishop, Henry of Winchester. He is King Stephen's brother, a man of tremendous influence in the kingdom, who holds six castles in the troubled south. A disappointed man, for he aspired to the Primacy; but Stephen passed him over and gave Canterbury to abbot Theobald."

My lord paused, and stared across the city to the marshes which lapped the northern wall. I followed his gaze, and remember how, during winter, the citizens disported there, binding shin-bones of oxen on their feet and skating over the vast expanse of ice.

"Humphrey, if you were king, how safe would you feel?"

The question abruptly recalled my attention. Geoffrey had outlined a political situation whose implications seemed clear to him as they were obscure to me. I searched my mind, and strove for a meaning. Bishops and wealth and castles. No – it was beyond me. I shook my head.

"My lord, to my thinking the kingdom is more secure than at any time since Robert of Bampton's revolt three years ago. The Scots are quelled, the Welsh subdued and the rebellious barons beaten. Bristol remains – Stephen, at Oxford, musters his army and will take the town this summer."

Far beneath, dwarfed by the height, a conroy of men-at-arms with arbalesters marched from the bailey, passed through the city wall by the postern gate and went to exercise on Smoothfield. From All Hallows church a bell tolled the hour of nones.

Geoffrey said languidly, "You disappoint me. I have given you all the clues – the threads which draw these separate warps together. Twice you have mentioned Bristol – which is Robert of Gloucester's stronghold. Do you see no connection?"

"Geoffrey Talbot holds Bristol," I said sulkily. "Count Robert lurks in Normandy."

"Robert renounced allegiance to Stephen a year ago and formally defied him. He and his ally, Matilda of Anjou, prepare for war."

Geoffrey leaned his elbows in an embrasure and gazed towards Walbrook, a meandering silver thread bisecting the city from north to south.

"My son Ernulf thinks only of war. Anything more subtle is beyond his mental grasp. I have tried to instruct him – and failed. Your sole interest, alas, is also war – which is but an extension of politics: a subject, if you remember, I once discouraged you from discussing. I have changed my mind. You will have to study politics very thoroughly indeed, because I intend that you, in Ernulf's place, shall become my instrument in certain designs wherein my hand must not be obviously apparent."

My lord smoothed his silken mantle, and smiled crookedly.

"Remember also that I am Constable of the Tower. Whoever holds the Tower commands London – and London is the sovereign city of England."

2

"And what, Ranulf, am I supposed to derive from these meagre hints?"

We sat in the lodgings I had taken for Saiva, in a street called Mincing Lane a quarter-mile from the Tower. Saiva had long abandoned her masquerade. Directly Ernulf's conroy arrived in London I dressed her again in woman's clothing – her sudden transformation from apparent catamite to veritable leman stunned my comrades but somewhat improved my own moral reputation. There was no place for her within the Tower: none among the highborn ladies of Lord Geoffrey's household, and certainly none in the gallery of alewomen and laundresses who served the garrison's needs. Her lodgings were far more commodious than those I had found in York. My lord's generosity allowed a certain luxury in their furnishings, and provided a tirewoman.

Saiva was contented and happy – but sometimes mentioned marriage: a ridiculous jest which I ignored.

Ranulf thoughtfully examined his fingernails. No longer the ragged varlet who accompanied me to Allerton, he wore a woollen gown, new and Flemish-woven, fur-trimmed at the hem though sober-hued, for he was still sufficiently a priest to eschew bright colours. He scrubbed no armour nor groomed horses, but supervised, with Anschitel, those of my retinue who performed those tasks. Ranulf had become my confidant, adviser and friend; and had grown a little plump.

He said, "I think the conclusions are reasonably clear. Here you have five powerful prelates who between them own half the country's wealth and fourteen strong castles, and command three hundred knights and a great company of men-at-arms. Too much power in too few hands."

"But why should it worry the king?" I asked, bewildered. "They are his men."

"He thinks they are." Ranulf hesitated. "I have spoken lately with a certain Frano, one of Bishop Henry's chaplains from Winchester, sent on an errand to London. He told me, indirectly, that the bishops are in treasonable correspondence with Matilda of Anjou."

"And that," said Odinel, lounging on the casement ledge, "fits the quarrell in the slot. There is the clue Lord Geoffrey mentioned."

"God's teeth! How could I know, or even guess? Henry of Winchester is the king's brother. Would Stephen realize his treachery?"

"Probably not," Ranulf said slowly. "Otherwise he must have acted. The bishops can bring formidable armies against him should Matilda ever land in England."

"Any moment now," Odinel said. "Count Robert has been preparing long enough." He swung his legs to the floor. "I am on duty in the third watch, and must return to the Tower."

Odinel's status had not altered since Allerton. After the battle he travelled to Prudhoe, spoke with his father, and returned to serve Geoffrey de Mandeville as a mercenary knight. I ensured that he lacked nothing in the way of accoutrements, clothing and silver. Although he owed allegiance to none save the baron of Prudhoe, in some strange fashion and with no words spoken he had given me his fealty, and served me faithfully in the Tower conroy.

He paused at the doorway. "A word of warning, Humphrey. Don't let your devotion to Geoffrey blind you to the fact that his own interests come first. I believe, from what you say, that he intends to interfere in matters of high policy. Before you become involved ask yourself: what does de Mandeville gain?"

He swirled his robe and clattered down the stairs.

Ranulf said, "I think Lord Geoffrey means to warn the king that the bishops may turn against him."

"That, surely, is overwhelming proof of loyalty to his suzerain," I exploded. "I do not like Odinel's imputations."

"Lord Geoffrey is a very clever man; his mind works in devious ways." Ranulf bit his thumb, deep in thought. "What does he gain?"

"Gain? My lord is a noble knight, honourable and true. Would he never serve his liege lord with no thought of profit to himself?"

Ranulf regarded me impassively.

"No, Humphrey. Never."

3

The Tower is a lofty quadrangular keep four stories high. Stone steps, like a huge mounting-block, lead to the first floor and the only entrance; a wooden drawbridge spans a gap between the topmost step and the narrow portal. The door opens on the armouries, where the sergeants live and sleep; here also is stabling for the garrison's destriers in time of siege. The basement floor below holds food and stores enough for a year-long leaguer. I climbed a twisting stairway to the hall, the knights' abode and communal dining room, and upwards to the fourth level and Lord Geoffrey's private chambers. Time had made me familiar with the internal complications of this tremendous castle, where every floor embraces several rooms and many convoluted passages. Often I remembered the stark simplicity of Bochesorne's wooden keep, and marvelled at Duke William's ingenious engineers.

But it was a dark and chilly place. Narrow slits in cavernous walls shed sparse daylight within. Only on the topmost floor, where the baron lived, could sunlight enter.

Lord Geoffrey led me to a room where no daylight penetrated. Candles flickered in silver sconces and draped deep shadows in corners. A polished table held parchment scrolls, quills and inkhorns and ponderous books.

He said, "Now, Humphrey, these are my plans – which you will reveal to nobody. Tomorrow I ride to Oxford to persuade the king against the Salisbury faction. This should not be difficult – there are others who think as I do."

"And the king's brother, Bishop Henry?"

Geoffrey's teeth gleamed in the candlelight. His blue eye glinted wickedly.

"Henry of Winchester, my dear Humphrey, is a very formidable man. Let us not, at this stage, show excessive zealousness in the king's cause: the consequences, for me, could be discomforting.

Think also on this: would it be quite wise to cut all ties with Anjou?"

I gaped at him, entirely lost. Geoffrey's train of reasoning ran far beyond my comprehension, both then and afterwards. Throughout our association I was like a man stumbling through dense fog, guided by a torch which showed the way ahead but revealed little of the pitfalls alongside.

"Do I accompany you to Oxford, my lord?"

"You do not. I am sending you to my castle at Walden, where you will find my lady and my younger sons. You will escort them to London."

He dismissed me. I descended to the hall, where I found Ernulf arguing with another knight over some intricate manœuvre. I told him of my errand and asked for an escort. When this was settled he said gloomily, "I scent trouble ahead."

"Why so?"

"I know my father. Affection doesn't call his family to the Tower. He just doesn't like leaving vulnerable hostages lying around the countryside."

I took a constabular to Walden, and met for the first time the lady Rohaise.

Describe her? Ask me to describe the noonday sun – her beauty was as blinding. A fine-boned face and dark, long-lashed eyes, and lips that curved in a smile to melt your heart. A delicate bloom like golden dust upon her skin. A sensuous body, deliciously curved; red-bronze hair which rippled like that tawny mane drowned in Bochesorne ford so long ago. Forty years old, yet ageless – an Eve contained for ever in the dawn of Eden.

She was the most beautiful woman that ever I saw.

For a time I fancied myself in love with Rohaise. Lord Geoffrey, whose indolent glance missed nothing, was perfectly aware of my sudden infatuation and remained serenely untroubled. The situation was not new to him: many knights knelt at my lady's feet. I think, however, he spoke once to Odinel, who later informed me with grim satisfaction that the baron some years since had found occasion to kill a knight who became importunate in his wooing.

"And if you consider yourself a better swordsman than Geoffrey de Mandeville," he said acidly, "I can assure you that you are quite wrong."

My lord returned from Oxford, and said nothing of his mission. Messengers rode from the Tower to unknown destinations and returned bearing letters which seemed to give him satisfaction. His mood was gay, his eyes bright, and he often laughed. He summoned from his fiefs in Essex the knights who owed him service; at night the newcomers' pallets crowded the hall's spacious floor. Geoffrey maintained over thirty household knights; there was also a changing flow of landed gentry from near-by fiefs acquitting their annual service – pleasant fellows, who talked more of hogs and harvest than war and weapons. We had some hard men, too: mercenaries hired to replace enfeoffed knights who paid shield-money rather than serve in person. These were a varied lot. Most were gently bred; others bore names whose lineage was difficult to trace.

On an evening later in June Geoffrey gave me long and detailed instructions which sent me marching two days afterwards to Oxford. I took twenty knights and forty men-at-arms. Oxford was the king's headquarters: pavilions clustered on the river-meadows like seashells on a beach. I avoided them and camped on the opposite bank. Presently a constabular bearing Count Waleran de Meulan's colours arrived and pitched tents near-by. I considered his identifying blazon to be incautious: our own shields were plain; no pennons carried de Mandeville's gold and scarlet. Anxious for the conduct of the enterprise – my own orders were precise – I sought the commander and found Waleran himself in his pavilion. He dealt sharply with my complaint.

"What is to be done has the king's authority – or at least his connivance," he answered contemptuously. "I see no reason to hide my hand. The chroniclers may write my name in their fables – and be damned to them."

He was a choleric man, rotund, with bloodshot eyes. His teeth were muddy fangs, and I flinched from his breath.

He indicated the encampment over the river. "There lie the knights and retinues of the bishops of Salisbury, Lincoln and Ely, summoned by the king to council at Oxford. The bishops themselves are lodged within the town. They do not concern us: Stephen's knights know where they dwell."

"We deal with hostelries and taverns, my lord count," I agreed.

"Just so. Four in the town are used by the bishops' knights. You take two; my men will cover the rest."

We settled details. Waleran departed for the castle, where the king and his court resided. Despite his outward indifference he seemed unwilling to be involved personally in the plot's performance. The air was cleaner for his going. I breathed more easily, and took Odinel and another knight within the walls to locate the houses which concerned my mission.

At sundown I led into Oxford twenty armed and armoured knights. Ten I left at a tavern near the castle, and went with my own detachment to a wattle-and-daub hovel crowded, at that hour, with Lincoln's knights, drinking and making merry. I left six men in the street – casual loungers lazily gossiping – and pushed through the door.

The rest was simple.

In beckoning the taverner I knocked a flagon into a drinker's face. It rattled against his teeth. He sprang to his feet, sputtering, and wiped wine from his beard.

"Christ's thorns!" he snapped. "You had better be less generous in your gestures!"

I contemplated him coldly.

"Too many peasants in here," I said. "and I do not like your smell."

He was a big, fair man, a little drunk but not yet quarrelsome. His helmet dangled between his shoulder-blades; wine-drops glistened on his hair. He looked at me owlishly, uncertain whether he had heard aright.

Odinel stepped between us, and shouldered him aside.

"Out of the way, oaf," he said pleasantly.

The knight bellowed incoherently; his hand went to his sword. I drew instantly and struck him on the arm. For a moment the company gaped; then the swords were out and a roaring fight raged in the cramped apartment. My men, blades sparkling, ran in from the street.

There was no space for sword-play inside the tavern. The struggle boiled into the street; knights thrust and slashed and shouted and thoroughly enjoyed themselves. The way was narrow; the fighting spewed along its length like floodwater in a ditch. Brawls erupted simultaneously from other inns. Within a little time a hundred knights were battling furiously in Oxford's streets, and the town rang in the summer twilight with all the violence of a storm and sack.

It could not go on for very long; nor was it intended to. Men fled, or yielded, or fell wounded or exhausted; one knight, I discovered later, was killed. The victors – of whichever faction – sheathed their swords, helped the fallen, congratulated erstwhile enemies and exclaimed over the excellence of an eminently knightly combat. The din subsided; the contestants, chattering and excited, returned to their encampments.

While we engaged the bishops' guardians King Stephen's knights took the unprotected prelates from their lodgings and imprisoned them within the castle. They botched the business: Ely escaped, galloped to Devizes, and closed the castle gates against the king.

Before dawn we broke camp and departed from Oxford as quickly and unobtrusively as we had come.

And so the king, at a stroke, eliminated a traitorous faction, won their castles and seized their wealth. Lord Geoffrey rendered his suzerain distinguished service and thereby gained much favour in his eyes. However, because of a discretion I did not then understand, his part was little known elsewhere.

I, in my first independent command, instigated a tavern brawl.

5

During that summer my lord stayed relaxed and contented. He spent long hours in the closet where no daylight entered. Usually, when he summoned me, I found him writing, or reading some missive, or poring over maps and strange cartographies. Sometimes he sat in darkness, the candles unlit, and answered my surprise with a laugh. "There is much to be planned, Humphrey; and I think better in the dark."

His messengers came and went on unexplained missions. Occasionally he admitted shipmasters from hoys moored at Billingsgate or Edrethshithe. Geoffrey never divulged what the seamen told him; once, pulling his long fingers till the knuckles cracked, he observed, "England is not all the world. A wise man keeps his lifelines to the Continent intact."

King Stephen, so we heard, besieged and took Devizes. Thereupon his brother Henry called a council of churchmen to Winchester, and debated the propriety of Stephen's move against the bishops. The king sent Aubrey de Vere to argue his case: Aubrey, in effect, said the thing was done and could not be undone; and announced the king's enactment that all war material and treasure in the bishops' hands should be surrendered – a transfer already accomplished. Stephen accepted a mild penance at his brother's hands; and went his way.

My lord said, "The world has seen Bishop Henry's wings clipped. He will not be pleased."

The thought seemed to give him satisfaction.

The king made good use of the treasure he had won. Part of the booty went to Louise of France, to strengthen the alliance against Anjou; at this time, also, Stephen betrothed his son Eustace to Constance, the French king's sister – a contract which, a little later, considerably affected my lord's fortunes. Some of the bishops' silver brought from Flanders a force of Flemish mercenaries under one William de Ypres – a heartless knight whom I came to know well.

In London the quarrellings of kings and princes sounded remote, like echoes from another world. Daily we practised warlike exercises on Smoothfield, and rode abroad with falcons on our wrists. We went into the city, frequented shops and markets, caroused in taverns – always in companies, for the citizens hated Geoffrey and all his works. The loathing was in part hereditary: my lord, his father and grandfather before him were castellans of the Tower; all were ruthless men, arrogant and impatient of opposition. Geoffrey had no direct authority over the city. But the citizens were a violent people, much given to brawls and rioting; the castellans, exercising their proper duty of keeping the king's peace, suppressed uprisings promptly and did not spare the sword. The Tower gallows were seldom unladen.

In September war flared again.

Baldwin de Redvers, exiled after the siege of Exeter three years before, landed without warning at Wareham, seized Corfe castle and raised Anjou's standard. Stephen moved swiftly to besiege him.

My lord said, "Here are the outriders of Matilda's army. Baldwin is a resolute man, and Corfe a strong place – but I think he needs a diversion." He rubbed his palms together, reflected for a while, and wrote a letter. I took the scroll to a waiting messenger and read with difficulty the superscription: John fitzGilbert, at Marlborough.

Ten days later John the Marshal closed his gates against the king. Stephen abandoned Corfe's siege and marched to Marlborough.

I am not clever, not given to deep cogitation or ponderous self-examination. But now I thought very hard indeed. Here was a sequence of cause and effect whose inspiration was undoubtedly Geoffrey's. Fealty and homage and stronger ties of admiration and gratitude and devotion bound me to Geoffrey de Mandeville. Where he led I followed; when he commanded I obeyed. I never doubted that whatever he contrived was for the best, his motives always guided by knightly usage and the laws of courtoisie. Where now was he taking me? In what murky waters of intrigue and treachery must his liegemen wade?

I took the problem to Ranulf. He considered for a long time before answering, joining his fingertips and resting his lips upon them.

"In midsummer, without advertisement, Lord Geoffrey gave the king valuable service and helped to establish his power in the kingdom," he murmured pensively. "Now, secretly, he does him harm and helps his enemies. The trend is obscure, but I think my lord is gambling for very high stakes."

Abstractedly Ranulf took from the floor a balance which Saiva, a careful housewife, employed to weigh her purchases in the market. He put iron ingots in each pan until the scales hung level.

"You take something from one side, so – and the pan rides higher in the world despite its loss. You abstract a little more from the other – now that one is on top. And so you may continue, turn by turn, until both pans are empty and all the weight lies in your hand."

He dropped the scales with a crash.

"The balance of power, Humphrey. Do you understand?"

"No," I said harshly, "and for this reason: Geoffrey de Mandeville does not hold the scales."

Ranulf sighed. "He holds the Tower, Humphrey, and with it London – the hook on which the scales are balanced."

I left him, my mind in turmoil, and sought Odinel. Ranulf, with all his learning, was not a knight: he could not comprehend the maze wherein my loyalties were lost. I found difficulty in stating the case without betraying my lord: I am not sure that Odinel was deceived. He grasped the point at once, because questions of fealty are dear to the hearts of knights, and endlessly discussed.

"Let me get this clear. This imaginary knight of yours once held land of the king, and owed him faith and service. Then he was dispossessed – I wonder how? – but never renounced his fealty. None the less he has since given that same fealty to another lord, and done him homage. To whom must he be loyal? A pretty stew, dear Humphrey."

"Yes," I said unhappily. "A pretty stew – which need not simmer until lord opposes king. What then?"

Odinel said, "A knight serves the king in return for his fief. If the fief has gone, how can service survive? If he owes no service, how can he owe fealty?"

I assented doubtfully. Odinel clapped me on the shoulder.

"Your question is answered, Humphrey. Your knight need have no more misgivings. Let him stay close to his lord, and follow his fortunes."

He grinned, and added, "You couldn't leave him if you tried."

6

On the last day of September Countess Matilda of Anjou and Count Robert of Gloucester disembarked at Arundel with a strong force and took the castle. King Stephen raised Marlborough's siege, marched to Arundel, surrounded the castle and trapped both his enemies inside.

Here the invasion should have ended; and the years of fighting and famine and pillage and misery which followed and continue to this day might never have been.

It happened otherwise, and the king must carry the blame.

Count Robert slipped through the besiegers' lines at night, outstripped a half-hearted pursuit and eventually reached safety in Bristol. Matilda remained, still in Stephen's grasp. The sequel is nearly beyond belief; the story, indeed, is not clear even now.

Apparently the king deemed warfare against a woman contrary to the usages of courtoisie and a stain upon his knighthood. Encouraged also, it is said, by his brother Henry of Winchester, he gave the Countess of Anjou a safe-conduct to join Count Robert in Bristol and provided an escort for her journey.

Legend has no part in my history; I try to relate nothing but the truth; I should not have dared to tell such an incredible tale had I not heard it later from Waleran de Meulan, who himself commanded the escort.

Here was courtoisie gone mad. The realm still pays a bitter price.

Robert and Matilda, reunited in Bristol, set the country alight. The banners of war flew at Gloucester and Wallingford, Malmesbury and Trowbridge, Cerney and Dunster. Like a broad-bladed spearhead whose point rested on Wallingford, the rebellion lunged at the heart of Stephen's England. No longer was this a revolt of discontented barons, but a full-fledged civil strife.

The pattern of warfare was always the same. Matilda's barons stocked their castles, strengthened garrisons and defences, and then sallied out to harry all the lands within reach. The lords of these devastated fiefs sent Stephen bitter complaints and hinted openly that unless he sent help they would abjure allegiance and change sides. When the king's armies arrived they, in turn, pillaged the enemy's manors. So every revolt, like a stone flung into still waters, spread ever-widening ripples of carnage and destruction over England.

Lord Geoffrey grew restive. "This could go on for ever," he complained. "Marching and counter-marching, castles and sieges. Stephen has lost the west, but eastern England stands firmly behind him. Nothing decisive has happened; nothing to show me which way the balance tilts."

Shortly before Lent a royal messenger brought a writ whose import stirred him into action – into a rashness normally foreign to his calculating mind.

"Constance of France, if the winds are fair, lands within three days at Dover, where Queen Maud receives her." Geoffrey read from the scroll. "Stephen of England to his faithful vassal Geoffrey de Mandeville. Greetings. We entrust to your care and custody the person of our lady queen, and the Princess Constance; and bid you lodge them within our royal castle in London until such time as we command."

He crumpled the parchment in his hand.

"The king at present is fighting in Cornwall. It will be some time before he can receive his ladies. Now this is what we must do."

"I myself shall go to Dover. I have sent writs to all the knights who owe me service, telling them to muster at the Tower within six days. You, Humphrey, will hire ten more knights – there are plenty in London, kicking their heels in taverns."

"Why these reinforcements, my lord? Queen Maud will have her bodyguard, and King Louis will surely send French knights to escort his sister."

"Precisely. And none will enter the Tower. You will pitch tents for them on Smoothfield, outside the wall. Rich pavilions, Humphrey, luxuriously furnished, so that they have no cause to grumble. The queen and princess, naturally, will live in the Tower – the lady Rohaise prepares their chambers."

I roved London in search of unemployed knights: a task less easy than my lord predicted, for the war absorbed them as a desert sucks rain. Geoffrey's liegemen arrived; Ernulf allotted watches and stations; soon the Tower's garrison, knights and sergeants, was stronger than at any time since Allerton.

"Why?" I asked.

Ernulf shook his head. "Some villainy afoot, if I read the signs aright."

My lord returned, and with him a glittering cavalcade : the royal ladies and their waiting women and tirewomen, in litters and on palfreys; knights and men-at-arms, servants and carts. The body-guard went without demur to the encampment I had prepared. The great barons – Waleran de Meulan among them – who attended queen and princess were allowed within the keep.

That evening Geoffrey held high revel in the hall and enter-tained his guests with a magnificence befitting their high station. Ernulf and I did not see these festivities : we were putting the Tower in a state of siege. By morning the destriers were in, draw-bridge raised, sentries posted and the garrison armed and armoured.

Waleran, recovering from his carousal, was slow to recognize the truth. Only when he tried to send some routine message to the camp did he realize that his communications with the world outside were cut. Angrily he sought Geoffrey and demanded an explanation. My lord appeared surprised.

"Surely this is reasonable," he protested. "The king has put his queen and future daughter-in-law in my charge – I cannot take too many precautions to ensure their safety."

Waleran raged. "Precautions against whom?" he spluttered. "Their own trusted knights? The loyal citizens of London?"

"How do I know her knights may be trusted?" Geoffrey inquired. "Was Brien fitzCount trustworthy? Was Miles of Hereford? No, my dear Waleran – you must let me do my duty as I think best."

The bodyguard knights, of course, sought admittance to the Tower. The barred gate, raised drawbridge, and men in battle stations on palisade and battlement puzzled them; Ernulf's shouted rebuff made them angry. They argued heatedly, realized they could not force an entrance and reluctantly returned to Smoothfield. Without their leaders they knew not what to do.

This peculiar siege without besiegers endured for two weeks. The deprivations of Lent did not make our restricted existence easier to bear. Geoffrey sent men secretly into the city to buy fresh fish, but reserved this luxury for himself and his royal guests. To them he was ever courteous; although the queen, a comely woman without great beauty but with much intelligence, must have delved in her mind for the motives underlying my lord's plausible excuses. Often I saw her reflectively contemplating Geoffrey's vivacious features while he conversed with Constance – a plain, pudding-faced girl, passively indifferent to her strange circumstances – or with Waleran, who grew more surly day by day. I think she alone had some inkling of my lord's purpose.

At the end of March the king sent from Oxford and bade Geoffrey deliver Queen Maud and the Princess Constance to his court. Scroll in hand, he sought the queen in her bower. Maud scanned the script, and lifted her eyes in polite inquiry.

"When do you set us on our way, my lord?" she asked.

Geoffrey shook his head.

"The roads are unsafe," he said in a worried tone. "I do not think that you should travel at this time."

The queen regarded him searchingly.

"Lord Geoffrey, it is the king's will that I join him. If my husband is prepared to take the risk, then your responsibility is at an end."

My lord shrugged. "In that case I cannot prevent you. Your train shall be made ready, and your escort warned."

Surprise flickered in Queen Maud's eyes. With something like relief she said, "Very well. The lady Constance and I will depart at daybreak."

Geoffrey sighed. "I regret," he murmured, "that the princess must not go."

The words dropped into a pool of silence. Ernulf hitched uncomfortably at his mantle; the silk rustled loudly in the quiet room. One of Maud's barons put a hand to a non-existent sword, and bit his lip: men did not come armed to council in a queen's bower.

Waleran lost control.

"By the bowels of Christ," he roared, "with whose authority do you prevent —"

The queen's gesture checked his spate. Enthroned upon her chair, she stared at Geoffrey's face as if striving to penetrate through flesh and bone to the workings of his mind. My lord stood before her, his head a little bent and a smile on his lips. Their glances locked and held like blade on blade.

"For how long, Lord Geoffrey?"

"Till Louis begins to wonder when his sister will be wedded."

"In this matter he is powerless."

"No. He has a weapon : his alliance with England against Anjou."

"You would humiliate the king of England?"

"I think, my lady, you recognize the remedy that will salve his shame."

Waleran rested a finger on his dagger. From the concealed portal where I waited I saw the movement, and silently unsheathed my sword.

The queen said, "King Stephen is an impatient man and will come with armies to seek his own."

"The king is not entirely his own master. He has formidable enemies."

"You increase their number, my lord. But you, like the others, will not last long."

"I am the king's vassal, not his enemy. And the Tower of London is impregnable."

The queen looked at her hands, resting in her lap, and remained for moments deep in thought. At last she raised her head.

"You are well armoured. Geoffrey de Mandeville, what is your price?"

My lord sighed faintly, like a gambler who sees the dice roll for a fortune. He knelt gracefully before his queen.

"My lady, you are wrong in thinking I coerce my suzerain. I try only to serve him according to my vows. I seek his interests, and further them with all my might."

He rose and strolled a little apart and stood chin in hand as though considering.

"In Essex," he said over his shoulder, "I hold of the king certain separate and widely scattered fiefs. The barons of that land are turbulent; their loyalty is wavering. Would not their allegiance become less indefinite if they were placed under one authority – my own?"

Queen Maud watched him, an icy understanding in her eyes.

"The County of Essex," she said with finality.

Geoffrey bowed.

"It shall be arranged. I give you, on the king's behalf, my pledge." She turned to Waleran. "My lord, prepare for our departure at dawn – myself and the lady Constance."

Geoffrey de Mandeville said regretfully, "The lady Constance is free to go wherever she wishes – when King Stephen's charter, sealed and attested, is in my hands."

Queen Maud turned swiftly, outrage in her face, and met Geoffrey eye to eye. In silence she gazed, and the hard furrows from mouth to nostril softened and, incredibly, she smiled.

"You bargain hard, my lord count."

A genuine amusement lurked in her voice.

7

I thought my lord, thus openly flouting the king's mandate, had gone quite mad. Ernulf agreed – with certain reservations born of experience. "My father," he said once, "is the sort of gambler who bets only on certainties. I doubt whether he has changed his practice."

Ranulf had no doubts at all. "Stephen has no choice. If he does not rescue the princess, King Louis and the world at large will see his shame – that he has no power to guard his own. The French alliance will collapse, leaving Normandy at Geoffrey of Anjou's mercy. And remember, Humphrey, that the Tower is not merely an inviolable fortress: it commands the port through which King Stephen receives supplies and mercenary reinforcements from the Continent. It is also an impregnable base whence an enemy may ravage far and wide. Can the king, fighting in the west, afford this dagger at his back?"

Glumly I considered this priestly exposition of military strategy; and found no flaw.

Nor could Stephen.

At Pentecost, riding with his barons and a bodyguard, he entered London. My lord received them ceremoniously and led them all within the Tower, and entertained the company in state. Throughout the festivities the king, a laughing man, smiled never once; his friendly eyes stayed cold and watchful, his manner courteous but withdrawn.

Princess Constance went to Oxford. The king marched for Norfolk, where Hugh Bigod stirred rebellion. Geoffrey de Mandeville, Count of Essex, reclined in his candlelit chamber and smilingly perused a parchment scroll. Idly he examined the seal whereon King Stephen's waxen image, mailed and mounted, charged for ever into battle.

In this manner my lord won his County, and made an unforgiving enemy.

12

January — February, 1141

In January my lord sent a secret mission to Count Robert of Gloucester.

He put nothing in writing; but rehearsed me in the message until I was word perfect. The contents I shall reveal in their proper place. That it was a political and military project involving treachery on a vast scale did not astonish me: I was no longer capable of shock at anything Count Geoffrey did.

The acquisition of Essex immediately increased his wealth; and he used the money to expand his power. Ten more fiefs and their revenues came into his hands, together with the services of fifteen knights. He gained two castles, which he promptly garrisoned; and doubled the number of knights bachelor in the Tower. In all, my lord at this time commanded nearly a hundred knights, five hundred sergeants and five castles, including the strongest fortress in the kingdom.

In December Count Ranulf of Chester had taken Lincoln Castle, ejected the king's men and oppressed the citizens so harshly that they sent Stephen an appeal for help. The king needed no spur, for Lincoln in enemy hands threatened his communications with the north. He gathered an army and soon after Christmas marched to Lincoln and began an energetic siege. The slippery Ranulf escaped, fled to Chester and there, so we heard, mustered a relief force.

All these alarms rang remotely on that January morning when I left London on the hundred-mile journey to Gloucester. I took Odinel and Ranulf, Anschitel and Warin and six sergeants. We travelled in moderate luxury: Odinel and I rode palfreys; varlets led our destriers; eight rounceys carried fodder and baggage.

Saiva also was with us. Using all the arts of a woman determined to get her own way she had persuaded me to let her come. I was not altogether unwilling. I loved her and enjoyed her companionship, and foresaw little danger in journeying through a countryside which at that time was reasonably peaceful. Again she dressed like a man – not for any reasons of concealment but because she could not abide riding in woman's clothes. After attempting to ride side-saddle, a fashion lately imported from the French court, she stripped her skirt and donned leather breeches, tunic and a short mantle. With a feathered cap set on shoulder-length golden hair she looked exactly what she was: a lovely woman inadequately disguised as a boy.

We took the Oxford road, and for two days rode through a snow-streaked land unravaged by war. The winter had not been severe; peasants prospered and worked busily in field and byre. Seldom did we see those emaciated corpses by the wayside or under hedgerows that told of famine. I felt a lightening of the heart, an uplift in my spirits that I had hardly known since the march to Allerton two years before. Freed for a time from the Tower's dank oppressiveness, from Count Geoffrey's dark machinations, I knew a happiness that bubbled like birdsong in springtime. So secure did we feel that Odinel and I rode unarmoured; hauberks rested in the rounceys' panniers. Odinel sang as we went, and Saiva carolled in harmony, and I growled a cracked accompaniment.

> *"Au plus hardi combateor*
> *De toz ices nos savons,*
> *Se fust Thiebaux li Esclavons."*

After Dorchester we entered the wastes of war, and took our hauberks from the panniers. The country had never properly recovered from Robert of Bampton's harryings four years before, nor from the more recent ravages round Cerney. We passed blackened rafters yawning to the sky, and rubbled mounds which had once been houses, and fields untilled and overgrown. The dead grass of winter sprouted like fungus between the ribs of yellowing skeletons. Gallows bore decomposing burdens. The few peasants we saw scratched a miserable living, and fled at our approach. We encountered armed companies who were suspicious and quick to inquire our business: in passing Cerney – a lonely, miserable castle, ringed by old siege entrenchments and scarred by the wounds of storm – an aggressive knight barred our path and demanded the courtesy of a joust. Odinel mounted his destrier and obliged. Then we set the dazed knight in his saddle again and escorted him with kindliness to the castle gates.

After Cerney we found a ragged couple sitting by the roadside: a raw-boned old man whose empty eye-sockets oozed bloody pus, and a youth with a haggard face furrowed by lines of suffering and privation. The youth listlessly held a frayed guide-rope attached to the old man's wrist, and gazed unseeingly on the ground. Human flotsam was not uncommon in these parts: war had left a plentiful tide-wrack; and I was about to pass on without remark. The old man heard our hoofbeats and raised his horrible burnt-out eye-holes and begged for alms. I flung a coin, and looked at the young man's face, and stared again without belief. Involuntarily I reined.

Drogo de Bevrere.

Odinel laid a hand on my wrist, and motioned me forward. Disgust and compassion struggled in his face.

"Nothing to be done for him," he muttered. "Outcast. Better he had cut his throat after Allerton."

We sang no more on the march. After a restless night in one of Cirencester's flea-ridden hostelries we gladly crossed the hills and descended the escarpment to Gloucester, six days since leaving London.

2

The town broiled with troops whose tents and horse-lines lapped the walls. The inns were full: we pitched tents in a scrubland clearing and mounted guards. I went to the castle to find Count Robert: a difficult matter, for I could not reveal my purpose or authority. While I still argued with the gate guard the count and his cavalcade crossed the drawbridge. I went to him, bowed over and in a low voice told him whence I came. Flint-coloured eyes examined me from a lined face; a black, grey-flecked beard framed sallow, sunken cheeks. He nodded, and bade his steward find a place for me at his board.

"Afterwards," he promised, gathering his rein, "we shall discuss your business."

Odinel met me on my return and explained the warlike assembly. "Count Ranulf has sent for aid against the king at Lincoln. Robert gathers an army; soon he will go north to join Ranulf, and the combined forces march to raise the siege."

"Campaigning at this season!" I exclaimed. A cold rain slanted viciously; sullen clouds covered the sky like a shredded pall; the fields where men and horses trod were a sea of mud. I dived thankfully into the tent and shook water from my cloak. "Luckily it doesn't concern us. Odinel, we dine at Count Robert's table tonight."

We donned our best tunics and mantles, which was as well, for Robert held splendid state in the castle hall and Matilda of Anjou sat beside him at the high table. From my lowly place I regarded curiously this woman whose claim to England's throne was destroying so much of the realm. I saw a full, high-coloured face, greying hair, glittering black eyes and a beaked nose, and a hard, thin-lipped mouth. Her manner was brittle and imperious; she spat her words like grape-stones. Not, I decided, a lady whom it would be comfortable to cross.

Count Robert summoned me after the meal and led the way to a chamber curtained from the hall. Here I found the Countess Matilda, enthroned in a high-backed oaken chair, and Brien fitz-Count, lord of Wallingford – a comely, smiling man, tall and lean and hard. I knelt before the countess, and greeted Brien. Count Robert bade me speak.

I said all I had ridden so far to say, uttering the words by rote; and answered questions as best I could. The count soon recognized that I was merely a messenger, without authority or ability to interpret my lord's proposals. He gave me an answer, fortunately short, which I memorized; then turned to lighter matters, inquired how I had fared upon the journey, and politely elicited something of my history.

"Disinherited, eh?" he said jovially. He drained his goblet – one realized he was no enemy to wine – and added, "You should march with us. A squadron of your like – dispossessed by Stephen because they fight for England's lawful ruler – rides in my train."

I smiled courteously. "The reason for my disinheritance is different, my lord count. I have not fought against the king."

"Guard your tongue!" Matilda snapped. "Stephen is not king by right!"

"Your pardon, my lady," I murmured. "But my fealty belongs to the Count of Essex, and he —"

"St Mary Virgin!" Robert interrupted. "You have just been telling me Count Geoffrey's plans. Is he faithful to Stephen?" He laughed explosively. "I think the highest bidder will always buy his homage – for a time."

My hand, unbidden, went to my dagger. Odinel, beside me, bore strongly on my wrist, forced down my arm. He said, "I think it would be a knightly venture, my lord. We will certainly go with you to Lincoln."

"Good! Good!" Count Robert flourished his goblet and belched. "Two more for the Disinherited."

Matilda of Anjou said, "You may leave us. And keep your steel and your temper for my enemies, my lord."

We stumbled through sleeting darkness towards our camp. I said to Odinel, "What have you done? Why have you committed us to this woman?"

"Firstly, to save your life. Brien was watching you like one of his own falcons, and as ready to pounce. You really must control yourself, Humphrey – you'll hear Count Geoffrey worse insulted before you've done. Secondly, I have no fancy to rot all winter in the Tower – the dampness racks my bones. And third, we have done no real fighting since Allerton: we grow rusty. What do you think knights are for?"

"Body of God! You must be mad! Count Geoffrey sent us here on a definite mission: how can we wander off to oppose the king, who is, after all, still his suzerain? What explanation can I give when we return?"

Odinel grimaced. "Must you always circle on Geoffrey's lunging rein, Humphrey? Can you never break free, even for a month? Who knows? in this faithless war, whether a knight serves his lord or fights against him? Your errand is accomplished. You bear a wolf's head on your shield, not Geoffrey's gold and scarlet. Be your own man for a time, not Geoffrey's. Let us ride errant, and find glory."

"And what of Saiva?"

Odinel said, "What of her? She is only happy when she is with you, Humphrey. And," he added comfortably, "this won't be her first campaign."

3

On the first day of February the army saw in the distance the spires of Lincoln crouched upon her hilltop. Between us and the city walls lay a canal called Fossdike; Count Robert sent outriders to reconnoitre a crossing. I went with a patrol and splashed through marsh and mud along the southern bank, examined gloomily the flooding waters, probed the depth with lances, eyed the spears bristling on battlements half a mile away. Eventually we found a crossing where the banks were fairly firm and the water no more than girth-deep. We reported our discovery: the two counts called barons to council, made plans for the morrow and gave orders. The night was disturbed. King Stephen's scouts probed the encampment and noisy scuffles exploded in the dark.

Dawnlight wreathed through lowering clouds and drizzling rain. I crouched beneath the tent's dripping roof, strapped the plastron's iron plate upon my breast and struggled into a quilted gambeson smelling of sweat and mildew. My squire dropped the hauberk over my head and guided my arms into wrist-long sleeves. The chain-mesh rustled like metallic silk: this was the fine armour I had won at Allerton. Saiva, cloak-wrapped, crouched unhappily in a corner; the wavering light of a horn lantern hung dark shadows beneath her eyes. I touched her brow gently.

"Do not grieve, my sweetling. There will be no battle today. The king, if he has any sense at all, will stay inside Lincoln's walls and withstand a siege which he is bound to win. For we are short of supplies, in a hostile countryside in midwinter, and cannot beleaguer him for long."

She nodded silently; a tear rolled down her cheek. The squire laced chausses round my legs, strapped long-spiked spurs upon my boots. I tied the helmet's chin-strap and buckled ventail round my jaw. The spreading nasal did not sit centrally; my squire clicked his tongue and deftly adjusted the cords. He was a handy lad, good with armour.

Odinel ducked beneath the tent flap. "Come on, Humphrey. The trumpets sound for assembly."

The squire draped baldric over right shoulder, shield guige upon left. I stepped into the drizzling dark; Chanson, led by a varlet, loomed like a black statue. I tested girth and curb-chain, climbed to the saddle. Saiva gave me the lance. I held her hand and spoke to Ranulf, who stood beside my stirrup.

"Strike tents, load the rounceys and go to the baggage park. Stay there until further orders."

I gripped his shoulder.

"Once more, my friend, I leave my treasure in your charge."

4

We rode six abreast towards the Fossdike crossing. Baldwin de Redvers, the hero of Exeter's siege, returned from a four-years' exile to Anjou, led the squadron. A commotion up front jarred the column to a halt. Horses collided muzzle to rump; men swore and peered anxiously into grey half-darkness. Baldwin thumped down the ranks.

"They've stationed a guard on the ford," he said curtly. "Form line. Prepare to charge."

We manœuvred clumsily. Now I saw Fossdike a hundred paces ahead, and indistinct figures moving before it like blots on an iron-hued ribbon. A trumpet moaned. Lances levelled and we trotted over squelching ground. Arrows whirred overhead; somewhere a horse screamed.

There was no proper charge, and no fight worthy the name. Marshland slowed the trot to a hoof-sucking walk. The enemy showed no desire to stand, and splashed hastily into the ford. Almost at a standstill, we prodded a few loiterers into the water. Baldwin quickly ordered a constabular over to establish a bridgehead on the farther bank. Then, re-forming column, we rode across without further hindrance.

"A witless fool stationed that lot," Odinel commented. "Had they opposed us on the far bank we'd have been fighting here all day."

I made no answer; I was watching Lincoln's western gate. The portcullis opened; a column of men emerged like a blackened log thrust through fire-bars. The voice of trumpets trembled faintly in the rain-mist.

I glanced to the rear. The army was still crossing. Count Ranulf's banner fluttered at the ford.

"Not the only fool in Lincoln," I said. "King Stephen is offering battle. Let's hope he isn't clever enough to attack us while we cross."

Baldwin de Redvers was of the same mind. Furiously he drove us forward to firmer ground and stationed the squadron athwart the ford. The knights, about seven score strong, dressed in a single rank. Sergeants formed in groups behind their lords and jostled for position: I heard Anschitel's oaths and Warin's whining complaint. At Fossdike Count Ranulf's bellows urged his men to greater speed.

He need not have worried. If King Stephen saw his chance he let it go. His notions were such that he may have considered it unknightly to catch an enemy at a disadvantage. His army issued from the gate and marched sedately in column straight towards us. Nervously we fingered lances. We saw knights in plenty, constabular after constabular; a swift charge now could scatter us like chaff. Baldwin watched them tensely. From time to time he glanced anxiously at Count Ranulf's progress.

When they were two hundred paces away the king's men swung left and right, halted and formed line of battle. The squadron breathed relief – a collective sigh of thanksgiving.

Ranulf's division arrived – dismounted knights and sergeants – and ordered ranks upon our right. Then Count Robert's horsemen spattered from the marsh and formed on the right flank.

The battlefield was this: from Lincoln's walls a half-mile distant the ground sloped gently to the Fossdike marshes we had crossed. We stood with our backs to the marsh; between us and the city's western battlements King Stephen drew up his army and barred our way. His three divisions exactly matched our own: infantry in the centre, cavalry on either wing. Leafless thorn-scrub and scattered trees speckled the ground between; rain-pools glinted like discarded spears. A plough-strip patched the frost-browned grass like a rucked blanket.

The drizzle had eased; a wizened daylight strained through clouds the colour of unburnished steel. Ice-barbed wind-gusts flapped the pennons. I blew on my fingers, soothed Chanson, talked in low tones with Odinel and tried to identify the enemy blazons. We saw Stephen's standard in the centre of his infantry, flanked by the colours of Bernard de Balliol and William de Aumale – our comrades at Allerton.

No one seemed in a great hurry to begin.

The cavalry opposite, flaunting polished armour and painted shields, made a painful contrast to our own rusted hauberks and mud-splashed chargers. Different, too, was their demeanour: while we stood fast in rank, motionless save for the sidling and curvetting of restless destriers, they were in continuous movement, walking their horses to and fro and chatting amiably.

"Like a carefree company setting out on a boar-hunt," Odinel growled. His destrier straddled; he leaned over the withers to help it stale. "I think I see Waleran de Meulan's shield."

I recognized Count Waleran's chevrons, gules on argent. Most of the devices were so newly invented by their wearers that they signified nothing to anybody else. A helmet painted blue – where had I seen that before?

Trumpets blew for onset. The enemy knights came on individually, lances aloft and pennons fluttering, cantering their horses and shouting. Only forty or fifty – the remainder stayed in position like spectators at a tourney. The outriders advanced within a hundred paces. We heard them calling taunts and challenges.

Few knights can resist an invitation to single combat, often a preliminary to the battle proper. Riders burst from our ranks, lances in rest. Suddenly I remembered everything about blue helmets, and collected Chanson between bit and spur.

Cursing like a madman, Baldwin de Redvers galloped down the line.

"Back! Back, my lords! Stay in rank!"

He rode athwart knights and barred their way, slammed lance-shaft across plastrons and made them halt. He stopped all but one: a baron on a bolting horse who, sawing at the rein and swearing helplessly, galloped towards the jousters. They saw his plight and laughed and let him through. The spectators struck him down. He earned a brief, derisive notoriety, but knights on 'shooting stars', as we called these hard-mouthed destriers, sometimes won an unwarranted reputation for reckless bravery.

The king's knights cantered nearer, and curvetted and jeered. I watched the blue helmet and wondered. Could it be the man I thought, or merely one of his vassals wearing his colours? The face behind the nasal, even at eighty paces, was unrecognizable.

Baldwin restored the line and did not spare his oaths. He walked his horse to the centre and said grittily, "My lords, have you marched two hundred miles in midwinter to engage in polite jousting, with ransoms given and taken? What ransoms can you give? You are the Disinherited – your fortunes and your lands are gone. You win this battle or you lose your lives, for you have nothing to offer in exchange. Nor can you flee – the marshes bar retreat."

He looked to Count Ranulf's standard, and saw trumpets lifting to the sky.

"There is the signal. Now, my lords, charge for your honour and your stolen fiefs!"

I sat down in the battle-saddle, pushed my spine hard against the high cantle and straightened my legs against stirrup-irons. Quickly I shortened rein and pressed my left arm close to my ribs; the curved shield embraced my body and the broad rim stroked my nasal. I tucked the lance firmly in rest beneath my armpit: the pennon's embroidered wolfhead snarled at the ground. Odinel glanced at me sideways and grimaced wryly; I saw apprehension in his eyes and answered it with my own.

No one is very brave at such a moment.

Baldwin flung down his lance and drew his sword – the signal for close combat.

"Forward!"

Chanson plunged at the bit, gathered himself on his hocks and reared. Power surged from him like a bursting dam. For a moment I fought him, and got him balanced and settled in his stride. He lowered his head and galloped.

The Disinherited raced into the charge.

A red mist hazed my eyes, and I yelled the war-cry of my House.

"Loup! Loup!"

An armoured horseman loomed behind a tall, spiked shield. With rein and spur I lifted Chanson on the line and aimed my lance. The shock wrenched me sideways in the saddle, jarred my back against the cantle. Chanson stumbled, recovered and swept on. I threw the splintered shaft aside and tugged at my sword.

The would-be jousters, trapped in the open, turned round and fled for their lives. The main body jostled in confusion, tried to form line, advanced uncertainly. The charge burst asunder, as charges do, into separate galloping meteors, like diverging fingers opening from a clenched fist. Odinel rode beside me, singing a wordless chant and twirling his lance. I heard Anschitel roaring obscenities. Destriers neighed shrilly; trumpets twanged in triumph; hoofbeats thudded and drummed; battlecries shredded to whispers in the wind of our speed.

A thunderous shock, a clash and recoil that flung men from the saddle. Then a whirling mellay and swinging swords and clanging and cries.

I rode down a knight who spurred across my path – Chanson's chest struck his horse and hurled both to the ground. Another I hacked between helmet and shoulder. A blade struck my shield; a blow seared my thigh. Then I was clear.

I reined savagely and swung Chanson on his hocks. The enemy were broken. A blue helmet flashed in the rout. I turned and followed.

He had a fleet destrier, and the uphill charge had tired Chanson, but the distance gradually closed. I drew to his girths and shouted. He turned his head and showed me his face an arm's-length distant.

I stood in the stirrups and slashed.

The knight threw his arms wide, toppled from the saddle, rolled over and over and sprawled on his back. I reined Chanson, dismounted and stood over him. His eyes looked into mine. He was in great pain, and spoke laboriously.

"I yield to you, sir knight."

"Do you remember me, my lord?"

"You shall have my ransom – a hundred marks, and my destrier and armour."

"Do you remember me?"

His eyes flickered to my shield.

"I do not know your blazon."

"Think hard, my lord. Bochesorne, which you sacked. An old man whom you hanged."

His eyelids drooped wearily.

"Yes. Visdelou. A long time ago."

"All time comes to an end, my lord."

I rested my sword point on his lips.

"Mother of God, I have yielded! You cannot kill me! Two hundred marks! Three hundred!"

I pressed on the hilt, and broke his teeth.

"Farewell, Hamo de Neufmarché."

The blade plunged deep into the ground through throat and skull and coif.

I leaned on the hilt and watched him die.

5

The pursuit penetrated far behind the battle-line. Had the Disinherited still retained cohesion they could have fallen on the enemy's rear – but they hunted valuable prisoners and were scattered far and wide.

The faraway noise of battle rolled unheeded.

I returned slowly through roving groups of horsemen, and found Waleran's choleric face was purple; he was dishevelled and in a Odinel in high fettle, for he had taken Count Waleran de Meulan.

bad temper; angrily he blamed his overthrow on an uncontrollable destrier and fumed at having to yield to a knight of inferior rank. Odinel explained blandly that no counts rode among the Disinherited; and inquired politely but pointedly about the prosperity of Waleran's estates in Normandy, which were vast. The count disgustedly agreed to an exorbitant ransom, gave his parole, and departed under Warin's escort to the wagon-park.

"And take that smile off your face," I told Odinel. "We don't know whether we have won this fight. Waleran may yet be freed."

We cast a wide circle, having no wish to become entangled with the enemy's centre, and found the battle in its last stages. The wings of both armies had vanished. Our exodus has been described; on the other flank, as I discovered later, a royalist cavalry charge scattered Count Robert's horsemen, but Ranulf's dismounted knights in the centre checked it stubbornly. Here Stephen was perhaps unfortunate. He entrusted his left wing to professional soldiers under a veteran commander: Flemish mercenaries led by William de Ypres. William saw that his Flemings made no headway against Count Ranulf's men, coolly assessed the damage being done to his soldiers – his stock in trade – and discreetly withdrew from the fight. They retired in reasonably good order, left few prisoners, and were not seen again that day.

This is one of the hazards of employing mercenaries – they know too much about war.

We came therefore on a dismounted battle where a thousand men fought shield to shield. Here stood the king among his bodyguard, and around them Ranulf's knights foamed like a mill-race. I looked at Odinel and shook my head: this was no place for cavalry. We approached warily, remained at a little distance and awaited the outcome.

An armoured ring encircled the king like iron battlements. Count Ranulf's knights attacked it like a castle. Storm after storm beat upon it, tore down part of the shield wall, flinched under whirling sword-blades and recoiled. The din was indescribable: clash and clangour and shouts and war-cries reverberated like rolling thunder and re-echoed from Lincoln's frowning walls. There was no respite, no breathing time: charge upon charge crashed on the shields like the surges of a roaring sea. And in the midst King Stephen fought in splendour like a paladin of old, and maimed and dying enemies garlanded his spurs.

He broke his sword on Count Ranulf's helmet, seized an axe and cleared a wider space. His liegemen toppled like trees on either hand, but none would dare the swathing butchery of his battle-axe. His enemies embayed him, panting, and shouted for him to surrender, and King Stephen fought on like a housecarl of Hastings, like Harold of England on another foundered field so long ago. From a distance beyond his reach some coward hurled a boulder which smashed into his face and brought him down. A knight leaped forward and gripped him like a wrestler round the helmet, and shouted, "Here! Here! I have taken the king!" They ran upon him and disarmed him, and made him yield.

The trumpets whooped for victory, and snowflakes drifted wanly from the sky.

6

Odinel said, "I suppose the war is ended."

We rode to London on snowbound roads through a white and silent countryside. A bitter wind stared the horses' coats, plucked at cloaks, raised flurries of snow like streaming smoke. Our company had increased: Count Waleran, and such of his retinue and baggage as he managed to retrieve, rode in the train. This of his own will – his ransom clinked heavily in Odinel's saddlebags and he was free to go wherever he wished. But the Battle of Lincoln had decided him that England held no future: he was bound for Dover and thence Normandy. "For," he declared, "Matilda has taken Stephen, and with him England's crown, and with England, Normandy. A wise man travels to protect his own." Acquaintance proved him to be an agreeable man, often witty, a pleasant companion provided one kept up-wind.

He answered Odinel: "No – and that, in part, is why I'm leaving. Too many barons have committed themselves irretrievably to the king's cause. For them there is no going back; they must continue fighting to save their fiefs. Stephen languishes in Bristol castle, but Queen Maud is still at large: they will rally to her like flies to a honeypot."

I said, "I wonder how this will affect Count Geoffrey's fortunes?"

Waleran grunted. "He has a foot in either camp, and can't go wrong. I wish I had a tenth of his cunning. If I know anything about him, he'll acclaim Matilda and send advice and help to Maud."

I resented the gibe, but said nothing, for Waleran did not speak ill-naturedly. Moreover, he probably spoke truth. I glanced at Ranulf, who quirked an eyebrow and smiled.

Odinel sighed resignedly.

"More wars, then," he said. "Life would be more peaceful in Prudhoe. However," he added brightly, "perhaps I shall unhorse another wealthy baron, and become ever richer."

Waleran spluttered like an angry cockerel.

After entering Newgate we parted from the count, who lodged awhile with Walter de Clare in Baynard's Castle, and rode past St Paul's church to the Tower. We entered the bailey, left our horses and crossed the drawbridge. I put off my armour, inquired for Count Geoffrey and found him on the battlements talking to his lady and some household knights. I bent my knee; he greeted me courteously but, I thought, a little coolly.

"Come below, Humphrey. It is too chilly to linger here."

He led the way to his candled chamber. His politeness dropped from him like an outworn cloak.

"Now," he inquired icily, "where have you been?"

I related baldly our adventures, and gave him Count Robert's message. He sat for a time in thought, and drummed his fingers on the table.

"I already know most of this," he said at last. "My spies made better time from Lincoln than you did. As it happens, you have done no harm. You never wore my blazon nor advertised my hand. But, Humphrey, in your small way you are becoming quite famous. Bochesorne's stubborn leaguer is a legend; men speak respectfully of your gallantry at Allerton. Do you realize that, at Lincoln, you overthrew and almost killed Count Hugh of Norfolk, a renowned warrior, and left him and his ransom to be gathered by another? Such deeds are the essence of courtoisie, the doer a pattern of knighthood. You have a reputation, Humphrey, and more people know you for my man than you might think. You fought openly against the king. Had he prevailed at Lincoln I should certainly have disowned you, and probably had you killed. Fortunately for you he lost, and I shall let you live. I may need you yet to help me restore the balance. But you might have wrecked my plans."

Count Geoffrey rose to his feet and towered above me. His eyes were cold and cruel; anger snarled his mouth.

"On your knees, dog."

I knelt before him. His foot crashed in my face.

"That for your blunder."

I grovelled on the floor and wept. He kicked me again.

"And that to teach you obedience."

He snuffed the candles, sauntered from the room and left me to the darkness and my shame.

7

I nursed my humiliation in the hostile streets of London, because no place was private in the Tower, thronged always with knights and men-at-arms and servants. I walked the crowded alleys all day and half the night, and knew not where I went, for my mind was empty and my eyes unseeing. Scullions elbowed me into the gutter, and drabs screamed insults. I heard them like far-off noises in a dream. Snowflakes rimed my hair; the cold plunged ice-blades into my cloakless body. I felt nothing, and thought nothing, and knew only the hopeless void that yawned like a bottomless pit – a world without Geoffrey de Mandeville.

At dawn I went to Saiva's house, and sobbed wordlessly on her shoulder. She nursed me like a child and soothed me till the shaking ceased, and stripped my sodden clothes and put me in her bed. She asked no questions. Presently I slept.

Count Geoffrey stood beside the pallet. His tunic was cloth of gold, his fur-lined cloak of purple silk. A smile transfigured the lean brown face.

I thought I dreamed, and closed my eyes.

His fingertips lightly caressed my brow. He stooped, and gently kissed the caked bloodstains on my broken lips.

"Come to me when you are well, my Humphrey, well in body and in mind."

Then he went away; and I lay and stared at the tattered thatch that bulged between the rafters.

A radiance like a summer dawn still lingered in the room.

13

June – September, 1141

Count Geoffrey said, "The bishops have proclaimed Matilda queen. She has come to London for her coronation and holds court at Westminster."

Once more a teeming garrison thronged the Tower. Once more my lord had called to arms the knights who held his fiefs and owed him service; he shut the Tower gates and men stood at battle stations.

The bailey basked in sunshine. Varlets hissed and curried in the horse lines; knights inspected destriers, ran fingers over hocks and fetlocks. Grooms led horses in procession on the exercise track. A farrier, shoe-nails between lips, danced on the hind leg of a refractory palfrey and mouthed curses. Fires roared in the smithy; hammers clanged on iron. A sergeant changed the watches; his orders snapped like breaking sticks.

Geoffrey leaned on the stockade and gazed over the river. "Robert of Gloucester, of course, is with her. Bishop Henry has decided to support her. He is in London and has declared himself openly at last – I did not think him so foolish. Other barons and prelates also. I, too, have done her homage." He grinned. "But Matilda has made a mistake. She is so encouraged by her reception since Stephen's capture, so confident that the realm is at her feet, that she has come to London without an army – with only the household retinues of her nobles : possibly a thousand men in all. A serious miscalculation – she doesn't know London's temper – and for me a providential opportunity."

He hawked and spat forcibly into the moat. The globule curved in the air and plopped in the water.

"Now, Humphrey, we must work fast. Three separate parties are concerned in my schemes : the Countess of Anjou, Queen Maud, and the people of London."

"And you, my lord?"

Count Geoffrey smiled radiantly. "I intend to act the mummer manipulating his puppets' strings, and benefit from all three. Here in the Tower I am secure, surrounded by my faithful liegemen." He regarded me with a kind of ironic affection. "My homage to Matilda has begun the play. It's going to be a complicated business, Humphrey – we must be careful to keep the strings separate and disentangled. Therefore I shall personally guide the enterprise with Countess Matilda; you will deal with the Londoners; Ernulf I have already sent to Queen Maud."

I felt the mesh of intrigue weave around me like the clammy tendrils of a spider's web. I shook my head and tried to clear my mind.

"Where is the queen, my lord?"

"In Kent with an army. William de Ypres is her adviser and commands her forces: his Flemings are the backbone. Ernulf's persuasions have had effect – already she is marching on London."

"And I?"

"You will convey to one Gervase fitzRoger, justiciar of London, certain advices which I shall make known to you. Calm yourself, dear Humphrey – don't look so distressed. Your part will be straightforward, your instructions simple. Moreover, I have yet to persuade the countess to my way of thinking. I wait upon her today, and you go with me."

Count Geoffrey rode splendidly to Westminster with fifty knights. We went through Eastcheap, along the street called Candlewick, and left the city walls at Ludgate. Matilda's encampment sprawled on the meadows of Westminster: she herself lodged within the palace, her barons in the precincts. Seneschals received my lord with honour, and led him to audience inside the hall. Sunlight lanced through lofty windows and lighted gaudy paintings covering lime-washed walls, where knights Templar slew infidels and charged Jerusalem's battlemented spires. Mighty oak-beams vaulted a high ceiling; fresh rushes strewed the floor. A table stood on trestles before a stone dais, and stools and benches leaned against the walls.

Matilda occupied the royal throne – Geoffrey's lips twitched in a secret smile – and on her left stood Brien fitzCount, on her right Count Robert of Gloucester. Bishop Henry of Winchester was there, and the bishops of Ely and Lincoln whom King Stephen had handled so roughly. The barons' ceremonial robes, the silks and furs and jewels, blazed like flowers in a gorgeous garden – but knights in mail formed a sombre background, and knights in mail stood behind my lord.

Count Geoffrey knelt and made formal greeting, and exchanged the courtesies proper to a state occasion. Impatience twitched Matilda's ruddy features; her black eyes glinted and she brusquely interrupted the stilted phrases.

"My lord count, you have given me your homage. You did not then swear the oath of fealty. I remind you that I am your queen by right of succession, by lineage, by the vows sworn to my royal father, and finally by conquest. I hope you have come to repair your omission."

Geoffrey said with surprising meekness, "My lady, all I have is yours – my knights and fiefs, my castles and revenues – everything I lay between your hands. I am your man."

"And the Tower?"

Geoffrey spread his hands. "I hold the Tower for England's sovereign. It is yours, of course. I am only surprised you have not accepted my humble hospitality."

Matilda studied him intently, and spoke without turning her head. "Count Robert, send a conroy to augment Count Geoffrey's garrison."

Robert of Gloucester's stony eyes examined Geoffrey's face. He made no move to implement the order.

My lord said regretfully, "The Tower is fully garrisoned. There is little space for extra troops. And, under the circumstances, it might be unwise to weaken your own forces – even by so much as a single conroy."

"What circumstances?" Count Robert barked.

Geoffrey said softly, "Queen Maud's army is approaching London."

There was a little silence. Bishop Henry plucked his lip and looked thoughtful.

Matilda said, "Maud is no longer queen." She spoke from habit, absently, her mind elsewhere. "How far away?"

Geoffrey said negligently, "Two marches distant. William de Ypres commands."

The barons stirred and whispered anxiously among themselves. Count Robert's sallow face was suddenly careworn, his cheeks more sunken. "Foolish," he muttered. "We were foolish to come without an army."

"We have men under arms at Oxford, at Winchester, at Wallingford," the Countess said. "Count Robert, we must summon them without delay!"

"No time," Robert said tiredly. "Two marches – thirty miles or less. We have no time."

Count Geoffrey said, "You have soldiers nearer at hand, my lady. The loyal citizens of London, the city bands, the watch and ward. Could they not be mobilized on your behalf?"

Matilda stared at him. "By the Rood, Count Geoffrey, I almost begin to trust you! Can this be done? It should be your business – will you see to it?"

Geoffrey sighed. "My lady, I am merely Constable of the Tower – I have no power to muster London's citizens for war. For this, and the gathering of provisions and money, I must be given authority – your authority."

"Authority? You have the Tower, and a hundred knights. What powers do you require that you don't already possess?"

My lord stated his terms.

I listened aghast. Count Robert's frown grew blacker. Bishop Henry looked faintly amused. Matilda sat rigidly, her lips compressed, her nose jutting like a beak. When Geoffrey had finished she said, "And this is your price?"

My lord said mildly, "I am not merchandise, my lady, to be bought and sold. I have merely proposed a remedy for the predicament in which, unfortunately, you now find yourself. And I would remind you, with submission, that I have offered you aid in the past."

"That plan!" Matilda exploded. "Circumstances have changed – Stephen is finished. It does not now arise."

"Who knows the will of God?" Geoffrey inquired piously. He dropped his beguiling manner. "My lady, do I have your authority – or not?"

She glared at him. "I have no choice. I give my promise. Now go – and rally the wards of London to my standard!"

"In writing, my lady. The citizens are but merchants. They have little faith in promises – they prefer the written word."

The haggling was over. Scribes were summoned, and parchment, quills and inkhorns. Matilda pretended to ignore the proceedings. She talked with her lords while Geoffrey dictated to the clerks and they inscribed his terms in legal language. At length it was done, and wax and tapers brought. Witnesses – bishops and barons –

appended their seals. Clerks unrolled fresh parchment, and copied another document to the address of Gervase fitzRoger, justiciar of London, which set forth Countess Matilda's instant requirements of men and supplies and money. Heavy demands: I knew the temper of London's citizens and heard Count Geoffrey's dictation with astonishment. He saw my unease and smiled serenely – and was careful to see Matilda's seal attached.

The chatter ceased; prelates and barons gathered in order behind the throne. My lord knelt. Countess Matilda formally presented the charter, heavy with dangling seals, and the lesser document addressed to Gervase. We made our farewells and left the chamber. Matilda's eyes snapped venomously at Geoffrey's departing back.

We returned in state through the city streets. My lord was happy, and hummed a tune, as befitted a man who, within an hour, had doubled his possessions of land and money and enfeoffed knights. He thrust a scroll into my hand.

"Take this to the justiciar, Humphrey. Listen carefully – this is what you must say and do."

He spoke clearly and precisely. I took a dozen knights and went to find Gervase fitzRoger.

2

The justiciar lived on Cornhill in a considerable mansion embowered in trees. Gervase, a rotund man, clean shaven, shrewd eyes embedded like raisins in a pudding face, showed little surprise at the formidable deputation which clattered into his courtyard. I took him aside, made no mention of Queen Maud's march on London, and gave him the scroll containing Matilda's demands. Gervase read silently, his face expressionless.

He said, "My lord, I am chosen by the citizens to represent the king's interests in the city. To this end I assess and collect the ferms and taxes which are properly due to him, year by year, and send them to the royal treasury at Winchester. I know what London owes to the king; I know also that our taxes have been paid in full. Beyond that neither the king nor anyone else has a right to tallage London, far less to conscript her citizens in arms. These privileges we secured under King Henry's seal. They have not been rescinded since."

I shrugged. "I know nothing of that. I merely bring you the queen's demands."

Gervase frowned. "The Countess of Anjou," he said emphatically, "is not yet queen. Nor does London favour her claim. We are Stephen's men, my lord."

"Stephen is a prisoner." I let impatience edge my tone. "Matilda of Anjou is queen in fact; coronation will soon make her queen in name. You split hairs, Gervase. This is her mandate – what is your answer?"

The justiciar thrust the parchment into his wallet. "My lord, I cannot decide this alone. I must consult the aldermen. May I send you our decision tomorrow?"

I remembered Maud's approach and Count Geoffrey's instructions, and answered vigorously. "No. You can see the matter is urgent. Go now and confer, if you must. I shall stay here until you return."

Gervase puffed his lips; reluctantly mounted a palfrey and ambled off. I walked the cobbled courtyard, and chafed, and avoided the knights who sat at a table beneath an elm tree's shade, gulped the justiciar's wine and victuals, caroused and toyed with his serving wenches. Servants came hastily from kitchen and vintry at their call – but the mansion's door was closed, the windows shuttered. Count Geoffrey's knights had an evil reputation for violation and pillage.

The elm tree's shadow crept towards the house. At evening Gervase returned. His eyes were unhappy, his plump jowls sagged dolefully. He said, "My lord, the aldermen protest against these unprecedented exactions. They seek an audience with the Countess Matilda, to represent to her London's privileges and safeguards which her father enacted. I cannot persuade them otherwise."

I tugged my ear. This was a development whose effect on the train of events I could not foresee. Nor had Count Geoffrey mentioned it. Foolish to act without his guidance. I called Odinel, gave him instructions, detailed for his escort two knights who still seemed reasonably sober and sent them galloping to the Tower. Soon he returned, slid grinning from the saddle and gave my lord's answer. "Count Geoffrey said, 'By all means let them talk to the hell-bitch. She'll bite their ears off.'"

As always, he was right. Countess Matilda granted the burghers an audience next day. By noon Gervase was back in the courtyard, flushed and furious. I listened contentedly to his description of

Matilda's blazing rage, of her tirade against the Londoners' support of Stephen and her demands that they should now contribute as much and more to her own cause.

I said, "What will you do?"

Gervase collapsed exhaustedly upon a settle. "I do not know. How can we resist? At Westminster a thousand men are under arms. Between them and your Count Geoffrey in the Tower" – he spat – "we shall be cracked like a louse."

"Mobilize your bands," I answered. "The countess will see and be satisfied. But they will be employed in a manner different to her reckoning."

Gervase raised his head from his hands and scrutinized my face.

"What do you mean, my lord?"

I told him that Queen Maud marched on London, and was no more than fifteen miles away.

"Is this the truth? It could prove a vicious trap if it were not."

"You have my word as a knight."

"Will the queen know that we may rise in her support?"

"She has been told already."

He scuffled his foot in the dust, and pondered.

"And Count Geoffrey?"

"He will not stir from the Tower."

Gervase rose, strolled a little way, regarded distastefully my knights who again were wasting his substance, returned and stood before me. His eyes, bloodshot from sleeplessness and anxiety, examined me curiously.

"What is your part in this, my lord? You are Count Geoffrey's man – he has done homage to Matilda. For whom do you act?"

"Gervase," I said gravely, "do not concern yourself with policies beyond your scope. All that matters is that you should understand the situation as it affects you and the men of London, and act upon it speedily and decisively. Have I made myself clear?"

"You have. I shall do as you . . . suggest. This is a dangerous business, and will require much contrivance. With your permission I go to consult the aldermen." He paused, and added inconsequentially, "My lineage is part Norman, part English. There are times when I thank God for my English blood."

My lord wove the complex threads of his design with the smooth efficiency of a master-armourer meshing the links of a chain-mail hauberk. At nightfall Queen Maud's army arrived and camped beyond the Thames. At daybreak they ravaged Southwark very thoroughly. Count Geoffrey surveyed the coiling pillars of smoke, the leaping flames, the glint of spears where soldiers pillaged; and was angry. "Stupid sons of misbegotten whores!" he raged. "Do they want to alienate the Londoners? Is Maud insane?"

Ernulf, who had ferried secretly across the river during the night, peered from an embrasure and gloomily explained. "Bloodstained Flemings," he said. "Quite uncontrollable except in battle. Show them a whiff of loot and they go mad."

The harrying continued all day, and smoke drifted in clouds across the Thames and obscured the sun. London hummed like an overturned hive; from the battlements we saw furious activity in the streets and armed men on the walls. They stationed a guard on the bridge, but Maud's men made no attempt to cross. Ernulf sighed relief.

"Obeying some of my instructions, anyway," he grunted. "Told them to leave the bridge alone. They should be sending a diversionary party to the ford above Westminster to lure Matilda's knights away. Hope they have."

Count Geoffrey chewed his nails, and never left the battlements. Sunset shot emerald streamers through the smoke-pall; the dying fires of Southwark glowed redly in the dusk. Torches flared in London's streets. A loud murmur, the vibrating roar of an angry town, thrummed like lute-strings.

St Paul's bells gave the signal. The tocsin was repeated by the bells of all the churches. The air reverberated and the ringing re-echoed from distant hills. The torchlights swept to Ludgate, and the citizens of London poured forth to battle amid the clanging of the bells.

My lord sighed deeply, and turned to Ernulf. "I think they will prevail. Send out spies. Tell them to follow quick, and bring me word."

They returned at dawn. There had been no battle, practically no resistance. William de Ypres' noisy demonstration had lured half Matilda's knights to a futile watch on the ford; the remainder, surprised by the fiery torrent that exploded from the town, scattered and ran in panic. The Countess of Anjou, escorted by a handful of knights, fled to Oxford. The men of London burned the encampment, ravaged the mansions whence the nobles fled, looted the palace.

Queen Maud's army marched in ordered ranks across London Bridge.

My lord smiled contentedly and retired to his bedchamber, and slept like a new-born child.

4

"Let her bump her head against the Tower for a while," Count Geoffrey said. "A little bruising will do no harm."

"My lord," I protested, "you speak of the Queen of England. Would you withstand Maud, and London, and all the resources of the realm?"

Geoffrey scanned the brilliant procession, escorted by citizens running alongside, cheering and throwing caps in the air, which wound towards the Tower from Eastcheap. "A ceremonial visit," he murmured. "Not many troops with her. Well, Humphrey – you know what you have to do."

The count left the battlements and went below.

The Tower's defenders stood at battle stations. Knights and sergeants, bowmen and arbalesters manned the stockade. The bailey was cleared for action, all litter and impedimenta removed. Wet hides covered the thatched roofs of sheds and outbuildings. The horse lines were half empty; all destriers were stabled in the keep.

From the lip of the moat Queen Maud's outriders demanded admittance. My lord's seneschal, perched above the gateposts, made reply. A rowdy argument followed. Presently a throwing-spear curved from the stockade and landed harmlessly at the heralds' feet. A knight unbound the parchment wrapped round the shaft and took it to the queen. Maud read, and gave it to her barons. I heard voices raised in anger, and saw threatening gestures. Still sitting on their horses, they held a sort of council. I spoke to the trumpeter beside me; he rested elbows on a merlon and raised his clarion. The cavalcade swung about and returned the way it had come. I let my breath out slowly, and shook my head. The sergeant eased the trumpet from his lips.

No message came from Maud next day. My lord was unperturbed. "My proposals, doubtless, need leisure for digestion," he observed.

On the fourth day came a single herald, a knight bearing the green-leaf wreath of truce upon his lance. We let him enter. He spoke with my lord, who smiled happily and gave orders. Presently Count Geoffrey rode from the gates with Ernulf and a hundred armoured knights; the count himself was mailed and helmeted. "I do not really expect treachery," he assured me, "but you never know with a man like William de Ypres. Close the gates after me, Humphrey, and lift the bridge: I leave the Tower in your keeping."

At evening he returned, and went straight to St Peter's chapel, and remained for an hour on his knees in prayer. Awed knights watched from the shadows beyond the altar's flickering candles. They had reason for wonder. This was the sole occasion within my knowledge when my lord communed alone with God. He was not a religious man; although strict in attendance at daily Mass he yawned his way through the offices; and judged a priest's worth entirely by his speed in saying a Mass. Now he prayed long and earnestly, and offered thanks to God.

He had much to be thankful for. Queen Maud surrendered all that he demanded.

And here I must make clear what Geoffrey de Mandeville's intrigues and stark treachery had brought him, bid by bid. Before he won his first grant from King Stephen he was already a great baron, holding manors by hereditary right in eleven counties, and the services of knights enfeoffed upon them, and two castles besides the Tower. The forcible detention of Princess Constance, a year before, compelled the king to give him the dignity of count and one-third of all the revenues of Essex. From the Countess Matilda he then extracted enormous grants of land, additional fiefs affording the services of twenty knights, the right to build another castle anywhere in his domains, and the offices of sheriff and justiciar of Essex – offices which made him virtual governor of the county. Now to Queen Maud he raised his bid: she confirmed him in all that he already held and added the fiefs of sixty knights, conceded yet another castle, trebled the grants of land and gave him the shrievalties and justiciaries of London, Middlesex and Hertfordshire.

Count Geoffrey's power now was unsurpassed by any baron in the land. Huge revenues flowed into his coffers, he governed

London and three counties, commanded the services of a hundred and thirty landed knights – besides those he hired – and held four castles and the Tower. In theory, of course, it all belonged to the king. But the king was a prisoner, and Geoffrey's possession of manors and castles and knights strengthened his power as arbiter between the rival claimants to the throne.

London and the Londoners were placed firmly beneath his yoke. I think that pleased him most of all.

5

Throughout July my lord's emissaries travelled the roads of southern England.

How much of the trap at Winchester was due to Count Geoffrey's plotting, how much to William de Ypres and the queen's barons, how much to sheer chance, I never discovered. Bishop Henry made the opening move: he changed sides, fortified his palace of Wolvesey in Winchester and laid siege to Matilda's garrison in the castle. The Countess of Anjou reacted swiftly. Enraged by Henry's desertion she gathered an army at Oxford, marched to Winchester, relieved the castle and in turn besieged the bishop in Wolvesey. Henry escaped before the siege-lines closed, and came to London.

Queen Maud received him gladly and called a council of war in her bower chamber in the Tower, where she resided since her pact with Geoffrey. Nothing could soften the Tower's stark interior, but Count Geoffrey had done his best. Embroidered hangings, brightly woven, hid the grim hewn-stone walls; cloth of gold and silver covered tables; silken cushions padded the chairs. The queen's feet rested on a precious drugget brought from the spoils of Antioch. A miserly daylight, mellowed by candles in branched holders, struggled through close-fisted windows. The fortress seemed to wear this finery with contemptuous resignation, like a mailed warrior bedizened in a gaudy cloak.

"And now, I think, we have them," Geoffrey said. "My lord bishop, your garrison can hold for a week or two?"

Henry of Winchester nodded. Bushy eyebrows over his hooked nose, the ashen face, gave him the look of a brooding owl.

"Yes, for a certainty. They had trouble at first. Winchester's buildings crowded close upon the palace: the enemy could attack under cover almost to the walls. However, the knight I left in charge waited for an east wind and showered fire on the rooftops. I regret to say he burnt half the town and several churches, but he cleared the ground and destroyed the covered approaches for Matilda's sallies."

William de Ypres hitched his robe inelegantly over his knees. "A sound tactic," he approved. William, in manner and appearance, was hardly the image of a famous captain – a short, bulging man with yellow greasy skin and muddy brown eyes. His chin was shaven and his hair cropped close. Although a great noble – son of the Count of Flanders – he looked like a base-born peasant. He prayed a great deal, invoking divine approval for all he did. Some of his deeds were of a nature that made God's blessing extremely doubtful. ,

"The army is ready to march," he continued. "My Flemings, the Breton mercenaries under William de Warenne, the barons of Kent with their knights. Under God's will, we shall be at Winchester inside five days."

"And you, Count Geoffrey?" Queen Maud said gently.

My lord put his fingertips together and gazed at the massive beams that crossed the ceiling. "Let me see. I can spare from the Tower fifty knights and two hundred sergeants. The Londoners, I think, must share in this venture. They can raise a thousand men, if pressed. And pressed they shall be – but it will take a little time. I can follow you within seven days."

The queen smiled. "Waiting on the fence again, my lord?" She seemed to bear him no animosity. Queen Maud was a woman of great intelligence, never fretting over her reverses, determined always to profit from the goods she bought, whatever the price. "Do you doubt Lord William's ability to ensnare my enemies?"

Geoffrey lowered his gaze and smiled into her eyes. "My lady, you read my motives wrongly. None the less, I always like to ensure that a trap is sprung before I put my fingers near."

The queen laughed. "The sentiment becomes you, my lord. I know you for a very careful man."

Her army marched next day. My lord sent edicts, backed now by all the force of law and royal authority, to Gervase fitzRoger, who mobilized the city bands. Geoffrey paraded and drilled them on the open fields outside the city walls, and went daily to inspect their progress; not until ten days had passed did he declare himself satisfied. In mid-August, after receiving certain communications from his spies at Winchester, he led twelve hundred men from Newgate.

6

A ditch and ramparts encompass Winchester's half-mile square. A river washes the eastern wall and feeds the moat. At the south-east corner stands Wolvesey, a stone building heavily fortified; on the south-west the castle's wooden keep rises on a high mound over-looking an extensive bailey. Between them the church of Holy Trinity, which had survived the fire, towered like a crag in a waste of blackened rubble and charred timbers.

Count Geoffrey pitched his tents outside the eastern gate, on a hill called St Giles which commands a prospect of the town. With William de Ypres, encamped near by, he rode a circuit of the walls, inspected the siege lines and heard William explain his dispositions. My lord found little to criticize.

"You have them fast?"

William slowly closed his fist. "If God so wills," he answered, "we hold them just like that."

This was a remarkable siege within a siege; nothing like it was ever heard of in our times. Matilda's forces from the castle closely invested Wolvesey and were themselves encircled and besieged by Queen Maud's army.

William de Ypres pointed to the castle. "They are all there, the countess and her adherents: Robert of Gloucester, King David of Scotland, Brian fitzCount and many other barons. They have flocked to Winchester like crows on carrion."

"Couldn't resist the bait," my lord agreed. "Bishop Henry in arms against her, and the royal capital and treasury in peril. Now we must make sure they don't escape."

William, always careful of his men, conducted a total blockade rather than a regular siege with all its trappings of trenches and mantlets, fire-storms and saps. His troops picketed every road and track leading to Winchester. Wolvesey was no longer in serious danger; William had opened communications with the palace and delivered reinforcements and supplies whenever he wished. The garrison, thus encouraged, made periodical forays across the cindered wasteland and kept the castle's defenders occupied.

My lord examined the road-blocks and approved.

"I'll send my Londoners to man some of these, and relieve your knights," he said. "You need plenty of infantry for this work."

The operations settled into routine. The days were fair and warm; the sun rose in glory and sank in splendour. For long periods nothing happened; conroys went in turn to relieve road pickets; knights prowled on regular patrols and observed trackways and probed woodlands. When we were off duty we hunted boar with berselets in the forest, or flew our hawks. Food and wine were plentiful: wagons carrying provisions thronged the roads from London. With them came merchants and mummers, pedlars and harlots, who infested the army like maggots in a wound. I ate fresh tender meat and wheaten bread, drank wine of Artois and bedded a Southwark drab – for Saiva stayed in London and a man must guard his health. The enemy's growing privations were a sauce to our enjoyment.

"The countess must be losing weight," Odinel reflected.

Odinel had run into trouble, and this was the way of it.

The younger and more frolicsome knights, to lighten the tedium of leaguering, began riding beneath the castle walls and shouting challenges to single combat. At first the whip of arrows was all their answer; after some days and many taunts had passed the garrison's knights, probably equally bored, came forth to joust. Beyond the moat lay open fields, grey with ashes of burnt-out corn. This plain saw many a gallant career, spirited clashes and splintered lances. The loser, naturally, was held for ransom, and also forfeited his armour and destrier – a custom creeping into the usages of tourney which I deprecate, for I do not think a man should lose the tools of his trade. We did not demand large ransoms of Matilda's knights, nor they of us, because these were contests of courtoisie quite separate from our warlike enterprise. Therefore we often entertained enemy knights, as they did ours – though rather less hospitably: supplies were running low in the Countess of Anjou's castle. Sometimes a knight was badly wounded in these contests, or even killed, which was sad since nobody profited – one did not, in tourney, strip armour from a knightly corpse.

In an early joust I acquired a piebald stallion named Baucan, silken-mouthed and sensitive to rein and spur. He lacked the massive strength and speed which made Chanson a superb battle-charger, but handled better for the individual skills of tourney. Thereafter I won many ransoms, and hauberks and destriers – which I sold –

until the castle's knights became shy of the wolf's head. I wore my own blazon, because these were private affairs.

The counts on either side never fought – they had too much to lose – but one met barons experienced in war and famous for skill at arms. So it happened that, one sunny afternoon, Brien fitzCount of Wallingford answered Odinel's challenge and hurled him from his saddle at the first career.

Odinel, leaning on the arm of Brien's squire, limped glumly into the castle. Nobody would ransom him for a long time, since he was a penurious hired knight – and Prudhoe was England's length away. I foresaw a long separation from my friend. Politely I pleaded with his conqueror for the courtesy of a joust. Smilingly Brien agreed. We separated and ran together.

I laid Baucan on the line, whence he deviated by not a hand's-breadth. Brien's destrier yawed and rolled, and wavered his rider's lance. I struck the lord of Wallingford true upon the helmet; his lance-point scored my shield. When he became conscious I asked merely for Odinel's release. Brien shakenly agreed

"And that," I told Odinel, "hast cost me thirty marks, the finest chain-mesh hauberk I ever saw, and a destrier I wouldn't ride if I were paid. Mother of God, are you worth it?"

Odinel grinned. "Of course. I'm your jester. Without me, my solemn Humphrey, would you ever laugh?"

I swallowed my retort, and pondered awhile on the nature of truth.

The serious fighting happened in the incinerated no-man's-land between the castles, and at the road-blocks. Bishop Henry's constable in Wolvesey was an energetic knight who, despite William de Ypres' strictures, insisted on harassing the opposing garrison at every opportunity. William, a mercenary captain, disliked seeing good soldiers unnecessarily wasted. Only a careful watch and a strict blockade, he insisted, were needed to reduce Winchester castle. The constable nevertheless persisted; his sallies met counter-sallies; savage little fights flared amidst the ashes. Corpses littered the ground, and death's sickly-sweet smell overlaid the summer stench of Winchester's drains and sewers.

August's golden sunshine lingered into September. Within the castle starvation sharpened hunger. Matilda's knights ignored our challenges, and no longer came forth to joust.

7

In the darkness before dawn John fitzGilbert the Marshal led three hundred knights and sergeants from Winchester castle, dodged across country to avoid road-blocks and vanished into early morning mist. A sleepy outpost heard their passing, mounted hurriedly and gave chase. They lost the enemy but found a laggard, a frightened sergeant whom they brought to Count Geoffrey.

"Where are they bound?" Geoffrey snapped.

The man cringed beneath his anger. "Wherwell, my lord. The Marshal rides to meet a convoy from Devizes – a wagon train carrying supplies enough for half a year."

"If that gets through our work is wasted." My lord chewed his thumb. "An hour's start, or more. We must move quickly."

He strode to William de Ypres' pavilion, ignored the sentry, snarled at a squire, and roused the occupant from slumber and the arms of a tousled slattern. He spoke urgently. William emerged, rubbing sleep-gum from his muddy eyes. Orders flew, and the camp on St Giles's hill awoke. Count Geoffrey armed and waited impatiently. William, on his knees before a priest, received the sacraments and confessed his sins. I peered inside the tent: his cropped head bowed devotedly, his thick lips moved in prayer.

"A very pious man," my lord observed sardonically.

We took the Roman road to Wherwell – all Geoffrey's fifty knights and four hundred mounted Flemings. Sunrise gilded the mist; a million dew-gems glittered on leaves and grass. The squadron extended on both sides of the road in line of constabular columns. William whirled his arm. We rode ten miles to Wherwell at a swinging canter over prickling stubble, across scrub and grassland, through woods and thickets, like huntsmen trailing a running wolf.

A river ford closed the squadron into column, and we came from the east on Wherwell, a scattered village dominated by the greystone walls of a church and nunnery. Horsemen crowded round wagons that thronged the dusty trackway; they spilled into fields and rode carelessly between cottages. Some were dismounted, girths loosened, watering their horses, or reclined at ease with reins looped over arms and lances stuck in the ground.

Surprise was complete.

William de Ypres raised his eyes to heaven, joined hands and gave thanks to God. Then he swung his destrier and shouted orders. The constabulars formed line unhurriedly on the harvested fields. William watched critically, and shouted unintelligible reproof in the Flemish tongue. He turned to face the wagons, dropped his lance and drew his sword.

The charge lacked the insensate fury of Lincoln's mad career. You cannot ride down laden wagons. We hit the Marshal's knights at a controlled canter and met no counter-charge: the enemy, hopelessly unready, milled in utter confusion. The onset quickly splintered into separate mellays. Dust rose in clouds and gritted between my teeth. The Flemings showed no mercy and gave no quarter. The unarmed wagoners, I think, were slaughted to a man.

John fitzGilbert's knights had nowhere to run, no shelter save the stone-walled nunnery. Thither they fled, such as survived the ruthless swords. We surrounded the place, and drove the enemy within as dogs herd sheep. Soon none but the dead was left in Wherwell village.

The nunnery was an oblong, thatch-roofed house with a portal at each end. The Flemings battered the doorways, forced the doors, and met the enemy sword to sword on the thresholds. They got no farther.

William de Ypres leaned on his saddle-bow and observed the fight. He saw his men being killed, and frowned. He gave orders and they came away, dragging their dead. We heard fitzGilbert's knights cheering their short-lived triumph, and the nuns' terrified screaming. The Flemings hauled wagons from the road, and blocked the doorways.

William said, "Bring fire."

We sat our horses in a ring and watched the torches hurled to the roof. The dry straw caught readily; flames rippled like flying pennons along the thatch.

Count Geoffrey said, "The women?"

William turned his head. "What women, my lord?"

Geoffrey clenched his teeth. Muscles bunched on his jaw like walnuts. "Can't you hear their screams? Would you burn alive the Sisters of Christ?"

William shrugged. "Yes, my lord. It is most unfortunate – but what can one do?"

"Holy Mother of God! Call a truce, man! Get them out!"

"A truce?" The fire's redness glinted in William's eyes. "My lord count, we are not playing games. I am a soldier. I have the enemy at my mercy – and this is war."

He returned an interested gaze to the building, and watched benignly. Fires spurted merrily from eaves to roof-tree, crackled and caught hold, leapt skywards in a sheet of flame. Men struggled in the doorways and wrestled with the wagons. They were heavy and held firm. A few escaped and ran blindly on expectant blades. The Flemings laughed delightedly. A shrilling agony of pain and terror blended with the fire's roar.

The roof collapsed in an inferno of smoke and flame and hurtling sparks. The crying ceased. A stench of roasting flesh clogged our nostrils.

William de Ypres bowed his head. "May God in His mercy receive their souls," he murmured. He crossed himself, dismounted and wiped soot-grime from his face. A squire approached, bearing a platter of bread and meat.

"My lord, it is past noon. Will you not refresh yourself?"

William's eyes bulged in horror. "Christ's thorns!" he shouted. "Meat? Do you want me damned for ever in hell? Do you not know today is Friday?"

8

Count Geoffrey avoided William's company during the return to Winchester. He spoke only once – and I do not think the subject he mentioned was that on which he brooded.

"This affair has destroyed Matilda's final hope of replenishing her supplies. Now they must either surrender or go. We must watch them very carefully."

They broke out five days later, on the 14th of September.

14

September, 1141 — October, 1143

Inevitably we had forewarning.

Spies said that wagons were being loaded in the castle court, that the last reserves of food were issued to the garrison. They said Matilda would escape on the Salisbury road by way of Stockbridge. The spies – mostly priests, who passed freely between the contending armies – were certain a break-out was imminent, but could not tell us when.

William de Ypres conferred with Count Geoffrey. He then put pickets on the Stockbridge road, well mounted on fast horses, and withdrew the road-blocks. "For," he said, "we do not want to stop them going, but we must know directly." He forbade any more hunting and hawking expeditions, confined everyone to the siege-lines, and put the army at an hour's readiness.

The weather broke. Rain hammered on tent walls; wind-gusts lashed the forests. The dusty, hoof-pocked battlegrounds round Winchester became muddy quagmires. Three days passed with no sign of movement from the castle. William harangued his priestly spies, flogged a couple to encourage the others, and dispatched them to gather more detailed information. Naturally enough, they did not return. My lord scowled, summoned two of his agents who passed as sweetmeat pedlars – a tempting bait for hungry men – gave concise instructions and sent them to the castle.

Soon after dawn on the fourth day riders came hastily from the outposts to William on St Giles's hill. He listened to their tidings, shielded his eyes from the rain and peered across the town. A dark column coiled from the western gate. He gave orders, and trumpets called to arms. One of the pedlars, muddied from head to heels, appeared from the mist and spoke urgently to Count Geoffrey, who asked a single question.

"Where does she ride?"

"With the vanguard, my lord."

Geoffrey swung to the saddle, and his face wore the intent look of a falconer throwing his hawk.

William de Ypres divided his pursuing army into two wings. His own Flemings, and the Breton mercenaries under William de Warenne, swept north of Winchester. Geoffrey, on the south, led his knights in the van of Bishop Henry's vassals and the Kentish barons. My lord found the river swollen by rain, the ford impassable. He fumed, and sent outriders to discover a crossing. This they did; but the delay and extra distance brought us late to the road two miles beyond the western gate, where battle was already joined. The Flemings had fallen on Matilda's rearguard, commanded by Count Robert himself.

Geoffrey halted his squadron and watched the fight from a distance. Count Robert led two hundred knights, half on foot, half mounted. The infantry formed a compact, shielded orb retreating at a steady walk; behind them lurked the cavalry. Their tactics were simple and effective: when William's knights charged they halted and engaged them sword to sword; cavalry swept from the rear and fell on the Flemings' flanks. Then they resumed the slow retreat until the next attack developed.

My lord pensively stroked his nasal and flicked water from his fingers. "Count Robert knows his business," he murmured. "This could take a long time. Humphrey, go to William and ask if he needs help."

William de Ypres was mud-splashed, nursing a wounded hand, and in a blazing temper. He finished cursing an unfortunate banneret whose onset had been bloodily repulsed, and heard me impatiently. "No!" he snapped. "I can deal with this. We'll get Robert sooner or later. Tell Count Geoffrey to go after the other one – Matilda. We want her too. Now, my lords," he said to his chastened followers, "let's see if you can retrieve your reputations. Form line and follow me!"

He spattered off to lead another charge.

Count Geoffrey skirted this mobile battle, led us south of the road at a fast pace over thorn-scrub and fields, past woods and solitary steadings. Soon we overhauled the enemy's main body, a four-mile trail of wagons in broken clusters on the road, and knights and sergeants in troops riding or marching alongside. Our appearance set them prancing and shouting, but my lord made no attempt to close, and demanded greater speed. We rode on, passing the column a half-mile distant. Behind us Bishop Henry's knights and the Kentish barons attacked the wagon-train. We heard the clash and cries of conflict. Odinel muttered and glanced hungrily over his shoulder.

"A wealth of plunder for the taking," he said. "Must we miss our share?"

"Count Geoffrey seeks a bigger booty," I grunted. Baucan stumbled in a furrow; impatiently I collected him, and longed for Chanson, lamed by an overreach during the affair at Wherwell. "A prize that will end this war – no less."

We drew level with the head of the main body; my lord edged nearer and closely observed the conroys which escorted the wagons. He shook his head and raindrops flew.

"Not here," he said. "They have a long start. Faster!"

We left the wagons and the squall of strife behind. Count Geoffrey called me to his side, and gave abrupt orders. With twenty knights I went ahead, galloping like riders whipping to a winning-post. We were halted by a river, and followed the bank northwards to the road, which spanned the water on a wooden bridge just wide enough for a wagon's passage. Here we took our stand, and cosseted our blown and spume-flecked horses.

Outriders spurred from the rain-veil and ran almost on our lances, thinking us to be their friends. One we unhorsed and took, and set him free to wander dismally away. The others returned and gave warning. A little later a constabular of knights, some twenty strong, approached us on the road. Their lances were in rest, their shields enarmed. A woman rode among them. We braced for the charge.

Count Geoffrey's squadron cantered from a spinney and dressed in line across the road, so that the enemy were hemmed between us, able neither to retreat nor advance across the bridge. Quickly they formed in a cluster and faced both ways. We stood thus for a while, unmoving, and there was no sound save the patter of rain and the wind's wailing.

My lord walked his destrier forward. He carried his lance athwart the saddle bow; the rain-soaked banner, gold and scarlet, drooped limply from the shaft.

"Do you yield, my lords?" he called.

A knight answered from the centre of the group. "We do not. We await your onset. Why do you hesitate – are you afraid?"

Count Geoffrey's voice hardened. "You are outnumbered three to one, Brien fitzCount. Would you sacrifice the lives of your knights and the lady whom you guard?"

A muted drone, like the distant clamour of a market place, drifted on the breathing of the wind. A riderless horse, muzzle high and tail flaring, trotted past, balked at the river, dropped its head and began to graze.

Brien said, "We are not alone. Our army follows close behind. You have laid your head in a snare, my lord count, and the noose twists round your throat."

A cloud of horsemen burst from the mist. Our rear ranks, alarmed, turned on their hocks to meet the attack they feared. Destriers fidgeted and collided; their riders swore. Count Geoffrey gave them never a glance: all his mind was on the prey within his grasp.

The horsemen saw a squadron massed before the bridge, and swerved away. They rode helter-skelter to the river, slid down banks, wallowed through water. Some rolled beneath the flood-browned torrent and disappeared; some were unhorsed and, wading neck-deep, scrambled up the farther bank, labouring beneath the weight of armour and soaked gambesons, throwing away their shields. Footmen followed, plodding exhaustedly over miry fields, and more knights flogging tired horses.

The Rout of Winchester had started.

Geoffrey's lips twitched. He thrust his lance-butt into the ground beside his stirrup and slung his shield aback. No triumph showed upon his face.

"My lord, there goes your army – what seems to be left of it. I think that now you have no alternative."

Brien did not stir. "My lord count, you must take us if you can. We do not yield."

Geoffrey hunched his shoulders irritably. "Your defiance exceeds the imperatives of honour," he said harshly. "May I speak with your lady? No one will lay a hand on her."

Brien spoke over his shoulder. A palfrey sidled through the line of shields. Countess Matilda, with Brien beside her, advanced into the open space between the levelled lances. I left my place and stood beside my lord.

Count Geoffrey said quietly, "My lady of Anjou, it were better that you should surrender. You will spare much bloodshed, and save yourself from hurt."

Matilda listlessly regarded her hands crossed on the saddle-peak. Defeat and despair graved furrows round her mouth; her lips trembled.

"And if I do, my lord, where will you take me?"

"I must deliver you to my liege lady, Queen Maud of England."

Matilda raised her head. Her dark eyes glittered.

"You swore to me not long ago, my lord!"

Geoffrey said, "Do you yield, my lady?"

"I do, because I must."

Brien raised a hand, and let it fall resignedly. A dismounted knight ran past, mouthing incoherent cries of warning. He stumbled to the water's edge, frantically stripped his hauberk and plunged in. A sick disgust twisted Brien's mouth.

Geoffrey said softly, "I swore no fealty, my lady. I gave homage for my fiefs – which are no longer yours to bestow. Yet my homage remains."

He smiled.

"Therefore I shall let you go."

I thought I had not heard aright, and slapped my coif to clear raindrops from my ears. Brien stared in disbelief. Matilda gazed levelly into Geoffrey's eyes.

"And what reward do you demand this time, Count Geoffrey?"

He slowly shook his head. "None, my lady – save remembrance and, perhaps, a little gratitude."

She turned without a word and threaded through her knights. Brien sent Geoffrey a curious glance, began to speak, checked his utterance and followed. My lord gave orders: his knights opened a passage to the bridge. Hooves drummed hollow on the planks.

Despairingly I grasped Count Geoffrey's arm. "My lord, you must not set her free! You cannot throw away the prize that you have won! You must hold her – she is the key to lock the gates of war!"

"You grow poetic in your passion, my good Humphrey." Fastidiously he removed my fingers from his wrist. "Don't you remember how King Stephen, two years since, had the countess in his grasp and let her go? Must I be less particular in the niceties of courtoisie?" His lips curved wickedly. "True knights do not make war on women – or not often. Let us leave it there, dear Humphrey – my gentle knight."

2

The journey back disclosed an expansive spectacle of pillage. The Countess of Anjou's army, routed and panic-stricken, fled in all directions, seeking sanctuary in forests and hovels, in byres and copses. Bretons and Flemings hunted them, and Bishop Henry's knights and the men of Kent. They made prisoners of any knights they caught and gained plunder which was littered everywhere for the taking. You saw fine destriers, riderless and straying, and shields and hauberks and arms of every kind strewn on the ground, and cloaks and vessels of gold and silver and other valuables flung in heaps. Pillagers flitted like swarming wasps. Count Geoffrey waved a generous hand and gave his knights permission to take part.

Depressed and sick at heart, I went on alone, ignoring the excited shouts and quarrelling scrabbles over booty. I rode Baucan on a slack rein and let him walk, and bowed my head against the wind and rain. My suzerain and liege lord had wrought treachery of the basest kind. The long months in his company, the many occasions when he had opened his mind to me, had taught a sort of wisdom. I no longer needed Ranulf's sidelong hints to unravel the twisted skeins of his designs. I knew him to be merciless – why then this act of mercy? I saw the reason plainly as the blazon on my shield. Matilda's capture would upset the balance, the scales of power which my lord tilted this way and that to suit his ends. The war must go on – because only in a state of lawless anarchy could men like Geoffrey de Mandeville prosper and become invincible.

A thought struck me like a blow. My rein hand jabbed the bit and Baucan snorted in protest. Was he aiming at the crown itself? No – that was fantastical. Geoffrey's noble lineage I knew well – but no royal blood of Normandy or England flowed in his veins: no baron or bishop would support his claim. He sought a position more puissant than the king: he would be kingmaker of the realm of England. And for this end the filthiest sludge of betrayal was not too foul to handle.

A Flemish knight trotted past, grinning jovially. A bulging sack bumped on his saddle bow. I wiped the streaming moisture from my face and laughed without mirth. Who was I, a humble landless knight, to concern myself with high policies of power? I was Count Geoffrey's man, my duty but to follow him. Why should I care that corruption slimed his soul?

I had to care. I loved him.

Odinel cantered up, gleefully brandishing a golden chalice. "I lost you, Humphrey. Did you know we've taken Count Robert? What ails you, man? Come with me and gather riches! There's been nothing like it since the sack of Lincoln!"

I shook my head. He saw my face and said no more. Silently we rode together through the rain. Presently the din of pillage faded. We slid down the embankment of a sunken lane, and found an abandoned cart with a broken wheel. Oxen still stood patiently in the shafts. Odinel tore aside the sackcloth cover and probed, and stared wide-eyed.

"God's bowels!" he muttered. "Here's all the wealth of Christendom."

It was not that, yet riches enough were there: thuribles and chalices of gold and silver, jewelled rings and bracelets and silver coins in bags; enough to ransom a king or pay an army. Odinel replaced the sackings and firmly bound the ropes.

"Stay here, Humphrey. I'll fetch a wheelwright, and an escort. Guard it with your life!"

He galloped away. I dismounted, eased Baucan's girth, leaned against the cart and thought about my life. A hare crossed the lane, her fur bedraggled, and paused and shook herself before leaping to concealment in the grassy bank. A blackbird chattered noisily from an elder-tree. It was a lonely place. No one came near.

I had plenty of time to think.

3

Count Geoffrey said, "Why do you wish to leave me, Humphrey? Tell me the truth."

I stood in his pavilion on St Giles's hill. All about us was the bustle of departure: tents were struck, picket pegs uprooted, fodder stacks dismantled and wagons loaded. Winchester lay below, hazed by smoke and utterly destroyed: the men of London, left behind the pursuit, had made a thorough business of the sack. The army was decamping with its plunder. The greatest prize of all, Count Robert of Gloucester, had gone to imprisonment in Rochester castle.

Wretchedly I straightened a hauberk hanging on an armour-stand, examining the ring-mesh as if it were some strange creation never seen before. A rivet had worn loose; I pressed the swages together and dropped my hand.

"My lord, I have served you faithfully for three years and more. I am a landless knight: the fortunes of war have now given me a chance to recover my fief. With the treasure I have won I can hire soldiers, fortify a castle, buy ploughs and cattle, rebuild farmsteads and restore the husbandry."

"Tell me the truth, Humphrey." His voice was soft, sheathing an iron edge like a scabbarded sword.

"There is no more," I said sulkily. "The House of Visdelou once held manors; it is not fitting that I should live for ever as a soldier – a landless hireling."

Count Geoffrey thoughtfully joined his hands together and gazed at me over steepled fingertips. "You are my man," he said mildly. "Do you intend to abjure your fealty?"

"No, my lord. I shall not break my vows."

"You held Bochesorne of the king. If you recover the fief he becomes once more your suzerain. How can you serve two masters?"

I shrugged helplessly. "My lord, in times like these what does it matter? Matilda by election is England's ruler, Stephen a captive – is he still my overlord? Who can tell what fealty is owed by any man? Who can distinguish the faithful from the faithless. You yourself —"

I stopped.

Geoffrey smiled. "Yes. I, myself. At last we touch the skirts of truth. In a word: abhorrence. You still cling, my Humphrey, to fading vestiges of knightly conduct, to the stained caparison of courtoisie. A threadbare garment, easily rent in times of stress. I had thought, in our acquaintance, to prove to you the farcicality of vows and oaths, homage and fealty and all the trappings which encumber knighthood. I hoped to teach you something of high policy and the ruthlessness of power. I have failed. You cannot stomach my contrivances. Therefore you are no longer useful to me."

He sauntered to the door and raised the flap. A wagon trundled past. The driver cursed his cattle and flailed a whip. The bells of Holy Trinity tolled mournfully for the dead; the muffled peals rang like a knell for all my hopes.

"I shall not hinder you. You may go and stock your farms and plough your fields. A knightly occupation – truly fit for such as you."

I stumbled to his side and seized his hand. "My lord," I babbled, "I am still your man. I serve you with my sword at your behest. Whenever you should summon me —"

"You are indeed my man," Count Geoffrey said. The devil's mask sat on his face; his eyes were cruel and cold. "You leave me because you think me faithless. I am. But from you I demand that fealty which is your ideal. If you are untrue, Humphrey, I shall come to you and tear the remnant of your manhood, and put out your eyes, and burn you living at the stake. Do not break your oath, my friend."

I sank on my knees, and held his hand in mine, and cried bitter tears.

"Too late for weeping, Humphrey." His tone was suddenly brisk. "You will rebuild your castle. That is an order. Matilda still holds Oxford and Wallingford. Winchester is a ruin. I shall need an outpost on Anjou's marches, the constable a liegeman I can trust, ready to raid or desist at my command. That is your charge – a dangerous one. Go now and fulfil it!"

I raised a stricken face to his. "My lord —"

"A different concept from your peaceful farmer's life?" His voice was savage. "You fool! Did you think I would not use you to the end? Will you never realize what I am?"

I blundered from his presence, tripped on the threshold and fell.

Count Geoffrey laughed.

4

I enlisted a constabular: twelve knights, their sergeants, and a dozen extra men-at-arms. The campaign was over and mercenaries sold their swords anew. I had more offers than I needed. Men seemed eager to serve beneath my banner. "Why should you wonder, Humphrey?" Odinel answered my surprise. "You have a famous reputation as a true and valiant knight. Even in these days men prefer the best when they can find it."

Odinel, of course, shared the booty we had found in the sunken lane. Now that he had more wealth than many a baron I expected he would return at last to Prudhoe, but he wagged his head and laughed. "No, Humphrey – I should be foolish to leave you. In your company I have become a rich man – first Waleran's ransom, now this. Who knows where it may end? – we have not yet sacked Matilda's treasury in Bristol. Besides, you suit my humour and make me laugh. I have quit Count Geoffrey's service – now I enter yours." He added with a twinkle, "How much will you pay me?"

One week after the Rout I led fifty fighting-men from Winchester. I had no more speech with Count Geoffrey since that hateful scene in his pavilion. He returned to London before I left. I tried to forget his cruelty, with little success, and strove to ignore the numbing sorrow which festered like a mortal wound. Sometimes I wakened in the night and roused my servant and called for wine to drown the pain. Morning found me heavy-eyed, with a throbbing head, and misery aching in my heart.

We came to Bochesorne at the first streak of dawn. The years had blurred my memory of the once-familiar scene, like a painting on a church-wall smeared by rain. Then all at once it was there again: the river drifting like a wisp of smoke through grassy meadows, red-berried thorn-scrub on Rood Hill, an October-mellow tree-cloak mantling the slopes beyond. The same yet not the same: shapeless, nettle-grown humps where once a village stood, the fields of wilderness, the Hall's flaked walls and broken thatch; and no life anywhere, no beasts, nor hearth-smoke mingling with the mist. Jagged stumps like severed fingers crowned the castle mound; scrub elder raddled the slopes.

We picketed our horses and unyoked ox-carts in what had been the bailey – a tangled waste of thorn and bramble – cleared a space and pitched tents.

I began rebuilding the castle.

Labour was our main difficulty. I sent horsemen to scour fields and woods. They collected a score of frightened peasants, survivors of the harrying, who scratched a living from untilled fields or lived like outlaws in the forest. The sergeants worked with a will; even knights swung axe and pick, since they knew that without defences we were vulnerable. I did not know what lay beyond our marches, whether to expect interference or not. News of our arrival would travel slowly from this deserted fastness, and we could rely at least on a few days' grace.

Within three sunsets we had uprooted the blackened, greasy stumps of the old keep, and cleared undergrowth from mound and bailey. More English came, like cockroaches from crevices at nightfall, because I broke all laws and gave the villeins money for their labour – the word spread swiftly and lured others from hiding. The work went faster. I built a more commodious keep with stouter wall, three oak-trunks thick; a new stockade girdled the mound's summit. The moat was dredged and deepened; the bailey palisade rebuilt. I cleaned the well – a skeleton mouldered in the depths – and sank another in the keep. Within fifteen days the work was done.

I set my lance on the battlements. The wolf's-head banner snapped bravely in the wind and snarled at all the world.

Visdelou was home again.

I sent to London for Ranulf; and told him to bring Saiva and Anschitel.

5

Saiva descended from her palfrey, curtsied and kissed my hands and gave me formal greeting. Her cheeks were flushed, her green eyes sparkled. I led her into the keep, to the first-floor chamber which was both armoury and living-room, where a sergeant scrubbed a haubergeon and a serving-woman laid a fire on the flintstone hearth. The chamber, lit only by a trapdoor to the battlements, was very dark : after the experience of Hamo's siege I allowed no arrow-slits in the walls. In a corner I had built a planked partition, just large enough to take two pallets and a coffer. This was our bedchamber. We went inside.

Saiva flung her arms around my neck and kissed me passionately. "Humphrey! Never have we been apart so long! Be quick, my sweetling – I am parched for love!"

I ripped her robe. She lay on the pallet, legs spread wide, and panted. "Hasten, my love, hasten! Why do you dally?"

I fumbled in my wallet. Saiva laughed tremulously. "Must an armourer rasp his file upon my belly? Send for him, Humphrey – I can wait no more!"

I found the key, unlocked the girdle and slid the iron gently from her thighs. I stroked the welts it left upon her skin. She gasped, and wrapped her legs around me like a wrestler.

We stayed there for a day and a night, and in that time I gave to her my son.

Ranulf rode round the manor, and talked to the villeins. Naturally I appointed him bailiff. He chose a reeve, and field-work began

219

under proper supervision. He authorized tree-felling to build cottages, cut rushes for thatch, started rebuilding the mill. He took carts to Hungerford and Reading, and returned with seed-corn, bill-hooks and sickles, cows and a bull, sheep and hogs and plough-oxen, and sacks of grain for the peasants. There had been no harvests: they had lived on acorns, berries and roots, snared birds and dug grubs from tree-bark. Little by little he subtracted from the treasure – now safely bestowed in the keep – jewels and brace-lets and other valuables, and sold them to merchants for silver. He never made an unprofitable bargain.

By mid-December the fields were ploughed and harrowed, the wheat and barley sown. Cattle lowed in byres, sheep grazed the last of the season's grass, and children played at cottage doors. The manor, like bracken after winter's frosts, uncurled the tendrils of a new existence.

Anschitel had grown old. The Tower's chilly, stone-walled damp-ness, the Thames-side fogs, had seeped into his bones and racked his joints. The square, sturdy shoulders were a little bowed, the leathern visage pinched and pallid. I restored him to his former place as steward of my household, and was careful to appoint a capable sergeant – a Breton who had once marched with William de Warenne – as his underling and assistant. Gradually, without ostentation or offence, the Breton took over the old man's duties; and Anschitel contentedly became my armour-bearer and horse-master – my squire had gone with Count Geoffrey – and took charge of three destriers and three chain-mesh mail-coats. Some-times, when I saw him seated on a hay-truss in the bailey, happily burnishing armour, I wondered whether he remembered my father's ancient disc-mail hauberk, and Chanson's predecessor who was burned alive.

I built a hall inside the bailey, a wooden house where we ate our meals and the garrison slept. We were very crowded, but this was nothing new: castles were always crammed – even the Tower. The war was all around us; the habit of castle life had grown strong over the years; without the protection of stockade and moat, mound and keep, I felt naked and defenceless.

Cautiously I probed the fiefs upon our marches. Little was changed. Gervase de Salnerville still ruled at Donnington; my sister Isabel, given in his charge, had wedded, a year since, a wealthy London goldsmith. She now lived in Chensnetune, a village near the city. Gervase was apologetic, but I shrugged – worse things happened to women in these times than marriage to a base-born merchant.

After Hamo de Neufmarché's death a freebooting knight called Payn de Chaworth raided his fief, ejected his vassals and settled on the land. He built a castle at Newburgh and thereafter seemed content, since he made no effort to extend his territory and left his neighbours unmolested. I remembered the Neufmarché family's power, the many fiefs they held in England and the knights they led, and wondered how long Payn would be permitted to enjoy his lawless acquisition.

Ranulf, from the markets, brought news of the world outside. In November the two mighty prisoners, King Stephen and Count Robert of Gloucester, were exchanged; and at Christmas Stephen, to cleanse the tarnish from his majesty, celebrated a second coronation at Canterbury. So the balance rested level, and four years of war had gone for nothing. I reflected on Count Geoffrey's satisfaction, and found, surprisingly, no rancour in the thought. Bochesorne's comfortable routine healed bitterness; the shadow of de Mandeville was lifting from my heart.

I restored the church, an ivy-creepered, roofless ruin; and hinted to Ranulf that he should resume his priestly duties. He shook his head.

"I have done too much that is unholy, and condoned more. Never again can I administer the Church's sacraments to sinners when I myself have sinned beyond redemption. This sacred burden I am no longer fit to bear. My lord, I beg you to excuse me."

I had not forgotten Ranulf's bloodied spear at Allerton. I pressed him no further. He travelled to Abingdon, and spoke with the abbot. What he said I do not know; but he returned with a clerk, a lettered man and able, although English, and installed him in the church.

In March I married Saiva.

I took no advice and suffered none. A knight does not wed his leman. Men of my rank regard as criminal the sullying of noble blood. Saiva claimed nobility – she may well have spoken truth, though I have small regard for English ancestry. But I loved her, and she bore my child within her belly. Better, I thought, that a half-Norman Visdelou should reign at Bochesorne after I had gone than none at all. I knew my time was short: Count Geoffrey held my fealty, and the realm was still at war.

A knight who sneered and failed to bend his knee before my lady got my dagger in his throat. I hung his body on the gallows. That warning ended reservations – knight and sergeant, varlet and tirewoman accepted Saiva as the baron's lady and their mistress. She was well content, and ruled her household with a firm but easy hand.

Bochesorne followed a fair course to prosperity. Benham remained. I rode there on an April day with Odinel and surveyed the desolate fields and ruinous hall whence peasant squatters fled at our approach. We dismounted, gave our horses to attendants, and picked a way among fallen rafters.

"All to be done again," I said. "Clearing the undergrowth, ploughing, rebuilding – everything. Too much for me to undertake at this season."

I tugged my ear, and hesitated.

"Odinel," I said, laying a hand on his shoulder, "would you hold this fief of me? If you will, you shall have it without obligation – I shall not demand your homage."

Odinel's face for once was serious. He said formally, "You do me honour, my lord. But no man can hold land without doing homage and owing service – it would be against all usage and custom."

"You refuse, then?"

He knelt and put his hands in mine, and bowed his head.

"Umfrai Visdelou, jo sui vostre liges hum par fei e par humage."

I raised him to his feet. He said, "I can refuse you nothing, Humphrey. We both know who holds my true allegiance – I have been your man for many months. For Benham manor I do you homage. To yourself, my shining knight, I give my fealty and heart."

Tears stood in his eyes. He rubbed his nose savagely and added, "You do not realize your own quality, Humphrey – that strange attraction which compels men to follow you for love alone. If Geoffrey de Mandeville had not so ensnared your soul —"

I said, "A man must have a star to guide him – he is mine."

"God save you when your star falls from the heavens. Your way will then be truly dark."

Odinel spat, and turned to survey Benham's crumbling walls. "Persuasion is useless – you will never change. We become gloomy, Humphrey. Look at that gaping roof! This is a pretty ruin you have foisted on my back!"

In July my son was born.

Saiva pouted and declared him matchless among children, his beauty marred only by a single blemish: a cast in the left eye. I laughed, and squinted vilely at her, and told her she was fortunate, for the tiny squint was proof of chastity: only a Visdelou could beget the Visdelou brand.

I named him Walchelin.

Remembering my brother William's fate, I insisted that Odinel build a castle at Benham. He demurred, and spoke of royal licences. "King Henry is seven years dead," I told him. "His peace is gone. Stephen cannot control his barons – each man must guard his own, with or without a licence."

I gave him five knights and fifteen sergeants, and thereby relieved Bochesorne's congestion. The tides of war lapped far away and we were not disturbed. Once a small conroy – sergeant mercenaries – looted an outlying steadying. I turned out Bochesorne's garrison, pursued and caught them, killed three and hanged the rest. Only five years since, I reflected grimly, watching the bodies dancing upon air, such summary justice would have brought on me a royal writ and all the processes of law. Times indeed were changed.

One crisp October morning I had warning that knights and men-at-arms in full panoply of war were traversing my land along the Bochesorne trackway. I fired the beacon on Rood Hill to warn Odinel, closed the castle gates and manned the palisades. The constabular crossed the marshy causeway where Hamo's knights had once plodded to disaster at the ford. I saw gilt and scarlet shields – the heralds of the summons that I dreaded.

Ernulf rode in the van. I opened the gate, dropped the bridge and made him welcome. Seated on a trestle in the bailey hall, he explained his presence.

"On my way to Oxford. Matilda's there. King Stephen's taken the town. Besieging the countess in the castle."

"And Count Geoffrey?"

"With the king. I go to join him."

"So. My lord is faithful to his latest oath. You surprise me, Ernulf. He swore to Queen Maud over a year ago. I did not know he could be trusted for so long."

Ernulf sent me an odd look. He took his goblet and stood. "Let us be private, Humphrey. Something to tell you."

We strolled from the hall, across the bailey bridge, and went to the tilt-yard where my knights, relieved from battle-stations, sported happily with sword and lance.

Ernulf said, "Miss you, Humphrey. You used to carry the burden of my father's plots. I could get on with my proper job – commanding his troops. Now he confides in me. Tricky. Try to follow the convolutions of his mind. Like riding an assault-course in a bog, blindfolded, without reins."

He paused and took a sip of wine.

"The king was sick this summer. Like to die. Many barons read the writing, as they thought, upon the wall. Hastened to Matilda. Swore allegiance. Count Geoffrey among them."

I nibbled a grass-stem. The stalk's fresh sweetness soothed a bitter taste that suddenly fouled my mouth.

"Why, therefore, is he now with Stephen?"

Ernulf broodingly watched a knight who charged the quintain. "That destrier's going short. Lame off-fore. Why? Remember that message you took to Count Robert, before you went gallivanting off to Lincoln?"

"I do. Count Geoffrey can't carry out that scheme at Stephen's side."

"Can and will, when the time is ripe. The plot has burgeoned since last you heard. Hugh Bigod of Norfolk is in it with my father. They'll both strike from Anglia, at Stephen's back, while Matilda hurls her armies at him from the west. Crack the king between them like a nut."

He gulped his wine. "Good stuff, this. Better than the campaigning brew I live on now. I must admit," he said regretfully, "that Geoffrey's strategy is sound – if he chooses the right time to strike."

"Which," I said, "will be when Stephen looks like winning the war outright."

"Correct." Ernulf crowned a straw dummy with his empty cup. "The king recovered from his sickness in July. The rest had done him good. Went on the rampage. Took Wareham, Cirencester, Bampton and Radcot in a row."

"And Count Geoffrey changed sides again?"

"He changed sides," Ernulf agreed grimly. "Obviously you understand his bent. Supports the faction with the upper hand. Until it grows too strong. The king at present has Matilda pinned in Oxford

224

castle. Her prospects don't look bright. But Count Robert is loose. Raising new armies in Anjou. When he lands again in England I think my beloved father might fulfil his grand strategical design."

I spat the grass-stem from my mouth. "Ernulf, has King Stephen no inkling of this?"

Ernulf fumbled between his shoulder-blades for the dangling helmet, and set it on his head. "Must get on – lingered here long enough. Stephen," he continued, "is a valiant knight. Also a political idiot – or so my father says. But the king isn't blind. I think, sometimes, Count Geoffrey underestimates him."

We walked to the castle. Ernulf called to his men to tighten girths.

I said hesitantly, "Has my lord no message for me? I expected his summons long before this."

"Never mentions your name. Seems to have forgotten all about you."

I bit my lip. Ernulf looked into my face. A frown sat on his swarthy face, but his eyes were kind.

"If you're wise, Humphrey," he added gently, "you'll do nothing to remind him."

7

The war was nearer to my marches than I liked. Like ants contending for a lump of dung the armies swarmed round Oxford, less than thirty miles away. Yet we were left in peace. No highways crossed my land, no fortress guarding some important place frowned over the empty downlands that surrounded us. The region held no value in the eyes of captains who directed war. For so much I was thankful – we could not withstand armies. There were other dangers, less predictable: marauding barons waging private war, or freebooting soldiers. Against such lesser menaces I had built my castle and enlisted knights.

In January I heard that Stephen had taken Oxford castle, but lost Matilda. The story of her escape sounded improbable, although the wandering troubadour who brought the news assured me it was true: she was lowered from the battlements on a rope and fled, white-clad in surrounding snow, to Wallingford and safety. Count Robert landed in England, and recaptured Wareham.

The war went on.

Winter waned, and work resumed on the fields. I settled some of my best sergeants on smallholdings, and thereby saved my silver. One knight, bored by inaction, left my service. The status of the others changed imperceptibly over the months. Our rib-to-rib existence in the castle planed the edges of formality: I got to know them well and liked them better. From hired soldiers they became household knights, bachelor companions of hawk-flight and hunt, tilt-yard and carousal, recipients of my bounty rather than a settled wage. They all kept lemans in the bailey huts, tumbled serving wenches and seduced my villeins' daughters. But they were gentlemen and knew discretion: they left the wives alone.

My second son was born in June. I named him William. Odinel married our neighbour Gervase de Salnerville's daughter Athelais, a demure brown-eyed girl who laughed dutifully at his quips and, I suspect, bullied him in private, for he was a soft-hearted man. The celebration of their nuptials lasted two nights and a day; on the second day's dawning a pedlar on a donkey could have taken Benham – even the sentries slumbered drunkenly on the battlements.

Haystacks towered in meadows high as castle keeps; the wheat and barley harvest was abundant, the wool-crop heavy; fifty head of cattle grazed the meadows. Prosperity lapped the Honour like a comfortable robe; we felt happy and secure in our lives. Someone told me, one August afternoon, that the king was heavily defeated, his army scattered and his castles lost. Wilton, where it happened, lay more than fifty miles away. I yawned. The day was hot. My feet were itching badly – could it be lice? Should I cool myself in the river? I had not had a bath for months. No – unwise, perhaps: cold water in the heat might bring a fever.

I settled lower in my chair, and dozed peacefully.

8

The beech-leaves were yellowing when Ernulf came again. Sweat dewed his face; mire-stains of hard travel spattered his armour; lather and spur-rowels streaked his palfrey's flanks.

"De Mandeville summons his liegemen," he said without preamble. "You have sworn fealty, Humphrey Visdelou Do you ride with me?"

226

I turned my eyes from his exhausted face and gazed over green meadows, the ochre fields where peasants ploughed, the sunflecked golden mist above the river. A herdsman called his cattle: the lingering cry wailed like a sad farewell.

"Count Geoffrey has my faith," I answered quietly. "I obey his summons. What crisis calls me to his side?"

Ernulf said, "He's been outwitted. Stephen called him to council at St Albans. I told him not to go. Heard rumours – plots against him. Geoffrey thought himself inviolable – the king's writ of summons is supposedly a guarantee of safe conduct; and St Albans, in demesne of Holy Church, is sacrosanct. Made no difference. Stephen arrested him. Took him to the Tower, Walden, Plessy. Put a noose round his neck and forced him to order the garrisons out. Lost all his castles."

He slid wearily from the saddle.

"Count Geoffrey fled into the Fens of Anglia. He gathers an army to make war against the king – war of a kind that England will for ever remember."

Ernulf buried his face in his hands.

"Rage has bereft him of all reason. I think he's going insane."

15

October, 1143 — September, 1144

"So the king," I said, "that paragon of courtoisie, has himself muddied his hands in the midden of betrayal."

Clouded twilight of an autumn evening darkened the hall. Firelight flung grotesque shadows on timbered walls, tinted rose and russet the faces of knights and squires. Servitors socketed torches in cressets, and placed a girandole on the table where we sat.

Ernulf stared wearily into the candles. He said, "Of course. He has fought my father with his own weapons, and overreached him."

Odinel said, "Humphrey, why are you going? You hold no lands of the count, and therefore owe him no service. Moreover, if you are taken in arms against the king, you are likely to forfeit your manors. Have you thought of that?"

"I have." I gazed down the crowded tables. My knights, enlivened by the presence of Ernulf's companions, raised a boisterous din. Servants zealously refilled wine cups. Fire-smoke and torch-fumes hung like a storm cloud below the rafters. "It makes no difference, Odinel."

He sighed. "I didn't think it would. When do we march?"

"I leave at dawn with Ernulf. You remain here."

Odinel set down his goblet carefully, and glowered. "What are you saying? Why —"

"You remain here. You are my vassal and obey my orders. I leave Bochesorne and Benham in your charge. No, Odinel. There can be no argument about this."

I left him speechless, and walked across the bailey. Rags of sunset splashed like scarlet flames across a dark horizon. I climbed the ladder and entered the keep. My children slept together in a coffer-like cradle placed in a corner. A tirewoman, sewing on a stool

228

beside them, rose and brought candles. For a long time I gazed on the faces of my sons.

Saiva came softly from the bedchamber. She put her hands on my shoulders, and laid her face against mine.

"I cannot dissuade you?"

"No, my love. I must go."

Her body quivered. I felt the tears upon her cheeks.

"I think that you will never return, my Humphrey."

"If God is merciful —"

"No!" Her nails dug into my flesh. "You have abandoned God and yielded your soul to a devil from Hell. His dominion over you defeats the understanding of poor mortals like myself."

I stroked her hair; and reflected sombrely that Saiva's bewilderment was not unreasonable. No material compulsion forced me to Count Geoffrey's side; a fugitive in Anglia, he could no longer reach me; the fearful threats he had uttered at Winchester were empty as the wind. Yet I could not think for one moment of forsaking him.

Saiva sobbed against my shoulder. I led her gently to the bedchamber, and comforted her sorrow.

At daybreak Anschitel roused and armed me. I descended to the bailey, to a cold and cheerless dawn where men and horses moved like grey phantoms in the mist. Ernulf, already mounted, grunted a brusque greeting. I inspected my retinue – three sergeants and five varlets who led rounceys and two destriers: Chanson and Baucan – and balked at a ninth figure, in haubergeon and helmet, who flanked the line. I peered into the soldier's face.

"What foolishness is this?" I demanded harshly. "Get down from that palfrey, Ranulf, and return to your accounts!"

"I have instructed the English priest, my lord," he answered mildly. "A lettered man – well competent to figure and to tally."

"Do you disobey my orders? Dismount!"

"I am a free man, my lord, free to go wherever I will." He leaned from the saddle and whispered in my ear. "I am also your brother, Humphrey. I think, in this adventure, you will sometimes need my help."

Ernulf called impatiently. I said no more. One cannot argue with an obstinate man in the half-dark bustle of departure. Also, strangely enough, the fury roused by his defiance was mingled with a gladness and a lightening of my heart.

We clattered across the bridge, and left Bochesorne behind.

At Fordham Count Geoffrey had built a castle, and there his vassals gathered.

This was a countryside whose like I had not seen – flat, nearly treeless, desolate, where the slightest hill towered like the ramparts of a fort. The earth was heavy, yellow and sodden, a dreary waste-land fringing marshland solitudes of reeds and rushes, roadless, almost trackless, the secret ways known only to the English who lived like water-animals in the watery wilderness. A more improb-able country for the vagrancies of war I could not imagine.

Count Geoffrey had no intention of waging regular warfare.

He received me in the bailey, at the entrance to his dwelling – a mere hut, quite unlike the luxurious pavilions he usually in-habited. I knelt before him, and murmured a greeting. His eyes flicked my face. He replied tonelessly, the polite phrases cold upon his lips. Then he resumed his discourse to the knights assembled in council.

"We march to Ely, but not to battle. Bishop Nigel is no friend of Stephen's – his knights will receive us kindly. They will hold Ely castle, and Aldreth also, on my behalf; thus securing the Isle of Ely as my base."

I listened to the outline of his plans, and studied the man I served. Count Geoffrey had greatly changed. His eyes, sunk deep into his head, glittered feverishly. Deep furrows scored his pallid cheeks from chin to nostrils. A brittle intensity, a jerkiness of speech and gesture, replaced the languid calm that I had known. He never smiled, and seldom frowned: his face was still, like a corpse or graven image – compulsive, arrogant, and merciless.

"From Ely we go north and west, and build castles to engird the fens which are our shield and refuge. We shall meet no opposi-tion, for no armies are yet ranged against us. Nor do we seek en-counter till the castle-ring is ready."

A hundred knights were in his audience, all Geoffrey's vassals, and four hundred sergeants camped on puddled fields beyond the moat. I wondered that King Stephen, when he took Count Geoffrey's castles, had not escheated his fiefs and so deprived him of a follow-ing. Possibly he had; probably my lord summoned his liegemen before the writs arrived.

Geoffrey continued, "We shall not seek the enemy; we shall let him come to us. And come he will, for I shall wreak such havoc in the lands beyond our castles, in the fiefs of Stephen's barons, that he must hasten to his vassals' aid.

"When his armies arrive to seek us we shall not oppose them in the open, but try rather to lure them into the watery fastnesses we guard, and there ambush and destroy them."

Someone in the crowd said, "A hundred knights against King Stephen's armies? Lengthy odds, my lord. What do we live on? Fish?" He pointed to the dreary flats beyond the bailey wall. "This waste of reeds grow nothing to feed man or beast."

"We are not alone," Geoffrey said coldly. "Count Hugh will send supplies from Norfolk. To south and east our lines of communication are open. At Walden, once my castle" – his lips curled bitterly – "King Stephen's constable is my friend: he keeps the road to Essex for my wagon-trains. For what else you lack, the country to the west – when once I give the word – is yours to harry as you will."

He paused. A muscle quivered in his cheek.

"This you must know: I fight my war without scruple or remorse. I shall spare nothing, neither man nor child, hall nor hovel, church nor chapel. If any among you fear the Pope's anathema let him now depart, for in a little time we shall all be surely damned."

Geoffrey turned sharply and went into his hut.

3

We left a garrison in Fordham, and marched to Ely. On this journey I saw something of the difficult country where we had to fight. We went through reed-forests taller than a horseman, and rode in single file on narrow trackways that wound erratically over marshland and squelched malignantly beneath our hooves. Here a man could lose himself within a pace, and suffocate in a quagmire or drown unseen in a hundred rivulets that coiled like brown worms among the rushes. Count Geoffrey bought guides, English peasant dwellers in the fens, and paid them well – on them his projects and our lives depended.

The Isle of Ely, eight miles long, wallowed in the marshes like a waterlogged hulk. Towards the northern end stood Ely's abbey church and village, guarded by a castle; in the south Aldreth castle overlooked the fens. On the Isle were cultivated fields, ploughed and sown, and villages and steadings and cattle in the meadows. We lingered for a time while my lord inspected the forts, well garrisoned by Bishop Nigel's sixty knights of the Honour of St Etheldreda.

I seldom accompanied Count Geoffrey on these excursions. An intolerable itching afflicted my hands and feet, and an intermittent fever kept me to my tent.

In December Count Geoffrey led his army to Ramsey, sixteen miles west. On a freezing morning we surrounded the abbey buildings, overcame a few unready knights, and stormed into the monastery. From dorter and infirmary, chapter-house and cloister – where later we stabled our horses – we ejected monks and left them, lightly garbed, to wander homeless over frost-rimed fields. The abbot alone resisted: a knight threw him in a ditch. Then we pillaged church and monastery, stripped altars, and piled the treasure high on the cloister sward. The haul was rich. My lord divided the plunder justly; and at the end stood hands on hips and regarded his knights as they gathered up the spoil.

"Enjoy your booty, my lords," he said. "You and I – all of us – are henceforward excommunicate."

They blenched and dropped the loot they held. These knights were not soldiers: all were Geoffrey's vassals, decent gentlemen who farmed their fiefs, inured to warfare but shuddering from sacrilege and the Curse of Christ. Geoffrey looked at their awed faces; a faint trace of the old sardonic humour flickered in his eyes.

"The thing is done, my lords. There can be no going back."

He allowed no time for reflection, but commanded them immediately to start converting the abbey into a fortress. Stray monks who had not strayed far enough were rounded up and put to labour. The church tower made a formidable keep – Anglia's only stone-built castle north of Colchester – and cloister and chapter-house formed natural bailey wards. Beyond these boundaries Geoffrey ordered extensive demolitions, throwing down rere-dorter and chapel and other buildings which might hinder his bowmen's field of view or afford approach to an enemy. Walter the abbot, muddied from his sojourn in the ditch, raised hands to heaven and lamented that the House of God was become a den of thieves. Count Geoffrey impassively agreed – and took from Walter's finger a garnet ring incautiously displayed.

The work was finished in three days. My lord detailed a garrison

232

and put me in command. He said, "I have intentionally given you more men than you need, so that you can form a striking force – a flying column to ravage when I send you word."

He departed to Walton, six miles west, built a castle there and appointed Ernulf constable. Then to Benwick, five miles north by east, and another castle. In January he returned through Ramsey, and went to Ely.

The castle ring was set, his dispositions ready. Outriders brought the message we awaited.

"Go forth, and burn, and harry, and destroy."

4

I aimed first at religious houses. They always contained a wealth of gold and silver, and offerings left at shrines by generations of worshippers. The common people deposited valuables there for safety: a precaution lately encouraged by Stephen's edicts against sacrilege, which simple countryfolk foolishly accounted a guarantee against profane marauders.

I conducted the raid as a military operation, carefully planned beforehand. This foray, and others after it – the battles of more orthodox warfare – was vital to the success of Count Geoffrey's campaign. I threw a cordon round the monastery, and set pickets to watch the roads to Huntingdon and Cambridge. I did not really expect interference. A vassal of Scotland's king held Huntingdon – he was unlikely to interest himself in the tribulations of St Benedict's monks five miles away.

A storming party axed the doors and charged into the church and priory buildings. I had appointed certain knights to seek and dispatch, if necessary, the abbey knights – tenants on the monastic demesnes who sometimes, for the brethren's protection, resided in the chapter. They lived soft lives, were seldom valiant, surrendered easily, and afforded us some useful ransoms.

We broke into all the buildings, smashed open cupboards and coffers and snatched everything of value. Sergeants detailed for the purpose roved adjacent steadings, collected carts and draught-oxen, grain and animals – few enough in this winter season when only breeding stock was left alive – and salted meat and human captives. A comely peasant woman rarely escaped. We loaded our

233

plunder on carts and fired the village – a mistake, as I discovered later, since valuable trinkets hidden beneath earth-floor or in thatch, could often be discovered after a little compulsion. Then, guarding the long train of carts, and driving the animals we left the pyre behind and returned to Ramsey.

Such was my first foray: a quick in-and-out raid when fear of retaliation dictated speed. Later, after experience showed that reprisals never came, I adopted more leisurely methods and roved for days from church to church, village to village, and became much more thorough in extracting the last fistful of plunder from every crevice. Occasionally Ernulf joined me with a conroy from Walton. I learned from him ingenious ways of persuading recalcitrant peasants to disgorge their little hoards. He hung them head-down over smoky fires, or strung them by the thumbs from rafters and tied hauberks to their legs until the increasing weight ripped muscle and sinew. When pressed for time, or just impatient, he thrust a red-hot spearhead up the anus: a most effective stimulus which no one ever resisted.

These interludes sickened Ranulf. In Ramsey he managed my armour and horses. When he accompanied me on raids he kept an inventory of the treasure we took, and saw to my comfort – such as it was – in huts and stables where I camped at night. Once, watching a prisoner squirming in the fire, he muttered, "For the love of Christ, my lord, have you no pity? These men are God's creatures, created in your own image, feeling pain as you do."

At that moment, unfortunately, the peasant strained at his bonds, shuddered, and died. He had not told us what we wanted to know. The man was English. Despite living all my life among the English they were, to me, still alien, barely human. I could feel no remorse.

"Ranulf," I said briskly, "Count Geoffrey must feed his army, and pay for his soldiers. These wretches possess what he must have – need only speak to avoid being hurt. I do not torture for amusement."

He went behind a cowshed. I heard him vomiting. Afterwards I discouraged his presence on my raids. After all, he was not a knight, and could not really understand the necessities of war.

My ravages spread farther and farther, to Peterborough and Oundle and Kimbolton. I did not destroy every village: when the local landholder – knight or sergeant – seemed sufficiently prosperous I saved time and trouble by demanding protection money to reprieve his estate. If he could not find the bribe – which we called 'tenserie' – I told him to raise a mortgage on his property and held him prisoner until he paid his ransom. Some of these men were very obstinate – particularly the Normans – and had to be persuaded. One of my sergeants invented a new trick, the crucethus – he half-filled a coffer with sharp flints, put the victim in, and piled more stones on top. Then he closed the lid.

Meanwhile, in the south, Count Geoffrey rampaged from Ely. He descended without warning on Cambridge, sacked churches, plundered and fired the town. A royal castle guarded Cambridge: the constable closed the gate and watched helplessly while a holocaust raged round him. My lord then roved farther afield, and harried to the Essex borders.

His exploits, and mine, and the prospects of endless spoil, attracted mercenary knights and sergeants. Elsewhere in England the clamour of war was muted: we heard only of minor affrays, mostly indecisive. Soldiers lacked employment; they swarmed to Count Geoffrey's banner, and he sent them to his castles. Some came to Ramsey. They were iron men, predatory and ruthless, the knights base-born and mannerless. Urged by a craving for loot, they gave a new impetus to my harrying, and ardently devastated the few localities I had left untouched. Tenserie no longer availed; they plundered the donors despite their contributions. I could not approve, for I had given my knightly word that they should be spared; but for a time I was unable to control the soldiers' depredations. Fever racked me again; rust-coloured blotches whose itching so tormented me that I could not sleep, appeared on hands and feet. I called Ranulf, and did not understand the horror on his face, nor why he should cross himself and hesitate to touch my skin. He pulled himself together, rubbed ointment on the sores and bandaged them. Then he fell on his knees and prayed. I watched him in wonder, but the fever ran fiercely and bemused my mind, and I forgot to question him.

After a time the blemishes faded, the fever cooled, and I recovered.

By the end of March the army's character was altering. Count Geoffrey's enfeoffed knights, on completing forty days' service, began returning to their manors. The farming year had started: they wished to supervise the husbandry on their estates. Because booty had enriched them they could not be persuaded to fight on for pay. The vassals that remained were the hard men, knights who loved war above all else, whose greed for plunder was insatiable.

Soldiers replaced those that left: men born to warfare, competent and merciless – but impatient of discipline and difficult to control. They fought for profit, and often killed for fun.

The rivers of loot flowing eastwards from the ravaged lands began to ebb. Nothing was left. This was the season of ploughing and sowing, but you could easily go a day's journey without finding a village inhabited or a field cultivated. The people starved. Their granaries were ransacked, empty, even the seed-corn taken; their breeding-stock – cattle, sheep and pigs – was gone; no oxen remained to draw ploughs – for a space of thirty miles from Ramsey neither ox nor plough was to be seen. Emaciated corpses, torn by wolves, lay unburied in fields. Nor, lacking physical subsistence, could they gain spiritual comfort: the churches, burnt and broken, yawned rafterless to the skies.

Men said openly, in those days, that Christ and His saints slept.

5

Count Geoffrey paid fleeting visits to his outposts all through the winter, riding from castle to castle, inspecting garrisons, checking provisions, listening silently to the histories of our depredations. Then he departed, sometimes taking with him part of the plunder, either to pay his troops elsewhere or buy supplies which still trickled to Ely from Hugh Bigod's Norfolk or from Essex. To me he was not unfriendly, but always chilly and withdrawn. I was the lowly vassal of a mighty count, no longer a trusted liegeman worthy of his confidences.

In the spring he came to Ramsey with a powerful conroy – thirty knights and a hundred men-at-arms – and made his quarters in the castle. He travelled eastwards, taking a small escort and an English guide, and vanished for two days in the marshes. Afterwards he summoned Ernulf from Walton, and called a council of his knights.

Count Geoffrey said, "King Stephen's armies are on the march. Spies tell me he intends to concentrate at Huntingdon, and afterwards will hunt us to destruction.

"The king's forces are far greater than mine. I lead ten score knights – he has five hundred. Therefore I cannot meet him in open battle.

"My intention is this: to lure my enemies into the fenlands, by

236

pathways I have lately reconnoitred, and there ambush and destroy them.

"I shall at once evacuate my advanced post at Walton. Ernulf, your garrison will join the conroy I have brought from Ely. Together we shall form a roving company to trail our mantles before King Stephen's men and lead them to their deaths.

"My castles here and at Benwick, at Fordham and the Isle of Ely, can withstand anything the king may bring against them. He will not, I think, waste time on leaguers – his object is to force a battle which will smash me and my army."

My lord gave detailed orders, and took his knights on reconnaissance deep into the fens. In this I was not concerned: as constable of Ramsey my duty was to ensure that the king did not overwhelm the castle when he advanced. Digging and re-fortifying, I devoted myself to this end during the days that followed.

On the ninth day Count Geoffrey's spies brought word that the king's army was camped round the castle at Huntingdon. My lord sent a dismounted conroy to prepare an ambuscade beside a pathway winding through the reeds, and included arbalesters – he had never disbanded them, despite the Papal edict five years before. With the ambush ready he led forth his knights, and disappeared westwards in the haze of an April dawn.

I heard later how he stirred the hornets' nest. Swinging in a wide arc, Geoffrey approached Stephen's encampment from the west – whence he was least expected – and fell like an iron cataract on the baggage-park. In a brief but furious spate of slaughter his knights speared horses and oxen, guards-knights and varlets. They finished in a headlong gallop through the fringes of the camp, slashing pavilions and killing all they met. Withdrawing in good order, they took the shortest route to the marshland.

The king's men, infuriated, found their destriers and followed close behind.

Count Geoffrey, riding fast but with discretion, so that his pursuers never lost the trail, led them far into the wilderness, into the place of ambush, where quarrells suddenly whirred and arrows whipped and swinging swords erupted from the reeds.

Of thirty knights only three escaped. A score of sergeants died.

This shattering reverse did not at once teach King Stephen caution. Thrice more, between Benwick and St Ives, he tried to penetrate the swampy wastelands that protected us, using English guides to find the hidden causeways. Our pickets were alert, our patrols active; always we had forewarning. Count Geoffrey's knights knew the secret ways better than they, and let them wander past redemption, until reeds swayed high above their heads and pathways trembled warningly beneath their hooves. Then Geoffrey struck. He killed a number and captured more – but his arbalesters lost him many a ransom, for men do not easily survive a quarrell wound.

From two of Stephen's expeditions there were no survivors.

The king switched his operations farther south, and sent his conroys between Aldreth and Fordham. Count Geoffrey left Ernulf at Ramsey to command the northern front, and took me with him when he hurried back to Ely. The pattern was repeated; the king fared no better. Day by day the hidden fighting flared among the reeds, and brave knights died where none would ever find their graves.

Before midsummer the attacks ended. My lord's outriders searched in vain for the glint of helmets on the tracks; his spies were mute. Stephen's army, still encamped at Huntingdon, growled like a wounded leopard and licked its wounds.

In June we saw the king's new strategy unfold. His conroys, circling the fenlands, marched north and south. They built seven castles in a ring that engirded us like a steel-studded belt. Stephen left strong garrisons, and provisions for a year, struck his tents at Huntingdon and marched away.

Count Geoffrey rode from Ely on a tour of reconnaissance, and inspected from a distance the king's new forts in turn. He returned to the Isle, and called his bannerets together.

"We are under siege," he announced flatly. "Stephen has set his castles to cut the roads which bring our supplies. I myself have seen them intercept, at Weeting, a wagon train the Count of Norfolk sent."

Ernulf said, "The castles can't stop us plundering beyond the fens."

"To what end?" Count Geoffrey asked. "There is nothing left to gather – not a single beast nor a grain of wheat. Only the Isle of Ely remains inviolate."

"Our fiefs are in Ely, my lord count," a knight of St Etheldreda said sullenly. "If they are harried we are ruined."

Geoffrey answered reasonably, "None spoke of harrying. Plunder we have in plenty – gold and silver and costly gems. Unfortunately they are uneatable, and we must eat. The provisions in my castles will not last beyond a month. I must ask you, my lords of Etheldreda, to give us of your harvests."

I said, "Won't the Countess of Anjou send us aid? We fight against her enemies."

"Aid indeed she promised, long ago – and none, as you have seen, has come." The vicious whiplash in his voice belied the expressionless face. "We are forsaken and forsworn, my lords, excommunicate and damned. None will risk his immortal soul to send us help."

Count Geoffrey took the island's harvests, and sent corn to his outposts. It was not enough. He seized plough-oxen and cattle, and bade his knights and sergeants scour the fields for more. The peasants hid their little granaries, concealed eggs and poultry in byre and thatch. The soldiers, with hunger gnawing their bellies, twisted knotted cords around the villeins' heads, and ground their testicles between stones, and flayed their skin in bloody strips. From such torments many died. Those that yielded starved.

Monotony increased the burdens. The stimulation of the king's attacks was ended; patrols moved listlessly along tracks; lethargic garrisons moped behind palisades. Count Geoffrey evicted the monks from Ely, calling them useless mouths, and ransacked the abbey store-rooms. Ernulf sent word from Ramsey that he must start slaughtering the horses. My lord shrugged. In Ely we had lived on horse-flesh for some time. Rounceys went first, then palfreys. I surrendered Baucan to the stew-pots; afterwards we mounted strict guards over the remaining destriers, for nothing eatable in those days was safe.

I had other troubles. Whether from lack of food, or the summer's heat, the rusty blotches on my skin returned, and swelled and suppurated. Ranulf, tight-lipped, applied salves and bandaged my arms and legs. The sores did not heal; he dressed them daily. Once, accidentally, when fastening the linen, he scratched a brooch upon my cheek, and begged forgiveness. I had not felt the graze at all, and told him so.

Ranulf wept, and would not tell me why.

In Aldreth castle St Etheldreda's knights, resentful of their ravaged fiefs, mutinied and closed the gates. Count Geoffrey deployed his siege-lines and starved them into surrender within a week. He hanged the constable and four bannerets from lofty gallows, and expelled the rest to wander in a land bereft of food. But these men knew secret trackways in the fens; they left the Isle and enticed others to desert: mercenary knights who foresaw no future gains – even Geoffrey's liegemen slunk away, furtive and ashamed. The trickle of desertions, once begun, swelled like the waters of a winter spate.

Hunger became a companion of our days, a devouring ache that griped our stomachs like poisonous acid. Sergeants who spoke some English, disguised as beggars, wandered by night from hovel to hovel pleading for food. They seized any man who produced the smallest morsel and dragged him to Count Geoffrey's knights, who devised artful methods to make him reveal his scanty store. Not even the dead were safe. Men crept stealthily by night to graveyards, exhumed the corpses of those who had lately died and feasted horribly in hidden places.

On a sultry August day Count Geoffrey called his knights together in the abbey cloister. Unusually for him, he sought advice, and listened still-faced to a welter of opinion. All were unanimous that, unless we took offensive action to break the blockade, starvation must compel surrender.

"I agree with you, my lords," Count Geoffrey said. "Unwelcome though it is, we have no other choice. Where shall we snap the chain? At Walden the castellan holds for me a corn convoy that Hugh Bigod sent. The king's fort at Burwell bars the way. We shall open the road and bring the wagons through. Burwell must be taken."

Next day we marched. Many knights trudged on foot, because their horses had been eaten.

6

The sun blazed from a cloudless sky. I sweated beneath the hauberk; the ring-mesh was so warm that it seared my bandaged hands. At a noonday halt Count Geoffrey rested supine beneath an ash-tree's shade; I saw myself the hot metal scorch the grass and leave an imprint of his form upon the ground.

We came to Burwell castle, and viewed the place despondently. King Stephen had not spared labour in building his forts. The bailey palisade was stout, the ditch steep-sided; a formidable tree-trunk keep surmounted a tall mound. The sun struck sparks from helmets crowding the battlements. The ground was flat and open; no hidden hollows or convenient copses offered covered approaches for an escalade.

Count Geoffrey pulled his lip, and called his bannerets. "Let us look closer," he said.

He rode forward and circled the defences. Trumpets sounded from the castle; we heard bellows of defiance. An arrow, almost spent, whipped over our heads. I glanced at Geoffrey anxiously. His head was bare. His helmet dangled by the coif upon his back.

"My lord," I said, "don your helmet. We are within range."

"Too hot," he answered. "Already I am grilled like a horse-meat steak. Ride on. Burwell is going to be a hard place to take."

I edged Chanson forward to interpose myself between Count Geoffrey and the castle walls. I heard a wasp-whirr, saw a sudden flash. My lord cried out, crouched over his saddle-bow and clasped hands to head. Blood trickled through his fingers.

His knights surrounded him. I put an arm around his shoulders, seized his rein and galloped. At a safe distance we halted. I parted his hands and examined the wound. The archer's barb had slashed his scalp and exposed the bone.

I took him to a coppice where his soldiers waited, laid him in shade, fetched water and washed the wound. I called Ranulf, who probed with tender fingers and wanted to trim the hair around the gash. My lord was impatient, and thrust him off.

"It is nothing," he said. "I was careless and have earned my lesson. Bandage it tight and let it be – I shall not be able to wear a helmet for a few days, that is all. Humphrey, you have seen the ground. Set the siege lines."

I ordered varlets to cut grass for a mattress, and spread Count Geoffrey's saddle-cloth upon it, stripped his armour and made him comfortable. We had no tents. I left him in Ranulf's care; and for two days directed the routine of investment, digging entrenchments and making road-blocks. On the third day Ranulf sought me. He looked unhappy.

"My lord is slow to recover," he said. "I do not like what I see."

I went to Count Geoffrey's pallet. His face was flushed, his eyes too bright. He twisted restlessly and complained of heat. Ranulf unwound the bandage. The wound gaped red and swollen, the edges blackened, the skin hot beneath my touch.

"I think his blood is poisoned," Ranulf whispered. He bit his lip. "Here I have no salves, except those I brought for your infection. There is little I can do."

Next morning the fever soared. The count muttered in delirium. An evil-smelling yellow liquid dribbled from his wound. I stood in thought and watched him for a while. Then I summoned his bannerets from the siege-lines.

"Count Geoffrey is gravely sick," I told them, "and, if he stays here, is like to die. Mildenhall, ten miles away, has a priory of his own foundation, with an infirmary and monks skilled in medicine. I shall send him in a litter there today."

"You will raise the siege?"

"I shall not. My lord wishes Burwell to be taken. That charge he has delivered into my hands. The siege goes on."

A fair-haired Fleming, a mercenary escaped from William de Ypres' hirelings, said, "An impossible endeavour, as I have seen from the beginning. We can't starve them out – they can endure longer than we."

I scanned the ring of gaunt faces, the hollow cheeks beneath the nasals, and inwardly agreed.

"Then," I said, "I am ready to lead you to an escalade."

The Fleming said, "A forlorn hope. No. We know you for a valiant knight, Humphrey Visdelou, but you are not our lord. Only the man who holds our fealty shall order us to our deaths."

His companions murmured vehement assent.

"Fealty —!" I swallowed my spittle, and acknowledged defeat. "Very well, my lords. We abandon Burwell. Quit your entrenchments after dark, lest the garrison see you leaving and make a sally. I trust your loyalty constrains you to escort your suzerain to Mildenhall."

It did not take them very far. During the slow, sweltering, day-long journey they began to go. I tramped beside Count Geoffrey's litter, and stopped from time to time to wipe his face, or give him water, or hold him by main force when he struggled in delirium. Knights came, looked into his face, shrugged, collected their retainers and left the column without farewell. Only a handful reached Mildenhall with Geoffrey.

My lord had founded the priory, so spared it in his ravages. I had thought to find the brotherhood grateful. When the prior recognized the man who raved on the litter his greasy jowls quivered and his pig-eyes popped.

"This is God's House!" he exclaimed. "Count Geoffrey lies under the anathema of Holy Church. He cannot enter here!"

I drew my sword and ended argument. We bore him to the infirmary, where some monks lay sick. I flung them from their pallets and bundled them outside, lest Count Geoffrey's infamy pollute their hallowed souls. I demanded that the prior find a monk learned in the arts of healing; eventually a reluctant lay-brother arrived, and tip-toed to my lord's bedside like a timid seraph approaching the portals of Gehenna. He fumbled clumsily, overcome with fear. Ranulf grimly watched his bungling hands. At last he intervened and thrust him out. He found herbs and ointments in the lazaret coffers, and dressed Count Geoffrey's wound afresh.

Those were days of scorching heat and black despair. I knew my lord's illness to be mortal. Fever wrenched him on a fiery rack; hard nodules swelled within his armpits; the wound was a gaping pit whence fetid corruption dripped. Seldom was he conscious. His face was like a mask of death, the livid skin stretched taut over his cheekbones.

With Ranulf I cared for Geoffrey, and watched over him night and day. The brethren never came near. Two red cross knights, Templars on pilgrimage to Outremer, stayed in the monastery awhile and gave us help. Sombre men, austere and taciturn, these military monks nursed him with skill and tenderness. They knew my lord was doomed; they knew him excommunicate, an object of abhorrence; never did they cease fighting for his life.

The fever left Count Geoffrey on an evening when sunset flushed the sickroom and a cool breeze freshened the tainted air. He opened his eyes. I knelt beside his pallet and held his hand. Slowly he turned his bandaged head.

"Humphrey?" he whispered. "Why are you here? Is Burwell taken?"

"No, my lord." My lips trembled. "We had to raise the siege, for you were very sick."

"My orders — You did not obey. And yet I dreamed —" His clasp tightened on my fingers. "I dreamed . . . that we prevailed. I dreamed of victory, famed and glorious. I dreamed that . . . I was . . . king."

His dying eyes gazed into mine

"Dear Humphrey. Faithful . . . to the end. I tried . . . to show you . . . what I was. You never . . . learned."

His eyes closed. He did not speak again.

I ran from the infirmary and found the prior, and demanded that he shrive my lord and give him absolution. Neither steel nor menaces would shift him. I thrashed him with my sword-flat, left him screaming, ran to the frater and threatened the monks. They cowered against the walls and refused to move. Despairingly I returned to Geoffrey.

He lay rigid on his back, eyeballs rolled into his head, the pupils gone. Breath rattled harshly in his throat. Ranulf and a Templar stood beside the bed. I gripped Ranulf's shoulder.

"For the Mercy of God —!"

He bowed his head. "No. I am not a priest."

My lord heaved on the pallet, and strove for death.

The Templar said, "He is going. Satan howls for his advent in the clefts of hell. And yet —" Gently he laid his blazoned shield on the writhing form. "For all your sin, Geoffrey de Mandeville, you were a peerless knight."

And so, beneath Christ's scarlet Cross, Count Geoffrey died.

7

Ranulf found me in the shadowed cloisters. Monks sang the offices of compline : the chanting mourned in twilit darkness like a requiem. He put an arm about my shoulders, and pressed me close; and thus we stood together for a while, and did not speak. The singing ceased. The monks, dim figures in the gloom, passed in procession to the frater.

I said desperately, "What is left for me, Ranulf? My star is fallen from the heavens. Where can I go?"

Ranulf stared into the night. Absently, he stroked the linen that swathed my arm.

"We must travel a long way together, my brother Humphrey, on a journey with no return."

Epilogue

October, 1144

Autumn in Savernake.

Last night's frost tarnished the forest. The trees, like knights arming for battle, are donning brazen scales for the final stand against winter's onset. A falling leaf drifts past my face. I try to grasp it, but my hands are useless. Yet I am comfortable enough, drowsing on a bracken mattress in the sunlight, a wolfskin covering my legs. The pain is not unbearable.

I can see Brand driving his plough. He is bent and greying, morose as ever, compelled once more to harbour fugitives. Fugitives? One cannot run far from my adversary. Brand is fearful, keeps his distance, and has built himself a hut in the farthest field. Ranulf gives him money, and has brought from Bochesorne a villein – a mop-headed, half-witted youth – to assist his husbandry. Never has the woodcutter been so prosperous.

Odinel rides over from time to time and brings me news. He has recovered from the horror of our first encounter and can look upon me calmly – though sorrow always lingers in his eyes. He guards my secret: Saiva believes me dead, killed in some affray in Anglia. I have a son whom I have never seen, just six months old. He bears my name.

Odinel says the manors thrive, the granaries are brimful from a plentiful harvest. He has promised to remain at Benham until young Walchelin is knighted. With that I am content.

Meanwhile I lie in the sun. Day by day Ranulf sits beside me, quill in hand and parchment on his knee. His arms are bandaged beneath his sleeves. I fear he has taken the contagion – but dare not ask. I relate the history of my times, and he scribbles while I talk. I have no skill with words; my narrative is bald. Ranulf, I think, embellishes the tale, and adorns my homespun sentences with the sort of imagery the minstrels use. The story now is told, which is as well: my throat becomes constricted, my nostrils clog and thicken, and I begin to find speech difficult.

This, then, is my confession, made to a man who was a priest – the nearest I can come to absolution. Ranulf, who can do no more for my putrescent carcass, is worrying about my immortal soul. He wants to bring a clerk to shrive me and purge the anathema which damns me still to everlasting fire. Always I refuse, and give no reason.

What use have I for paradise when my suzerain burns in hell?

I am happy to go, and meet again that transcendent spirit whom I loved. Why should I complain? I have known love's ecstasies, and felt my children's hands upon my lips. I have seen the lightning of battle and the splendour of spears. I am not afraid.

Leprosy, so Ranulf tells me, sends an easy death.

Author's Note

How much of this is true?

Geoffrey de Mandeville lived and died as I have described. The historical background is authentic. I have not altered the time-scale. All major characters – and most of the minor ones – are historical. The main events – battles and sieges and Geoffrey's complicated plots – really happened.

I live upon the fief that Visdelou once held.

Glossary

Arbalest	A crossbow.
Bailey	Outer ward of castle, extending from the keep.
Bailiwick	District under a bailiff.
Baldric	Belt worn pendent from one shoulder to carry a sword.
Banneret	Knight commanding 10 or 20 knights and/or men-at-arms.
Berselet	A hound, rather like a greyhound, which hunts by sight.
Blazon	An armorial bearing, usually painted on a shield.
Boon-work	Unpaid service due from a tenant to his lord.
Brachet	A hound which hunts by scent.
Castellan	Custodian or constable of a castle.
Chausse	Leg armour.
Coif	(see foot of p. 251).
Compline	Last service of the Catholic daily office, about 9 p.m.
Conroy	A mixed force, cavalry and infantry, about 50 strong.
Constabular	(see foot of p. 251).
Courtoisie	Chivalry.
Cresset	An iron torch-holder.
Destrier	A war-horse.
Dorter	Dormitory.
Enarmes	Straps on inner side of shield, for gripping.
Escheat	Confiscate.
Fascine	Long cylindrical faggot of bound brushwood.
Ferms	Fixed yearly taxes imposed on a town.

Forte	Strongest part of a sword-blade, nearest the hilt.
Fosse	A ditch or moat.
Gabions	Cylindrical wicker baskets filled with earth.
Gambeson	Military tunic of leather or thick cloth, sometimes padded, often worn beneath hauberk.
Girandole	Branched candle holder.
Glacis	A smooth sloping bank extending from outer fortifications.
Glebe	The land belonging to a parish church.
Guige	Shoulder-strap supporting the shield when not enarmed.
Guisarme	Long-handled hand-axe.
Haubergeon	Short, sleeveless mail-coat, extending to hips or mid-thigh.
Hauberk	A knee-length mail-coat worn by knights.
Hidage	Measurement of land area. (A hide varied from 40 to 120 acres.)
Honour	A seigniory of several manors held under one lord.
Liam	Heavily built hound, generally used for starting the quarry.
Mainpast	Household.
Mangonel	A siege-engine for casting stones.
Merlon	The part of a battlement between two embrasures.
Nithing	A vile coward, an outcast.
Palfrey	A riding horse or hack.
Plastron	A rectangular iron breastplate worn beneath the hauberk.
Prime	First service of the Catholic daily office, about 6 a.m.
Quintain	Target mounted on a post, to be tilted at with lances

Reeve	Minor official appointed by a lord to oversee his workmen.
Rouncey	A pack-horse.
Sarsen	Large sandstone boulder found on the surface of chalk downs.
Seax	A throwing axe.
Seisin	Possession.
Seneschal	A household official who controlled administration of justice and domestic arrangements.
Sergeant	A tenant by service, usually military, under the rank of knight.
Sext	Third service of the Catholic daily office, about noon.
Sutler	A camp follower who sells provisions.
Terce	Second service of the Catholic daily office, about 9 a.m.
Ventail	Flap of mail buckled across chin and mouth.
Verderers	Extension of the royal forests, with particular responsibility for the greenwood (vert).
Ward	Bailey.
ADDENDA:	Extension of hauberk, attached to helmet, to protect the neck and ears. A body of cavalry 10 or 20 strong.